Killing O'Carolan

Killing O'Carolan

A Mark Fairley Mystery

Walt Pilcher

First Published 2022 by Fantastic Books Publishing

Cover design by Gabi

ISBN (eBook): 978-1-914060-30-4
ISBN (paperback): 978-1-914060-29-8

To lovers of parody and satire everywhere who never,
or hardly ever, take themselves too seriously.
You know who you are. You will love this book.
The rest of you need it.

ACKNOWLEDGEMENTS

Thank you for reading *Killing O'Carolan*, or at least for picking up the book and thumbing to the Acknowledgements. It is the second in the Mark Fairley Mystery series. It takes a village to help prepare an author to write a book, and I had a big village for this one, going all the way back to my mother teaching me to read and write at a very early age. But we won't start there. Instead, let me thank some of the more contemporary contributors to my journey.

First, I want to thank my First Readers Carol Pilcher, Ann McKenzie, Jim McKenzie, Tom O'Shea, and Henry (Rocky) Colavita.

The "arts community" in Greensboro, NC, is varied, vast, and vibrant. Too varied and diverse to be compared to an ordinary village. To write a satirical novel about it might be considered sacrilegious to those immersed in that community, but I found theirs is a forgiving spirit and one which encourages, not condemns, an author's attempt to express his fondness with fun. I had the privilege of dipping my toe in the Greensboro arts pond long before having the thought of writing a book about it, but without that experience, I probably wouldn't have written any books at all.

Greensboro Writers, Musicians, and Artists:
* Chris Laney and Steve Cushman, teachers of the Write Motivation I and Fiction 101 classes under the auspices of The Creative Center, founded by Chip Bristol and through which I met and worked with several of the other musicians, writers, and artists mentioned here. Chris saw merit in my short story, "The Meeting at the Center of the Universe," and helped me polish it so that

it won a competition sponsored by Fantastic Books Publishing, beginning a relationship that led to FBP publishing it and four of my books, including this one.

- Writers Anonymous, founded by Write Motivation alumni Sharon Shepard, Stephanie Thomas, Amanda Cox-Lucas, Raef Mootassem and yours truly to meet monthly and critique each other's work in progress.

- Writers Group of the Triad (now folded into Winston-Salem Writers), especially Coventry Kessler, Diana Engel, Ellen Summers, Stephen Wessells, Rosalyn Marhatta, John Haugh, and Jean Rodenbaugh. Coventry, Diana, and Ellen edited WGOT's poetry anthology, *Fire & Chocolate*, and were kind enough to include my poem, "The County Library" (which later became a song and a 10-minute play), sparking my interest in poetry and my participation in a monthly poetry critique group sponsored by WGOT and attended by those listed in this paragraph, among others.

- The late Stephen Hyers, Director of the City Arts Drama Center and facilitator of the Greensboro Playwrights' Forum.

- Kathy Brusnigan, founder of the Creative Gathering at Center City Church

- Jim Dodson, founding editor of *O.Henry Magazine* ("The Art and Soul of Greensboro") which has published two of my poems.

- Kevin Dollar of Music Academy of North Carolina, my first and only formal guitar teacher.

- Vance Archer III, host of the weekly Bishop's Bridge band and music circle in his home, a generous man and talented musician who lent me one of his guitars while I was shopping for my own and then let me play in his band's gigs even though at first I could only find one chord and wait until it came around in the music at which time I would play it with gusto. It was through Bishop's Bridge that I first learned about Turlough O'Carolan and found that, as much as I love and respect ancient and traditional Irish music, it begs to be parodied.

- Other Bishop's Bridge regulars who took me under their wings: The late Steven Burns who helped me overcome my fear of changing chords, as well as Tom O'Shea, Chris Binkowski, Earl Inge, Holly Burdick, and Carol Michaelis, among others who encouraged me on my musical journey.

- Kristy Jackson, accomplished songwriter and teacher of a songwriting course I attended at University of North Carolina at Greensboro who saw merit in my first country & western song, "Fondest Heart," and helped me with the arrangement.

- Scuppernong Books, an indie bookstore gathering place, reading room, café & wine bar, and open mic venue that also sells a few books now and then and is the inspiration for the downtown Read-A-Spell Book Store in this novel.

- Carol Pilcher, an accomplished artist and my long-suffering wife (see First Readers) whose association with other artists in Greensboro and elsewhere has been a source of inspiration for my own creativity with the written word if not with paint. We have collaborated on a couple of small projects. Artist associates and acquaintances of influence to me include Connie Logan, Ken Hobson, and Dr. Steve Robinson, among others.

- Others who have been sources of inspiration and encouragement include writers and poets Shirley Coble, Lee Zacharias, Michael Gaspeny, and Miriam Herin.

Non-Greensburgers:

- Jeremy Sinnott, worship leader at the Toronto Airport Christian Fellowship, whose music, even though we've never formally met, inspired me to write my first song which was followed by many more.
- Steve Swanson of Maricopa, AZ, world-class composer, Christian worship leader, songwriting teacher extraordinaire, and overall musical genius.
- John Santa of Chapel Hill, NC, multifaceted musician, producer, author, encourager, and generous friend of Bishop's Bridge despite his cultivated curmudgeon façade.
- Rev's Coffee House in High Point, sometime amateur art exhibition and open mic venue.
- Of course, the Fantastic Books Publishing team under the leadership of CEO Dan Grubb who some years ago took a chance with this then-fledgling story writer, poet and novelist, for which I will always be grateful.

Some of the organizations, establishments, and venues listed here have become defunct since I experienced them. It's not that they were bad or poorly managed or failed to serve their purposes well. Times and people change, and with them the ever-shifting sands of an arts community, as I've tried to bring out in the book.

Now, if all these people would buy copies of the book for themselves and their friends and families and post five-star reviews on Amazon, we'd be well on the way to having a bestseller. Mark Fairley could use the royalty money.

PRAISE FOR *KILLING O'CAROLAN*

Someone is poisoning poets in Greensboro and there seems to be no rhyme or reason to it. Reluctant amateur detective Mark Fairley goes undercover in the arts community to learn whose muse has run amok and restore poetic justice to the city. All well and good until he discovers the future of this modern American town may hinge on the fate of a legendary 18th Century blind Irish musician and a hit man with a chip on his shoulder.

I wondered who was poisoning poets in Greensboro. There seemed to be no rhyme or reason to it. Then I read *Killing O'Carolan* by Walt Pilcher and found out. You should too.
   — *Durango Falcone, serial volunteer book reviewer*

Before I read *Killing O'Carolan* by Walt Pilcher, I heard about someone poisoning poets in Greensboro and wondered if reluctant amateur detective Mark Fairley, going undercover in the arts community, could learn whose muse had run amok and restore poetic justice to the city. Then I read *Killing O'Carolan* and found out. You should too.
   — *Lisa Condo, CEO, Al's Superior Oil and Juice Mining Company*

Lovers of parody and satire everywhere who never, or hardly ever, take themselves too seriously will love this book. You know who you are. The rest of you need it.
   — *Book Week, proud member of the Book Month / Book Day / Book Hour family*

Legendary blind Irish mystery writer Seán Ó Shéamuis once said, "The best mysteries are the unsolved ones." Unfortunately, there are none of those in *Killing O'Carolan* by Walt Pilcher. His reluctant but intrepid protagonist, Mark Fairley, solves them all. How disappointing. But you'll enjoy it anyway for the humor, the suspense, and the crisp writing that keeps you moving quickly from page to page until the very end where, sadly, everything is revealed.

   — *Bupkis Reviews*

Did legendary blind Irish mystery writer Seán Ó Shéamuis once say, "The best mysteries are the unsolved ones"? Not in my book they're not! I get paid for the solved ones. You can read where I solved a tough one in *Killing O'Carolan*. Although I had some help.

   — *Lt. Marshall Blue, Greensboro Police Department*

Better than any legendary blind Irish mystery *I* ever read! Funnier too! And Walt Pilcher is a great tipper.

   — *Sharon McDonald, floater, McDonald's Restaurant, 3301 Battleground Ave., Greensboro, NC*

Prologue

He is alone in a men's restroom at the Steven Tanger Center for the Performing Arts. A Broadway touring company is performing *The Wiz* on the main stage, and he can hear the music from speakers concealed in the restroom ceiling. It is a good show, but he has had to leave his front-row seat before the intermission and come here. Too much wine at the pre-show VIP reception, he supposes, and ruing the day he ever heard the disgusting expression he now can't get out of his head he needs to take a whiz himself.

Finished, he goes to wash his hands but, what's this? Two cigars in dark green wrappers on the floor in one of the stalls? He hesitates. Are they clean enough to touch? After all, they are on the floor of a public restroom. But this is a high-class public restroom, so maybe they are okay. He bends and picks them up. He sees they are not cigars but rather two of those cheap fountain pens Dylan Vivaldi has distributed all over town promoting The Gate City Playhouse, a competitor of the Tanger Center. He has two of them already, though he does not recall when or where he got them. He lays the pens on top of a washbasin while he washes his hands, and then he wipes each one with a damp paper towel. They have been on the floor of a public restroom after all. He pockets them, clean enough now, fleetingly thinking they seem a little heavier than the other Gate City Playhouse pens he has collected. No matter. They are probably made in China where quality consistency is not always a priority.

He exits the restroom without noticing the ceiling

speakers have gone silent. There is a commotion in the theater. He stops an usher, who tells him two of the actors have collapsed on the stage. He asks if it is part of the act; the usher says it is not. It is, however, literally a showstopper. People begin shouting and running for the exits, blocking his path back to his seat. Above the noise of the crowd, he hears sirens. Somehow, he manages to collect his wife and leave, just as a fire truck, two ambulances, and three police cars arrive.

Chapter One

Thursday

This story, like my previous one, began for me with a phone call. Only this time it was me making the call, and it wasn't to my erstwhile attorney, the estimable Frank Sheldon, Esq.

I was calling the Glowery Company, my former employer in Greensboro, North Carolina, from whom I'd been blindsided and "rightsized" out of my job about a year ago. I needed to discuss the rollover of my 401(k) to a private account. Not that I had a lot in it, but I needed to make sure it was protected from income tax confusion if I didn't handle it properly. If push came to shove and I didn't find a real job soon, the 401(k) along with loose change from our sofas and whatever I could get from melting down our wedding gift sterling might be all my wife Emily and I had to live on until our children could start supporting us. With all three still in college, that was likely a long way off. My severance package had been generous, I had to admit, but we had run through that and most of my earnings from my post-Glowery consulting gig with Spurr Nutritionals. Any proceeds from the expected appreciation of my stock after Spurr's planned IPO were still far away. Now we were living on accumulated savings from better days and a nice bonus the Spurrs gave me, but those funds wouldn't last forever. Thus, the call.

I was talking with Rhonda, an executive administrative assistant (not secretary) in the HR Department when apparently Bob the CEO happened to walk by and overhear that she was talking to me.

"Is that Mark Fairley?" I heard.

Muffled conversation.

"Hi, Mark! I thought that was you!" in my ear so loud I almost dropped the phone.

"Yeah, hi, Bob."

Bob, the guy who fired me. "Listen, you know, funny thing, I was about to call you. So, how ya been?"

"Well, not too bad, considering. Been fairly busy. You know."

"Ah, so Mark Fairley's been fairly busy, eh? That's a good one!"

"Yeah, I've heard all the 'fairly' jokes, Bob. Why were you going to call me?"

"Listen, I can't talk here, but can you drop by tomorrow, say around 2:30?"

Talk about "a bolt out of the blue." That is absolutely the last thing I expected to hear from Bob. I decided to play along.

"I'll have to look at my calendar, but provisionally let's say I can make it," I said. (My calendar looks like winter in Nebraska: flat, white, and blank.)

"Superb!"

"This won't affect my 401(k), will it?"

"Why should it?"

"No reason. See, that was a hint about whether you can give me a hint about why you want to see me."

"Ah, no can do, Mark. Loose lips sink ships, or so I've heard. But I think you'll like it. See you tomorrow!" he said and hung up. Or gave the phone back to Rhonda and she hung up. Whichever, it was hung up, and so was I—on speculating about what he wanted. Offer me my old job back? Emily would have mixed feelings about that ("He *fired* you, Mark!").

Like I should have nothing more to do with him or the horse he rode in on.

Invite me to join the country club? Probably not, but I've heard they're crying for new members to help finance a big renovation project over there.

The loose lips bit made it sound mysterious. What secret did he have that he couldn't at least hint at in front of Rhonda? Why would it involve me? Why would I like it? Or was he being ironic? But Bob wasn't the type for irony. And why am I still paranoid after all I went through over in Spurrville? Or maybe it's *because* of all that. Getting shot at in a dumpster by a fake Japanese moron with a stolen gun was no picnic even if things did turn out well in the end. And Emily still hasn't completely gotten over it.

But what the heck. At least it would give me something to put on my calendar.

Chapter Two

I worked at Glowery as Director of Strategic Planning for seven years, but Bob Ausländer wasn't the guy who hired me. It was Edgar Principle, the previous CEO. When Edgar moved to Atlanta to run a bigger company, the Board replaced him with Bob, an outsider, instead of promoting from within. Bob promptly fired all of Edgar's direct reports except me and brought in his own team. He kept me on because he needed somebody to explain and interpret the company's strategy while he figured out whether he liked it or not, and eventually I think he sort of forgot about me until we hit a downturn in the business. At that point he looked for expenses to cut, and Strategic Planning is always a prime candidate for sacrifice in hard times. Wiped out my whole department, small though it was.

Glowery Company is in the disaster recovery business. Competitors include After Disaster, Servpro and ServiceMaster, all fine companies as far as I know. If there's a fire, or a flood, or a tree falls on your house, or if an airplane or a meteor falls into your swimming pool, or a family[1] of bears hibernates in your den instead of their own while you're spending the winter in Florida, Glowery comes in and cleans up. In two senses of the word. First, your house, or your business, or your church, or whatever building suffered the disaster, enjoys a complete recovery, as if the problem never

---

[1] A "sleuth" of bears, to be correct. I looked it up.

occurred. Glowery does good work. After that, the company cleans up on its hefty fees. These are usually paid by insurance companies. The insurance companies haven't quite caught on to how much restoration work actually costs, which is less than they've been led to believe, and until that happens, Glowery's profit margins are … comfortable.

The company's service trucks are easy to spot as they sally forth on their myriad rescue missions around town. They're red, but not fire engine red, which would be illegal, but as close to it as they can come, with green trim, and they resemble ambulances. Again, as closely as they can without running afoul of the law.

On the side of each is a large blue "G" and a picture of a smiling bald, muscular man in a cape holding aloft a dustpan and broom and with the legend "G-Man" emblazoned on his form fitting T shirt. I'm surprised we never got sued by the Mr. Clean lawyers for trademark infringement. Maybe the cape, dustpan and broom make enough of a distinction. Also, unlike Mr. Clean's, the G-Man's eyes seem to follow you as you pass the truck or it passes you. Like the Mona Lisa.

Under the big blue "G" is the company slogan: Clean Up with the Glowery Glow!" (Bob's idea, against the wishes of the advertising agency and the Marketing Department who wanted to keep the previous slogan: Get Glowing Again with Glowery!" Six of one and a half dozen of the other if they'd asked me, but nobody did.)

We never did any research on what our customers thought the Glowery Glow was, exactly, much less whether anybody could say it three times fast, but to me it conjured up demonic images that once or twice gave me nightmares. Not something I'd want to pay money for, or an insurance deductible as the case might be.

Early on, some nitwit in the Marketing Department decided

they should name the trucks after famous accidental or natural disasters. When Bob took over, with his arrested sense of humor and nonexistent sense of irony, he didn't get it and wanted to end the practice (in this I agreed with him but for different reasons). But Bob is a pragmatist and when he discovered how much the employees liked the tradition, he let it stand and eventually warmed up to it. Now Glowery had trucks named *Katrina*, *Chernobyl*, *Titanic*, *Johnstown Flood*, *Krakatoa*, *Three Mile Island*, and *Exxon Valdez*, among others. Inspiring.

When they're not in use or at the end of the day, some of the trucks are parked here and there around the city, in plain sight, instead of in the company garage. Bob's way of getting free advertising. The police are clued in, so they leave the trucks alone.

Once in a while, teenagers will hotwire one of the trucks and take it for a short midnight joyride. Short because, in spite of their sporty ambulance-like color scheme, the trucks handle like drunken elephants and are no fun to drive. Short also because the police know they are supposed to be parked, and when they see one moving in the wee hours they take a closer look and arrest the miscreants. Occasionally Glowery will press charges, especially if the truck has been damaged, and that makes the *News & Record* and sometimes the Channel 2 news. Bob loves the publicity. One night somebody let the air out of the tires on four of the trucks. But it was Hallowe'en.

If it were up to me, I'd have long ago changed the name of the company and started all over with the slogans. Unfortunately, that couldn't be done because when the company was founded in Arkansas in 1915 by Amos Glowery, he specified in his will that the name must endure in perpetuity, surviving all changes of ownership. And indeed, the company changed owners many times over the years, and it faithfully kept the Glowery name.

Bob has a straightforward approach to most things, including business strategy. After he'd been with the company long enough to thoroughly think it through, he summed up his vision of our strategy one day in a staff meeting.

"Here it is, folks," he said inspiringly. "Shit happens. We fix it. Take notes if you want."

With a "strategy" like that, you don't need a Strategic Planning Department. Especially one led by me.

I held on as long as I could, but then the inevitable downturn came. It wasn't so much a downturn in the economy as it was a downturn in disasters. Shit stopped happening. A long stretch of unusually calm weather. An unprecedented epidemic of people remembering to turn off the stove before leaving the house. A rash of burglars piously, and inexplicably, cleaning up after themselves. Herds of animals remaining in their natural habitats. For Glowery, it amounted to an inexplicable run of bad luck. And it wasn't as if we could somehow go out and make shit happen again. We had no choice but to hunker down and wait until things got better, so to speak.

Which meant cutting expenses. Which meant firing Mark L. Fairley. Which … happened.

Chapter Three

Friday

Now here I was in Bob's office at 3:00, not 2:30. Typical Bob, he'd kept me waiting in the lobby twiddling my little plastic Visitor badge for half an hour before showing up, corpulently out of breath after a thirty-yard walk from the executive parking lot. He whisked me unapologetically into the elevator and up to the top floor and his well-appointed corner man cave. Ornate mahogany desk and credenza. Huge leather swivel chair behind the desk, looking more like a throne. Oversize leather wing back side chairs. Plush carpet, a literal step up from the industrial grade patterned burlap in the other offices and common areas. A round teak conference table with four comfortable chairs. A "conversation pit" complete with two easy chairs and a soft leather sofa, on which at Bob's beckoning I sat.

Bob sat on his throne, leaned back and swiveled a bit. Robert "Bob" Victor Ausländer (with an umlaut he proudly insists on using) is a pleasant looking man in his late fifties, clean-shaven but growing a beer belly even though I don't think he drinks to excess. His massive chair creaked a little but seemed to hold his weight easily enough.

On the walls, framed prints of signature golf holes from around the world. And the *pièce de résistance*, a 20-foot putting range, longer than you'd find even in a golf shop and complete with two gleaming Scotty Cameron Futura putters. Plus, one sad-looking fake ficus tree.

"How do you like it?" Bob asked, noticing my quick survey of his digs.

"Looks pretty much the way I remember it," I said. "The putting green is new, though."

"Just had it installed last month. Still waiting on Michaels to finish framing the life-size picture of me shaking hands with Tiger Woods at the 2018 Quicken Loans National up in DC."

Bob was my boss at the Glowery Company for 13 months before the end came in a black-fringed email my secretary, Janice, handed me one Friday afternoon. Yes, secretary. No executive administrative assistant for me, the lowly Director of Strategic Planning.

Just as Saturday is traditionally "moving day" in golf tournaments, when the pros with any chance of winning get as aggressive as they dare in order to better their positions on the leader board before the final round on Sunday, so Friday is the traditional "firing day" in corporate America. Friday afternoon. Late Friday afternoon. It's supposed to be the humane, compassionate way. Fewer people still around to notice you being escorted out by Security. Have the weekend to think things over. Don't have to be seen in public for two days. Assess the damage. Figure out how to put on a good face with smile on lips and British-like chin up while falling apart inside. Tell the wife and kids. Have many drinks, eat popcorn and binge-watch whatever stupid re-run TV show they're marathoning. Have nowhere to go on Monday.

Panic on Tuesday.

Still not have a real job a year later.

Come to think of it, Friday is "make the cut or go home" day in pro golf tournaments too. Sports imitating life? Or the other way around?

Of course, the email wasn't black-fringed, but the dark circles around Janice's eyes made up for that. She had read it and was sobbing. "What's going to happen to *me*?" she wailed, even before I had read the whole text of the doomsday missive. "I'm sure you'll be fine," I offered. "You've been doing a great job, and I'll bet one of the survivors has had an eye on you for a long time." Never mind I only gave her a "Good" review the last time around. At the word "survivors" she broke down completely and fled, presumably to the ladies' room. I never saw her again after that. Not even today. I looked.

Although straightforward about most things, even brash, for some reason Bob was averse to direct confrontation. He couldn't fire me in person, face to face, man to man. He sent an email.

But now here we were, late on another Friday afternoon, seated in Bob's office like in the old days. From his royal perch he was looking down at me, of course, but it was still more or less face to face. It's how I knew for certain he wasn't about to fire me again. If only there was something he could fire me from.

"So, Bob, how's the company doing now that it's the right size?"

"Oh, not too bad, not too bad, if I do say so my– … wait, that was a joke, right? Do I detect some hard feelings there, after all this time?"

"Well, that was the only reason you gave me in your carefully worded, black-fringed email."

"That *was* the only reason, Mark. We loved you. I loved you. Loved your work anyway. But it wasn't going to be a good fit longer term, bottom line-wise. I'm afraid Strategic Planning was a luxury we just couldn't afford anymore."

Cutting off your nose to spite your face. And he was lying. Bob didn't love me. Maybe he Liked me in a Facebook kind of way because my department did good work, but he never loved me. The chemistry was wrong.

10

"Whatever happened to Janice?" I asked.

"Who?"

"Never mind. And anyway, yes, I'm wondering why you called this meeting."

"Do you like poetry, Mark?"

"What?"

"Do you like poetry?"

"Only if it rhymes. Then it's good sometimes."

"Wow. Did you just say what I think you just said?"

"I think I did. But it's not something I've given much thought to."

"Well, give some thought to it."

"Right now, or do I get some time to mull it over?"

"Cheesh, Mark! If you weren't such a smart-ass, I'd have had my executive administrative assistant fire you in person."

"That'll teach me. What a treat that would have been. Almost makes me sorry I'm a smart-ass."

Bob scowled. It didn't look like he was going to throw me out, but there was a lull in the conversation.

So, it being late on a Friday afternoon I began to imagine people being fired here and there throughout the building. Getting their black-fringed emails, packing up their meager personal items—being careful not to be seen tossing office supplies like staplers and ballpoint pens into their pitiful little cardboard boxes—and being escorted to the front door by Security. But Bob hadn't sent any emails while I'd been here, so maybe my presence was giving some lucky underlings a week's reprieve.

"Okay, here's the thing," Bob continued through slightly gritted teeth, interrupting my reverie. "As you know, I'm chairman of the Greensboro Area Development Commission."

He paused to give me time to reflect on his magnificence. The GADC is a select group of business and community leaders chartered by the City Council to figure out ways of improving the area's economy.

"Since the textile and furniture industries went offshore, the banking industry went to Charlotte, and tobacco went in the toilet, Greensboro's been almost dead in the water," Bob continued. "Yes, FedEx made Greensboro a hub, and Hondajet builds airplanes here, and there've been some other bright spots, but they're not enough."

"Right. I know that."

Suddenly, I noticed I was slowly slipping out of the soft leather sofa. I corrected.

"We don't get paid for being on the GADC. We're funded by pledges from our members and affiliated companies and a modest grant from the City Council. About 40% of the money goes for advertising and promotion of the city and another 40% for travel and entertainment of prospective employers, which is our main focus. We're trying to recruit good-sized companies from out of state to relocate or open branches, divisions, subsidiaries or factories here, or whatever, so we can increase employment. The rest goes for research and administrative expenses. There's a staff of part-time volunteers who get paid time off from their companies, like Glowery and others, to work for the Commission. Of course, we pay their out-of-pocket expenses too."

"Okay, I know all that too. I've only been out of the loop about a year, and I still read the newspaper."

"Right. And how successful do you think we've been, not only in the past year, but for the past several years we've been at this? I mean besides FedEx and Honda."

"I'd say not very, from your tone of voice and the number of For Sale signs I see on houses in the $500,000 and above range when I drive around."

"Exactly. And do you know why?"

"I perceive that you're going to tell me." My latent detection skills kicking in. More alert, too, so as not to slip off the sofa again.

"Much as I might regret it down the road, yes, I am going to tell you."

Bob heaved himself up, went to the large west-facing window of the office and gazed out, probably not really looking at anything, but composing himself. That window has a good view. On a clear day you can see Pilot Mountain, north of Winston-Salem and about 42 miles away as the crow flies, according to Siri.

"It's the arts community, Mark."

"The arts community."

Silence from Bob, still at the window.

"You mean the artists, musicians, poets, writers and actors around here don't want economic development?" I ventured. "They don't want to sell more paintings, books and tickets? I've heard of 'art for art's sake,' but that's just silly."

"Well, of course, most of them want economic development as much as the rest of us," said Bob. "That's not the problem."

"Then what is?"

"What do you think is highest on the list of things top executives, like me, look for in selecting a place to plant a big company? I mean, after the usual economic stuff like tax incentives, a City Council with an 'open for business' attitude, a good labor force, access to interstate highways, a convenient airport, and so on? I'll tell you what."

"What?"

"Quality of life, that's what."

"Quality of life."

"For them, their employees and their families."

I agreed. But I thought Greensboro had that: a mild four-season climate within two to four hours of mountains or beach, friendly people, a flourishing downtown, robust nightlife, a coliseum, an Olympic swimming facility, a well-planned road system, excellent restaurants, beautiful residential areas, five colleges and universities and 23 more within 50 miles, an outstanding technical community college, wide choices of public and private schools, hundreds of churches, synagogues or other houses of worship, state of the art hospitals and healthcare facilities, eight public libraries, five YMCAs and one YWCA, five country clubs, 11 golf courses, an historical museum, a renowned International Civil Rights Center and Museum, a children's museum, the Greensboro Science Center and Zoo, movie theaters, a symphony, an opera company, a rock-solid United Way and other charities, a new Performing Arts Center, a minor league baseball team with a new stadium, parks with walking and bike trails and sports venues, and award-winning police and fire departments, among many other positive features the city could boast of, plus the arts community as Bob said. Didn't we have all that, and a big Costco with tasty samples and a liberal returns policy?

Of course, I didn't have that detailed a list in my mind as I sat there in Bob's sunny office—I looked it all up later—but I knew Greensboro had a lot to offer, in spite of my college-age offspring persistently referring to the city as "Greensboring."

"So you're saying somehow the arts community isn't holding up its end of the bargain, quality-of-life-wise?" I asked.

"You got it. Sure, there's lots of artsy stuff going on, but it's all over the place. It's disorganized. They don't communicate much with each other except in their own little groups. Their little groups don't cooperate with each other, and they've always got their hands out for donations. The 'starving artist' bit, you know? They're an amorphous bunch of temperamental prima donnas all doing their own thing."

That seemed a harsh judgement, and "amorphous" was an ambitious word for Bob, but I didn't say anything.

"Personally, I don't care what they do," he went on. "For one thing, I hate poetry. I mean, I just don't get it. You couldn't get me to the opera or the symphony on a bet, and I fall asleep standing up when my wife drags me to an art gallery—unless it's paintings of naked women. Those I can appreciate. Other than that, I guess all that stuff is better than eating glass, but I still don't like it. Anyway, never mind me. It's about prospective employers who might relocate here and whose executives, workers and families would want to see good performances or get involved in the arts themselves and wouldn't know where to begin."

"Okay," I said. Where was this going, and what did it have to do with me? And how much longer could I fight the slippery sofa without Bob noticing?

"And if that's not bad enough, there's a new wrinkle. About a month ago, the artsy-fartsy people started dropping like flies. I mean, they're not dying—at least not yet—but they're getting sick, they're having freak accidents, they're getting mugged, they're reporting suspicious characters lurking around in their neighborhoods, you know, like peeping toms. You name it.

"Nobody knows what's causing the illnesses. Some say it's the flu, but they all claim they've had their flu shots. Some think they've been poisoned, but the doctors can't find any poison in their systems. The police are stumped. They even called in the Centers for Disease Control, but they couldn't find anything. That, plus the accidents and everything, has got some of these people spooked, and I don't blame them.

"We've kept it away from the media so far, but it's only a matter of time before there's a leak, and then all hell will break loose. People will stop attending the artsy events and nightclubs and whatnot, panic will spread, and downtown businesses and restaurants will dry up like a cactus plant."

I didn't bother to point out that cacti are succulents and are always full of water, which is how they survive in the desert, but at least he was sort of on the right track with his simile. He probably doesn't even realize his ficus tree is fake.

"Worst of all," he again went on, "there are a few companies here—and you'd know them if I told you their names—that are already thinking about moving away. Not sure to where, but some of them are eying states like Colorado and Oregon where marijuana is legal and taxes still aren't too high. That's their definition of quality of life, I guess, though it makes no sense to me since it's not that hard to get pot around here."

"Or so you've heard," I said.

"Of course. Anyway, a thing like this could push them over the edge. And it would sure put a chill on anybody thinking of moving here."

Bob sat back down at the desk and looked at me across the vast expanse of the office. I knew what he was going to say next.

"That's not going to happen on my watch!"

Nailed it.

"I assume all this has something to do with why I'm here," I said.

"Even before all this stuff started hitting the fan, the GADC thought we should put together a big PR program for the arts. Let everybody know what's available. Encourage more participation. Add it to the Greensboro promotional efforts we're already doing. We've decided to go ahead with the planning and fundraising for it even though we might not launch until after the dust settles on this other business. It's probably about a six-month project."

"Uh huh …"

"I want you to head it up, Mark."

Another bolt out of the blue. The second from Bob in as many days. I confess I was expecting something, but not an out and out job offer.

"You fired me, Bob."

"Yes, and I'd do it again. But that was then; this is now."

"What's changed?"

"I haven't changed my mind about you if that's what you mean. And it's not like I'm offering you your job back with Glowery. You wouldn't be on staff; you'd be a 1099 contractor, a consultant, although you'd look like a regular employee for all intents and purposes. We'll even make up business cards with the Glowery logo. Pick your own title, I don't care, as long as it's not CEO."

A 1099 is the form companies file with the Internal Revenue Service to report the wages of a contract employee. It's like a W-2 but for consultants.

"What do you mean you haven't changed your mind about me?"

The phone on Bob's desk rang once and stopped. He ignored it.

"You're bright, Mark. You ran a good department. You worked hard, and you were loyal to the company. I appreciate things like that. But you're still a wisenheimer, as my grandmother would say, and I don't want you on my payroll again."

"Then why am I here? Why me? You know PR is a far cry from strategic planning. I don't know squat about it, and it seems like it's mostly on social media these days anyway, which is a foreign country to me."

"Yeah, I know. When it comes to that, I'm a dinosaur too. Anyway, don't worry about it. We've hired a local agency,

Upshot Marketing, to do the actual work. They've already started. You'll just be the front man."

This wasn't making sense.

Bob's executive administrative assistant, Frieda, stuck her head in the door.

"It's Mr. Vivaldi on line 1," she said.

"I need to take this," Bob said to me, with a thank you nod to Frieda. "I've been expecting it."

"Should I step outside?"

"No, it's okay." He picked up the phone. "Dylan! How are ya?"

Chapter Four

I'd never met him, but Dylan Vivaldi is a fixture in Greensboro, a mover-and-shaker entrepreneur and self-styled impresario who owns two nightclubs, three restaurants, the building leased to the Gate City Playhouse, and a golf driving range, plus probably more that I don't know about. Vivaldi is chairman of the Guilford Arts League, the largest and most comprehensive and influential of the arts organizations in town and the parent organization of many others. He finds time to be a guest conductor of the Greensboro Symphony occasionally. A creative guy and obviously a patron of the arts himself, as well as being a politically connected member of the GADC, he no doubt had as much of an interest in the suspicious goings on as Bob did.

I tried to look like I wasn't listening as Bob spoke to him on the phone. I rearranged my sofa position, trying to push my center of gravity as far back on the seat cushion as possible while still letting my feet touch the floor. I checked my cell phone. There were no text messages, only three new emails (none of them firing me), two Facebook notifications ("So and so wants you to 'Like' her page") and a news alert blaming the President for something.

All I did hear from Bob's side of the room was, "Yes, he's here with me right now. I think we're making progress." This while throwing me a big grin.

Finally, Bob hung up. The grin was gone.

"Well, again, why me?" I asked.

"When the weird stuff started happening to the artsy people, some of us in the GADC leadership met with the police to find out more about what was going on. Detective Marshall Blue. I think you know him."

"I do."

I had worked briefly with Blue when I was slinging clues back and forth between Greensboro, Spurrville and Raleigh for the Spurrt energy drink case, mostly Chinese takeout menus and photos of oriental-looking men skulking around my house. I didn't get to know him well, but he seemed like "a good cop," as they say.

"He told me about your work over there in, what, Sperryville or somewhere?"

"Spurrville. Near Siler City."

"Right. Whatever. Anyway, he told me about how you solved the murder case while posing as a company historian, which is sort of like PR in a way. Said you were perceptive. Discreet. Got along well with people. Said even the sheriff over there liked you a little."

"Always nice to hear. But still …"

I was beginning to get a creepy-crawly feeling, like this might be heading somewhere I wasn't sure I wanted to go. A six-month gig doing something I was unqualified for and working for somebody who maybe respected me but didn't like me very much? Also, it had no career path that I could see; I'd still have to keep up my job search. There had to be something else going on here. On the other hand, I did need money.

"I'd have thought you'd have figured this out by now," said Bob, "being so perceptive and all. Blue would be disappointed."

Suddenly, it was like *déjà vu* all over again. (No one ever says "*déjà vu*" all by itself anymore. It's a rule. Thank you, Yogi Berra.)

"You want me to go undercover in the arts community and figure out what's going on."

"Bingo!"

"No."

"Look, you wouldn't be working for me, if that's what's bothering you. And believe me, I wouldn't have picked you if Blue hadn't said he didn't know anyone else who could do it better, not even the police. Your client is the GADC. That's where your paycheck would come from even though you'll be carrying Glowery business cards."

"Living a lie. What fun."

"Aren't we all? You'll get used to it."

I had to agree with him there.

"Anyway, you won't have to do any actual PR work because the Upshot agency will handle all that. Frances Muldoon, the president over there, understands you'll be the spokesperson for their work and that you're just a … I don't know … a 'figurehead' or something, and she's okay with that. She gets that we need somebody with big company experience like you so the project will have credibility with the city's business leaders as well as the arts community. Frances is in on the undercover thing too, but her people don't know anything about it, so be careful what you say around them. As an added bonus, there are a bunch of writers and poets and whatnot on the agency staff, so you'll have an immediate entrée with the arts crowd from the get-go."

Although only two syllables, I thought "entrée" was as unlikely a word to escape Bob's lips as was "amorphous," at least in this context where we weren't deciding what to order at a restaurant, but I let it go. Maybe Bob was a little deeper than he let on.

"We'll pay you what you were getting when you worked here, plus 20%, translated to a daily rate. That means if you work a day you get paid for a day. Half a day and you're paid for half a day. Take a day off, no pay. Like a consultant. Plus expenses, of course. And maybe, and it's a big maybe, a bonus at the end"

"Seems fair, but …"

"No buts. That's a lot of money. Trust me, I had to beg for it. Our budget's not that big at the GADC, and I had to promise Glowery would underwrite any overages from what we estimated it would add up to."

"The 'but' wasn't about the money."

"What, then?"

"Getting poisoned, or whatever it is. Having a freak accident, getting mugged. That sort of thing."

"I wouldn't worry about that. If somebody's targeting artsy people, clearly you don't qualify. You're perfectly safe."

"I did write a book, you know. So someone might think I'm a writer. Artsy enough to be a target."

"Yeah, I heard about the book. Haven't had time to read it. I doubt if many other people have read it either, so you're still safe."

"Famous last words. Right up there with, 'What could possibly go wrong— BOOM!'"

"Very funny. Now, there is one other thing. This project can't take anywhere near six months. So, the upside is if you really are going to be exposed to any danger, which you won't be as I said, it won't be for very long."

It still sounded like Russian roulette to me, only without actual bullets. Maybe.

"Why less than six months?" I asked.

Bob suddenly looked more serious as his tone descended into a conspiratorial almost-whisper. "I trust you not to let a word of this get out, and I'll deny it if it does, but there's a big tech company up north we've been wining and dining for three years to move here. When I say big, I mean B-I-G. I can't tell you who it is, but, like I said, it's big. If they move here it will breathe so much new life into this town you'd think we were dead before they came. Which we basically are. We need them. We can't afford to see three years' work go down the drain. They're ready. All the permits and incentives and everything are in place. We were about to call a press conference with the Governor and the Mayor and make an announcement last week, but then they got wind of the trouble in arts-ville. Now they're on the fence. They're looking at Spartanburg too. And Columbia. That's all we need—losing to South Carolina again. Well, guess what?"

"Not on your watch?"

"You got it!"

My reluctant detective sense instantly made me wonder which big tech company from "up north" Bob was talking about, but since he clearly wasn't going to tell me I didn't ask. And I wondered where up north. As far as I knew, all the high-tech companies clustered along Massachusetts Route 128 in the Boston area near MIT, Harvard and other universities with think tanks were happy as Cape Cod clams and had no desire to move south. Could it be New York or the Washington, DC, area? Or maybe even the upper Midwest, like Chicago or Detroit? And maybe it was a different kind of tech. Pharmaceuticals? Defense industry or military? Aerospace?

And "quality of life" seemed a bit flimsy to build such a major decision on. Although, all other factors being more or less equal—like taxes, business climate, access to transportation, and so on—it could be the tipping factor. Not long ago, VF Corporation, another longtime leading Greensboro business, moved its headquarters out to Denver. Some of us wondered, with varying degrees of seriousness, whether the move was indeed because marijuana is legal in

Colorado and you can get a genuine John Denver-style Rocky Mountain high. Definitely a quality-of-life issue for many. Maybe if pot becomes legal in North Carolina, companies from up north will flock here. Maybe VF will come back.

"Now, here's the kicker," Bob continued, interrupting my dopey speculations, "They've given us 60 days from yesterday to get to the bottom of whatever is going on here and make Greensboro great again. And I know we can do it. With your help. So whaddya think?"

"I think I need to talk it over with Emily."

"Yes, talk to Emily. I want you to know I always thought you married up when you snagged that girl!"

"Thank you. Me too." What else could I say? It was true.

"But can you get back to me by Monday? Time is short, obviously."

"How about Wednesday? I want to talk to Detective Blue and Mr. Vivaldi too, if you'll make the introduction. Understand better what I'm getting myself into."

Bob thought about that for a moment.

"Yeah, you should talk to them. I'll set it up with Dylan if you'll call Blue."

"Back to you Wednesday?"

"Okay, Wednesday. And, uh, we'll pay you for your time talking with them too, since you'd have to do it as part of the project anyway. But only if you end up taking the job."

That sounded like desperation to me. Maybe I should ask for a higher rate. Or at least insist on sitting in a proper chair if we had another meeting like this.

"Fair enough," I said. I was leaning toward taking the assignment. Mostly, it was the money, but there were other aspects I found interesting.

But Emily wasn't going to like it.

Chapter Five

I got home from Glowery Friday afternoon in plenty of time for dinner during which Emily reminded me it was our night for Neighborhood Watch duty. This was supposed to involve driving around the area for three hours with a CB radio ready to report anything suspicious while presumably Don Bledsole, the amusingly bumptious chairman of our Neighborhood Watch Committee, monitored our transmissions and stood ready to relay our reports to the police if necessary, advise us of any new orders from Command Center (Bledsole's basement) or give us any reports he might receive from other sources so we could check them out. In reality, for Emily and me it meant driving around for 10 minutes and then sitting in the car in our driveway sipping Walmart wine, flipping between classical and oldies stations on the radio (I can't currently justify the expense of a SiriusXM subscription), and hoping the occasional static from the CB was caused by sunspots and wasn't heralding a report of nearby nefarious activity. Sort of like a police stakeout but marginally less fun than I imagined a stakeout to be, and usually without the traditional coffee and donuts.

The overzealous Bledsole had wanted to outfit the cars in the Neighborhood Watch program with GPS trackers so he could "come to your aid if necessary," but we all flatly refused. He pouted for about a month and finally let it go.

We weren't vigilantes, so if we saw something, we were supposed to let the police handle it. I still didn't have a gun,

25

and Emily wouldn't have let me bring one along anyway. In the year or so we had been doing this, we had never observed anything suspicious or used the CB to make a report except the one time, our first night on duty, when we discovered a burglary at our own house. It had happened before our shift officially started, so we didn't get any demerits from Bledsole. Otherwise, the year had been a quiet one in our neighborhood, no doubt because all the would-be criminals knew better than to mess with us rough 'n' ready official Neighborhood Watchers. The occasional raccoon raiding a garbage can or teenager setting off cherry bombs at midnight weren't as circumspect as the criminals, but they didn't warrant involvement by law enforcement.

It was as good a time as any to tell Emily about my meeting with Bob. Although bored with the inactivity, she was in a good mood, what with the wine and the music. It didn't take long for the mood to change.

"Mark, you *can't* work for that man! I don't like him."

"I don't much like him either, but sometimes you have to rise above …"

"And I don't trust him!"

"Well, that's a little different. Not sure I do either."

Sip of wine.

"When I found out you'd almost been killed by that … that stupid Japanese guy …"

"Hawaiian guy."

"Whatever. When I found out you'd almost been killed by that stupid *Hawaiian* guy, I was so scared I couldn't sleep for a week."

"I'll ask Marshall Blue if he thinks there are any stupid Hawaiian guys involved in this."

"You're not taking me seriously!"

"Well, actually I am. I don't want to rush into this any more than you want me to, and I want to assess the danger, if there is any, before I sign up. But it's not like it's a war, with snipers and everything, and nobody's been killed or even seriously hurt."

"Not yet."

"Right, but still. I think somebody's just trying to make a point, even though it seems a silly way to go about it."

Maybe there *were* some stupid Hawaiians involved.

"Who would want to hurt poets and writers?" Emily asked. "And so many of them."

A car went by, faster than the speed limit of 35 miles an hour. Then three more in rapid succession, with the emphasis on rapid. Our street is a thoroughfare through the neighborhood, so it's a busy one, and few drivers obey the speed limit, especially on the downhill portion in front of our house. But we weren't there to catch transient speeders.

"Maybe one of them posted a poem on Facebook or something that was so offensive to this guy, or woman or whoever, that he is out to get all of them. Mad at the whole community. It's far-fetched, and I doubt it, but who knows? That's what they want me to help find out."

Generous sips of wine.

"That's what worries me."

"But I'm not one of them. A writer or poet, I mean. Or an artist or a musician or an actor. None of those. I'm not the target. And anyway, I won't be working for Bob. The Glowery business cards are only a cover. I'll be working for the GADC."

"You'll be pretending to be a writer. No, come to think of it, yes, you *are* a writer. You wrote a book, remember? Someone is bound to notice," she observed.

She had me there. I wanted people to notice my book and buy it. That was the whole point of it. And the book's existence would blow my cover if I pretended not to be a writer. On the other hand, it would be a legitimate entrée into the good graces of other writers who wouldn't take me for an imposter, even if that's how I still thought of myself. On the *other* other hand, if they read the book, or only the cover blurb, they'd know I'd gone undercover to solve a crime, and that might make somebody nervous. Unless they thought it was fiction. But it wasn't.

Two more cars went by. Wine was poured from bottle to glasses. And sipped.

"You're probably going to write a book about this too, aren't you?"

"Thinking about it," I admitted. I was getting sleepy.

"You really want to do this thing."

"Well, yeah, I guess. We could use the money."

"Mark, I know you think you wrote that book just to make some money, but really, deep down, you want to be a writer. You've said so. You've spent your career doing business writing, and you're good at it. Those skills are transferable to book writing, aren't they?"

"Not much transfer required, when you think about it. You'd be surprised how creative most business writing is."

"Deep down, you'd love to hobnob with other writers, try writing different things, get critiqued, right?"

"I could learn a lot from them. Might be fun."

The CB crackled, but no command came forth. It was getting late.

"Promise me you'll be careful?"

"Promise. And like him or not, Bob is committed to making this work, and I know Marshall Blue and the police will have my back."

Truth be told, I still wasn't 100% comfortable with the whole thing, especially the part about everybody figuring out I had already done some undercover work, but my success with that had bolstered my confidence in my detective skills. I had talked myself into a boldness greater than my natural inclination, and Emily's resistance seemed to have withered with the wine and the lateness of the hour. So I guess it was a go, at least to take the next steps and meet with Blue and Vivaldi.

"You realize you had to get me drunk for me to agree," Emily said, looking through half-closed eyes.

"First time for that," I said.

Five minutes before our shift ended and we could put the car in the garage and go to bed, a basketball dribbled itself down the middle of the street.

"What was that?" Emily asked.

"What was what?" I was distracted by trying to push the garage remote-control button mounted on the underside of the car's rearview mirror in the dark without upending the wine bottle.

"That!!"

I looked in time to see a second basketball following the first.

"Aren't you going to do something?" Emily wondered sleepily.

"Absolutely," I said. "I'm going to sit here calmly and see if the Harlem Globetrotters come by next, followed by a band playing 'Sweet Georgia Brown.'"

They didn't, but two teenage boys did, laughing maniacally and running as fast as they could, trying to catch up with the basketballs they'd been dribbling without spilling the big red plastic beer cups they were holding. This was clearly a dangerous practice. They should have been dribbling on the left, facing traffic.

Hardly something to disturb Don Bledsole over. Although I was tempted.

We heard the cherry bombs a half hour later, but by then it was somebody else's shift.

29

Chapter Six

Typical of many to follow, this first 911 call had come at 7:32 p.m. on a Saturday from a cell phone at the Read-A-Spell Bookstore downtown during an open mic poetry reading event.

911: Nine-One-One; what is your emergency?

CALLER: I … I … she's just lying there!

911: Yes, Ma'am. What is the location?

CALLER: On the floor!

911: No, I mean what is *your* location, what address are you calling from?

CALLER It looked like she was trying to swallow the microphone, and then she threw up and fell down!

911: Please calm down, Ma'am, and tell me exactly where you are.

CALLER: Okay. Okay. I'm standing about ten feet from the back door right now, near the Children's section, but when it happened I was sitting near Self-Help. It's horrible but thank God I didn't get any on me! I got out of the way just in time. Now everybody's calling 911!

911: Yes, I know. All right, Ma'am, the GPS has you, and I'm dispatching the EMTs and the police. They should arrive in about seven minutes.

CALLER: OMG, I think she's dead!

911: Is anyone trying to help her? Does anyone there know how to perform CPR?

CALLER: Well, no one wants to get too close to her because, well, you know … the mess and all. We don't know what to do! 911:All right, Ma'am, please stay calm and stay on the line until help arrives. May I have your name. please?
CALLER: Her poem wasn't that bad!
911: What is your name please, Ma'am?
(Caller hangs up)

The poet wasn't dead. The EMTs took her to the hospital. The police interviewed the witnesses, not only those who were attending the monthly open mic event put on by the local writers' group, but also the customers in the bookstore at the time. Everybody said the same thing. It looked like she was trying to swallow the microphone, and then she threw up and fell down. Nobody saw anything else. She spent the night in the hospital and went home on bed rest for two days with a monster headache. Tuesday she was back at work as a cashier at Target.

She had no food allergies. Tests revealed no virus, no infection, no injury, no internal bleeding, no salmonella, no botulism, no controlled substance abuse—well, some, but nothing that would cause these symptoms—no needle marks and no detectable poison. Like the police, the doctors were stumped.

Sometime later, I read her poem. It *was* pretty bad. But I didn't think it was what made her collapse.

Chapter Seven

Monday – Week 1 on The Case

"I'm glad you're on board," said Detective Lieutenant Marshall Blue over a sausage biscuit, hash browns and coffee at the McDonald's on the corner of Battleground Avenue and Westridge Road. I had the Egg McMuffin and an Americano ("A simple, satisfying Americano made with hot water poured over our Rainforest Alliance Certified™ espresso"). It was early Monday morning and the restaurant was busy, but we found a corner booth and some measure of privacy. Better than sitting in his unmarked cruiser parked next door at the Village Tavern. A pleasant looking man I'd guess to be in his early 50s although I've never asked, Blue was in rumpled business casual with a dark jacket over an open necked light blue dress shirt and sporting a small neatly trimmed mustache that reminded me of Sheriff Belton's over in Spurrville except Belton's was bushier. His badge and gun were not in sight.

"I'm not there yet, at least not officially," I said. "My deal with Bob is I'll talk to you and Dylan Vivaldi and then decide."

"Bob said you were on board."

"Bob sometimes exaggerates."

"Well, crap."

"He likes to get his way, and sometimes he gets it by acting like he's got it."

"Could-a fooled me. And I don't fool easy."

"No, you don't. Anyway, I am leaning toward getting on board, so can we go from there?"

"I got a choice?"

My exposure to Blue was limited during the Spurrt case. As I said before, he seemed dedicated and efficient, but I didn't get to know him well. Now maybe I would. I hoped for the best.

"Anyway, thanks for recommending me."

"No problem. Last year I was on the Residential Property Squad, which is where I met you, but then I got promoted and now I'm in Criminal Intelligence—ain't that a joke—and I just caught this case. I'm getting a lot of pressure to clear it. Which I don't see happening anytime soon, what with all the victims and different kinds of crimes and trying to keep it out of the papers."

"Tough case, huh?"

"I've seen tougher."

"Oo-kay."

"Reason I'm glad you're on board is my guys don't have a clue how to handle this thing."

I didn't think the pun was intended. Or noticed.

"We do good undercover every day, but usually it's into stuff where we know the territory, right? Like drugs, gangs, gambling, ticket scalping. That kinda thing. With this, we're like a fish in deep water, you know what I mean?"

I nodded.

"We don't do painting or poetry and stuff, so we'd stand out, see?"

I waited for "like a sore thumb," but it wasn't coming.

"You, on the other hand, will fit in like a glove. You can be people like that better than us."

The puns and malapropisms were piling up, and so was the stifled laughter on my part, but I held it in.

33

"Although my grandfather took up water coloring after he retired from his police chief job up in Delaware," Blue continued. "Got pretty good too."

"I'm sure," I said. "Maybe we could start by …"

"So anyway, here's how I see the case right now," Blue said interruptingly. "The problem, like I said, is so many victims, from all over the map. But here's the thing—and nobody's figured this out yet except me because they haven't looked hard at it—there's a concentration."

"A concentration."

"Right."

"I mean, is that a criminology term or something?"

"If it is, I just made it up. It means like there's kind of a central thing all this is circling around," said Blue.

"Like what?"

"Are you boys doing okay over here? You need anything else?"

A small woman looking about 110 years old and wearing a McDonald's uniform shirt and a name badge that said "Sharon" had crept up on us during our own concentration.

"Hi, Sharon," said Blue.

"Morning, Marshall," she said, with a glint in her eye. "Ha! Every time I say that, I feel like I'm in a *Gunsmoke* episode. But, Pardner, you ain't Matt Dillon and never will be."

"… never will be," said Blue almost in unison with Sharon. "And glad of it."

"Who's your young friend here, sweetie?" she asked, rising on tiptoe to whisper in Blue's ear. "Another rookie cop, maybe? Is it training day?"

"Not this time. This is Mark. Just a friend."

"Hello, Sharon," I said.

"Well, Mark, I can tell you want to ask me, just like everybody else, what's an old woman like me doing working in a McDonald's? Right?"

34

"Okay, sure, I guess."

"'Cause I get ten bucks an hour, free food, a little exercise, talk to nice people like you boys, and it beats watching Fox News all day at home. They wouldn't hire me as a greeter at the Walmart. Got some kinda age limit, apparently."

"That's … admirable, Sharon," I said.

"And my name's not really Sharon," she whispered. "You think I'd use my real name in a place like this? No, sir. I don't need people knowing where I live. Take too long for Marshall and his rookies to get there and protect me."

"Smart," I offered.

"No, it's Evelyn," she whispered. "I can trust you, hon."

Then Sharon/Evelyn resumed her normal smallish height and her professional McDonald's demeanor.

"You boys need anything? Refills on your coffee? Take your trash?"

"No, we're good, Sharon," said Blue while I nodded in agreement.

"Thanks," I added. We both took sips of coffee as if to prove we were okay.

"Y'all just holler, now, y'hear?" she said and shuffled toward another booth.

I looked at Blue.

"Her great grandson is the manager here," he said. "Drives her to work from the nursing home on days when she's up to it."

"Wow."

"Yeah. Now, where were we?"

"Concentration. You were telling me the crimes all revolve around something."

"Yeah. Okay. Looks like a lot of the victims and crimes, but not all of them, have something to do with the Gate City Playhouse. I mean they either happened there or they happened to people who work there or perform there, know what I mean? Now that we've figured that out, I've told that guy Vivaldi to make sure somebody calls me direct if anything happens."

"Go on."

"That's it. I can show you the list and the numbers, but they're in the car."

"What do you think it means?"

"Last week that was for me to figure out. And I got some ideas, but now it's for you to figure out. Need you to get on the inside at the Playhouse, find out what's going on behind the scenes."

I waited for "so to speak" but, like the sore thumb, it wasn't coming.

"Okay," I said. "I get that. Here's my concern. I'll be going into this as somebody working on the GADC's campaign to publicize the arts community. I can do that, and everybody will be fine with it. But as soon as somebody checks me out on Google or Facebook or LinkedIn they're going to see I wrote a book where I go undercover and solve a homicide. They'll know it's not fiction because they can find the newspaper articles or talk to some of the people in Spurrville and Raleigh who were involved. You, even. You're in the book. Then they'll think I might be doing it again here. Spying on them for the police. Most of them will be okay with that too, although they might be a little wary and not open up to me right away, but the big risk is that whoever is behind this will get nervous and maybe do something rash. To me. To throw me off the trail or shut me up. Could be bad."

"I see your point. One good thing: Nobody knows we've spotted a pattern. Everybody still thinks this is only a bunch of random occurrences, a big bunch, for sure, but nobody knows how big, you know what I mean? They don't even realize it's mostly just with the artsy crowd, never mind centered on the Gate City Playhouse, because the media don't have the information we have, and they ain't drawn the dots yet. And maybe they won't unless there's a leak."

"That's another worry."

"Who's going to leak? Nobody knows but me and a couple of my guys who know I'll shoot them if they tell anybody. And now you. I ain't even told my boss. And I won't for a while because she don't need to know."

"You can get away with that?"

"You ain't read enough detective novels."

"Still, any ideas?"

"Tell you what. I'll make some calls over there. Jake Keil, Sheriff Belton, the Spurr family. Tell 'em if anybody asks it was all superior police work that solved the case and you just happened to be there as an observer trying to write—what was it—a history of the company or something?"

"Yes," I said.

"And the book is just a made-up story."

"I'm good with that, then. Mostly. At least it will confuse people."

Blue paused before speaking again. Took another sip of coffee. Grimaced.

"You say I'm in your book?"

"Yes."

"Did you spell my name right?"

"I think so."

"Okay then."

"Can we get back to the case? Creating confusion about my work in Spurrville is fine, but there's still some danger. Some of these events may be random, and I might just be in the wrong place at the wrong time. Or whoever's behind it may decide they don't like me for some other, who knows what, reason."

"You're right," Blue said. "It might be no walk to the park. All I can do is give you some pointers from how I'd handle myself if I was in your shoes. Okay?"

Blue spent the next five minutes doing that. Some of his suggestions were mundane common-sense kinds of things, but others were eye-openers, and overall they made me feel a little better. Still no guarantees, but ...

The breakfast crowd was thinning out and we had long since finished our second cups of coffee, discretely delivered by Sharon/Evelyn during a repeat visit. We covered a few more details and got up to leave. I noticed Blue put a couple dollars on the table, for Sharon I presumed since one doesn't usually tip in a fast-food place. After some hesitation, I did the same. He smiled.

"And by the way, you should know we *are* going to get this guy," Blue said on the way out. "Even though I'm in the Criminal Intelligence Squad, I don't think there is any such a thing as 'criminal intelligence.' It's like whatcha call an oxyclean or something. Criminals are just a bunch of dumbass scum bags as far as I'm concerned."

"Ticket scalping?"

"Don't get me started."

Chapter Eight

Let's talk about "community." The Merriam-Webster Dictionary has three definitions and 11 sub-definitions. They start with "a unified body of individuals such as the people with common interests living in a particular area broadly," and including "the area itself, a group of people with a common characteristic or interest living together within a larger society (example: retired persons), a body of persons of common and especially professional interests scattered through a larger society (the academic community), a body of persons or nations having a common history or common social, economic, and political interests (the international community), a group linked by a common policy, a social state or condition (the school encourages a sense of community in its students.)," and they end with "society at large (the interests of the community)." I have edited for brevity.

The venerable Oxford English Dictionary says the same thing but uses higher class words and slightly different spellings, as of course it would. One would expect agreement from two such esteemed and authoritative sources. After all, they are leading members of the dictionary community.

What all these definitions have in common is "common." So, you could say they are a community of definitions.

Those outside any given community naturally tend to think of that community as homogenous. Or, as Detective Blue might say, homogenized. This is dangerous. The "arts community," for example, is made up of a number of subcommunities, each representing a different art. This is what Bob Ausländer meant by "amorphous." The so-called "Black community" and the "Hispanic community," and others we could name, are no less heterogeneous. Nevertheless, we do lump them together, for better or for worse, mostly worse.

And what of all the communities in the world considered together? Not good enough to call them, mundanely, so to speak and pun intended, the World Community. No, I'd say they should be called the *Community* Community.

And then there is the Solar System Community, the Galactic Community (within which is the Delta Quadrant Community where the Starfleet vessel USS Voyager with its crew community was lost for seven seasons), and finally the Universal Community.

Well, maybe not finally. On the spiritual level, what about the Heavenly Community and the Hellish Community or whatever your faith tradition calls them? And then you lump all those together with the Universal Community and you get … tired of thinking about it.

Why was I having this absurd discussion with myself? Probably to get psyched up for my debut probe into the Greensboro arts community.

While I was at it, I looked up "tribe." These days, it's not uncommon at a gathering to hear somebody who is happy to be there proclaim, "I found my tribe!" as if they had somehow previously lost it or were wandering friendless and orphanlike their whole life searching for identity, love and acceptance, or maybe only for a bunch of like-minded people with tasty *hors d'oeuvres*. Sorry, I mean, a *tribe* of like-minded people with tasty *hors d'oeuvres*. I've also heard "it takes a village," but I don't recall ever hearing anyone declare, "I found my village!" I guess villages are harder to lose, whereas tribes can go wandering off willy-nilly, leaving no trace.

We have a missionary friend who recently discovered a lost mountain tribe in the Philippines. It has over 100,000 people. The Philippine government had no record of its existence. When presented with this fact, the tribal chief said he had no idea they were lost and he appreciated my friend letting him know.

Ironically for me, Webster's first example of using "tribe" in a sentence is, "a tribe of artists with wild hair and casual manners." Now I could hardly wait! Deep down, I'm all about wild hair and casual manners despite my mother's admonitions about grooming and deportment. I was ready to look for my tribe.

If my life were a TV show, at this point a narrator who could be mistaken for Rod Serling would say, "You are about to enter another dimension. A dimension not only of sight and sound, but of mind. A journey into a wondrous land of imagination. Next stop, The Greensboro Arts Community! You will be representing The Reluctant Amateur Detective Community. Good luck!"

Chapter Nine

I didn't have an address for the Greensboro Arts Community, but I did have one for Dylan Vivaldi. It was the Gate City Playhouse, located in a huge old house on Summit Avenue where I was told Vivaldi keeps limited office hours when he's not out visiting his entertainment venues or supervising backstage activities at the Playhouse. (Newspapers nicknamed Greensboro "the Gate City" in the 1890s because 60 trains used to pass through every day, providing a "gate" to the West and South. Far fewer trains these days, but the Interstates help, and the name has stuck.) I went there directly after my meeting with Lieutenant Blue without going home to change clothes, figuring I was already dressed casually enough to meet Vivaldi: chinos, loafers, and a short sleeve knitted golf shirt with an Adidas logo. I carried a legal pad in a light brown leather portfolio that sported a subdued version of the Glowery logo. The executive version.

I parked my aging crystal black pearl Acura TLX behind the building, messed up my hair a little so I would presumably blend in, checked my look in the rear-view mirror, decided my hair was wild but not too wild, got out and went in the back door, keeping my eyes peeled for clues.

Of course, I didn't have to worry about blowing my undercover cover with Dylan Vivaldi because he was in on it. I was thinking of the other arts people likely to be around. On second thought, maybe I should be dressed business casual with my hair neatly combed since that's what they might expect of a GADC representative. Too late now.

I hadn't gotten a half-dozen steps inside the door when Vivaldi himself greeted me affably.

"You must be Mark Fairley," he said with an outstretched hand.

We shook. Vivaldi was a short, balding man with a thick red beard and no mustache. I heaved an inward sigh of relief when I saw he was dressed similarly to me. Since he wasn't wearing green, I won't say he looked like a leprechaun in spite of his Italian surname.

"I'm Dylan. Welcome to the Gate City Playhouse!"

I was also relieved he didn't say, "Welcome to the Arts Community," or, "Top o'the mornin' to ya!"

"Thank you," I said. "Glad to be here."

"Watch out for poison and falling sandbags, and you'll stay glad, I hope."

"Uh …"

"Just a little theater humor."

"Oh. You mean like 'break a leg'?"

"Aye, like that. Here, have one of these."

I thought Vivaldi was handing me a cigar in a dark green wrapper, which seemed odd, but it turned out to be a pen.

"Unscrew the cap," he said.

I did. It was a fountain pen. With an old-fashioned nib, a word that hasn't been in much use since the 1950s before the ball point pen became popular. I touched the nib and immediately stained my left index finger with blue ink.

"Careful, the bladder's full," warned Vivaldi.

"Yeah, I see that now. But thank you. To what do I owe the honor?"

"Let's run up to my office, and I'll fill you in."

I pocketed the pen, and we trotted up some stairs and came out into a third-floor lobby with carpet, real ficus trees, framed posters of past shows at the Playhouse, and a reception desk complete with a receptionist. Or was she an executive administrative assistant? It was hard to tell.

"Marcy Melnick, meet Mark Fairley from the GADC," said Vivaldi. "He's come to help us."

I thought I detected a note of sarcasm in that last comment, as if maybe he wasn't completely sold on my involvement, but I filed it away and greeted Marcy, a pleasant looking woman of indeterminate age who did not have wild hair. Maybe she wasn't one of the real arts people.

"About time somebody came," she said with a smile. "Dylan's worthless."

"Nice to meet you, too," I said with a nod.

"Is it windy outside?"

"What? Oh, you mean the hair." I patted it down as best I could. "Maybe a little."

"Can I get you anything?"

"No thanks. I just had breakfast."

Marcy seemed relieved. Vivaldi seemed used to it.

His office was tiny, with barely enough room for his well-worn desk, a couple of mismatched side chairs and a bookcase laden with piles of manila folders but few books. The only natural light came from a dormer window that jutted from the roof of the building.

He switched on an overhead light, and we sat.

"Ever been here before?" he opened.

"I don't think so. My wife and I may have brought our kids to see *The Nutcracker* when they were little, but I'm really not sure."

"That was probably here. Before that, this place used to be a residence, which is why it still looks like a big old house."

"I wondered."

"It belonged to my grandmother, don't you know. Claire M. Vivaldi. Big patroness of the arts in Greensboro back in the

'30s. Textile money. When she died a widow 25 years ago, she willed it to my father, Connor, on the condition that he convert it into a performing arts venue. Between grants and donations, including some volunteer labor, Father raised enough to gut the place and rebuild the inside into the theater we have today. It typically seats about 750, but that can vary depending on the type of show. There's an orchestra pit in front of the stage, and parts of the stage can be raised and lowered. There's a small balcony. Plenty of space backstage and in the basement for dressing rooms, storage and whatnot, and we have a box office and a nice lobby out front with a big portrait of Claire, of course, and a small kitchen where we can prepare wine and snacks to sell during intermissions. Plenty of parking too."

"I noticed that," I said.

"Next door we have a nice guesthouse. We can put up visiting performers and celebrities from out of town. It's a lot more convenient than a hotel."

It came off as a recitation, as if Vivaldi had made this speech many times.

"Father was still trying to stay afloat in the textile business, which was going soft what with cheap imported goods coming in, and he didn't see how he could make much money off this place, so he signed it over to me about 15 years ago, and I lease it to the Gate City Playhouse Company for a dollar a year and a cut of the gate, and I help with the productions occasionally, you know, a little directing, someday maybe acting if I'm a good boyo. Might have to wait 'til we do *Finian's Rainbow* for that though. Except the leprechaun in the movie didn't have a beard." He gestured toward his own.

"I rent the building out to other groups when the Playhouse people aren't using it," he continued, "like between shows and during the off season. So, with ticket sales and advertising income, what little profit we make from the café, and the occasional donation or grant from the odd philanthropic foundation, we somehow get by. And all the while, I get this palatial office for free."

"What was Mrs. Vivaldi like?" I asked.

"Neither shrinking violet nor steel magnolia she, I can tell you. She was Irish and married to an Italian, so it was an interesting marriage. Parmesan on the Blarney Stone it was. She was quite avant-garde for a lady of her time."

"Casual manners and wild hair?" I ventured.

"Not exactly, but she *was* kind of a hippie before it was cool, if you get my drift, except she drank Jameson's whiskey, smoked cigarettes in a long holder and drove a Bentley. Entertained a lot. Mostly poets and starving artists. She'd have readings and art exhibitions in the living and dining rooms and invite the whole town, but it was during the Great Depression and not many people usually showed up. She'd wear a drab off-shoulder caftan and sandals, let slip an occasional well-chosen four-letter word, serve free wine and cajole people into buying the art. Some of it wasn't bad, but most of it wasn't ready for prime time."

"Did people call her a bohemian?"

"They might've except for the cigarette holder and the Bentley."

"You were going to tell me about the fountain pen."

"Aye, right," said Vivaldi, gesturing toward an oversize coffee mug on his desk that was full of them. I looked at mine again, admiring its glossy dark green color, and for the first time I noticed a design applied to the barrel, a musical staff with a few notes and the words "Gate City Playhouse Rocks!"

"See? It's an advertising gimmick for the Playhouse," he said.

"Cute."

"We do musicals and the occasional rock concert in

addition to plays, so it's to remind people. Get them thinking about the Playhouse."

I almost said, "And, hey, you could even sell actual Gate City Playhouse rocks in the lobby," but I didn't. Too early in our relationship for lame puns. Later, for sure.

I did say, "These are pretty fancy."

"Aye, not like those cheap Chinese ball points most people give out. Have another; we got tons."

"Thanks. For my wife."

As I picked up the second pen, I looked at it long enough to see "China" in teeny tiny letters on the side of the clip. Probably not a clue.

"Right now, we're trying to put together an Irish show, of all things. Not many of those going around apart from *River Dance* or *Lord of the Dance* and that *Celtic Woman* thing you see on PBS. But ours is an honest-to-God musical comedy with a story and some history even if it is mostly fictional, and some terrific original music as well as the traditional stuff. Not only my grandma and my father, who was half Irish, but my mother was Irish too, so I'm kind of partial to that side of things."

He was getting excited.

"Sounds interesting," I said.

"It's called *The Christmas O'Carolan Songbook, Volume 1.* Written by a guy named Foster Wood, from London."

"Sounds like a good Christmas show," I said. "Probably a lot better than *The Nutcracker.*" Trying to throw in a compliment.

"But see, it's not a Christmas show. You never heard of Turlough O'Carolan?"

He pronounced it "Ter-lock."

"No. Sorry."

"The Legendary Itinerant Blind Harpist of Ireland, boyo!"

"Was he a leprechaun?"

"O'Carolan was the most famous and enduring musician ever to come out of Ireland from back in the 18th Century. People all over the world are still playing his music today, or derivations of it. He was a contemporary of Johann Sebastian Bach, and my namesake Antonio Vivaldi too, wouldn't you know, but I don't think they ever met."

"Too bad."

"But he did meet Arcangelo Corelli at some point, and the story is they had quite the discussion about Irish music versus Italian."

"Who won?" I asked.

"Nobody knows, but given my own mixed loyalties, I'd have had to declare it a draw."

At that, Vivaldi started humming a tune for me, but it was unfamiliar. A nice one, but I never heard it before.

"You don't recognize that?"

"No."

"How about …?" Another round of humming.

"Sorry, still no. But I like it."

"Everybody does. Anyway, the story is about how Turlough has a son that history forgot, completely fictitious, of course, and he was born in December, so Turlough names him Christmas, and young Christmas wants to follow in his famous father's footsteps as an itinerant composer and musician and gain his approval and everything, and we learn about his trials and tribulations as he goes through all that to his final victory. Sort of an Irish *Oedipus Rex* but without the murder and incest."

"I should hope."

"And the music is wonderful! It's just started touring in America, and we were lucky enough to be only the third playhouse selected to produce it. First was Roanoke, then

Cincinnati where it finished up a few weeks ago, and now Greensboro."

"Where can I buy a ticket?"

"Well, that's just it. You can't yet, and I'm not sure you'll ever be able to if we don't get to the bottom of this poisoning business or whatever it is that's going on."

At last, we'd gotten to what I came for.

"How do you think we should do that?" I asked.

Vivaldi looked at me oddly.

"Isn't that what you're supposed to be figuring out?"

"Well yeah, in a way, but I thought I'd get your ideas to start with. You're here on the front lines. You know lots of the people involved, and you probably have some theories. I'm starting at the top, and then I'll work my way down."

That seemed to mollify him. "Makes sense," he said.

"And anyway, I haven't told Bob Ausländer for sure yet whether I'll do this. I want to see if I can make a contribution and how dangerous it might actually be. I had breakfast with Detective Blue, and now I'm here with you, and after I think about it some more and talk it over with my wife, I'll decide. Probably by tomorrow. And then you'll know if I'm really here to help."

"We do need some help, but you can't blame me for being skeptical. I don't see how dropping somebody in here who doesn't have any background in the arts will be much use. Bob explained it, and I agreed to it, but tell me again why the police can't do their job."

"Apparently, they don't feel they are artsy enough to go undercover."

"And you are?"

"No, but I have believable cover as the new PR guy for the GADC's arts promotion project, and I've done this sort of thing before. I do have some experience as a writer, and I don't mind trying to write some poems or whatever it might take to bolster my credibility with the community."

I understood Vivaldi's concern. He probably didn't know the term, but I was once what's called a "corporate seagull." That's somebody who swoops into your business, says, "Hi, I'm from Corporate, and I'm here to help," eats your lunch and then poops on you by flying back to headquarters to tell the big bosses how incompetent you are. I'm not proud of it, and that wasn't to be my role here.

"So you're like a chameleon then," said Vivaldi.

I nodded. A few steps down the food chain from seagull, but what the heck.

Vivaldi rose and motioned for me to follow him.

"C'mon, lemme give you a tour. Oh, and you might want to comb your hair, boyo."

This time, we took an elevator down to the lobby of the Playhouse. Auditions for the *O'Carolan* production were going on, so we were quiet in our exploration of the premises and discussion of the situation as Vivaldi saw it. No sandbags dropped, and no one threw up and fell down, but the specter of such events was evident.

The tour completed, Vivaldi looked at his watch. "Let's grab us some lunch, how 'bout it?" So, we did. Maybe that meant I was truly accepted even in spite of my wild hair.

Chapter Ten

Emily wasn't mollified. (If her name were Molly, would she have been emilified?)

Apparently, Bob forgot I told him I would let him know by Wednesday and he called my home trying to get in touch with me while I was still at the Playhouse. It annoyed Emily.

"He's trying to pressure you, and I don't like it."

There's not much Bob could do that Emily *would* like, and this move didn't help, which annoyed me as well. I didn't think going through another bottle of wine in the driveway that night was going to resolve anything, although it did get a smile from Emily when I mentioned the idea with tongue in cheek.

I called Bob back and basically told him to leave me alone.

"Just hoping, you know. Can't blame me for that," he said.

"I can, and I do," I said. "I told you I need time to sort this out, and my wife has to be on board or there's no deal. Wednesday."

"You da man."

It was as close to an apology as I was likely to get from Bob, so I left it at that. Now, even if I was ready by Tuesday, I wasn't going to call him until Wednesday. So there.

After the Playhouse tour, Dylan Vivaldi had taken me to lunch at one of his restaurants, a Greek place a few blocks from there. The wait staff had Greek names on their nametags, but most of them looked Hispanic to me. Our waiter was Miguel Dukakis. The food and the service were good.

On the way to lunch, I had checked my cell phone and

found an email from a company in Charlotte I'd sent my résumé to six months ago and forgotten about. They were inviting me to an interview Monday of next week. After about a year of unemployment it felt like a miracle even though it was only an initial interview and with a company I wasn't even sure I was very interested in. Nevertheless, it was something positive, and it's probably what buoyed my courage to talk to Bob as bluntly as I did.

The afternoon was spent taking my Acura for its annual state inspection and getting a long-overdue haircut. Long-overdue because I have become a penny-pincher since leaving Glowery, and I delay certain discretionary expenses as long as possible, small though some of them might be. Since my too-long wild hair didn't impress Dylan Vivaldi and I had a real job interview coming up, it was time to get shorn.

I spotted two red and green Glowery service trucks, one parked at a residence and the other at the Walmart on Wendover Avenue. No doubt dealing with more than clean up on Aisle 3. I was too far away from both for their G-Man's eyes to follow me. I didn't see any of the competitors' vehicles.

The afternoon's diversions gave my mind a chance to process what I'd seen and learned during the morning. It unburdened itself to Emily over dinner.

It was a pleasant evening, so we decided to brave the mosquitos and dine on the deck. Mac and cheese (with ketchup) and tuna casserole, my favorites. Emily's normal Monday night circle meeting at the church was cancelled because the head circle-ess was sick, so we had plenty of time to talk.

First, I filled her in on my meetings with Blue and Vivaldi. She listened patiently, smiling at this, frowning at that. Sipping iced tea, not wine.

"I'd like to meet this Sharon person at the McDonald's," she said.

"We can go tomorrow. Although I'm not sure she comes in every day."

"Whenever."

"I almost forgot something," I said. "Be right back."

I made a quick trip to the spare bedroom I use as an office and returned bearing gifts.

"I've returned bearing gifts, my dear," bending to give her a kiss.

"I see you didn't bother to wrap them," she observed. But she kissed me back anyway.

"They're not that kind of gifts. Dylan Vivaldi gave them to me."

"They look like cigars. Did he have a baby?"

I handed her one of the Gate City Playhouse Rocks fountain pens and a colorful booklet Vivaldi told me was an unfinished draft copy of the *Stagenotes* magazine for the *Christmas O'Carolan* production.

"It's a fountain pen," she exclaimed after unscrewing the cap. "I haven't seen one of these since forever."

"Careful, the bladder's full."

"Yes, I see that now." There was a blue stain on her index finger.

"It's a promotional gimmick for the Playhouse. I got one too."

"It's fun. I like it."

"The *Stagenotes* booklet speaks for itself, I guess. Vivaldi says it's the local version of *Playbill*. I'll read it later. Some of the pages are blank because they're still doing auditions and they haven't filled all the advertising spaces yet."

And if I read it, I thought, maybe some clues will jump out about why the accidents and poisonings seem to be concentrated around the Playhouse. Then I thought, uh-oh, apparently in my mind I'm already on the case. Best not mention it to Emily just yet.

"We haven't been to a show in forever either," she said.

"No."

"But I suppose it's hard to justify the expense right now."

"We could probably get free passes to the *O'Carolan* thing if I take the job. It would be part of my 'inquiries,' as the police always say on the British mystery shows."

"That reminds me, are you getting paid for your time this morning?"

"Yes, but only if I take the job."

"You're probably going to do it, aren't you?" she said plaintively.

I feigned slapping at a mosquito while I gathered my thoughts.

"I think I can do the job. It means getting to know a bunch of people—the Upshot Marketing PR people, artists, writers, poets, and so on—interviewing them without them knowing it's an interview—joining at least one writers' group, going to an open mic event or two, that kind of thing. Vivaldi knows everybody and can introduce me to the right people. He can be a little prickly, but we hit it off pretty well, I think, and I figure he'll be there to smooth out the political wrinkles too, if there are any and if he doesn't have enemies I don't know about. I'll probably find that out soon enough.

"Marshall Blue will have my back as far as police authority and muscle if it's needed, and he can warn me about criminal elements that may be lurking."

"What about Bob?"

"Forget Bob. He'll want status reports, and so will Vivaldi most likely, but one of my conditions is I only give those to Blue. This is a criminal investigation, and we don't need any leaks or armchair quarterbacking. It's a ground rule Bob and the GADC will just have to live with. All they can do is stop paying me, but then I stop working. That's the deal."

"I like that it's all in Greensboro. You won't be travelling, and you'll be home every night," Emily said.

"Yeah, I like that too."

The only thing left to discuss was the elephant in the room.

"I'm not ignoring the danger," I said.

"What are you going to do about it?"

"Be careful, obviously. I'll keep my eyes open, be aware of my surroundings, look for anything suspicious—some people call it 'situational awareness'—don't eat or drink anything unless I know where it came from, try not to get on anybody's bad side. Things like that. Blue gave me some tips this morning and I'll be in touch with him every step of the way."

"And of course, you could get hit by a bus, or an airplane could fall on you the next time you step out the door," Emily said. "You forgot to say that."

"Truly, I wasn't going to say that. Hadn't even thought of it." And truly I hadn't. An Uber or a drone maybe. Probably not a bus or an airplane.

"You're a lost cause, Mark Fairley."

She was in.

"Not with you in my corner, my love," I said. "I'll do the dishes and clean up."

"It's the least you can do."

"Oh, by the way," I said, "I have a job interview Monday in Charlotte."

"Mark! Why do you do these things to me?"

"What?"

"Wait 'til the last minute to tell me something like that!!"

"I thought the other stuff was more important, that's all. No, that's not true. Actually, I forgot."

"You're impossible!"

Chapter Eleven

STAGENOTES

The Gate City Playhouse Proudly Presents

Ⲧhe
Chriscmas O'Carolan
Songbook (1693-1760)
Volume 1

A musical comedy celebracing che life and works of
che liccle-known elder son of Ⲧurlough O'Carolan,
che Legendary Icineranc Blind Harpisc of Ireland
Ⲙusic by Ⲧurlough & Chriscmas O'Carolan
and concemporary 17th & 18th Cencury composers

Scage play, original music, biography
and commencary

by Foscer Ⲱood

Christmas O'Carolan (1693-1760)–The Man

Imagine if Turlough O'Carolan (1670-1738) (pronounced Ter-lock), the legendary Itinerant Blind Harpist of Ireland, had a son earlier than the one history records. Say he was born in December 1693 in Ballyfoulmouth, little more than a stone's throw[2] from his father's birthplace of Nobber, County Meath. And being a December baby, say it was natural for Turlough to name him *Christmas* O'Carolan.

This is his story.

Although he rarely saw his father, the latter being itinerant and all, Christmas was blessed to inherit his father's musical talent. This was discovered the first time he was allowed to attend Ballyfoulmouth's annual Throwing of the Stones Festival. One of the musicians broke a fiddle during an evening of revelry and gave it to the young Christmas as a joke. Christmas repaired it with an early form of duct tape[3] and began to sound out some of the simpler tunes. Soon it was almost as if he had been playing all his life.

Possibly the greenest leaf on the shamrock as a youth, Christmas took the references to his father as "the Blind Harpist of Ireland" not to mean that Turlough was blind and played a harp, but that he played an instrument called a blindharp. Christmas searched high and low for a blindharp and finally found one in a church, apparently left behind by Catholic missionaries from Venice. He took to it immediately, reveling in the mistaken idea that he might be following in his famous father's footsteps.

---

[2] Although a system of feet and rods for measuring distances had been in use in Ireland for many years during the O'Carolans' lifetimes (1670-1738 and 1693-1760, respectively), the common people were still in the habit of using "as far as the sound of a bell or the crow of a cock" or the popular "stone's throw" as their basic units of distance measurement.

[3] Called simply "tape," and made from potatoes. Ducts had not yet been invented. Scotch had been invented by then, but the Irish would have been loath to call it Scotch tape.

At some point, Christmas learned that his peripatetic father, Turlough, was indeed blind. Noting his father's success, as well as that of the many other blind itinerant musicians of that era, Christmas tried for a season to pass himself off as blind too in a bid to become "the blind blindharpist of Ireland." However, people quickly saw through the ruse, so to speak, and he gave it up after a few months of stumbling about with his eyes closed and inadvertently playing the blindharp upside down on several occasions, although this did lead to some interesting compositions.

Undaunted, on April 1, 1732, Christmas published a collection of songs he wrote under the name of a fictitious harpist, Blind MeLon O'LeMon. He created a biography of Blind MeLon and fictitious historical notes and stories to go with the songs, and he passed himself off as O'LeMon's biographer and business manager. Much to Christmas's chagrin, for a time these songs were more popular than those penned under his own name, but at least they brought in some money.

In all, it was a hard life, and Christmas did not marry until he was almost 50, having also endured the emotional pain of a birth defect that stalked him for years until he finally came to terms with it by celebrating it in a song ("Two Left Feet"). His marriage produced no offspring.

In October 1760 at the age of 67, Christmas O'Carolan (1693-1760) choked to death on a small potato, the tragic victim of a failed O'Heimlich Maneuver.

Because Christmas resembled his famous father, he was often mistaken for him on the occasions when he ventured forth from Ballyfoulmouth. During the 22 years between Turlough's death in 1738 and that of Christmas in 1760, rumors abounded of Turlough sightings throughout Ireland. We now assume these were either rare sightings of Christmas or simply wishful thinking by Turlough's over-imaginative admirers. Christmas did nothing to dampen their enthusiasm in this regard. More intriguing are the occasional sightings that continued to be reported even long after Christmas's death, some as far from Ireland as Memphis and as recent as last Thursday.

It is our firm position that both Turlough O'Carolan (1670-1738) and Christmas O'Carolan (1693-1760) are, in fact, dead.

Christmas O'Carolan (1693-1760)
"The spittin' image of his father" [4]

---

[4] The painting of a man with a harp, above, is by Francis Bindon of Doonass in County Clare, according to some scholars. Most believe it depicts Turlough, but some say it depicts Christmas and is by M. Neverdon of Doontel in Count Meath. The "Is it Turlough or is it Christmas?" debate has become known as the "Doonass, Doontel Conundrum."

Chapter Twelve

Tuesday

Tuesday was quiet in the Fairley household. I paid some bills. Sweet Emily went grocery shopping and created more bills, but we had to eat. Between the robocalls on our house phone that seemed to come every 30 minutes or so despite our being in the Federal Do Not Call Registry, I thought about my plan of attack. I briefly considered running over to the Upshot Marketing offices to meet with Frances Muldoon and get a head start on that side of things but discarded the idea. Better to wait until Bob made an appointment for me, even though she already knew who I was and would be expecting me at some point.

Bob didn't call. But Dylan Vivaldi did.

"Are you in?" he asked.

"You mean like, 'the doctor is in'?"

"No, boyo, I mean are you the lad who's going to help us with this mess?"

"Yes, I am, but I haven't told Bob yet."

"I'll talk to Bobby. I was wondering if you and your wife were free tonight after dinner to meet me at the Comedy Club. I'm trying out a new comic there named Lenny Monahan, and Tuesday's a slow night, so the three of us would be padding the crowd a little for him, plus I want you to meet some people. No charge as my guest, and you'll be on the clock. Don't worry about ol' Bobby."

After a quick hand-covering-the-phone consultation with Emily, who was thrilled, I accepted.

We arrived at the Comedy Club on Spring Garden Road at about 7:45. It turns out it's the Ꙅomedy Ꙅlub, spelled with Ks turned upside down and backwards and slightly askew, all to say, "Hey, we're terribly zany, madcap and wacky in here!" Like some kindergarten day care place that turns the Rs, Ss and Es around on its sign to make it "childlike" and cute. Or substitutes Zs for Ss, as in Kidz. The now bankrupt chain store Toys "Я" Us went even further, substituting a skewed, cartoony backwards letter for a whole word and never mind how confusing that must be to a four-year-old who is just learning to read.

I'm convinced that in the same way trailer parks cause tornadoes, cutesy kindergarten day care signs cause lysdexia.

I wanted us to walk backwards into the place, but Emily refused.

"Maybe we should cry at the good jokes instead of laugh," I said.

"Get hold of yourself or I'm not going in there with you."

I gave our names to the doorman, and after finding us on his list he ushered us in. It was dark, but when my eyes adjusted I spotted Vivaldi talking to the bartender.

"There you are!" he said, bounding over. "And you must be *Mrs.* Mark Fairley!"

"Emily," she said demurely.

"Charmed," he said. I thought for a moment he was going to kiss her hand, but he didn't.

"Your timing is perfect. Show starts at 8:00. Freddy, my MC, will start it. Four comics doing standup, and Lenny is number two, followed by a young lass I think you'll like, then an intermission and then the headliner, Morrie Milburne outta Toronto. Only one show tonight. The first lad's a rookie, but I think he's got possibilities. I put Lenny second because he's new around here and I've never heard his act before, but he's got some chops according to my sources. Plus, he's Irish. Or says he is. I want you to give me your honest opinion after the show, okay?"

I didn't want to do that unless Lenny was very good, but we nodded anyway. ꓘomedy ꓘritics.

"Then, like I said, we finish with Milburne. Have you ever seen him?"

We confessed we had never even heard of him.

"You'll love him. Part of his schtick is he wears these ridiculous eyeglasses—different ones for each show—sort of like Elton John but funny. Bills himself as The Spectacular Morrie Milburne."

"A pun on the eyeglasses? Spectacles? Maybe they still call them that in Canada."

"Aye, you've got it. You'll see."

So to speak. (Why am I the one who always has to add that?)

Over the sound system we heard, "Last chance to get your orders in before the show! Show will start in fi-i-i-ve minutes!"

"Let's get you both set up with something to drink and some munchies," Vivaldi said, "and you can sit at that table for two in the middle of the room. I'll be here and there, you know, managing. Feel free to get refills."

Emily got a glass of red wine. Monet, I think. Or is it merlot? I get them confused. I got a draft Miller Lite ("a fine pilsner beer").

We sat with our drinks resting on flimsy little paper cocktail napkins, nibbling from a bowl of complimentary munchies that looked like a combination of beer nuts and Chex mix and tasted good. Fifties doo-wop music was playing almost-but-not-quite too loudly over the sound system.

63

The place wasn't full, but it was a respectable crowd. We wouldn't stand out. Emily noticed there were two Gate City Playhouse Rocks fountain pens next to the flameless tabletop votive candle that provided what little light there was for us. Not enough light to take notes by, it seemed to me, but probably adequate for signing one's bar tab and adding a generous tip. There were pens on all the other tables too. Good cross-promotion by Vivaldi.

I pocketed one, and Emily slipped the other into her purse. Why not?

The prices on the drink menu seemed high to me, even for "Toss Back Tuesday" with everything 20% off and no cover charge for ladies, but then I hadn't been to a nightclub in a long time. Inflation. I was glad we weren't paying.

Suddenly, I shifted into situational awareness mode. Not because anything triggered it, but rather because I happened to remember that's what I should be in now that I was "On the Case." I looked around furtively. Anyone here could be a suspect. Except Emily. And maybe Vivaldi; it was too soon to rule out even him.

"Show will start in threeee minutes!"

The stage was small, and it backed up to a plain red brick wall with a large Komedy Klub sign mounted on it but off to one side so it wouldn't distract from the performers. They would use the microphone mounted on a stand next to a wooden stool in the center, bathed in the glow of a bright spotlight. We had a good view.

Promptly at 8:00 the music stopped, the lights went even lower, a drummer I hadn't noticed before did a drum roll building to a cymbal-crashing climax, and a muscular man in a top hat and form-fitting black Komedy Klub T-shirt bounded on to the stage and grabbed the microphone. Freddy the MC, I guessed. Maybe Freddy the Bouncer too, with that physique. He pretended the spotlight was blinding him. Maybe it was.

"Hi-ya folks, I'm Freddy McIntyre, and wellll-come to the Xomedy Xlub, Greensboro's happiest place to meet and greet and eat and beat the heat, where our slogan is 'Funny you should say that!!' And don't worry, just like in the old Doritos commercial, drink all you want, we'll pour more!"

The drums went bada-boom. The audience laughed a little.

"We've got a great lineup for you tonight, folks. First up, Dickie Rafferty direct from Orlando, Florida. Dickie's a newcomer to the comedy scene but funny, funny, funny, and tonight you'll be his gracious guinea pigs. I know you'll make him feel welcome. Next up, an old veteran of standup but also new to our fair city, Mr. Lenny Monahan with some brand-new material. You'll love him! Then, Miss Rwanda Forsythe direct from Pearl at the Palms in Las Vegas where she spent the week wowing famous Hollywood stars who couldn't stop laughing at her impersonations. And finally, after a short intermission, we'll have the distinct honor, privilege and pleasure of presenting the great Morrie Milburne, that crazy, crazy, literally spectacular man from north of the border who needs no introduction, but we'll give him one anyway!

"Are you ready to laugh?"

A few "yeah"s and some applause went up from the audience, and Freddy was not impressed.

"I *said*, are you ready to laugh??"

"YES!!" the audience roared.

Drum roll, cymbal crash.

I noticed the drummer was also the bartender. Vivaldi stewarding his resources. I liked that.

Freddy yelled, "Let's give it up for Dickeee Raff-erteee!" and we were off and running.

Rafferty had some funny lines, but his timing wasn't the best. Worse, he felt he had to be lewd, crude and rude to get a laugh, and it was awkward with Emily sitting right there. Most people didn't seem to mind, which was both surprising and disappointing. Changing times, I guess. But as Vivaldi said, he showed promise, and some coaching would help. I hoped the rest of the evening wouldn't be as uncomfortable.

It wasn't. Lenny Monahan was down-to-earth, clean and reasonably funny, but instead of his material being new, as Freddy the MC had promised, I felt it was a bit too derivative and even a little corny here and there, although he did throw in some clever improvisations. Maybe it was new material to him, but I doubted it. Emily agreed when we talked about it later. We also agreed he did it in such a way that it was funny almost in spite of itself. A remarkable feat. He also had Lenny Monahan souvenir T-shirts to sell after his performance, from a table in the back of the room. I assumed Vivaldi was getting a cut.

Monahan seemed likeable enough, a pleasant looking if slightly overweight man in his late fifties or maybe early sixties with an oversize nose and going bald under the blue pork pie hat he occasionally doffed when delivering a punch line. He was indeed getting on in years, especially for a standup comic. On the other hand, George Burns was booked for Caesars Palace at age 100. Still, there was something about Monahan or his routine that seemed a little off to me. I couldn't put my finger on it, and I don't think it was the T-shirts, but it was vaguely unsettling, whatever it was. My situational awareness? My detective Spidey sense? Even though my views about him were generally positive, I wasn't looking forward to expressing them to Vivaldi, but we'd promised.

Miss Rwanda Forsythe was … different. You don't see many women doing impressions of well-known celebrities. Probably because most impression-worthy celebrities are men.

This was not a problem for Rwanda. She cheated, cleverly. All her celebrities were historical figures of whom there are no videos or recordings and whose statues, if they have any, are stone cold and silent, so she was free to make everything up. Who could disprove her authenticity?

Moses having a hilarious conversation with an imaginary burning bush and later when Aaron tells him the golden calf just sort of popped out of the fire. "Oy vey!" he says, surrounded by shards of the shattered Ten Commandments tablets, "If that calf really just popped out on its own, I'll worship the damned thing myself!" Julius Caesar getting stabbed to death, but hilariously, on the Ides of March. She did Brutus' part too, using a rubber knife. George Washington eating corn on the cob with wooden dentures. Abraham Lincoln feverishly rummaging through his coat and pants pockets looking for the Gettysburg Address he wrote on the back of an envelope and realizing he must have left it on the train. There were others equally well done, one of whom was a woman, Marie Antoinette having her cake and eating it too as the last meal on the eve of her execution, complaining that it's not chocolate devil's food, her favorite. Rwanda didn't do Jesus, which was a relief.

We had to agree, Miss Rwanda Forsythe, direct from Las Vegas, knocked it out of the proverbial park.

After the intermission, during which Vivaldi introduced Emily and me to Lenny Monahan and we all agreed to get together after the show, it was time for the much-vaunted Crazy Canadian, Morrie Milburne. The lights went down again as Freddy the MC bounded on to the stage and gave Morrie a flamboyant introduction that was almost as funny as Lenny Monahan's routine, not that that was too difficult. It wouldn't take much for Morrie Milburne to top it, and I suspected that was the point.

To another drum roll and cymbal crash, The Spectacular Morrie Milburne, the Crazy Man Himself, bounded out from backstage and took the microphone, bowing to the audience applause as Freddy the MC bowed low to Morrie in feigned reverence and bounded off.

Apparently, it's a Komedy Klub rule that you can't walk, run or jump on and off the stage. You must bound.

Tonight, Morrie was sporting oversize Groucho Marx disguise glasses—bushy black eyebrows mounted on thick black rims with a big plastic nose and a broad, bushy mustache mounted below. I doubt many Americans under 40 know who Groucho Marx was. Maybe he's still big in Canada.

When the applause died away, Morrie stuck the microphone in his mouth as if he was going to swallow it. Then he vomited and fell down, breaking his glasses.

In the ensuing silence, some in the audience apparently thought it was part of the act, and there was scattered laughter.

"Cleanup on Aisle 3!" someone shouted. More snickering.

Dylan Vivaldi and I knew exactly what had happened, and it was going to take more than a few flimsy paper cocktail napkins to clean up Aisle 3. Vivaldi bounded on to the stage yelling, "Call 911! Call 911! Turn up the lights!" as the now bewildered audience sat in stunned silence, squinting in the newly-bright house lights.

I remained in my seat but whispered to Emily, "Don't worry. He'll be fine. And so will we."

She looked unconvinced but said nothing.

Freddy the MC bounded on to the stage, sans top hat, and addressed the audience without the microphone, which was on the floor soaking in Morrie Milburne's half-digested dinner.

"He'll be okay, folks! We've seen this before, and he'll be okay. Maybe he forgot to take his meds! The ambulance is on the way, so try to remain calm until they get here and then we can call it a night and go home."

"We want our money back!" someone shouted. "Yeah!" others joined in.

"No problem, no problem! Everybody gets a refund on the cover charge! Just stop by the bar on your way out!"

Already, I could hear approaching sirens. I guess it pays to locate your nightclub near a fire station with EMT personnel on duty.

As the first few customers headed for the bar, EMTs and police barged through the door simultaneously, and everyone froze. The EMTs bounded on to the stage to tend to Morrie, and one of the police officers, a big one, also bounded on to the stage and said, "I'm afraid I'm going to have to ask all of you to return to your seats until we have a chance to sort things out here. We can't have anyone leaving the premises just yet. We'll need to talk to each of you about what happened. If you have an emergency at home or something, see one of the uniformed officers at the door." Then he bounded from the stage to give the EMTs more room as they gathered Morrie up on to a gurney along with his broken comedy glasses, bounded carefully off the stage and wheeled him out the door.

Apparently, the EMTs and the police knew about the bounding rule. They'd probably been to the Χomedy Χlub before.

Detective Lieutenant Marshall Blue arrived around ten o'clock, looking not too happy to have been roused from whatever he usually does on a Tuesday evening. After talking to the big officer and then Vivaldi, he made a beeline for me.

"Fancy meeting you here," I said. He was not amused. I introduced him to Emily, and he softened a little. I couldn't tell what Emily was thinking, but she certainly wasn't bored, especially since Blue had shown up and she was now "in on" things.

"How is it you 'just happen' to be here?" he asked me. "Not that I mind, you understand."

"Of course not. Dylan Vivaldi invited us, and I thought, why not gather a little 'criminal intelligence' while I've got the chance?"

Blue looked askance at me. Probably thought I was making fun of him. Which I sort of was, but only because it was late and I was tired and the evening had stopped being fun. I was mostly laughing with him, not at him, but he might not catch the difference.

"Anyway," I continued, "I might ask the same of you."

"I'm on call for whenever there's an incident involving artsy folks," he said. "It's my case, if you'll remember. And I'll ask the questions, if you don't mind."

"Of course. But you'll be happy to know I'm officially On the Case now," I said. "I told Bob Ausländer already. Or at least Vivaldi said he would tell him."

"Well, I'm tickled to pink."

"Don't you mean 'tickled pink' or 'tickled to death'?" asked Emily.

"Yes, Ma'am, I probably do," said Blue, a little miffed.

"Please, call me Emily."

Emily had a few things to learn about Detective Blue. I would explain them to her later. She would appreciate it.

It was midnight before the police finished taking statements from everyone in the place, amidst not a little grumbling from those patrons who were among the last to be released, including us. Blue had long since departed.

Vivaldi stopped by our table to apologize and say obviously our get together with Monahan would have to be postponed.

Emily and I drove home without saying much. I didn't notice any Glowery trucks parked along the way. Traffic at that hour was light, and I found myself thinking about something I had noticed but, in the confusion, had forgotten, about Morrie Milburne as he lay motionless on the Komedy Klub stage. There was a blue stain on his index finger.

Chapter Thirteen

Lenny Monahan's Standup Routine (excerpts)

(Recorded live at The Komedy Klub in Greensboro, North Carolina. Transcribed by Marcy Melnick. Subscribe to Lenny's channel on YouTube.)

FREDDY THE MC: All right, people, let's give it up for comedy's newest Greensburger, the one ... the only ... Lenneee Monahan!!

(Audience applauds as Lenny bounds from backstage to the microphone wearing sneakers, jeans, a blue pork pie hat, a blue sport coat, and a white T-shirt picturing his smiling face leaning out from behind a barred jail cell door and the words, "Lenny's Out!" MC exits.)

LENNY (in an Elvis imitation): Thank you. Thank you very much. (Applause dies down)

LENNY: And good evening, ladies and germs. Or, since I'm Irish, maybe I should say, "Top o' the evenin' to ya!" Anyway, how do you like my T-shirt, eh? Whaddaya think? My parole officer said I shouldn't do it, but I couldn't resist having a few made up. If you don't like the prison motif, I've got another one that just says, "Lenny!" But, hey ... "Lenny's Out!"? And I only got out a few months ago. Get it? Only 20 bucks, your choice of sizes and colors, and they'll be on sale in the back right after the show.

Actually, I was never in a jail. It was a "detention center".

A detention center. Do you have those here? What happened to good old-fashioned jail? Now it's a *detention* center. You know, nowadays they've got euphemisms for everything. A secretary is "an executive administrative assistant." A short person is "vertically challenged". (Laughter)

So, a detention center. When I was a kid and they made you stay after school for being naughty, you got "put in detention." *That* was detention. They were going to "detain" you for an hour so you'd miss the school bus and have to walk home or get your mom to pick you up, or maybe catch a ride with your hoodlum friends. Detention was in an empty classroom near the principal's office, and there'd be maybe 20 other kids in there. Studying, clock-watching, reading *The Catcher in the Rye*, making out (Laughter), whatever. That was detention. Something you could look forward to. Something you could aspire to. (Laughter)

So I was in a detention center. And you know why I was there? Because they said I shoplifted a watch. From Walmart. It was one of those watches with the hands that glow in the dark, you know, so you see what time it is at night when the lights are out. But you gotta expose it to some bright light first, you know, sort of charge it up. So I took it outside. Wouldn't you? I tried to explain I only wanted to expose it to the sunlight for a minute, then bring it back in and see if the glow in the dark hands worked before I bought it. They didn't believe me! Can you imagine?! I guess maybe since it was a rainy day, that didn't help. (Laughter)

So, the judge says, "Okay, you're going to serve time in the 'detention center.'" I'm sure she must have said how long I was going to serve, but I was playing a game on my lawyer's iPhone (Laughter) and didn't hear that part. I thought, "detention center," that sounds good. Be there an hour or two, find some new friends. Maybe make out. (Laughter)

Well, I was there a long time. And it sure seemed a lot like jail. Not that I've been in jail a lot, you understand. Just from what I've heard. Detention center. Can you imagine: Clint Eastwood rounds up the bad guys in Dry Gulch and says, "Okay, I'm takin' you boys to the *detention center*!" The bad guys are all looking at each other like, "What did he say? 'Detention center'? Hey, could be fun, right? A lot better than jail. We'll find some new friends. Maybe make out. (Laughter) Let's go!" And before ol' Clint can say, "Go ahead, punk, make my day," they're already halfway there. (Laughter/applause)

Okay, I know you came here for a good laugh, so enough about jail, and let's get to the really funny stuff. Hey, hey! A rabbi walks into a bar. But he doesn't order anything. It's a bar mitzvah! Hey, hey! (Tepid laughter)

I just flew in from the Coast, and boy are my arms tired! Hey, hey! (Groans)

Take my wife. Please! (Tepid laughter)

I admit I borrowed those jokes, but they're so old maybe nobody here has ever heard them. Right? Hey, hey!

You can probably tell I'm not from around here. Where are we again? Milwaukee? Philadelphia?

AUDIENCE: Greensboro! North Carolina!

LENNY: Oh, right. Greensboro. Hello-o-o, Greensboro! Hey, hey! Are you all from Greensboro? (Audience applauds, tepidly)

LENNY: Hey, hey! A fine city, a fine city. I've been there. (Tepid laughter) Okay, who here's *not* from Greensboro? You? You, sir? Where you from?

MAN: Cleveland.

LENNY: Say what? Speak up a little so we can all hear you.

MAN: Cleveland!

LENNY: Cleveland! Wow, Cleveland! I flew over Cleveland once. Boy, were my arms tired! Hey, maybe you know my cousin Lonny? Lonny Monahan? He's actually *been* to Cleveland. You know him?

MAN: No.

LENNY: Okay, well, he's been in a detention center over in Dayton for a while, so it was a long shot, but I had to ask. He's got about two more years of detainishment. Do you have a business card, sir? I'll give it to Lonny and ask him to look you up when he gets out. I've got a feeling you guys'll get along great! No? Well okay, anybody else?

WOMAN: Venezuela!

LENNY: VENEZUELA! Wow! That's like somewhere way down in Mexico, right? (Laughter)

WOMAN: No! South America! South America!

LENNY: South America? Like in (sings) "Don't cry for me, Venezuela-a-a"?

AUDIENCE: That's ARGENTINA!

LENNY: Potato, potahto, tomato, tomahto, right? Hey, I did a show once in Mobile, Alabama. I thought *that* was South America! Everybody talked funny. Even funnier than you folks, y'all. Hey, hey! Well, welcome to Greensboro, Ma'am. Or should I say Senorita?

WOMAN: I'm married.

LENNY: Okay, welcome, *Mrs.* Senorita. (Laughter) ¿*Como estas*, and *Hasta la vista*!

Hey, hey! But you know, now that we're talking nationalities, and potatoes too, did you hear me say I'm Irish? (Slips into Irish accent) Aye, that I am, born on St. Patrick's Day, and Monahan is a fine old Irish name! Any more Irish in here this lovely evenin'? (Scattered applause)

I thought as much. We like our music and our whiskey, don't we? So, drink up! And our potatoes too, as long as they're not *French* fries! (Laughter)

And as quick as we are to tell a joke or two, we can take a

joke or two as well, don'tcha know. Fer example, I went out drinkin' last St. Patrick's Day, so I took a bus home. That may not be a big deal to you, but I'd never driven a bus before. (Laughter)

What's Irish and stays out all night? Paddy O'Furniture! (Tepid laughter, groans)

Aye, 'tis a terrible pun fer sure and all—the lowest form of joke, but harmless enough and not too insultin' like some I've heard, especially the terrible limericks. We don't much like those, now, ye know. You say, "Don't mess with Texas." We say, "Don't get my Irish up!" There'll be a shillelagh in your future now, fer sure 'n' all. Just you ask my two daughters, Fait' and Begorrah! (Laughter) We're God's people, we are! *Éirinn go Brách* and all that, you know.

Here's another good one then: What happens when a leprechaun falls into the water?

ANNOYING MAN IN AUDIENCE: He gets wet? (Laughter)

LENNY: Thank you, kind sir! Your check is in the mail! (Laughter)

LENNY: I'm thinkin' you're all Irish tonight, all right! (Loses accent) But seriously, folks, and speaking of hearts as we were, you know I had a heart attack way up north in Philadelphia a couple years back. I did! It was a tough crowd that night. (Laughter) You guys are much nicer, thank you very much. Not that I'm looking for sympathy. Or mercy laughter. Hey, hey.

Anyway, it was February. Cold. Cold.

ANNOYING MAN: How cold *was* it?

LENNY: Again, thank you, sir! Why, it was so cold the Philadelphia lawyers were keeping their hands in their own pockets! (Laughter)

But, hey, I got really good treatment. My only complaint is they never used the siren on the ambulance. I thought I should deserve a siren. You know, being sort of a celebrity and all. But they said, "I'm sorry, sir, Obamacare doesn't cover that." (Laughter)

Don't you know, actually the police got to me before the ambulance came? I said, "Why?" They said I was under cardiac arrest. Hey, hey! (Laughter interspersed with groans)

But seriously, my heart attack was from years and years of abusing fatty snack foods. They found a Frito in my one of my arteries. (Laughter)

So, they put in what they call a stent, to keep the artery open, right? So, now the Fritos can flow more freely. (Laughter)

You know, after a heart attack they ask you a bunch of questions—see how you're doing psychologically and all. My doctor asked me if I ever had suicidal thoughts. Suicidal! What is he, nuts? Would I be doing standup if I *wasn't* suicidal? Or I could be a politician. Same thing! (Laughter)

But my doctor is happy … with the new boat in his garage. (Laughter)

I feel good, and I can do just about anything I want. And if there's stuff I don't want to do, I can play the Heart Attack card and just say no. It's great! (Laughter)

Now, where was I? Oh, yeah—a priest and a minister go into a bar. They don't order anything because—Hey, I could go on, but you know what? I had a heart attack! (Laughter)

Hey, you've been a great audience! I've got to go rest my arms up for the commute back to my apartment, so thank you! Thank you very much! And don't forget about the T-shirts! For you, only 20 bucks!

(Audience applauds. Lenny bounds off the stage and jogs to the back where the T-shirts are. Freddy the MC returns.)
FREDDY THE MC: How about that Lenny, huh? Lenneee Monahan, ladies and gentlemen! Yeah! Let's hear it again for Lenny!

(Applause continues. Lenny bounds back on stage for a bow, says "Hey, hey!" and then bounds off and jogs back to the T-shirts.)

Chapter Fourteen

Wednesday

Bob called promptly at 8:00 a.m. Wednesday morning.

"I hear you're on the case," he said. Not "Hello."

"Looks that way."

"You could've called me."

"Didn't get on it for real until late last night. Thought it might be past your bedtime. Besides, Dylan Vivaldi said he'd let you know."

"And he did, but still ..."

"Did he tell you what happened at the Жomedy Жlub last night?" (I assumed Bob knew the Ks were supposed to be backwards.)

"No."

I told him.

"Sounds good! I mean ... you know, for the case and all."

"Right."

"What's your plan?"

"Well, it's basically your plan. I'm going to start by meeting the folks at Upshot Marketing to get that part moving, and then I'll work my way through the Usual Suspects and see where things lead."

"The usual suspects?"

"Yeah, Bob, there are always Usual Suspects."

"You're nuts, Fairley. Anyway, I'll set it up with Frances Muldoon."

As much as I was looking forward to immersing myself in the Usual Suspect Community, I did want to get to know the PR people first, to establish my GADC credibility. Early afternoon found me and my Glowery executive leather portfolio in the spartan offices of Upshot Marketing, located in a modern office campus off Piedmont Parkway southwest of downtown, waiting to meet Frances Muldoon and her merry band of benevolent propagandists. Both she and Donna Majors, the Project Director, greeted me in the lobby—a good sign—supplied me with a clip-on plastic Visitor card and escorted me to a small conference room. A little sign on the conference table said, "Welcome, Mr. Farly! We're glad you're here!" A nice gesture, but the "Mr. Farly" made it mildly problematic.

I gave each of the ladies one of the new business cards I'd picked up at Glowery on the way over. They barely glanced at them before handing me their own. No evidence they noticed any inconsistency. I decided to let it slide. It was the thought that counted. And the "Mr." was nice, if a little more formal than I'm used to.

Coffee was offered, and soon a smiling gofer whose ID badge said "Brandon" served it efficiently and withdrew. I wondered if he was Frances' or Donna's executive administrative assistant but decided not to ask. He probably wasn't. I hoped he wasn't the person responsible for the spelling debacle, because he seemed like such a nice, quiet young man. Which means he will probably turn out to be a serial killer.

Anyway, we got down to business in a hurry. Frances, a pleasant looking woman of about 50 with graying red hair and freckles, welcomed me to "the team," announced she had another meeting in five minutes (Bob, characteristically, must have disrupted her schedule), gave me a brief history and overview of the Upshot agency, which I appreciated and told her so, turned things over to Donna, and left. Donna, a pleasant looking black woman probably in her early thirties and wearing an engagement ring with a diamond half the size of Gibraltar, rolled her eyes but with a smile.

"I love working for Frances, but she *is* driven," she offered.

"So was Miss Daisy."

She missed half a beat but laughed and said, "Not exactly what I meant, but I guess it's close enough. She knows what she wants, and she gets it, but usually in a nice way. And I've learned a lot from her."

"And what does Miss Daisy want for this project?"

I needed to speak carefully from this point on because although Frances Muldoon was in on the undercover thing, I had to assume Donna wasn't. I had forgotten to ask.

"Basically," said Donna, "we want to glorify the arts community. Make it seem bigger than it is, make it seem like a lot of fun, that it's fulfilling for the highly talented yet safe and welcoming for beginners and hobbyists, that it's contributing greatly to the quality of life in Greensboro. We want to encourage more participation by both the artists and the public, and garner more financial support for it by the more economically favored among us."

Basically, it sounded like she'd made this speech before. And basically, it wasn't bad. Extra points for "garner." And "economically favored."

"Not bad," I said. "How much is true, and how much lying do we have to do?"

"What?"

"Sorry. But I know marketing and PR involve a lot of spin, maybe some exaggeration from time to time, you know, just to get a point across."

"Oh. I see. Well, that's right, but we do adhere to standards of honesty and integrity here at Upshot."

"Of course."

"Let me take you to my pod and introduce you to the rest of the team."

"Your pod?"

"We don't have a lot of offices here, and the teams work in together-circles we call pods, out in the open where everybody can see what's going on. It's very welcoming and conducive to creativity."

As far as I know, pod is the term for a social group of whales or dolphins. I awaited my introduction to Donna's with eager anticipation.

Donna's pod, which had a little sign on a music stand that actually said "Donna's Pod," was indeed near the center of a large open room that appeared to have two or three other pods scattered around. Floor to ceiling windows admitted copious amounts of light on three of four sides. Donna's pod boasted a couple of sofas (not leather, I was happy to see), a coffee table strewn with squeeze toys and comic books, a raised drawing table such as an architect might use, a couple of small desks with chairs, and a stationary exercise bike. Three young people stood amidst the furniture, all holding laptops or iPads and wearing eager-to-meet-you expressions. This failed to make me think I'd found my tribe, but it did feel good.

Until Donna said to the smiling group, "Boys and girls, meet Mr. Markell Farly from the Greensboro Area Development Commission!"

"Call me Mark," I said. They smiled all the more.

She'd pronounced it "Markell. "As in "Mark L."? Why was she using my middle initial for an informal introduction? And why Farly again?

I had three of my business cards out and ready to hand to her people when it dawned on me I hadn't bothered to look at them myself when I picked them up at Glowery. The pot calling the kettle black. Maybe I should look at them now. I did.

Markell Farly, Vice President, Special Markets, The Glowery Company, they said, followed by my contact information. Apparently, someone at Glowery had verbally asked Siri, Alexa, Cortana or one of those other ubiquitous AI thingies to order my cards, and she (it?) ordered what she thought she heard. I'd be stopping off and having a word with that someone at Glowery on the way home, it appeared. It wouldn't be Bob.

I nonchalantly palmed my cards and slipped them into my pants pocket. No one seemed to notice. How the misinformation got to the Upshot people was a mystery for another day.

"This is Brad, our graphics guy," said Donna brightly, indicating a slender, smooth-faced boy who looked about 14 to me but was probably in his late twenties with a master's degree from the Rhode Island School of Design.

"He has a master's degree from the Rhode Island School of Design," she said. Brad nodded modestly, and we shook hands.

"And this is Sarah, our media and computer guru, who comes to us with a degree in integrated marketing communications from the Medill School at Northwestern University."

We shook. I could imagine Liking Sarah on Facebook and enjoying her Tweets and Instagram posts, being so all about media as she was. A pleasant looking brunette with oversize horn rim glasses, Sarah didn't look any older than Brad.

"And finally, Nigel, our writer. No master's degree but a master of the King's English."

"That would be the Queen's English, surely," said Nigel in a perfect "posh" (I learned later) accent and with a grin, as if they had rehearsed this routine more than once. "I'm from

Yorkshire but studied in London." His dirty-blond muffin-top haircut bobbed a little as he nodded when we shook hands.

"Nigel published two novels before he was 30," added Donna proudly.

"Wow," I said. "I'll have to look them up."

"They're nothing much," said Nigel.

"And," said Donna, "he's auditioning for one of the leading parts in the *Christmas O'Carolan Songbook* production at the Gate City Playhouse."

"I can do the Irish accent, me lads and lasses" said Nigel, demonstrating.

"Good luck to you. And what about Donna?" I inquired. "A Ph.D. in applied psychology from Harvard, I'll bet."

"No, just a bachelor's in business from Greensboro College," she said. "The rest is OJT University."

I stared at her.

"On the Job Training. OJT?"

"Got it."

Nobody offered business cards.

"We'd love to tell you our thoughts on the project," said Donna.

"And I'd love to hear them."

This was not a pod of whales, but they weren't guppies either.

"Of course, we're just getting started, but we already have some exciting ideas. Our first presentation is at the Greensboro Country Club in a couple of weeks, so we're putting in some extra hours."

Donna gestured that I should have a seat on one of the sofas. I sat and opened my leather Glowery executive portfolio so I could take notes, or pretend to, on the legal pad. I pulled out my Gate City Playhouse Rocks fountain pen and held it poised over the pad. Classy.

"Hey, I've got one of those!" said Brad, spying the pen.

I smiled at him. Brothers in arms, the pen being mightier than the sword and all.

One by one, Brad, Sarah and Nigel stood before me and described their exciting ideas. They used charts and graphs, mockups of ads, rough storyboards, and other props and exhibits to get their points across. I nodded and said "uh huh" and "right" a lot, threw in a question here and there, and generally engaged in what's called "active listening." It's a practice I first learned of during some down time with Tadashi Tanaka, a Japanese college student I met during my previous assignment over in Spurrville. It's a leadership technique widely taught in this country too. There are seven parts to it, but it boils down to pretending to care greatly about what someone is telling you. I can do that if I don't have to do it for long.

After about 20 minutes of this, Donna stepped in and shared her exciting ideas for how to employ the others' exciting ideas in an expertly coordinated way so as to create and execute one grand overall unstoppable absolute Jonah's whale of an exciting idea that would glorify the heck out of the arts community.

In fact, it did sound good. These were bright, committed professionals, and I respected that.

When Donna finished, I summarized (Active Listening, Part 7) to make sure they understood I understood what they had said. I praised them—me, the big cheese from the Glowery Company and the Greensboro Area Development Commission. They glowed (but not with the Glowery Glow. I know the difference.). Then it was time to clarify my role in all this.

"So, Donna," I said, "what do you see as my role in all this?"

Donna hesitated a moment before saying, "Well, uh, Frances said you would be a sort of a, you know, a figurehead, kind of." She looked at me as if seeking my approval. Which I gave.

"That sounds about right," I said. Donna relaxed.

"It's not that we don't want your input, you understand," she said. "Far from it. We'd love to know your ideas and get you to critique what we're doing. It's just that ..."

I held up my hand, palm forward, and shook my head. "No, no, don't worry. What you presented is exactly how I see it. You are the professionals, and I'm not even qualified to critique you except as a consumer, if you will, of the campaign you're putting together. Which already looks great as far as I can tell. I'll attend some of your presentations when you meet with the movers and shakers to pitch this, like at the country club, and I'll nod approvingly and make 'Isn't this great!' gestures and noises at appropriate places and generally put the GADC stamp of approval on everything to give it the credibility you need.

"Also," I continued, "I'm going to go to some of the arts community activities and events and meet some of the people so I'll have a better understanding of how things work at ground level. Maybe that will turn out to be helpful to you too. How's that?"

Donna and her pod mates smiled and nodded approvingly. "Welcome to the team," she said.

No one can accuse Mr. Markell Farly of not being a team player. I'd found my pod, if not my tribe.

Chapter Fifteen

The Music

Only a precious few of Christmas O'Carolan's (1693-1760) songs, or those attributed to Blind MeLon O'LeMon, have survived. Some had no lyrics, and for many that did, the lyrics have been lost or are illegible either because the pages got wet or Christmas did. Here is a small but representative sampling of his works.

Fallen and Can't Get Up

Christmas O'Carolan (1693-1760) wrote many drinking songs, of which this is perhaps his most famous. A teetotaler himself, which would have made him a pariah among the Irish of his day if he weren't also a musician (although some would say that made it even worse), he still enjoyed visiting pubs for the entertainment value as well as to perform in them from time to time. He often wrote songs and tunes about what he saw there.

Verse 1
Here's a fresh tankard of Irish ale,
Keep filled and I'll tell my tale.
My health, may it never fail;
Spirit of courage must needs prevail!

Verse 2
Crossed swords with the best of men,
'Though I can't remember when.
Hard fighting from glen to glen,
Ever returning to drink again.

Chorus
I would stand if I was able.
Pass the bottle and pass the cup.
Raise the floor up to the table;
I've fallen and can't get up.

Verse 3
Well the ale's done what a blade can't do.
I'm floored after just a few.
Fair maid with your skirt askew,
Aye, from down here it's a lovely view.

(Repeat Chorus)

The Robbers of Nobber

Every year, Christmas O'Carolan (1693-1760) made a sort of pilgrimage from Ballyfoulmouth to Nobber, County Meath, the birthplace of his father, Turlough O'Carolan (1670-1738) and the site of the annual All-Ireland Sad Song Competition. Each time, when he had scarcely got to within a stone's throw of his destination, he was stopped by robbers who beat him and took his money and clothing, leaving him only his underwear and his blindharp, the latter probably because no pawn shops would take it. Christmas assumed they were men who had taken offense at a song he had written about their loutish behavior in a pub (possibly "Fallen and Can't Get Up"), but they wore masks so he could never identify them.

However, on the journey of 1749 he decided he had had enough. He prepared by sharpening the slats on his blindharp, intending to use it as a defensive weapon. It worked, and the robbers retreated with severe lacerations about the arms and masks, never to harass Christmas again. So he wrote another song about them.

Part 1a
I was on my way to Nobber,
Innocent as could be.
Crossed a band of robbers,
Low, lying in wait for me.

Part 1b
This time I was ready,
Ever my blades were sharp.
Made the robbers bloody!
Aye, blindsided by my harp!

Part 2
Fo fum, here they come,
Now, I'm going to have some fun!
Hi ho, there they go,
Hey, look at the robbers run!

Never Moor

Desolate and cold even in the summer, the windswept moors of County Tyrone are among the most inhospitable lands in the otherwise breathtakingly beautiful country that is Ireland. Some say they resemble crater-pitted moonscapes, with scant vegetation, little potable water, and barely enough sod to build a house.

Only a few diehard farmers and herders continue to eke out a living there, many of them sheltered in caves, wedded to the land because it is where their ancestors settled in the days before they found out there were better places. In short, they are morons.

Christmas O'Carolan (1693-1760) never visited County Tyrone, but he must have heard about the area in travelers' tales. In a song he imagines a place called Never Moor and the emotions of one whose lover has departed, presumably for a more agreeable clime.

"Never Moor" won the top award in the All-Ireland Sad Song Competition of 1736 for "Sad Song of the Year."

Verse 1
Look how the wind sweeps across to the sea,
As it bears you forever e're farther from me.
Grass turning amber like old sheaves of grain;
Aye, the moor mocks me gently to add to my pain.
For I know in my heart nevermore will there be
Aught but bittersweet sorrow you've set yourself free.

Verse 2
Gone and no reason, no recourse to save,
Off to find you a new world, a new road to pave.
No more the comfort we shared as of old,
Now my hope's rendered brittle; it shatters with cold.
As the sun dimly sets behind clouds dark with rain,
Fading dreams are the last place I'll see you again.

Nevermore

After the success of Christmas O'Carolan's (1693-1760) "Never Moor" at the All-Ireland Sad Song Competition of 1736, many contestants in subsequent years entered songs with the same or similar names, hoping the judges would presuppose the songs were good, and sad. And many were. Notable titles included "Ever

Moor," about an unattainable Irish Eden, the opposite of "Never Moor;" "Never Mare," about a barren racehorse; "Liver Moor," a mythical place where alcoholics go to die; and "Morenever," a metaphysical song no one really understood, including its composer.

None of these songs ever won until Christmas himself entered "Nevermore," in 1739. His own career by then on the wane, he planned to enter the song under the name of Blind MeLon O'LeMon, hoping thereby to resurrect the once thriving parallel career of the fictitious blind harpist alter-ego he had created in his younger years. However, his supportive if mostly absent father, Turlough, convinced him to enter it under his own name.

When the judges heard "Nevermore," their emotional reactions and those of the attending barflies were strong but mixed. Everyone had an opinion, and after listening to the song several times (the first time ever that an entry had received such treatment), the judges realized they had to create a whole new prize category.

Thus, "Nevermore" was the first winner of the So Sad It Makes You Laugh prize and was awarded the Pewter Funny Bone.

Verse 1
Nevermore will the sunshine pour over the rain,
Nor for me will the flowers be open again.
And I'll see no more rainbows in skies up above,
Nevermore taking joy in the arms of your love.

Verse 2
Nevermore will I hold you from sunset 'til dawn,
As we dance in the moonlight 'til all fears are gone.
Oh my passion will smolder but nevermore burn,
For I'll ne'er love another lest you should return.

Chorus
There's a place, far away, where lost lovers have gone,
When the ways of the world sing a bright siren song.
I can see them adrift on that far distant shore;
It's the land of lost lovers that's called Nevermore.

Chapter Sixteen

Figuring Detective Blue had probably interviewed Morrie Milburne in the hospital Wednesday morning since he was supposed to fly back to Toronto as soon as he was released, I called on my way home from Upshot to see how it went.

"Pretty much a bust," he said disgustedly. "He'll be okay, just like the others, but he don't remember anything that might explain what happened. No strangers approached him. Nobody touched him before the show, or all day for that matter—he was mostly in his hotel room making calls and writing new stuff for his act, and he ordered room service for lunch and dinner. Backstage before the show he says he only saw Vivaldi and the other three clowns. The lab says there was nothing strange in his stomach or his blood, so it ain't food poisoning, and he wasn't on drugs. He's healthy as a fiddle. They're releasing him this afternoon."

"Did he say how he felt right before he stuck the microphone in his mouth? Or why he did it? Did he feel nauseous, or was sticking the mic down his throat what made him throw up?"

"I asked him all that. He said he felt normal until he grabbed the mic. Then he said all of a sudden the mic looked like a chocolate ice cream cone and he needed to eat it all in one bite. 'Devour it,' is what he said. He wasn't hungry, but he couldn't control himself. He said with the mic in his mouth he started to gag, and that's when he puked. He don't remember passing out."

"How does that match up with what the other victims say?"

"Some said they felt vertigo, like they lost their balance or were spinning or falling, but otherwise pretty much the same as Milburne except for the ice cream cone thing. That's new."

"So you think nobody else had that?"

"Or they were too embarrassed to admit it."

"Maybe. Or they saw something else. Candy bar? Fudgesicle? Rocky Road? Cherry Garcia? Chunky Monkey? Beef jerky?" I was reaching.

"Possible. Still, maybe too embarrassed to admit it," Blue said.

"So, what do you think?" I asked.

"I don't know, Shylock, what do *you* think?"

Shuddering at the misplaced epithet, I plowed on. "It's a clue, Detective Blue."

"Clever, Fairley. I can see why I always knew you were the right guy for the inside job with the poet-people."

I assured Blue the impromptu rhyme was unintentional. It just popped out, like the golden calf. Although I kind of enjoyed it.

I plowed further. "I mean, it says there are hallucinations involved. Maybe that will help the forensics people figure out what kind of poison is being used."

"Good point," he admitted. "I already ran that by the lab folks, and they're all over it."

Dueling detectives. Blue could win the duel all day long for all I cared, but it didn't hurt for me to gain a little more of his respect along the way.

"No clue too small, we'll find 'em all, y'all," I said.

"You're a hooter."

"But I think it's too early to bring in Ben and Jerry for questioning."

"Who?"

"Never mind," I said, barely managing a straight face even though Blue couldn't see me, we being on the phone and all. "Were there security cameras at the Xomedy Xlub? And does the Xlub videotape the performances?"

"Yes on both counts, and we've been all through them but we didn't see anything suspicious."

"Could I have a look at the performance videos?" I asked. "Especially Morrie's."

"Sure, knock yourself out. Extra eyeballs won't hurt."

I didn't have any extra eyeballs, although my mother always claimed to have two in the back of her head. I didn't inherit the trait, so it must have been a recessive gene. I don't know what I expected to see in the videos, but something was gnawing at me, something just out of reach.

"Okay, one more thing," I said. "Actually, two things. Looking at Morrie on the floor last night, I noticed a small blue stain on his right index finger. Mean anything to you?"

"It was on some of the other victims too, but mostly on their left hands. Didn't think much of it until now, but it could be a common denomination."

Stifling a snicker yet again, I imagined Blue's superiors reading his reports and struggling to translate his idiomatic gaffes into standard police-speak. He was a courageous, intelligent and perceptive man, but there was a tiny screw loose somewhere. Maybe as a tot he'd gone to one of those kindergarten day care places that turn their letters backwards. At least he tried. Emily was sympathetic when I brought it up after we got home Tuesday night, and she didn't resent my clueing her in on it, so to speak. She was more concerned with the dramatic spectacle we had witnessed, and what it might mean in terms of danger for me.

"Do you have one of those fountain pens from the Gate City Playhouse?" I asked him.

"No, but I've seen a few. Why?"

"Dylan Vivaldi's handing them out all over the place to promote the Playhouse. Gave me one the other day, and I took another one home to Emily. They were on the tables at the Ҟ omedy Ҟlub last night too. We both got ink stains on our fingers playing with them. On our left index fingers, not the right."

"Makes sense. Milburne must have one. You and your wife are right-handed, right?"

"Right."

"Milburne's left-handed, so that might explain the difference."

Chalk up another point for Blue's observational skills.

"No idea what it means, if it means anything at all," Blue concluded.

"Everything means something," I said.

"Words to live with," said Blue. "I'll send one of the uniforms over to the hospital to ask Milburne to give us that pen so I can have the ink analyzed. I think he's still there."

"Good idea."

"What was the other thing?"

"Can you give me that list of victims with whatever information you have on them, how they're connected to each other and the Playhouse, or not, and any notes you've made about them? You said you had some ideas about the case, and now that I'm on it I'd like to hear them."

"Sure. I'll get all that emailed today. My notes are scratchy, but I guess you're smart enough to figure them out."

One more call and I figured I'd be done for the day. My cell phone battery was getting low, and I'd forgotten to put the charger cord in my car. I would call Vivaldi to see if he still wanted to reschedule the visit with Lenny Monahan for Emily and me. Also, I wanted to ask him to introduce me to somebody in the local writers' club so I could join a critique group and also start attending some of their open mic events. And, as a by-the-way, to ask him how the *Christmas O'Carolan Songbook* auditions were going at the Playhouse. Maybe I would show up at one of them and look for clues.

He was out, so I left a detailed message with Marcy Melnick and asked her to have him call me back.

Then it was home to dinner and a good night's sleep so I would be physically and mentally prepared for the real work to come, part of which was pretending to be the right guy for the inside job with the poet-people.

Chapter Seventeen

Thursday

Blue's email was waiting for me the next morning, which was Thursday, and I pulled it up after breakfast. His "scratchy" notes were there and also a link to a restricted police website where I could view the Komedy Klub performance videos. I was mainly interested in Morrie Milburne's.

In the four weeks following the first 911 call, there were many more such calls involving victims connected to the arts in one way or another. There were so many in such a short time that it aroused the suspicions of Guilford Metro 911 Call Center personnel who reported their concerns to the Greensboro Police Department. (Greensboro is in Guilford County.) Under Detective Blue's direction, investigators sifted through all of the approximately 50,000 911 calls received during the relevant one-month time period, weeding out 376 duplicate calls for the same events, and identified 34 separate incidents that seemed to be connected in that way. Thirteen more incidents occurred in the week since I got involved.

The list of victims was staggering. Thirty-four and 13 made 47, and that included only the ones the police knew about. There might be more. There was no way to tell how many other incidents may have occurred that didn't result in someone calling 911. Looking at emergency room admittance records was only marginally helpful because some victims may have self-treated or been helped home by friends and quietly stayed there until they recovered. That was fortunate because otherwise somebody would have said something to the newspaper by now.

I read some of the 911 call transcripts myself. Sobering, but somewhat entertaining in a macabre way, like the first one.

By far, most of the incidents were like the one at the Read-A-Spell, but not all. There was variety. Simple accidents like falling off a ladder while changing a light bulb backstage at the Gate City Playhouse or tripping on the stairs after a meeting of a writers critique group. Freak accidents like getting clobbered by a sandbag falling from above the stage—a classic murder ploy in popular fiction. Some that weren't accidents at all, like being almost run down outside the downtown public library by a masked, black-clad, helmeted figure on a motorcycle or being mugged behind the Weatherspoon Art Museum by a masked, black-clad, helmeted figure who escaped on a motorcycle.

Too many incidents with victims connected by their involvement in the Greensboro arts scene for all this to be happening by chance.

Fortunately, no one had been killed. So far. Whoever was responsible, they apparently weren't out for murder. Intimidation maybe? But why? A prejudice against creative people, maybe driven by jealousy or resentment? "Stop being so damn artsy!" didn't strike me as a particularly worthy motive for mayhem or even a sensible protest slogan. But these days you never know. I didn't rule it out.

A ploy to drive artsy people closer together against a common enemy? Too far-fetched for me, and too much like herding cats anyway, as I was about to learn, but again, these days you never know. I didn't rule it out.

A ring of unhinged practical jokers? They'd have to be so dedicated to their "craft" that it didn't seem reasonable. I ruled that out.

Far too many suspicious incidents and only one lead, and it was tenuous. A mysterious masked, black-clad, helmeted figure on a motorcycle who might be involved or might as easily have absolutely nothing to do with any of it. But clearly someone or some group was behind it. Whoever they were, they were putting an awful lot of effort into it. How long before they made a mistake and a non-lethal apparent poisoning, "accident," or assault turned into murder?

Knowing the media monitor police scanners and check hospital records trying to uncover newsworthy events or any goings on that could be embellished and sensationalized, the police had adopted a special variation of their 10-codes for the incidents to throw them off the scent.

Greensboro and Guilford County law enforcement agencies have a set of 100 10-codes. We all know a few, like "10-4 (Acknowledgement)" and "10-20 (Location)" because of TV cop shows and trucker CB slang, as in "What's yore twenty, come back?" and "Ten-four, good buddy!" Ever wonder about 10-5? It's "Relay." I don't know if there are track shoes and a baton involved. 10-21 is "Call by telephone." 10-0 is "Use caution," and 10-100 is "No assist car available." And so on.

A few of the 10-codes have status codes after them, like "10-7, Code 3 (Out of service, Court)" or "10-24, Code 4 (Assignment complete, Assistance provided)." You can Google this.

I'd have suggested adding "10-101 (None of your business)," but that probably wouldn't fly. It would draw a "10-23 (Stop transmitting)" or a "10-22, Code 5 (Disregard, False call)."

Detective Blue's variation was to have everybody go Canadian. Whenever there was a call about one of these poisonings or any other suspicious incident involving someone in the arts community, police officers and Sheriff's deputies were instructed to add "eh?" at the end of each code. For example, "10-52" would normally be a routine call for medical assistance ("EMS needed"). But "10-52, eh?" would mean the incident involved an arts person. The police thought this was hilarious, and so did I, and so far no civilians had caught on, including the media.

Blue and his team of detectives[5] had sliced and diced and grouped the victim list the proverbial six ways to Sunday, looking for patterns. The only one that emerged, as Blue said, was a concentration of victims with some connection to the Gate City Playhouse. There were 19 of those, and the others seemed randomly distributed, yet almost all within the arts community. Blue's team interviewed all the known victims and then re-interviewed the 19. Besides being victims, all were considered suspects as well because the perpetrator could easily have poisoned him- or herself to throw off suspicion.

None of the 19 had jumped out to the investigators as being of more interest than the others, but at least maybe we were getting closer to identifying a motive. Something to do with the Playhouse. ("A brilliant deduction, Shylock," I could hear Blue saying.) Not much of a lead, for sure. And it could all still boil down to coincidence. Since there was so much activity at the Playhouse anyway, those 19 victims could be associated with it just by chance. Anyway, it was a start. Maybe. And in detective stories, the detective always says, "I don't believe in coincidences."

I looked at the list of 19 and read the interview reports, trying to decide which ones to get acquainted with. First, I ruled out those I considered "happenstance" victims (a euphemism for coincidence, I suppose, but justified). One was

---

[5] Why not a "sleuth" of detectives? Like bears.

a homeless man whose only connection to the arts was that he routinely slept alongside the dumpster behind the Playhouse building. Not a suspect. Another was a pizza delivery guy who had shown up to feed the stage crew. Still another was a plumber hired to unstop a toilet in the Playhouse ladies' room. He got some dirt on his bifocals, and after finishing the job he washed them in the sink and tried to dry them with the electric hand drier. Unfortunately, it was a newly installed Xlerator® high speed model that puts out a tornado-force wind for quicker drying, and with his glasses off he didn't realize it until it was too late. They were hurled to the floor and smashed. And so on.

That narrowed the list to six. I was surprised to find Nigel Wilson on it—the copywriter and novelist from Upshot Marketing who was trying out for a part in the *Christmas O'Carolan* show—but it made sense. The mugging victim was on the short list too, but not as a suspect. She was taking Playhouse audition notices to the Weatherspoon Art Museum when she was attacked. Hers was the only recorded instance of a victim being a specific target, again assuming the mugging had anything to do with anything and wasn't just a random act. The mysterious masked, black-clad, helmeted motorcycle rider rummaged through her purse and got away with $12.37, her Visa Card, a York chocolate mint patty and two Playhouse fountain pens. Did her work for the Playhouse make her a target?

So far, the police had not apprehended the motorcyclist. A definite suspect, but probably a long shot.

Then I pulled up the security camera video from the Ҳ omedy Ҳlub. The quality of picture and sound was good. Vivaldi hadn't skimped. I watched all the footage, from the time the Ҳlub opened that evening until the camera was cut off shortly after Milburne's literal downfall. Like the police, I saw nothing suspicious. Nothing jumped out at me. I watched Milburne's part four times. There was Morrie in the spotlight each time, blithely starting his routine, just as we'd seen in person. Then, without warning, he sticks the mic in his mouth, upchucks, and falls down as the audience sits stunned for a moment before pandemonium breaks loose. I was getting nothing.

Yet, there *was* something. Something. But what?

Chapter Eighteen

I made a few more notes about the most interesting victims (the "Artsy 6?") and was putting my pen down—a Bic ballpoint, not the Gate City Playhouse Rocks fountain pen—when the house phone rang. I was hoping it was Dylan Vivaldi returning my call, but according to Caller ID it was only another robocall, so I let it go to voice mail. Of course, they didn't leave a message.

I guess I should be more appreciative of the helpful folks who want to reduce my credit card interest, sell me cut-rate insurance, or offer technical help should my computer crash. Not so appreciative of fake threats "from the IRS," announcements that there is a warrant out for my immediate arrest, that my auto warranty has expired, that my accounts at banks I've never done business with in my life will be frozen, that my computer *will* crash or that my grandson will be held indefinitely in a Guatemalan jail unless I send money right away in the form of Walmart gift card serial numbers, plus my bank account number, my passwords, a facsimile birth certificate and my shoe size. I don't even have a grandson. I do have three children in college, as I've said, but none has yet expressed an interest in spending a semester in Guatemala. Paris maybe. Not Guatemala. As if we could afford either one anyway.

The phone rang again, but I ignored it. Except this time, somebody *was* leaving a message, and it was Dylan Vivaldi. I grabbed the phone and caught him in midsentence.

"Sorry," I blurted, "I thought you might be the IRS."

"Oh, do they call often, then?"

"It would be the third time this week, except it's you instead. For which I'm grateful. I was about to call you again anyway."

"Well, I was just returning your call, boyo. If it's about you and Emily getting together with Lenny Monahan, can we do it tomorrow morning at 11:00 in my office at the Playhouse? Most mornings Lenny sleeps in, as you can imagine."

Resting up from a strenuous night of ⅀omedy.

"Yeah, that'll work," I said. "Afterwards, if the *O'Carolan* auditions are still going on, maybe we could sit in for a while. You know, get a feel for the show and the people involved. Atmospherics." And maybe clues.

"Actually, we've just started rehearsals, and you're welcome to watch."

"Thanks, that's even better. Also, could you get me an introduction to whoever heads up the writers' group so I can figure out how to get involved there?"

"That would be Betty Wright-Moore, the president."

"You're kidding."

"About what? Oh, the name. What can I say; it's her real name. Anyway, I've already taken the liberty of calling her, and you're now a provisional member of Writer's Block and entitled to attend their monthly poetry critique group that, as it happens, meets next Tuesday night at 7:00. I told her you're with the GADC but genuinely interested in trying your hand at some poetry. She was happy to hear it."

Vivaldi told me where the poetry critique group was meeting, said the moderator was a guy named Ryman Stanza, and gave me Ryman's email address along with Betty Wright-Moore's phone number in case I wanted to get acquainted enough to ask her about her name. And maybe Ryman's.

How many more artsy people in Greensboro had names like these? Was this a clue?

I thanked Vivaldi and went to tell Emily about our appointment with him and Monahan.

And then it hit me. I was going to have to write a poem by Monday for Tuesday's critique group meeting. Actually, before Monday since Monday was when I had to be in Charlotte. Would my creative muse deign to grace me with her ephemeral presence over the weekend? Or would my fledgling poetic skills see me in the doggerel house come Tuesday evening?

Chapter Nineteen

Friday

Friday morning at 11:00, Marcy Melnick met Emily and me at the back door to the Playhouse and took us up to Dylan Vivaldi's office. Although right on time, we were the first to arrive. We hadn't rehearsed exactly what we were going to say to Vivaldi by way of a critique of Monahan's performance at the Komedy Klub, and we were hoping to get away with a few complimentary comments offered to Monahan himself and hope Vivaldi had forgotten our promise.

It was not to be. Monahan showed up a few moments later sporting a mild case of bed head (or was he being Webster's "artist with wild hair and casual manners"?) and without his trademark blue pork pie hat. He wore jeans, sneakers, and a navy-blue Notre Dame sweatshirt, presumably over a "Lenny's Out!" T-shirt, but I couldn't be sure.

"Hey, hey," he said as we re-introduced ourselves and shook hands. "Nice to meetcha, you know?"

"Right," I said. Since I didn't know if Vivaldi had explained why he wanted Monahan to meet with us, I filled him in on my role with the GADC, our goal of promoting the arts in Greensboro and my need to get acquainted with some of the key players. He seemed surprised to be considered a key player, especially since he was in town only temporarily, but without Vivaldi there to explain it himself it was the best I could come up with on the spot.

"We did enjoy your show the other night, Mr. Monahan," offered Emily, too soon in the conversation for my liking, but the subject had to be broached sooner or later. Might as well be sooner.

"Thanks. I get that a lot," said Monahan with a grin. "And hey, hey, please call me Lenny."

"Lenny," I said.

"Lenny," said Emily.

Nothing was said about the incident involving Morrie Milburne, and we hadn't spoken to Monahan again that night. After the police interviewed everybody, Monahan had gathered up his T-shirts, having sold none, and vanished into the night. I imagined him flying to his apartment with only one arm flapping, the other cradling the shirts.

There were more chairs in Marcy's reception lobby than in Vivaldi's cramped office, so we sat out there and made small talk while waiting for Vivaldi.

"Of course, my real name is Séamus. You know, pronounced 'Shame-us' and with one of those funny little marks over the 'e.'"

"Like an umlaut?" I ventured.

"No, that would be German, which I definitely am not. 110% Irish, that's me."

"Right."

"Of course, I don't go by Séamus. It doesn't sound too good for a guy who's been in jail to call himself 'shame us' now does it?"

"Right. And the word 'shamus' is slang for detective," I said. "There was an old Burt Reynolds movie by that name. In the '70s."

"Yeah, I saw it on TV. Didn't like it. Don't much care for cops."

"Right."

"As you can imagine."

"Right."

"Plus, when I was little, I got tired of the other kids calling me 'Shameless' all the time at every foster home I ever lived in."

"Of course."

"And anyway, most of your good standup comedians have catchy, fun-sounding, friendly-type names like Jackie, Johnny, Buddy, Jerry, uh, Richie, Freddy, Eddie, Jimmy, Jay, Reggie, Bernie, Gary, Danny, uh, Woody. And Andy. Even Morrie. Not to mention Amy, Kathy, Lisa, Susie, Lucy, and so on. There's something funny about the 'y' or 'ie' sound at the end of a name."

It was sounding rehearsed.

"But not Vinnie or any of those kinds," he added. "Sends the wrong signal, you know?"

"Wrong. I mean right."

"What about Marcy?" said Marcy from behind her reception desk.

"Yeah, Marcy would work too, for a girl. You wanna try standup?"

"No thanks. Just thought I'd ask."

"By the way," said Monahan, "how is Morrie?"

"We heard he was okay," I said.

"Well, good. Glad to hear it. Anyway, my point was, as a society we've learned to expect people with devil-may-care nicknames like that to be funny. Séamus is Irish for James, so I could have picked Jimmy, but I didn't like it. I picked Lenny because it's kind of edgy. Had it changed legally. Leonard Monahan. Lenny for short. Lenny is actually Irish too, but most folks don't know that because it's also English, German and Dutch. Or they think it's Italian; you know, like Leonardo da Vinci. Means 'lion heart.' If it reminds anybody of Lenny

Bruce, I'm sorry, but he's been dead since 1966 and his foul mouth with him. Who really remembers? The 'Monahan' says it all anyway. Hey, hey!"

"Right."

Small talk with the stars. What a treat!

"Ah, I see you're already getting acquainted!" called Dylan Vivaldi, stepping out of the elevator a good 20 minutes late but very welcome at that point.

"Marcy, any calls?"

"Not a one."

"Nuts. It's almost 11:30 and I haven't made any money yet today. Well okay, has everyone had some coffee?"

"I was waiting for you," said Marcy.

"I'm here now."

"Fine. Coffee, anyone?"

Our coffee mugs filled and doctored with the sweeteners and creamers of our choosing, we all settled back in our chairs for the discussion I had been dreading. Monahan kicked it off.

"So, you say you liked my show, but what did you really like? Specifically. Be honest now!"

And we were, mostly. As Emily and I had discussed after our evening at the Komedy Klub, our reaction was positive overall, but not enthusiastically so. We praised Monahan for using clean jokes and witty improvisations but diplomatically chided him about how some of the jokes seemed a bit corny. He took it well and even made a few notes.

"I take it the both of you didn't have much to drink that night, am I right?" he asked when we finished.

"Right. Just a glass of wine for Emily and a beer for me."

"Guinness, of course," said Vivaldi.

"No, it was a Miller Lite. Sorry."

"Guinness next time," said Vivaldi. Monahan grinned.

"Yes, sir," I said.

"Anyway, we had to drive home," added Emily. "No designated driver."

"Okay, well, see, here's the thing about standup. In a comedy club, everybody comes expecting to laugh. They're presupposed to it from the start. Then the MC sets them up some more. That's his job. They have a few drinks, which lowers their inhibitions and makes them even more ready to laugh. So, if the first comic was any good, at least by the time the second comic comes on stage, the audience starts laughing just because he walked up there. Put a few drinks in people at a show and they'll laugh at anything. It doesn't have to be very funny.

"Listen to the comedy channels on SiriusXM. Most of the stuff is really not so funny even though you can hear an audience laughing. And why should it be? You're sitting in your car, perfectly sober we hope, keeping your eyes on the road ahead, with no crowd around you to take cues from and no MC to get you in the mood. It's flat. The jokes are mostly lame, but they get laughs because the audience is drinking and the comedians talk loud or use funny voices or accents. Or catch phrases, like 'Hey, hey!' They make faces and use hand gestures too, or props, like my hat. Or gimmicks, like my T-shirt schtick. Or Morrie Milburne's 'Spectacular' glasses. You can't see those on the radio. But they all add up to an entertaining performance even though it's basically an illusion."

I still couldn't afford SiriusXM, but as I thought about what Monahan was saying I realized he was probably right. Also, these were good tips in case the Reluctant Detective thing didn't work out and I decided to become a comedian. Maybe I would try them out if I ever got to perform on an open mic night, although those venues are usually libraries that don't allow drinking, or bookstores that might offer beer or wine but no hard stuff. I did have one or two hats at home that some people might think were funny. And some amusingly incorrect business cards I could hand out. And I could make faces.

I was impressed with Monahan's thoughtfulness and sincerity about his craft, and I could tell Emily was too. Vivaldi hadn't said a word during this whole exchange, but his expression indicated approval as well. Like he'd made a good choice giving Monahan a tryout at the Xomedy Xlub. But none of this was getting me any closer to solving The Case. Time for some real investigative work.

"That was very educational, Lenny," I said. "Thank you. Where did you learn all that?"

"I've been doing it a long time. Had some good role models."

I was afraid he'd launch back into the laundry list of disarming nicknames, but he refrained.

"How did you happen to come to Greensboro?" asked Emily. "This isn't exactly Las Vegas."

"Hey, hey, I'll show up wherever I'm asked. Uh, no offense."

I thought I caught the beginnings of a frown from Vivaldi.

"But actually, I read somewhere that Mr. Vivaldi here was putting on some kind of Irish thing at his theater, and since I'm attracted to all things Irish, I emailed him and introduced myself."

"Call me Dylan," said Vivaldi.

"Dylan," said Monahan. "And thanks again for giving me a shot. I hope I can, you know, schtick around for a while. Hey, hey!"

"No problem," said Vivaldi.

"Obviously, you saw what happened to Morrie Milburne," I said, forging ahead. "Did you know he's not the first performer it's happened to around here?"

Lenny seemed surprised. "I should say no because I just flew in from, uh, Cincinnati actually—and boy are my arms tired—but geez, Dylan, do I need to be worried?"

"Not if you keep bein' as good as you are," said Vivaldi without missing a beat.

"Small comfort," said Monahan. Then, looking at me, "What's going on, anyway?"

"You really haven't heard?" I asked again.

"Not a thing. Tell me."

He seemed genuinely upset. I downplayed it by telling him a few people around town connected to the arts had had similar episodes, but all recovered completely, and I'd heard somewhere that the police were looking into it but didn't seem to think it was a big deal. Morrie was the only professional performer who had had a problem, so it was probably a fluke and Lenny shouldn't be too concerned. Vivaldi nodded encouragingly in agreement.

Of course, I was downplaying for Emily's benefit as well, even though she knew I was lying. I couldn't tell if Lenny was buying it or not. First he nodded and looked thoughtful. Then he seemed to shrug it off. Clearly, I wasn't going to learn anything from him today.

"Well listen," said Vivaldi, "Time's marching on and we've got the rehearsals of our 'Irish thing' downstairs we can sit in on if everybody's ready."

"Thanks, Dylan," said Monahan, standing up, "but I'd rather wait and see the show on opening night, if that's okay."

"I'll set you up in the front row," said Vivaldi.

"Thank you, kind sir. Anyway, I've got a lunch date waiting and then it's back to my little apartment to sharpen up my act with the comments I just got from Mr. and Mrs. Fairley here."

"Emily," said Emily.

"Mark," I said.

113

"Right," said Monahan. "You sure'n it was never '*Mc*Fairley'? Or '*O*'Fairley'? Ye could be Irish, y'know."

"Positive," I said. "I think it's Scottish, actually."

"Ah, so maybe we're Celtic cousins, like."

"Maybe. I do have another question before we split up, if it's okay."

"Hey, hey, shoot."

"There was this one point in your act that I thought was, oh, maybe a little negative and didn't quite fit. It was the bits about bad Irish jokes, 'Don't mess with Texas,' 'Don't get my Irish up' and the mention of a shillelagh. Nobody else seemed to mind, but I found them a little jarring."

Monahan hesitated and then said, "Yeah, sorry about that. Probably just my Irish pride gettin' the best of me. I'll lose those for the next show. Still, *Éirinn go Brách* you know!"

Then with a parting "Hey, hey!" from Lenny it was off to see *Christmas O'Carolan.*

Chapter Twenty

Because the day's rehearsal was already underway, Vivaldi, Emily and I crept into the Playhouse auditorium as quietly as we could and took seats in the back. Things seemed to be going smoothly, which meant none of the actors or musicians had swallowed a microphone, vomited, or fallen down so far. As on my previous visit, however, there was a certain vague tension in the air on stage. I wanted to chalk it up to the fear of impending disaster, but maybe that's true at any new show even when poisonings are not expected. I asked Vivaldi about it later and he agreed.

"Well, what did you think of Lenny Monahan?" whispered Vivaldi, directing his question to both of us.

"Seems nice if a little strange," Emily whispered back. "But I've never met a comedian before, so I didn't know what to expect. Are they all like that?"

"They're all strange, I'll have to say, but all in different ways, of course," said Vivaldi.

"I picked up on that too," I said. "I mean, I like him, and the audience liked his act, but still … I don't know. I felt that way the other night too. Do you think maybe he pushes the 'I'm Irish' thing a little too hard?"

"Of course, I'd be biased in that regard," said Vivaldi. "And like I said, he came well recommended."

I was suspicious, nevertheless, but still it seemed stupid to put somebody on my suspect list simply because he was Irish. If that were the case, I'd have to add Vivaldi too, although he was only half Irish, so maybe he was in the clear. Besides, what motive would he have for jeopardizing part of his livelihood by attacking people in the arts community and sabotaging the success of the Komedy Klub and the Playhouse?

"Uh-oh, we've been noticed," said Vivaldi, pointing to the stage down from which hopped a diminutive man in a safari jacket, red scarf and riding boots who began striding purposefully up the center aisle toward us. "That'll be Cecil Miller, the director."

"Good morning, Dylan," said Miller, stopping in front of Vivaldi but looking down his nose at Emily and me. "I see you've brought some visitors to my theater?"

"Indeed, I have," responded Vivaldi brightly, "and not just *any* visitors, because I know you hate interruptions during your rehearsals. Cecil Miller, meet Mark Fairley and his wife Emily. Mark is with the GADC and is helping get the word out about how important the arts are to the quality of life around here. Maybe bring in some big donors."

Emily and I stood, and we all shook hands, Miller somewhat reluctantly, his facial coloring almost matching his scarf, although its fierceness faded as he took in Vivaldi's words about my worthy ostensible mission.

"In that case, you're more than welcome," said Miller, now looking *up* his nose at us because we towered over him. We sat back down.

"Mark just wanted to get the flavor of things here by watching for a few minutes, and then we'll be out of your hair before you know it," said Vivaldi.

"No, please, stay as long as you like. We're just getting started, really. Reading the parts and doing some stage blocking, and so forth, so there are no costumes yet, but you'll get the idea. We're doing the opening scene right now."

"Thanks, Mr. Miller," I said. "We look forward to seeing it."

"Please, just call me Cecil B.D."

With that, Miller turned and strode back down the aisle.

"*Cecil B.D. Miller?*" I asked Vivaldi.

"Actually, his middle name is Barton. He added the D which I don't think stands for anything, liked the S in Harry S Truman, but you know how it is. He was a plumber, and a good one at that, until he tried out for a play here a few years ago and fell in love with the whole process. He's a good director and the get-up makes him feel like he's also acting, so everybody humors him."

Back on the stage, Cecil B. D. Miller resumed directing. "Places, everyone! We have distinguished guests today, so best behavior now. Let's take it from the top!"

The stage went dark. Music in the form of a sprightly, familiar old Irish tune came from offstage as an actor who turned out to be the narrator entered and took the center in a spotlight. What follows is from the script Vivaldi gave Emily and me as we were leaving. I thought if I read it some clues might jump out at me.

Act 1
Narrator's Introduction

NARRATOR: Good evening, and welcome to *The Christmas O'Carolan Songbook, Volume 1*. Our pleasure this evening is to treat you to some history, some fable, some philosophy, and some laughs, and mostly some rollicking good music from the down to earth folks of 18th Century Ireland.

First, let's set the stage. How many of you have heard of Turlough O'Carolan? That's right, it's spelled like it should be "Ter-LOW," but it's really pronounced "Ter-LOCK." O'Carolan was born in 1670 and was an Irish harpist and composer who wrote beautiful music. He was blind, and a wealthy patron provided him a horse and a companion to accompany him on his travels through the land spreading musical joy. Today we know him as ... The Legendary Itinerant Blind Harpist of Ireland. We're listening to one of his compositions now, called "Hewlett."

We know a lot about Turlough O'Carolan, but what about his little-known elder son, Christmas O'Carolan who was born in 1693? What of *his* life? What of *his* hopes and dreams? What was it like to live in the shadow of his famous father? Yes, Christmas O'Carolan, whose unsung talent might have eclipsed his father's if only he had found a proper forum in his time. It is a touching and tragic, yet strangely uplifting story, grounded in the tradition that The Irish are Happiest When They are Sad.

Return with us now, back to a land where the men were men, the women were women, the music flowed as freely as the beer and the whiskey, and the potato was king. Actually, it was a queen, Queen Anne, who ruled in that day, but some of the Irish do say she resembled a potato when she was angry. I can't say I've ever seen an angry potato myself.

Our scene opens with Turlough the father, blinded by the smallpox since the tender age of 18, toiling away at a new and no doubt achingly beautiful musical composition.

(Narrator exits as the offstage music fades.)

SCENE ONE

(Irish pub interior, 1694. Bar, tables, chairs, etc., and space for musicians and dancing. Potatoes scattered here and there. A sign over the bar says, "O'Donald's Pub – 100s Served". Other signs advertise Old Harp Ale and specials on various potato dishes. It is early morning.

PADDY is behind the bar drying tankards with a dingy towel. TURLOUGH is seated alone at a table facing the audience, alternately playing a few notes on an Irish harp and scribbling on foolscap with a quill. A commotion offstage, and MICK, SEAN and JACK enter, in good spirits.)

PADDY: Ah, finally you're back! You get up early, but still you don't come here first?

MICK: Don't take it so personal, Paddy, me boy. There's two dozen pubs in Ballyfoulmouth, and it takes a while to make the rounds, but we always come back to yours in the end. We were just over to the IHOP for breakfast, and now we're back for something to wash it down with.

PADDY: Looks like you've been doing some washing down already. Besides, what do they have at the Irish House of Potatocakes that I don't have? You well know you can get a proper meal here anytime.

SEAN: Aye, so long as it's potatoes!

(Sean picks up a potato and tosses it to Mick, who fumbles it and then notices Turlough for the first time.)

MICK: Well, as I live and breathe, look who's here! It's THE Turlough O'Carolan himself, the Legendary Itinerant Blind Harpist of Ireland! And what brings you back to our fair city?

TURLOUGH: It's hardly a city, Mick, and never will be with a name like Ballyfoulmouth and only a fast-food potato recipe to distinguish it.

SEAN: Ah, so you're slummin' then, is it?

119

TURLOUGH: Truth to tell, Sean, 'tis family business brings me here.

JACK: Oh aye ... that's right. And have you named that little boy of yours yet?

TURLOUGH: Not yet. Didn't want to rush things, you know.

JACK: But he's almost six months old! Born in December if memory serves.

TURLOUGH: I've been away. Bein' itinerant and all.

JACK: Never seen a man travel as much as you. And blind too! Where's Barry, your faithful companion?

SEAN: And your horse, Silver?

TURLOUGH: Down at Mrs. O'Leary's barn, of course. They'll be back in an hour or so.

MICK: Well, then, what is it you're workin' on so hard there?

TURLOUGH: It's a song in honor of his birth — my firstborn son. It almost makes me want to cry. Hard to believe he's truly mine. But an Irish mother wouldn't lie.

   (They share a sentimental moment, their eyes tearing. They bring out handkerchiefs.)

JACK: They say he looks just like you.

SEAN: Aye, the spittin' image.

TURLOUGH: I wouldn't know now, would I?

(They quickly recover from the embarrassing, unmanly sentimental moment.)

JACK: Turlough, how can you write, bein' blind and all?

TURLOUGH: The same way you get to The Great Hall in Dublin, Jack – Practice, my boy, practice!

SEAN: Well, you do write some beautiful tunes. Let's see what you've got this time.

(Sean grabs the foolscap from Turlough.)

SEAN: Hey, gather 'round, boys, and look at this! Whaddya think?

(They gather 'round.)

MICK: I think we can do it.

JACK: Aye, let's try it!

(They bring out instruments from behind the bar and tune up, including Paddy. Paddy brings out a music stand for the foolscap, and they gather around it, facing the audience.)

PADDY: Lead us into it, Turlough, me lad!

(Turlough plays a few introductory measures on the harp, and then they all join in. They play "Carolan's Welcome," an instrumental.)

TURLOUGH: Not a bad job, lads!

JACK: You know, that sounded like a Christmas carol, but we're in the merry month of May!

SEAN: Only 210 shopping days left!

(They all briefly look at Sean quizzically, except for Turlough who is deep in thought. He stands up and slaps his forehead.)

TURLOUGH: I ... I don't know why I didn't think of it before! I must be blind!

(Mick, Sean and Jack look at each other.)

TURLOUGH: Of course, the boy's name will be ... will be ... *Christmas* O'Carolan!

(After a moment's reflection, they all cheer and thump Turlough on the back.)

JACK: Well, you know now, the lad's got mighty big shoes to fill.

MICK: Aye, but who's to say he'll want to?

SEAN: Fait' and begorrah, what *will* become of young Christmas?

(They continue to congratulate Turlough as the stage goes dark. Offstage a baby cries. Music up from offstage ["Carolan's Welcome" reprise].)

Emily and I didn't stay for Scene Two but quietly took our leave, Vivaldi showing us the way out of the darkened auditorium. Nothing untoward had happened. If there were any clues in the script, they didn't jump out. The only oddity I noticed was the quill pen the Turlough character was using to scribble on the foolscap appeared to be a Gate City Playhouse Rocks fountain pen with a feather glued to it.

We headed home for lunch, stopping only to pick up my corrected Glowery business cards at the company's reception desk. They looked fine. Emily stayed in the car.

Chapter Twenty-One

Monday – Week 2 on The Case

"I read your book, Mark," said GK3, a vice president in the company I was interviewing with in Charlotte.

At least that's what I thought he said.

"*The Accidental Spurrt*?" I ventured.

"Uh, yeah, of course. That one."

"What did you think of it?"

"Well, like I said, I've only read your bookmark.

"My book*mark*."

"The one that came with the book you FedExed us. With a picture of the cover and a little description of the book. I haven't had time to get into it. Nice bookmark though."

This wasn't going well. Strains of "Monday, Monday" by the Mamas and the Papas ran through my head. Moments before, I was ushered into the august presence of this the third gatekeeper of the day at the Charlotte company. It was the first interview I'd had for a real job in almost a year since being rightsized out of Glowery. Seventy-two résumés cast to the four winds (18 per wind) with zero responses, not even one, until these guys emailed and invited me to their headquarters for the day.

All the male gatekeepers were dressed in "business casual," meaning permanent-creased but comfortable slacks (not jeans yet, but that's where it's headed), black or brown wingtips or tasseled loafers but with rubbery injection-molded soles like on running shoes, a dress shirt open at the neck, no tie, and sometimes with a jacket hanging on a door hook or the back of a side chair in their offices. By contrast, I was in a brand-new dark suit and tie. New shiny black wingtips too, with real leather soles. And black socks. My mother would say, "Better overdressed than underdressed," and "Always put your best foot forward," and stuff like that. But times have changed, Mom. Today the wingtip on my best forward foot served only as a pedestal for a glaring sartorial error that made me look desperate (which I am, but why show it?) and a dinosaur to boot. And some of the people here were indeed wearing boots.

If I ever do get another interview, assuming this one doesn't pan out, which it now looks like it won't, maybe I'll wear camouflage. That way, I'm guaranteed to fit in. But even then, I'd still have to decide: jungle, forest or desert?

Emily, my darling and ever-supportive wife of 23½ years, told me to dress business casual and obviously I should have listened. But no, I thought, Emily's never been on a job interview since the one she had for waiting tables at a popular sports bar in college. What does she know of today's grown-up world of work? Formal attire was not *de rigueur* for women employed by the sports bar. In fact, the less you wore the better. Fortunately, that was before we met, and she's matured since then. Quite wonderfully too, I must say.

Even my business cards were overdressed. While carrying only the simple inscription, "Mark L. Fairley, President, Fairley & Associates, Strategic Planning," followed by my contact information, they are glossy and embossed and have a four-color rendering of a protractor spanning a globe of the earth occupying the whole left half. Compellingly evocative of Strategic Planning, at least to the clerk at Office Depot who helped me design them. Again, Emily warned me they were too fancy, but I was in best-foot-forward mode when I ordered them. When these people in Charlotte handed me their cards—simple blue type on white matte finish with a tasteful company logo in the upper left-hand corner—I pretended I didn't have any.

As a last resort I suppose I could have used my new fake Glowery cards, but I didn't want to confuse things even though they now showed my name correctly.

Gatekeeper 3, or GK3 as I'm calling him, was indeed a vice president of something or other—strategic planning, I hoped, since that is my forte. His business card said, "Gatekeeper 3." No, actually I don't remember what it said, and I've since misplaced it, but as I recall it was a euphemism for what could have been anything, so it was hard to tell. I asked him, but his answer was so roundabout as to be unintelligible as well.

Responding to their email, I had called GK1, a minion in Human Resources, and asked what position they wanted to interview me for. She was evasive and said the company was growing fast and had more than one position they might consider me for and until they interviewed me they wouldn't be able to decide. A visit to the company's website wasn't enlightening either. It was AFC Corporation, a conglomerate of food processing plants contract-manufacturing private label brands for grocery chains. I assumed AFC stood for Amalgamated Food Conglomerate. Or maybe American Food Conglomerate, or something equally undistinctive and uninspiring. Or All Foods Considered, which would be distinctive but still not inspiring. Maybe the "A" was for Ajax. Or maybe Acme, the unreliable supplier of everything from anvils to dynamite to impossibly long rubber bands which Wile E. Coyote outlandishly misuses in the Roadrunner cartoons. "Beep-beep!" The website didn't say, and I forgot to ask while I was there. At least it wasn't Foods "Я" Us.

GK3 was pleasant enough and tried to make me feel

comfortable, at least at first, although I'm not sure how comfortable he felt himself. His not-a-secretary-but-an-executive-administrative-assistant had brought me up to a large and luxurious top floor conference room from the sterile basement company cafeteria where I had lunched with GK2, a department head with a fondness for Jell-O fruit salad and no talent for small talk. The executive administrative assistant introduced me to GK3, and after he and I shook hands (firmly but not too firmly, yet not tentatively either, and not held overly long), she handed him a manila folder and tiptoed off for parts unknown without offering coffee, tea or water. GK3 made an "after you" gesture that brought us to a long conference table surrounded by comfortable-looking chairs, and to his comment about my bookmark.

Company gatekeepers have one function: to prevent anyone from being hired. Most people you interview at a company do not have hiring authority. Most are not capable of discerning who should be hired and who should not, and they know this. It is risky to recommend hiring someone who may turn out later to be "not a good fit," as it will reflect poorly on the recommender. The safe course is to say no, or at best to express reservations and concern, deferring to the superior wisdom of the person with the actual hiring authority. Gates are best kept closed. Who knows what kind of riffraff will come in if they are left open? Think of company gatekeepers as walking stop signs.

Somehow, I must have passed muster enough with both GK1, and GK2 that they decided not to send me home after lunch, and after all, GK3 was a senior person here, so that was encouraging. Maybe he had hiring authority, or enough clout with whoever did that he could risk a favorable recommendation. On the other hand, he looked about 18 years old.

We sat. Or rather, he sat, at the head of the table. I dithered.

What will he read into my choice of where to sit, I pondered paranoidly? If I sit on his left, will he think I'm a liberal? Would that be bad? Or good? But wait, his left would be my right, so maybe I'd appear conservative. Would that be better? Or not? What if I sit across from him? But no, that would put me at the other end of the huge table, practically into the hallway. What will my dithering signal to him? And will I have squandered what I believed to be a perfectly good first-impression handshake?

In the end, as it were, I sat on his left, but with one empty chair between us. I reasoned we wouldn't thereby be in each other's space. He probably saw it as a defensive move, almost but not quite submissive. Right then I knew I hadn't spent nearly enough time on the Internet researching interview seating protocol, much less how to dress. What would Emily have advised? Why hadn't I asked her? (Oh, that's right, I don't value her opinion in these matters.) Would common sense prevail? Hard to say, these days.

At least there was no slippery leather sofa.

I looked at GK3 expectantly because it was his prerogative to begin the conversation.

He looked at me.

Me. Overdressed and seatingly challenged. Then the exchange about my bookmark. Then he peered into the manila folder and slowly took out what I presumed was my résumé. It had notes written all over it. I couldn't read them upside down at the one-chair distance.

"So, Mark, it says here …"

Ping.

My cell phone. A text message. Just great! Did he hear the ping? I confess I saw the sign at the conference room door that clearly said, "Please Silence All Cell Phones and Other Devices

Before Entering," but being all wrapped up in the drama of greeting and seating etiquette, I had unintentionally failed to heed it.

If I didn't look at the message, the stupid phone would only *ping* again in a few seconds. I shot GK3 the "I'm as sorry as if I've tracked in dog poop, but I need to check this" look and dug the device from my pants pocket. The message was from Emily. Detective Blue had called and needed to talk to me. Apparently, there was an accident at the Gate City Playhouse this morning during rehearsal. That would make it the umpteenth incident involving the Playhouse, not to mention all the other poisonings or suspicious events elsewhere. Incidents and accidents, hints and allegations, as Paul Simon wrote in "You Can Call Me Al," that lyric now replacing "Monday, Monday" in my mind.

A terrorist plot, a medical epidemic, or *Arsenic and Old Lace* reimagined?

I put the phone on Vibrate and turned back to GK3 who gave me the "It's okay, but I sure hope that's the last interruption" look and dove back into the interview.

Time passed. Working our way through my résumé. My references. Information about the company. Obfuscation about what position they might consider me for. Questions. Answers. Worry in the absence of details about what Detective Blue and Dylan Vivaldi would have to say about this latest development. Which reminded me, I still had to write a poem when I got home. I had procrastinated over the weekend, reviewing the victims' lists again, preparing my first week's hours and expense report for Bob Ausländer, and looking up more companies to send my résumé to while awaiting my muse. She never showed up.

The interview's grand finale was approaching—those annoying questions interviewers save to the end just to make you uncomfortable for the fun of it, and to make them look sophisticated and professional even though they've already decided what they think of your candidacy.

"We've talked a little about the strengths you would bring to the position," said GK3, "but now let me ask you: What would you say some of your weaknesses are?"

"Well, I have weaknesses for grilled cheese and tomato sandwiches, dark chocolate, fuzzy coffee, and Dilbert."

"Ha ha, but seriously …"

"Okay, here's something," I offered. "I have this sort of love-hate relationship with authority."

"I think I've picked up on that."

"See, on the one hand, I respect authority, whether I'm under it or have some of it myself. It's important. Structure and organization are important. But I tend to question authority. A lot. I've seen it abused, and I think it needs to be kept on its toes. It needs to be a little uncomfortable. Some people see that as a weakness. So, you're wondering: 'Will he be a Dilbert—a smart but cynical, sarcastic, intractable pain in the butt? Or will he be a useless, spineless toady who looks to see what the boss is thinking before he commits? Or is he a team player who thinks outside the box and demonstrates leadership, perseverance and loyalty to his colleagues and the company?'"

"And what do you think I would conclude?" he responded.

"Well, I hope it would be the loyal team player and all that. Outside the box. It's one reason I sent you the book. It will show not only that I'm creative but also that I communicate well, I understand how a business works, and I can contribute to yours."

"Fuzzy coffee?"

"Long story."

"Okay, well thanks very much for coming in. We'll be in touch."

I thought, "I won't hold my breath," but I didn't say it.

Chapter Twenty-Two

Breathing normally, except when sandwiched between 18-wheelers doing 90 miles an hour, I carefully worked my way home on the always challenging I-85 from Charlotte to Greensboro, made more treacherous than usual because it was raining and the trucks were throwing up so much water from the road it was hard to see even with the wipers going full speed.

I tried to put the interview behind me and focus on the next big challenge in my Reluctant Detective career: writing a poem. The critique group's protocol was that I should submit my poem to Ryman Stanza the moderator by email no later than the day before the meeting so he could distribute it to the other group members along with their poems, and everyone would have time to read them and make notes. Theoretically, that gave me until midnight, but I doubted Ryman was going to wait up for me. I would have to come up with something sooner.

Steering uncertainly with one hand, I fumbled with my cell phone until I found the dictation app. In North Carolina it's against the law to text while driving, but I assume that doesn't extend to verbally composing poetry.

"Roses are red,
   Violets are blue.
   Why that should be,
   I haven't a clue."

And that won't do.
I'm on the road, so how about a highway poem?

"The wheels on the trucks go round and round,
And with my luck'll pound me into the ground."

Evocative but not very inspiring.

It did need to be something simple, however. No sonnets or epics. No odes on Grecian urns. A limerick? No, too risky, especially with a group of strangers.

Haiku! That was it! Five syllables, followed by seven, then five again, in three lines. The Japanese had it right. Easy-peasy. I could do that.

I only needed one poem, but by the time I got home, I had dictated several. I typed them up, polished them, and sent half of them to Ryman by dinnertime, keeping the other half in reserve in case I needed them for the next meeting, if I ever went to a next meeting. All along, my muse must have been right there in the backseat. Or the glove compartment. Maybe it's no coincidence I drive a Japanese car.

I'd be debuting my poetic talent with not just one, but a plethora of haikus. It would be memorable. Assuming they were any good.

Chapter Twenty-Three

Tuesday

I hadn't returned Lieutenant Blue's call on the way home because of my selfishly inconsiderate preoccupation with staying alive while dodging trucks and composing haikus, but I figured he would have already handled whatever needed handling in the latest "accident" at the Playhouse and was only calling to fill me in on it. That could wait until Tuesday morning. Sure enough, he called again right before breakfast.

"It was that director, Whatshisname Miller," said Blue. "Stepped off the stage into the orchestra pit and sprained his ankle."

"It's C.B.D."

"What is? Oh. You think he was high? That CBD stuff is everywhere, but you don't get high from it."

"That's his initials. His name. C.B.D. Miller."

"That's what I said. Are you okay?"

"Yes, fine, so go on."

"So, he would have broken it except for how thick his boots were. Could've been a lot worse."

"But why is that so suspicious? Anybody could have tripped up and fallen like that."

"Yeah, that's right, but it fits in with all the other stuff that's been happening. And you know what we real detectives hate."

"Right, coincidences."

"You got it. We hate coincidences. We don't believe in coincidences. And neither should you."

"I don't."

"Good. And that's my tip of the hat for today."

"Okay. Thanks."

"Plus, get this now, *plus* he claims he was distracted by some kind of flashing light in the balcony. Claimed it startled him because nobody was supposed to be up there. One of the actors heard a door slam right after. Another one went and took a look but didn't see anybody or find anything. Neither did my guys. So, no hard clues. We talked to everybody who was there and got their stories. Miller wasn't too thrilled about how long it took, but we had to be thorough."

"What did Vivaldi say?"

"He wasn't there when it happened. His assistant … Marcell or something, same one who called me … called him on his cell and he came right back from wherever he was, but he didn't say much."

"Okay."

"I have to say, that guy bothers me a little," said Blue.

"Vivaldi?"

"Right. Can't put my finger on it yet. Just seems a little squirrelly to me."

"I had the same reaction when I first met him," I said. "It's probably the red beard, but I don't see why he'd want to sabotage his own Playhouse, or his Komedy Klub. Or the city, for that matter."

"I know, and maybe you're right. So, you got anything new on your end?"

I told Blue about meeting with Vivaldi and Lenny Monahan and attending the uneventful rehearsal on Friday and that I was going to meet some new people at the poetry critique that night. He didn't seem impressed with my progress. I didn't bother to tell him Emily and I thought the dialogue in Scene One was only so-so, but the music was good. Probably not germane to The Case.

I did mention my concerns about Lenny Monahan.

"Like you with Vivaldi," I said, "I can't put my finger on it, but something seems a little off with him. Maybe it's the Irish thing. He seems too militant about it."

"I'll have him checked out," said Blue. "See what turns up."

"Thanks. Let me know."

Blue didn't ask to see the poems I was going to bring to the critique meeting, and I didn't offer. With a cheery, "Good luck, poetry boy," he was off, presumably to catch some ticket scalpers.

Normally, Emily wouldn't have been too excited by my suggesting a lunch date at McDonald's, but when I reminded her that Sharon/Evelyn the elderly floater lady might be there, she was all for it. Also, it would be inexpensive, which we both appreciated. In addition, for Emily it was sort of a step up from her frequent practice of grazing among the food samples at Costco. And since I was soon going to be getting a paycheck of sorts, I felt we could afford it. Even so, another trip to Costco was in the offing anyway because our pantry was getting so bare we'd recently discovered a fruitcake we hadn't seen for at least 12 years. It tasted pretty good.

I ordered the Quarter Pounder® with Cheese ("deliciously juicy"), medium World Famous Fries˙, and McCafé Iced Coffee ("refreshingly cool") while Emily had the Filet-O-Fish˙ Meal consisting of a "wild-caught" Filet-O-Fish˙ sandwich, Sprite (medium), and medium World Famous Fries˙. I toyed with the idea of getting a Big Mac˙ with "mouthwatering perfection," but the last time I ate a whole one, about 15 years ago, I spent the afternoon feeling like there was a bowling ball in my stomach. No more eating like a teenager.

135

It was crowded, but we got our condiments and found a booth near the Indoor PlayPlace but yet far enough away that we weren't likely to be too disturbed by the muffled but blood curdling screams emanating from it. I had glanced around looking for Sharon as we came in but didn't spot her. Being short, she wouldn't stand out, so I wasn't concerned. I could ask for her later. Or she could be in the restroom or something. Just not in the PlayPlace, where she wouldn't have lasted 30 seconds.

"I have a detective question," Emily said as we unwrapped our sandwiches.

"Okay, shoot," I said, quickly shifting into On the Case mode.

"Do you think it's true that the criminal always returns to the scene of the crime?"

"Hmmm, isn't there a proverb or something that says a dog returns to its vomit? I doubt it applies here, even with, come to think of it, all the vomiting involved in these incidents. For criminals, I think it's mostly a myth that's used for adding drama to crime stories in novels and movies, but I could be wrong. Still, I'm sure some criminals return to the scene, and I've heard that arsonists sometimes do because they have an insane craving to see the flames they've created. Pyromaniacs. There are stories of bystanders jumping in to assist in firefighting and rescue efforts who later turn out to have started the fire. But I'd imagine most criminals want to stay as far away as possible for fear of getting caught."

"Yes, probably. I wonder what Detective Blue would say about it."

"Maybe I'll bring it up if you're that curious," I said. "Why do you ask?"

"Oh, I don't know, it's just that something's been nagging at me about all this since you've told me what's been happening."

"Go on."

"Well, a lot of the poisonings and accidents and so on have happened more than once at the same places," she said. "Like the Playhouse, the bookstore, and wherever, although so far only once at the Xomedy Xlub, but it could happen again."

"Right, so …?"

"Well … and I know we don't even know how the crimes are being committed. I mean, does whoever is responsible have to be at the scene to commit the crime, or can they somehow do it by remote control—like you always see the terrorists on TV shows blowing things up by using their cell phones from a distance? You know what I mean?"

"Yeah, so …?"

"So I was just wondering if you have looked at the lists of the witnesses who were at each of the crime scenes to see if any names appear on more than one list, that's all."

"Hi, sweetie!" came a raspy female voice from behind and a little below my head. "I assume your name's not Kitty, so who are you and what have you done with the Marshall?"

The interruption stopped me in mid-forehead slap as my steel-trap mind instantly saw what Emily was getting at. The voice belonged to Sharon, who'd snuck up behind me and was fixing Emily with a menacing glare that was contradicted by a wide smile.

"You must be Sharon," said Emily, deftly napkining World Famous Fries® grease off her fingers and extending her hand, which Sharon shook warmly.

"She knows me already?" said Sharon, turning to me. "Sounds like you've been telling tales out of school, rookie!"

"Only the good stuff," I assured her. "Besides, it says 'Sharon' on your name badge."

"Yeah, well it's Eileen actually. Don't tell anybody I said so. I know I probably told you Evelyn before, but I didn't really know you then."

"Okay, well this is Emily, my wife," I said. "And it will still be Emily the next time she comes in."

"Nice to meet you, darlin'." Ignoring my little jab. Or not getting it.

"Likewise," said Emily.

"Did you know I was on *Jeopardy!*?" Sharon/Evelyn/Eileen interjected. "I was a champion for one day and my two-day total winnings were nine thousand four hundred dollars. Seven thousand five hundred twenty dollars after taxes. That was in 1986. I still have the cancelled check. The bank let me have it back. Did you know, the first show was in 1964? March 30. I watched it. I don't consider it a show about trivia. I think it's important stuff and I still study it all the time. I'll be 90 in September. The 14th. I chalk it up to a love of knowledge. Ask me anything!"

"I'm game," I said. "How about–?"

"A common plant that means lion's teeth in French. Why, what's a dandelion, of course? George Washington had this many horses shot out from under him at the Battle of the Monongahela on July 9, 1755. Plus, four bullet holes in his coat. What is two? Because of the bulge at the earth's equator, the beaches of this country are farther from the earth's center than is the top of Mount Everest. What is Ecuador? People should know these things."

"I couldn't agree mo–"

"Do you know how many versions of Trivial Pursuit there are?" she went on, oblivious. "Even I don't know, believe it or not, because the number keeps changing. It was 68 last time I looked, and that's just the American versions. People keep giving them to me. Birthdays, Christmas, Hanukkah, Valentine's Day. Whatever. I give the duplicates away to nursing homes. Except the one I live in. They've got too many already. I've given the rare ones to the Historical Museum, where I worked for 58 years before they made me retire. I get tax deductions.

"And that's not to mention all the online trivia games you can play. Nobody knows how many of those either. I have all the main versions of Trivial Pursuit and a great many of the imitations, and I've memorized most of the answers. Just ask my kids and my grandkids. And my great grandkids. And my hairdresser. And my one sister who's still living. And all my friends, although I fear I've driven most of them away. The ones who haven't died already. They love me, but they don't understand. I was crushed when Alex Trebek called it a trivia show. It's just not! And now he's passed, poor thing."

"Yes, we all miss him terribly," said Emily gracefully while my brain was still reeling from this unexpected influx of important stuff.

We all three observed an impromptu moment of respectful silence for Alex. Contentious, high-pitched shouting could be heard from the PlayPlace, but muffled.

"Uh-oh, here comes Lester, my great grandson, to scold me," said Sharon.

"Sharon, are you being nice to these fine people now?" said a pleasant looking young man with a badge that said "Lester McDonald, Manager."

Sharon looked sheepishly at me.

"We're fine," said Emily.

"Yes, she was telling us about her exploits on *Jeopardy!*" I added.

"Oh yeah, the *Jeopardy!* story," said Lester. "She's got one for every day of the week. Yesterday it was how she came in first on *Wheel of Fortune* but missed in the Bonus Round. Tomorrow it will be how she helped Neil Armstrong suit up at Cape Kennedy for the Moon landing when she was with NASA."

"Entertaining though," I said.

"Some people enjoy them, but not everybody likes to have their lunch interrupted like that. Or hear the same story for the third or fourth time."

"Well, we think it's really sweet that you bring her here whenever you can," said Emily.

"Thanks. Okay, you be nice now, Maw-maw, or I'll have to take you back to Abbotswood."

"Not unless you promise me I can take an Egg McMuffin home for the microwave in the morning," Sharon said to Lester's retreating back. Then to us, "He's a nice kid, but he still doesn't know what he wants to be when he grows up."

"We liked your story anyway," I said.

"You folks need anything? Refill on your Sprite? Take your trash?"

"No, we're good, Sharon," I said. "Thanks."

"Y'all just holler, now, y'hear?" She shuffled toward another booth.

From a distance, barely understandable above the shrieks (but muffled) from the PlayPlace, "Did you know I was on *Jeopardy!*?"

Emily and I looked at each other and decided not to laugh. At least not right then.

Now suddenly back On the Case, I completed my forehead slap.

"I'll ask Blue if he's cross-referenced the witness lists to see who's showed up more than once."

"Of course, there will be some because these arts people do attend a lot of events," said Emily, "but there might be a pattern or something."

"Yeah, and since Blue and his people aren't artsy—by his own admission—they might have missed something. Maybe I'll have a look at the lists myself to see if anything jumps out at me now that I'm beginning to worm my way into the community."

We finished our beverages, left a tip for Sharon/Evelyn/ Eileen/Maw-maw, took our trash to the receptacles by the door, waved goodbye to her and left.

I was starting to think maybe Emily was more suited to this detective thing than I was.

Wait ... Lester *McDonald*? Seriously?

Chapter Twenty-Four

There are hit men, and there are miss men. Norman Shartly was a miss man. But it wasn't always so.

Growing up in rural Oklahoma as an only child, little Norman—or Shorty, as he was called by the other children even though he was of average size for a boy his age—learned to be a crack shot with his Daisy Red Ryder BB gun by age nine, scaring rabbits, squirrels, crows and other varmints from his mother's vegetable garden and never once shooting his eye out. At 13, he graduated to his father's 12 gauge and started scaring the varmints to death, literally. Then he started scaring the kids who called him Shorty. This made him sort of a loner. In spite of admonitions from his parents, and even the local sheriff a time or two, this behavior persisted, and his parents finally saw no alternative but to take away the shotgun and send him off to boarding school at age 15 for some discipline.

It was a military academy run by a retired Green Beret colonel named Harrison "Hotshot" Hoffman (his students' play on the nickname was not as grandiose), and there in the school's Junior ROTC program Norman learned real marksmanship with a real rifle, albeit only a reconditioned Army surplus M1 Garand left over from the Korean War. He won several shooting competitions for the school. No one called him Shorty. Still, he kept mostly to himself until he graduated and went off to college at Oklahoma University (located, ironically, in Norman, not far from Oklahoma City) where he majored in Art because he thought the courses would be easier than other majors and because he did have some skill at drawing, having practiced doodling a lot while not socializing with his classmates in middle school. He made average grades and continued with his ROTC career, winning more rifle marksmanship awards, this time with modern weapons.

Upon graduation, Norman received his commission as an Army second lieutenant and began a military career that eventually saw him qualify for the Army's Special Forces and don his very own Green Beret. He served tours in Iraq and Afghanistan. Along the way, he participated in various "black ops" from time to time, honing his marksmanship as a sniper, now with state-of-the-art weapons. He had several kills to his credit. He had enjoyed them. No one called him Shorty.

Rifles were a snap for Norman, but for some reason he found it difficult to master the handgun, and that was the beginning of his downfall in the military.

"I'm a sniper," he said to his commanding officer. "You can't very well snipe with a pistol."

"The point is," the colonel countered, "if something goes wrong with your sniping engagement and you have to use your handgun in the process of getting away, you need to be able to shoot straight. Right now, you'd be lucky to hit the proverbial broad side of a barn at ten meters."

Norman knew the colonel was right, and he resolved to improve his handgun skills, but it was an uphill battle. The targets at the practice range were far smaller than a barn.

Maybe the situation had taken a toll on his confidence, or maybe he was having a bad day, but whatever the reason, while carrying out his next sniper engagement somewhere in Eastern Europe Norman did the unthinkable. He missed. Worse, as the local authorities closed in on his sniper "hide" in the belfry of a church 2,000 meters from his intended target, he had to fight his way out with his 9mm Glock 19. He made it, but only after confusing his pursuers by emptying two magazines of the pistol while firing wildly, screaming maniacally and running zigzag like crazy, finally losing himself in a dense crowd of shoppers at an outdoor bazaar before making his way to the border and crossing into friendly territory using his counterfeit credentials. In all the shooting, his bullets had hit no one. And he'd left his rifle behind.

"It was all part of my plan," he insisted during the debriefing, "except for leaving the rifle, of course. I just needed to scare them, and obviously it worked."

The Army was unimpressed and cut Norman loose with an honorable discharge but docking his final paycheck for the cost of the rifle.

Two weeks after the incident, a farmer about a quarter of a mile from the church belfry noticed two strange holes in the broad side of his barn. He reported this to the local police who investigated and dug two 9mm slugs from an inside crossbeam. Unfortunately for Norman, the Army is not big on irony, and even if they had known about this it still would not have saved him.

A bereft Norman cast about for a new career. He had no skills or experience except with a rifle … and doodling of course, but that was hardly marketable. However, in this fallen world there are clandestine, non-governmental interests who occasionally have need of such skills as Norman's and who are less worried about their agents escaping successfully from tight situations than is the Army. One such contacted Norman and, reluctantly at first but unable to ignore the generous pay, he succumbed. His employer and handler was a go-between, brokering assignments from clients of all kinds. Norman never knew who the clients were, although sometimes he had his suspicions.

He accepted several engagements, mostly domestic but occasionally overseas. Surprisingly, most of the time nobody seemed to care whether he hit his targets or missed. The mayhem he created either way seemed to be enough. And lately he was missing more than he was hitting. His confidence was shot (so to speak). He took no pride in the work, and he was beginning to fear people would start calling him Shorty again even though he used aliases most of the time. And disguises too, when necessary, in spite of being naturally nondescript.

As previously noted, Norman wasn't actually short. In fact, witnesses would often describe him as "an average-looking guy," which wasn't very helpful to detectives investigating a murder or assassination he carried out. He took some comfort in that, but he still wasn't happy.

And this latest gig was weird. There were multiple targets, none of whom seemed especially important to anyone except maybe friends and family. No rifle either. Instead, a weapon using technology like he'd only seen in science fiction stories he'd read as a teenager. It wasn't a pistol, but it felt close enough to one that it made Norman uncomfortable. So, he missed a lot.

Norman Shartly was a miss man, not a hit man. A comedown for sure. Still, nobody seemed to mind.

Chapter Twenty-Five

On the way home from lunch, I called Lieutenant Blue and asked him about the witness lists.

"Of course we checked the lists against each other. What didja think, we suddenly remembered it was something they mentioned at the Police Academy?"

"Sorry, I know it's 'Basic Detecting 101,' which is probably why even I thought of it. Well, actually Emily thought of it. Anyway, what did you find?"

"No joy there. Some of these people must go to every artsy event they can find. I get the part about mooching the refreshments and all, but I mean, when do they work? When do they find time to write their own poems and draw their pictures and stuff?"

"Beats me, but would you mind if I take a look at the lists myself? I've become a little more artsy in the last few days, and maybe something will jump out at me."

I thought about what I had just said. It seemed all I was doing on this case so far was wandering around and hoping clues would jump out at me. They weren't going to keep paying me much longer if I didn't start doing more than that.

"Okay, I'll email you the file this afternoon," said Blue, "but in all honestly, I think you're barking at the wrong dog."

"Thanks. I'll have a look at it as soon as I can."

"By the way," Blue continued, "the tests on Morrie Milburne's ink came out negative. No poison."

146

"I expected that, but thanks,"

"You still going to that poem thing tonight?"

"Yes."

"Well, have a rhymin' time!"

"Thanks. I'll try."

Wow. Detective Lieutenant Marshall Blue of the Greensboro Police Department's oxymoronic Criminal Intelligence Squad made a joke. Sort of. Maybe there was hope for him after all.

Blue's email came an hour later, but I couldn't spare the time to look at it just then because I needed to review and make notes on the poems submitted by the other members of the critique group that Ryman the moderator had sent out. I should have taken the time to Google "how to critique a poem," because it turned out to be one of the hardest things I've ever had to do in my life.

There were three poems in addition to my little collection of haikus. The first one I looked at was by somebody named Eleanor Cutty, who called it "Springlyness."

Springlyness
By Eleanor Cutty

Mission bold from aft the cold
of winter oft depressing,
taking hold to slow unfold
a season's reassessing.

'Twixt and 'tween it doth careen
among the equinoxes,
growing green but not too keen
for Nature's fickle boxes.

147

Soon there's calm like soothing balm,
a springly reconciling:
Not like a bomb but with aplomb,
a happy domiciling.

But comes some heat the calm to meet,
another new upheaval,
summer's torch about to scorch
since early times primeval.

Nothing stays for endless days.
The seasons keep a'moving.
But this one plays, the one I praise:
It's spring that I'm approving.

At first, I was at a loss for what to say about this poem. For all I knew, it was brilliant, and Eleanor Cutty should be the next Poet Laureate of North Carolina. I should call the Governor immediately to alert him, since he makes those appointments.

It had an interesting story and progression of ideas and some good poetry-type stuff in it, at least to my untrained mind, like "aft," "oft," and "doth," apostrophes in place of cleverly omitted letters, omitted words and suffixes but you know what is meant anyway, and lots of good rhymes.

On the other hand, I couldn't help wincing at the way the word "bomb" was tossed in, so to speak, like she was reaching for a rhyme. It was jarring. Like a bomb. The expression "a'moving" seemed like it would be more at home in a cowboy song than in a statelier poem like this one. "Keep a-movin' Dan don't ya listen to him Dan, He's a devil, not a man and he spreads the burning sand with water" from "Cool Clear Water" by Bob Nolan (I looked it up) came to mind. Also, although the word "springly" is okay as a made-up adjective, shouldn't the title noun "Springlyness" be spelled with an "i," or "Springliness"? Like "lovely" becomes "loveliness"? Was poetic license involved here? I certainly don't want to mess with that, but maybe I'll hold off on calling the Governor for now.

The next one was called "Poetry Heaven," by Michael Brennan.

Poetry Heaven
By Michael Brennan

I wonder where old poems go to die …
Or do they have a life that's not their own –
a different fate from things of flesh and bone,
not fade away nor vanish in the sky?
Is poem heaven like the one we know –
All imperfections edited divine,
all meter, rhyme and cadence in align,
so close to God in perfect form and flow?
Or maybe freedom reigns in such a place,
with structure cast aside like shackles tossed
away along with criticism's cost,
as if abandon won't in fact abase.
But truths once written never will be gone;
not buried with their authors, they live on.

Another nice progression, with poetry-type incomplete sentences, good rhymes, an interesting central idea and a good finishing thought. Somehow it seemed familiar, but maybe it was the form, not the content. I liked it. I later learned it was a sonnet, a form often used by Shakespeare and other famous poets, so it was in good company. However, again the Governor would be spared a call.

Finally, I came to "Athabasca" by Sillveeya Constance. I imagined her real first name was probably Jane, but she changed it for poetic reasons, although she could as easily have gone with Jayne, or Jaine, unless one syllable wouldn't cut it.

Athabasca
By Sillveeya Constance

Cool petals mounting forth indelibly,
a wind for sixpence falling softly through panes and seas
with memories of youth, older now but smoothly.
Where did we go?
I know, right?
Rattled branches reaching.
Forgotten vistas long remembered and caution not
forthcoming as one but more and not in touch.
Tangibly.
Daybreak.
Yes no.
Leaning on the breast of time, and longing.
Why?

What the heck was this? A lament on the plight of indigenous peoples in Canada? An homage to nature's beauty and diversity one hasn't fully experienced? A cry for help? Or a last-minute belching of words and phrases from a random poetry generator so as to be ready with something to take to a critique group meeting? I suspected the latter, but being a poetry novice, I was ready to give it the benefit of the doubt. Maybe I would learn something at the meeting. I hoped so. But forget about the Governor. Sheesh!

Chapter Twenty-Six

From the website: "The Kathleen Clay Edwards Family Branch of the Greensboro Public Library system is located in the 98-acre Price Park, which includes a bird and butterfly meadow, reading garden, walking trails, ponds, and wetlands. In addition to popular collections, the library also has an extensive collection of nature, gardening, and environmental resources for children and adults."

There are two meeting rooms that can be reserved for private use. The Writer's Block Monthly Tuesday Evening Poetry Critique Group would meet in the smaller of the two, starting at 7:00 p.m. I arrived at 6:50 carrying the poems in my leather Glowery executive portfolio and found Ryman Stanza the moderator, Eleanor Cutty ("Springlyness") and Michael Brennan ("Poetry Heaven") already there. All were pleasant looking people dressed casually, as was I. Ryman I guessed to be in his mid-forties with salt & pepper hair going thin in front but with a small ponytail and a goatee, Eleanor a bit older but with jet black hair that was probably dyed, and Michael definitely younger with dark curly hair and the scruffy 10-day mustache and beard popular with so many young men these days.

I introduced myself to Ryman and we shook hands.

"Nice meeting you, and welcome to the group," he said. "Betty Wright-Moore tells me you're with the Greensboro Area Development Commission."

"Well, that's right, the GADC, but I am also really interested in trying my hand at some poetry."

Then we shook hands all around. No one seemed to suspect I was On the Case, although when Brennan and I made eye contact during the handshake I thought his gaze stayed on me a moment longer than normal. Or was I being paranoid?

Sillveeya Constance ("Athabasca") was expected at any moment. I couldn't wait.

Until then, we made small talk during which I dutifully probed to see if anyone had any opinions about the mysterious poisonings I assumed they had all heard about. They were aware but seemed only mildly concerned. All said they had not been present at such an occurrence, and nobody professed to have any idea what was behind them. Nothing jumped out at me.

As only the three poems plus my haikus had been circulated, I assumed Ryman had not submitted one this month. He confirmed it and offered "too busy with the divorce and custody mess" as an excuse for not having written anything. Apparently, having a poem for every meeting was not a requirement. That was something of a relief, even though I had a goodly supply of additional haikus in reserve. After that, I'd be in trouble because I probably couldn't get away with bringing haikus every time. But maybe The Case would be wrapped up and I could quit the group long before that became an issue.

We sat around a large steel table with six chairs. There was plenty of elbow room. Another set of table and chairs sat empty at the other end of the room. There were two huge picture windows facing into the main reading room of the library, the view partially obscured by the fiction stacks. From time to time, other library patrons, especially children, would look through the windows at us as if wondering what we were up to. Sometimes they would wave, but mostly they would frown and walk away. The smaller children would creep along under the sill and pop up suddenly as if playing peek-a-boo until called or ushered away by an adult, who waved or frowned. We ignored all this, but it was disconcerting until I got used to it.

At 7:05, Michael spotted Sillveeya approaching. Unexpectedly, for me, there was another woman with her who turned out to be her cousin Feebee Constance and who, as I learned later, although a member of Writer's Block and a regular attendee at the poetry critique meetings, had never to anyone's knowledge actually written a poem. Privately, I imagined her real first name was Joan. Spelled "Jone."

With everyone assembled, my moment of truth was about to arrive. I confess I was nervous. I have been in many meetings. I have run many meetings. I have made speeches before audiences large and small, some less than receptive to what I had to say. They never made me nervous. But this was new territory. This was personal. Would I be accepted? I had to say nice but constructively critical things about other people's poems and, worse, I had to listen to whatever they had to say about mine. Their babies. My babies. And, un-detective-like, I didn't have a clue how to go about it.

But then I thought, what the heck, following the traditional advice that's given to novice public speakers, I will simply imagine everybody else in the room is naked. No, seriously, I thought, how bad could it be? There's no microphone to swallow and then vomit and fall down and, hey, I'm getting paid for this, which in a way I guess makes me a *professional* poet, so who cares if they don't accept me.

It didn't help. Nothing to do now but wait for Ryman to get things going and then let the chips fall where they may.

They started falling quickly.

"Normally, I would ask one of you to read your poem

aloud to the group," Ryman began, his goatee bobbing up and down as he spoke, "and then I'd go around the table and ask each of you in turn for any positive things you have to say about it. After that, I'd ask for your questions and comments, including criticisms, and then I'd let the poet respond, followed by any further discussion.

"But tonight's a little different," he continued, fixing his gaze on Michael. "Michael, I think we have a problem."

All eyes on Michael.

"What's that?" said Michael, somewhat defiantly I thought.

"I had a suspicion after last month's meeting that you weren't being entirely honest about the poem you brought. It sounded vaguely familiar to me, but since you're a fairly new member I thought maybe you'd just modeled it on some other poems you'd been reading, so I let it go. Plus, everybody liked it."

"That's right, I was trying to capture a style I liked," answered Michael. "Just like your famous painters started out by copying the works of other painters so they could learn."

"Well, I spent some time Googling some of the lines and phrases in your poem and I discovered most of them can be found in 'Looking for a Sunset Bird in Winter' by Robert Frost. It's hard to believe that's a coincidence."

My ears perked up. Detectives don't like coincidences, and obviously Ryman didn't either.

"Well, maybe I got a little carried away there," said Michael, "but Frost's a good one to learn from. I like him."

Michael wasn't giving an inch.

"Really?" said Ryman, stroking his goatee. "Can you name another one of his poems besides 'Stopping by Woods on a Snowy Evening' or 'The Road Not Taken'?"

"Umm, well not offhand, no. But I've got one of his books

and there's miles to go before I sleep," said Michael with what I thought was a slightly mischievous grin. Trying to deflect with humor.

"Okay, well here was the clincher for me," said Ryman. "Your poem 'Poetry Heaven' is word for word the same as 'Poem Paradise' by Walt Pilcher from his book, *On Shallowed Ground*. Page 166, to be exact. See, I brought a copy. He's a local writer, and I just happened to have read it recently."

"Well, I did use a different title and changed some of the punctuation. What's wrong with that?"

"Unfortunately, everything. If you had brought the poem and said, 'I didn't write a poem this month, but here's one I like and would appreciate your opinion on,' that would have been fine. But instead, you tried to pass it off as your own. That's a no-no at Writer's Block. I'm afraid I'm going to have to ask you to leave the group."

The rest of us sat in stunned silence while Michael glared at Ryman for a moment, then slowly stood and walked to the door, leaving his copies of tonight's poems on the table. He turned and said, "Thanks for embarrassing me in front of everyone!"

"You can appeal my decision to Betty Wright-Moore," said Ryman, "but for now, good evening, and we wish you well."

"I'll just bet you do. This isn't over," said Michael, opening the door. We watched as he stomped with head held high through the fiction stacks and out toward the main entrance, library patrons glancing at him curiously.

"Well, maybe I should have done that in private, and I'm sorry you had to see that on your first visit with us, Mark, but I really felt an example must be made if we are to maintain the integrity of Writer's Block," said Ryman after we had sat there in silence for another moment.

"I have to agree," said Eleanor. The rest of us nodded. Ryman absently stroked his goatee.

I was thinking, wow, these poetry people are tough. Not your stereotypical artsy-fartsy pantywaists. Now I was truly nervous.

On the other hand, I now had a possible suspect. And not only because he had an Irish surname, which would obviously be a flimsy reason to put someone on the suspect list. For example, I could probably rule out Lester McDonald and his great grandmother Sharon/Evelyn/Eileen/Maw-maw as suspects. The other problem is that many surnames are common to England, Ireland and Scotland, so pure Irishness in a name isn't always guaranteed.

Anyway, Michael's plagiarism didn't seem innocent to me. Was he a for-real wannabe poet and merely stupid, or was something else going on? Would banishment bring on more attacks, if in fact Michael was behind them at all? His parting shot of "This isn't over!" bothered me a little even though I know these days the aggrieved party in this type of situation is culturally required to hurl that declaration at his tormenter, at least on TV. So, it could have been nothing more than a lame attempt to save face, but you never know. Would there be a headline reading "Disgruntled Poet Attacks Critique Group Leader in Vicious Rhyme Crime"?

And thinking about microphones as I had been a few moments before, I suddenly remembered from the witness accounts that microphones were not involved in all of the incidents. Sometimes the victims were speaking or performing without a microphone, and sometimes they weren't performers but members of the audience or venue staff or simply passersby who weren't directly involved in the artsy event at all. Like bookstore customers who happened to be in the store when an incident occurred. So maybe it wasn't a gag reflex from attempted microphone-swallowing that caused the vomiting and falling down, but something else.

Eleanor read her poem "Springlyness" first, and it was discussed. Then Sillveeya went through the process with "Athabasca." I noticed Ryman, Sillveeya and Feebee making notes on their copies with Gate City Playhouse Rocks fountain pens. I didn't notice any ink-stained fingers.

On the whole, the critiquing was objective, kind, and compassionate, not brutal at all. Nobody cried or got mad and went stomping out of the room. True, I detected a latent hurt feeling now and then, but I had expected worse. I confess I didn't understand a lot of the comments about rhyme schemes, slant rhymes, meter, tempo, iambic this and pentameter that, "feet," "music," word choices and so on, and a weird thing called enjambment which isn't what it sounds like, but I refrained from asking too many questions. I would have to look some of it up. When I did ask questions, they were welcomed. Even the poemless Feebee made comments that seemed intelligent. I cautiously offered my own comments, and nobody laughed at me.

The group liked both poems but surprisingly (to me) preferred "Athabasca." Maybe someday I'll understand why. I thought it was plain silly, but what do I know?

"I've saved your haikus for last, Mark," said Ryman when we'd finished with the others. "I thought it would be helpful for you to see how we do things and get comfortable before being thrown to the wolves."

"I don't see any wolves here, but I appreciate that," I said. Then I read my little poems.

Lucky Number Haiku
By Mark Fairley

I'm outside the box,
and do you know what I think?
I want back inside.

The emperor has
virtually no clothes since
he buys them online.

At night, where's the sun?
Of course, it's looking for you.
You're the one who set.

When the wise man asks,
"What is the meaning of life?"
the wise-ass answers.

Night begins the day,
slowly slipping away to
reveal morning bright.

Indian legend:
Great Spirit wakes up at last,
sees whites buffaloed.

The metric system:
Now a miss is as good as
a kilometer.

Poetic bow to
multiculturalism:
Haiku! Gesundheit!

Silence. Not stunned silence, I thought, just silence. Ryman looked at each of the women in turn. They didn't look back. Nobody spoke. Then Ryman said, "Eleanor, any positive comments?"

Eleanor shifted a little in her chair before responding in a soft voice, "Well, they certainly are … different. Uh, unique I'd have to say. And, uh, interesting. The syllable counts are correct too." She stopped.

"Sillveeya?"

"Yes, I agree with Eleanor. And some of them are sort of humorous, I guess. And the title is interesting." She stopped. Then added, "But I'm not sure what you're trying to say with these."

"Let's hold the criticism for now," said Ryman. "Feebee?"

"Well," said Feebee more brightly than the others but ironically it seemed to me, "you have a special talent, Mark. I could never write anything like that." She stopped then, and everyone nodded agreement.

"Okay, well I like them," said Ryman to my amazement. "They're clever and mostly funny, and I assume the title is a reference to there being eight poems in the set and eight is a lucky number in Japan, right?"

I nodded.

"Do the rest of you have any other comments before we let Mark talk?"

Now that Ryman had let them know where he stood, it was like a dam had burst. They all started talking at once, and Ryman had to jump in and referee. It was clear they *wanted* to like the haikus but simply couldn't wrap their minds around them. Technically, they were legitimate poetry, but beyond that they were like strange creatures that had popped into existence without benefit of proper zoological provenance. Or magically, like the golden calf. Creation versus evolution right there in the Kathleen Clay Edwards Family Branch Library.

When there was a lull, Ryman said, "Actually, these are more like *senryū*, similar to haiku but tending to be about human foibles and often satirical, while haiku are more serious and tend to be about nature and man's response to it."

"I didn't know that," I said.

"Well then, you've sort of stumbled upon something new to most of us, and we thank you for that. It was a learning experience, and that's what we're all about, right, everyone?"

Nods and yesses all around.

"Now it's your turn," said Ryman, looking at me.

"Ah, well, let's see," I began.

I thanked them all for their comments and told them about my death-defying drive home from Charlotte because I had procrastinated and was reduced to composing haikus into my cell phone in torrential rain while blinded by semi-trailer backwash. They seemed to enjoy the story. No doubt they were happy I hadn't been killed and could therefore bring them these terrific poems.

"You should write a poem about that!" said Feebee.

"In fact, I did," I said, reaching into my portfolio. "I didn't include it because nine is an unlucky number in Japan. Is it okay if I share it?"

Ryman said, "Sure."

I handed out copies and then read it.

> Dangerous business:
> Dodging trucks and composing
> haikus in the rain.

They all thought it was wonderful. But it was, in fact, number nine.

Chapter Twenty-Seven

Tuesday night & Wednesday

When I got home, Emily and I discussed my debut literary triumph over small glasses of amaretto. Not that we can afford expensive liqueurs, but this was a bottle left over from better days. She was surprised to hear about Michael Brennan but relieved that nothing untoward had happened. No vomiting or falling down, although I hadn't been sure something like that wasn't about to happen during the initial silence after I read my haikus. And I was happy that I appeared to be accepted by at least a tiny portion of the Greensboro arts community. Presumably, word would get back to Betty Wright-Moore, and maybe others, that I was okay. Maybe Dylan Vivaldi would hear about it too, in case he had any lingering doubts about my involvement in the investigation.

Lieutenant Blue would be pleased as well, I hoped, since I could point to real, if slight, progress on The Case. I was a success with the poet people, and I had a possible suspect we could check out and keep an eye on.

After dinner we watched a documentary about Sir Arthur Conan Doyle on PBS, one of only about 13 channels left to us since I cut back to the Basic cable package to save money. I took mental notes of some of Sherlock Holmes' methods. Emily fell asleep. After that, we went to bed.

Wednesday we slept in a little, had a leisurely breakfast, in my case topped off with a fuzzy coffee in my WFDD-FM

161

commemorative mug.[6] It was to be a day for taking stock and planning next moves, one of which was to sign up for an open mic event so I could use my haikus, or *senryū*, to meet and expose myself to a wider circle, maybe see if more clues would jump out at me.

Vivaldi had given me a copy of this month's Greensboro's Got Talent calendar, published by a loose consortium called Greensboro Arts Alive! (GAA!) and consisting of Writer's Block, Stringing Along (stringed instrument musicians), Singing Along (choruses and barbershop quartets), Painting the Town (artists), Shape Shifters (sculptors and metal workers), Tutu Wonderful (ballet and dance), Buttons & Bows (sewing, needlepoint, knitting, crocheting and quilting), Bluebirds of Happiness (bird watchers) and more, including groups within groups, each one trying to outdo the others with an enviably clever name and mostly failing. Writer's Block itself included Tall Tales (fiction writers, formerly Angst of Green Fables), Small Tales (memoir writers), Matinee Idolatry (playwrights, actors and production people), and Rhyme 'n' Time Again (poets, obviously, of which Tuesday night's group was a part). I have no idea how the birdwatchers got in there unless it was a desperation move resulting from failure to get noticed any other way.

---

[6] Recipe for Fuzzy Coffee: Gather ingredients – approx. one cup water (may be left in tap or container until needed), instant coffee (in jar until needed), one packet artificial sweetener (sugar may be substituted if desired – one or more teaspoons to taste). Fill one WFDD-FM (or other NPR radio station logo mug of your choice) with water. Place in microwave oven and press Beverage. Wait. When microwave dings, remove mug. Open the jar of instant coffee, remove one teaspoon of coffee (level or heaping to taste) and pour into mug. Do not stir. Foam will form on top of the liquid (Thus, fuzzy coffee). Open one small packet of artificial sweetener and pour contents into mug. Sweetener will momentarily ride on top of the foam but will eventually sink. Milk or creamer may be added to taste. Stir. Enjoy. Serves: 1

GAA! is sort of a United Way for the arts and does not include such organizations and venues as the Greensboro Symphony Orchestra, The Greensboro Opera, the Steven Tanger Center for the Performing Arts, Dylan Vivaldi's Gate City Playhouse, his Komedy Klub, and other professional or semiprofessional enterprises that are strong enough to stand mostly on their own. Those, along with GAA!, are part of the overarching Guilford Arts League.

This was not to mention groups that do not choose or weren't invited to belong to the consortium or to the Guilford Arts League. No one has a complete list of those or knows how many there are. They pop in and out of existence like Schrödinger's cat anyway, so it's pointless to try to keep up with them.

As Bob Ausländer said, a confusingly organized potpourri. Except he didn't use the word potpourri. He said amorphous.

The calendar showed an open mic scheduled for Saturday evening at the Read-A-Spell bookstore, so I called the number provided and fearlessly signed myself up.

An open mic is where amateur poets and writers get a chance to perform excerpts of their work in front of a small audience, typically in a bookstore, coffee shop or library. A few experienced readers, sometimes called "headliners," are invited and usually go first, and then the microphone is declared "open" for the others, provided they signed up in advance and were accepted by the host of the venue—usually the bookstore or coffee shop owners or the sponsoring literary club. In this case it was Writer's Block, and Betty Wright-Moore herself was to be the MC. I looked forward to meeting her.

For Thursday, the GAA! calendar showed a multi-artist event at one of the local galleries, The Framery, on State Street, open to the public. I invited Emily to attend both events with me. She said the art gallery might be fun but she'd have to think about the open mic. I understand (from experience now) that if you are not a poet, listening to some people read their poems can be challenging (read boring), but I agreed we'd both enjoy the gallery event, if only because we could leave as soon as we got there if we didn't like what we saw. I would introduce myself to some of the artists and see if any clues jumped out at me.

When it came to taking stock, there was a lot of stock to take.

- Multiple poisonings and accidents in the arts community beginning about six weeks ago and ongoing since then, seemingly concentrated around the Gate City Playhouse, currently in rehearsals for *The Christmas O'Carolan Songbook, Volume 1*, a musical comedy about the fictitious son of an ancient Irish musical hero, set against a background of national sadness, potatoes and alcohol, and no other helpful connections among the victims.
- No trace of any identifiable poison in any of the victims. A black-clad masked motorcycle mugger.
- Ink stains on many victims' index fingers from fountain pens promoting the Gate City Playhouse, but no trace of poison in the ink (a good play on words there waiting to be milked later. See if you can guess what it is). Of course, if the poison were untraceable, there understandably wouldn't be any trace of it. A conundrum. (Okay, the play on words is "This gives a whole new meaning to the expression, 'poison pen.'" Did you guess it?)
- Lenny Monahan, a moderately-funny-but-strange new-in-town standup comedian who might be a suspect if only because he acted super-Irish to the point of being

chauvinistic, which was suspicious in this day and age in someone apparently not a native of Ireland. But I checked the timelines and saw that Monahan had arrived about two weeks *after* the troubles started. Maybe that ruled him out, but still …

- The video of Morrie Milburne's act at the Komedy Klub, about which something was nagging at my subconscious.
- Michael Brennan, a plagiarist poet with an Irish name but also with a clear reason to be alienated from the arts community.
- My "Artsy 6" list of victims I needed to interview.
- A witness list Lieutenant Blue had cross-checked but that I needed to have a look at.
- A fledgling campaign by Upshot Marketing and sponsored by the GADC to unify and promote the arts community, but which might have to be put on hold if the media found out about the poisonings and accidents, and maybe should be put on hold anyway—I would have to make that suggestion to Bob Ausländer.
- Time pressure because a mysterious "big tech company from up north" was delaying its move to Greensboro and threatening to go to a rival city unless this mess was cleared up in 60 days, about two weeks of which had already flown by without much progress. But at least I was getting paid.

I had a lot of questions. Here was my list:

1   What the HECK is going on?

No, sorry, here is the actual list:

1   Why the Gate City Playhouse? Could it have anything to do with *The Christmas O'Carolan Songbook* production?

2   What kind of light did C.B.D. Miller see that caused him to fall off the stage?

3   What is the poison?

4   Do the ink stains mean anything? Or should I ignore them for now?

5   Should I ignore the black-clad masked motorcycle mugger for now?

6   Are Lenny Monahan and Michael Brennan legitimate suspects, and if so, what do they have to gain by causing all this trouble? How could Monahan be responsible since he arrived two weeks after the trouble started? Will I find either of them on the lists of witnesses to the incidents (besides Monahan's presence at the Xomedy Xlub, obviously)?

7   What is bothering me about the Morrie Milburne video?

8   Can any of the "Artsy 6" victims shed light on things? Did they see any lights?

9   Will I learn anything from the cross-checked witness lists? Did they see any lights?

10   Why is there so much Irishness being thrown around? And so many people with Irish names. Is that a clue? It does sort of jump out at me, after all.

11   Who is the big tech company from up north? Maybe that would be a clue. And will they give us an extension if the investigation takes longer than 60 days?

12   Will I ever find a real job?

Which reminded me, I hadn't yet heard anything from the company in Charlotte. It had been less than a week and these things often move slowly, but still I was mildly curious.

From my excellent list of perceptive questions, I painstakingly developed a to-do list:

1 Find out what the HECK is going on.

No, actually it was:

   1 Follow up with Blue on his promise to check out Monahan.

   2 See what Blue can find out about Brennan.

   3 See if Emily can spot anything odd in the Morrie Milburne video.

   4 Interview the Artsy 6 victims.

   5 Double-check the cross-checked witness lists. Look for Brennan and Monahan.

   6 Get Bob Ausländer to tell me who the big tech company is.

   7 See what he thinks about delaying the Upshot Marketing campaign.

   8 Ignore the ink stains and the black-clad masked motorcycle mugger for now.

   9 Crime scene investigation: Conduct a thorough inspection of the Gate City Playhouse theater area and see if any clues jump out at me. Strange lights?

  10 Attend the art gallery open house event on Thursday.

  11 Read at the open mic event on Saturday.

  12 Attend the Upshot Marketing presentation at the Greensboro Country Club (check for date & time).

  13 Update the list sometime next week.

  14 Bread, milk, dozen eggs, peanut butter, potato chips, toilet paper

Oh, and:

  15 Get a real job. Probably not in Charlotte.

I ran the lists by Emily. She liked them, mostly. Except number 14 on the second list, which she thought was dumb. She had only one question:

"Why are you ignoring the poison?"

"Seems like a dead end, so to speak. Nobody can find any."

"Is that possible?" she said.

"I suppose it's possible there exists a poison that leaves no trace," I said. "But I've searched the Internet and can't find a reference to one that's truly untraceable, and I'm sure the police and medical forensics people have searched much more thoroughly than I."

"So maybe it's not possible?"

"Maybe."

"You thought I was asleep during that Arthur Conan Doyle program last night, didn't you?"

"Well, you *were* sort of snoring."

"But I remember one thing I heard. A quote from one of his stories. I looked it up this morning. Hang on."

She went to the bookcase and pulled down our copy of *The Complete Sherlock Holmes*, which we'd both read some years ago.

"Here it is," she said. "The original quote from 'The Sign of the Four' is, 'How often have I said to you that when you have eliminated the impossible, whatever remains, however improbable, must be the truth?'"

"So, what are you saying?" I said.

"I'm saying if an untraceable poison is impossible, as far as we know anyhow, maybe there is no poison."

"Although that's 'improbable.'"

"Right."

"So maybe we should be looking for something else?"

"Right."

"But what?"

"You're the detective."

Chapter Twenty-Eight

Three First National Plaza in Chicago is a prestigious address. It is a 57-story office tower located at 70 West Madison Street. Completed in 1981, the building is one of the tallest in the city at 767 feet. Tenants include companies you've heard of and many you haven't, but all are leading lights in key industries with national and worldwide influence. It is only five blocks from Michigan Avenue's opulent Magnificent Mile, an area densely populated with upscale shopping and dining as well as luxury hotels boasting room rates of $500 per night and above. Nosebleed territory for most mortals, but not those in the 51st-55th floor corner offices of Tribulette Corporation.

These worthy executives and their employees also enjoy halls decorated with one of the world's largest and most prestigious collections of Impressionist art, including masterpieces by such artists as Pissaro, Degas, Renoir, Braque, Matisse, Picasso, Bonnard, Giacometti, Moore, Maillol, Kandensky, and Léger, works which would be worthy of any museum. Tribulette's longtime Chairman personally chooses and manages the collection in what he believes to be an ideal way to bring the worlds of art and business together. Why he believes it is important to do that is anybody's guess.

Tribulette is in the defense industry. It is in many ways a stealth-type corporation. Although it has roots in a startup launched not long after the Vietnam War ended, few people have heard of it outside of the Federal Government, and precious few even within it. *You've* certainly never heard of it, until now, and even now you can't be sure it actually exists. But it does. Nobody knows the full extent of the products and services offered or the complete list of defense contracts held by Tribulette at any given time, not even the corner office executives, who should. Not even the Pentagon.

It is privately held. There is no annual report except a three-page executive summary memo generated by the Accounting Department (which also doesn't know the extent of the corporation's activities but thinks it does), signed by the Chairman and the President and read aloud via secure satellite telephone by the President to each of the members of the Board of Directors one at a time in order of their tenure on the Board. None of the Board members even knows who all the others are. No hard copies are distributed. Quarterly Board meetings are held via Zoom using encrypted audio feeds, filters to mask the faces, and pseudonyms in the participants' boxes in place of real names. You would recognize the names of the Chairman and most of the Board members, and you would be astonished at how such a diverse group in terms of educational and professional backgrounds, not to mention political leanings, could work so well together.

Visitors are few, which means, to the Chairman's chagrin, the extensive art collection goes unseen by the public and is practically unknown outside the company except to the top tier of art critics and historians who have seen it only by invitation and only after signing nondisclosure agreements.

Tribulette has no website, and there is no publicity. None. Not even a listing on the directory of tenants displayed in the building's lobby. In spite of Tribulette's incalculably valuable contributions to America's security over the years, its Chairman will never see his (or her, Tribulette not bowing to political correctness by resorting to the term "Chairperson") name in print in connection with the corporation, much less be named, politically correctly, Person of the Year by *Time Magazine.*

However.

There are subsidiary companies. Some of these are not so secretive about their own existence even though much of their work is highly classified. Most are scattered hither and yon around the country and the world, but some are headquartered at Three First National Plaza, a near enough proximity for convenience while at the same time, by being on much lower floors, far enough not to betray an obvious relationship to the parent company. Private elevators facilitate physical communication.

One such company is RayDact Corporation, its headquarters taking up half of the 14th floor. RayDact is in the forefront of nontraditional weapons development and custom manufacture. They make nothing that explodes. Agents of chemical and biological warfare are eschewed. Their products are far more discreet. Most testing is done in laboratories under stringently controlled conditions, but sometimes field testing is also conducted.

Jerome Fostridge, president of RayDact, rarely rides those elevators to the corporate stratosphere. They are for underlings—vice presidents, lawyers, engineers, IT people, accountants, clerks and such. He was seriously thinking about doing it now though, having just received the third missive in six weeks from Tribulette's Chairman asking about progress of plans to move RayDact's Chicago headquarters and its main manufacturing facility now located in the industrial part of town, to Greensboro, North Carolina, a move the Chairman believed would benefit Tribulette's bottom line. It was time for another of Jerome's infrequent face-to-face meetings with the Chairman, and this might not be a pleasant one.

On the other hand, it would provide an excuse to roam

the halls and enjoy the art collection, which he loved as much as the Chairman did. Which was one of the reasons he had no intention of moving his company to a cultural backwater like Greensboro. He had visited Greensboro. He knew what kind of art could be found there. Shallow. Amateurish. Self-absorbed. Nothing rising even to the level of Grandmas Moses' celebrated but overrated primitivism, for example. Never mind that she won countless awards and that her art appears on US Postage stamps. One or two steps above cave paintings, in Jerome's opinion. There were exceptions in Greensboro of course, but precious few. Further, he and his wife, now empty nesters, were loath to abandon the attractions of the Magnificent Mile, the joys of Chicago's rich cultural and social life with its many museums, galleries and theaters, and their luxury high-rise condo on Lake Shore Drive.

He would explain this to the Chairman. He would say that the other executives in RayDact felt the same way about the proposed comedown in quality of life. He would update the Chairman on current events in Greensboro, especially the recent increase in the crime level. He would also of course diplomatically and in a businesslike manner demonstrate to the Chairman with charts and graphs and irrefutable data why it made no sense economically to move his company.

The Chairman would understand and agree.

Otherwise, current events in Greensboro might take another turn, and not for the better.

Chapter Twenty-Nine

Working my to-do list, I called Lieutenant Blue. Did he have anything to tell me about Lenny Monahan? No, not yet. Did he happen to know the identity of the big tech company up north? No, but he agreed it might be helpful to find out. I said I'd press Bob on it.

I told him about Michael Brennan and how he was banished from the critique group for plagiarism. He said he'd have a look at him, get some background and so on.

He agreed to let me interview the Artsy 6 victims and also agreed that I should do so without police involvement, using my GADC cover. My story would be that I was gathering background to help Upshot Marketing write an article about the arts scene and I needed their perspectives on things. They would be flattered and therefore cooperative. Until no article ever came out, but by then I hoped to be gone from said scene. Fortunately (or presciently), I had mentioned to Frances Muldoon and Donna Majors at Upshot that I would be getting to know people in the arts community as part of my GADC assignment, so they would presumably back me up if any of the victims or witnesses I interviewed called them to check up on my story.

I filled him in on my plans to attend the art gallery event and the open mic. He muttered something unintelligible but in what I took to be an approving tone.

"One more thing," I said.

"I'm listening."

"You know how we've been assuming there's some kind of poison involved in the attacks, right?"

"Right."

"But nobody can find any trace of it, right?"

"Right again."

"So … what if there's really no poison at all?"

"No poison?"

"Right."

"Okay, maybe you're on to something there," said Blue. "No poison, huh?"

Chalk another one up for Emily.

"So if there's no poison," I said, "what do you think it could it be?"

"Hey, you're the detective."

Echoing Emily. He had me there, but I knew he'd think about it.

Next, I called Bob Ausländer. He sounded harried but happy to hear from me.

"Well as I live and breathe," he said when I was finally put through to him after a two-minute wait during which I was treated to James Taylor singing "Fire and Rain," apparently Bob's idea of evocative "on hold" music designed to build business for Glowery. "It's my favorite undercover guy. I was wondering if you were still on the planet."

"I like your new hold music, Bob."

"Don't you just love it? What did you hear … the James Taylor?"

"Right."

"We've got it in rotation with 'Ring of Fire' by Johnny Cash and 'Light my Fire' by the Doors. Oh, and 'Great Balls of Fire' by …"

"I know, Jerry Lee Lewis."

"Right! Great tie-ins to the business, don't you think? I

thought it was a stupid idea when Marketing first brought it up, and the royalties we're paying are pretty steep, but the employees like it, so here we are. Gives the customers something to smile about in the midst of their troubles too, so I guess it's worth it."

"Well, sounds like you're 'burning' through a lot of cash," I said.

"Oh, that's real funny. And artsy too, sort of, I mean with the pun and everything."

"You seem to be in a good mood."

"I was until you called. No, just kidding. I can't wait to hear your report. But, yeah, I'm happy. But busy. Business has been good the past couple weeks. Kitchen fires, burst waters heaters, arsons. You name it. I love it! But nothing involving artsy folks."

"And naturally you're sorry about all those people who've had so much damage."

"Sure, but business is business. You know that."

"If business is so good, are you thinking of adding staff, like maybe some strategic planning professionals?" (Not that I would even seriously consider working for Bob again, but I had to get the dig in.)

"Thought about it. For about a split second. The thing is, when business is bad, we can't afford a strategic planning department, and when it's good we don't need one. But that's not why you called, is it?" he went on. "Tell me what been happening in undercover detective world."

"It's still early days, but I'm making some progress," I said, determined not to give Bob any details. "I'm attending some events, meeting some people, getting briefed by the Upshot Marketing team, working with Lieutenant Blue. You know, that sort of thing."

"Blue seems to think you're doing okay, for a tinhorn."

"Was that his word for it?"

"Yeah, why?"

"Don't you think he meant 'greenhorn'?"

"Now that you mention it …"

"Nice to hear, anyway."

"Yeah, but the problem is, we're getting pressure from the big guy up north. Says he wants to see some action on getting this mess cleared up. So naturally that means I'm getting pressure from the GADC and the Mayor, and so on. What's your outlook?"

"Like I said, it's early days, but I've got some ideas and a few leads which of course we have to keep under wraps for now, but I'm glad you mentioned the company from up north. That's mainly why I called."

"Oh?"

"I need to know who they are."

"I told you, no can do, Mark."

"Look, I'm just trying to turn over every stone I can think of here. Somebody's benefitting from all these attacks, if that's what they are, unless it's some nut case out for a lark, which I doubt, so it behooves me to make sure there aren't any connections with the people up north since that's what the whole urgency of the case seems to hinge on. Right?"

"Well," said Bob, "if it 'behooves' you, how can I say no?"

"Sorry, I got carried away. But thanks."

"I was just kidding. It's still no."

"Bob, how many people here know who that company is?"

"Let's see, there's only me, Frieda my executive administrative assistant, the Mayor, three of her cronies on the City Council, the City Attorney, most everybody else on the GADC which is 14 people right now, including Dylan Vivaldi. But that's all. Except my wife and maybe some of the other spouses. But that's definitely all."

176

"Now I'm surprised the *News & Record* hasn't run a feature in their Sunday business section yet!"

"Goes to show you what a good job we've done keeping it a secret."

"Okay, maybe, but you've also hired me to keep a big secret too. Two secrets in fact: One, that there's something fishy going on in the arts community and, two, that there even *is* a big company on deck that won't move here unless we get to the bottom of it. Those are big secrets, if you ask me. Are you telling me you can't trust me to know who the company is?"

"Silence."

"You still there, Bob?"

"I'm thinking."

This could take a while, I thought. But it didn't.

"All right, you win. Ever heard of RayDact Corporation?"

"Who?"

"RayDact." He spelled it for me. With a capital R and a capital D.

"No."

"Well, they're big. Really big. Defense contractors. R&D on new sophisticated weapons for the military, stuff like that. They have a big plant in Chicago and their parent company wants them to move here because it's cheaper to operate in the South. Their president, a guy named Jerome Fostridge, doesn't want to move because of the poisonings and whatnot. So I'm getting pressure from the Chairman."

"Who's the Chairman?"

"Don't know."

"You don't know?"

"I don't know the name of the parent company either. Very hush-hush obviously. Must be into black ops and all that secret government stuff or something. But this guy keeps calling me about when we're going to solve our 'crime problem,' says to call him Mr. Phillips because he can't use his real name. I ask Fostridge, and he confirms it's him all right. Uses Phillips as a fake name with everybody he talks to, apparently."

"Does this 'RayDact' have a website?"

"Yes, but there's not much there, and no mention of a parent company," said Bob.

"Is this for real? Or are you just making it up to avoid my question?"

"I wouldn't do that, even to you."

"Then I apologize. But this is weird, you have to admit. Anyway, I won't tell anybody. Except Detective Blue. He needs to know everything I know."

"Okay, just Blue," said Bob reluctantly. "But no one else, right?"

"No one else."

Except Emily.

Chapter Thirty

Before settling into reviewing the cross-checked lists of witnesses, I couldn't resist checking out the RayDact website. Sure enough, there wasn't much there. The home page bore not much more than a large, flag-shaped red, white and blue RayDact logo over a patriotic landscape: Amber waves of grain, a fruited plain, and purple mountain majesties under spacious skies from sea to shining sea. That sort of thing. And a slogan, "Where Exceptional R&D Stands for Readiness and Defense." Not as catchy as DuPont's old "Better Things for Better Living through Chemistry," one of my all-time favorites, but at least it did suggest a ballpark of possible activities.

The About Us page wasn't much more enlightening: Several paragraphs of meaningless fluff with "state of the art in highly sophisticated countermeasures" being the only clue as to what the company might actually be up to. The client list was short, consisting of a few Government agencies I'd never heard of but whose names sounded military in nature, the governments of a handful of other countries, presumably friendly ones, a well-known aircraft company, and two US weapons manufacturers I'd also never heard of.

No products or specific services were listed, so I was on my own to imagine what they might be. Electronic surveillance equipment? Laser weapons? Electromagnetic Pulse (EMP) technology to knock out an enemy's electronic equipment? Star Trek-type phasers with settings ranging from the ever popular "stun" to the rarely and reluctantly used "blow to kingdom come"? Memory-wiping neuralyzers like they use in the *Men in Black* movies? Training in how to use such devices? Customer service on them, including repairs? It was impossible to say.

The Our Team page featured a photo, presumably authentic but who knows, of Jerome Fostridge, the president. No one else. A one-man team, apparently. The photo showed a no-nonsense-looking man in his fifties with broad shoulders, a receding hairline and wire-rimmed glasses wearing a dark suit with a white button-down shirt and a blue tie. This was accompanied by two paragraphs of fluff about his background, making him sound like a tough but affable one-man Defense Department.

Finally, there was the Contact Us page. There was no mailing address, no email address and no phone or fax number. Not even the name of the city where RayDact was located (but Bob had said Chicago). To contact RayDact, one had to fill out the form on the page with one's own name, company affiliation, contact information, and reason for wanting to make contact and then click a "Submit" button. I refrained for now. What would be my reason for making contact? "Hi, I'm in the market for some highly sophisticated, state of the art countermeasures. Can you please send me your catalog?"

I Googled Jerome Fostridge. Nothing. I looked him up on LinkedIn and Facebook. Also nothing.

While I was at it, I looked up Michael Brennan and Lenny Monahan too. Not much on Brennan. His Facebook page showed an avatar instead of his photo and that he had 23 Friends, which my daughter Judy would consider "pitiful." Other than "Lives in Greensboro, NC," there was no basic information such as schools or where he worked. He had few posts, the most recent being a poem by Robert Frost. He posted it the day after the debacle at the poetry critique meeting, maybe as a way of thumbing his nose at Ryman Stanza. The online White Pages gave his local address and phone number. He was not on LinkedIn or any of the other social media platforms.

Monahan had a zany website touting his stupendous "funnyness" (shouldn't it have been "funniness" with an "i"?) and giving his appearance schedule and information on how to book him for a performance. The About Lenny page had a publicity photo of him in his signature blue pork pie hat gleefully brandishing a shillelagh at the camera and some lamely humorous words extolling his Irish pride. His LinkedIn presence was similar.

Wikipedia has articles on most celebrities, even minor ones, placed no doubt by themselves or their agents. Nothing on Monahan.

I hoped Blue would be able to find out more.

Facebook was still showing me ads for detective gear, even though it had been over a year since I went online looking for such things out of curiosity. Facebook is relentless. Maybe because I never bought any actual detective gear, the ads had started to include semi-related products. That day it was ghost hunting equipment. Type that into Google and it will return 12,300,000 results. The most prominent company boasts 107,400 followers on Facebook, but with over 12 million other choices, you certainly don't have to go with the first company that comes up.

If I did go with that company, however, the Spirit Box Ghost Hunting Kit was on special for $225.95, plus I'd get 100 Reward Tokens. The Kit includes the basic S Box Ghost Scanner, the Rook EMF Meter, the EVP Wrist Recorder, and a flashlight, presumably to blind the ghosts (or is that only for vampires, I don't remember). Purchased separately, the cost would be $235.85, but I'd get 125 Reward Tokens. So, I'd save $9.90 but give up 25 Reward Tokens. Batteries not included with either option. A quandary. What would you do?

Maybe if the amateur detective thing doesn't work out, and if I don't get a real job soon, I'll explore ghost hunting opportunities more seriously. In the meantime, let me assure you, this book isn't ghost written. I know you were wondering. Besides, if you don't believe me, who you gonna call?

I phoned Blue again and filled him in on RayDact and what little I'd learned on Google, Facebook and LinkedIn. I left out the ghost hunting part. He thanked me. Then it was on to the witness lists.

Chapter Thirty-One

I had been putting off getting into the witness lists because I thought it would be a tedious and boring task. Lieutenant Blue told me that most police work was tedious and boring, and Sheriff Cecil Belton in Spurrville and Detective Jake Keil from Raleigh said the same thing. "It's like they say about being an airplane pilot," Keil said. "Hours of utter boredom punctuated by brief moments of sheer terror. We try to spice it up by playing practical jokes on our colleagues. And in my case, laying traps for the dumbass criminals to fall into before I collar 'em." Keil and Belton certainly had their fun with me a time or two, so I knew what that meant.

The rest of it was following useless leads, interviewing witnesses with conflicting stories or who hadn't really seen anything, poring through pages and pages of records, overnighting in fruitless stakeouts, sitting in court for hours of dull testimony, avoiding donuts except in secret so as not to contribute to the stereotype, and filling out reams of daily paperwork, all the while wondering if the next minute somebody was going to take a shot at you. I could see where there would be tons of satisfaction in solving a case after all that effort and risk (and sacrifice when it came to the donuts), but I also appreciated the courage and dedication it took to do the job. And I could appreciate Emily's concerns about me. For them it was a calling. Not for me. I sort of fell into this and was doing it because we needed the money, but I hoped some of their skill, and their integrity, was rubbing off on me just the same. Maybe someday I would be enough of a colleague to start playing practical jokes on them, but that was probably a long way off.

Fortunately, when I finally got into the material he'd sent I discovered Blue and his people had already done most of the tedious and boring part. A list of witnesses, including any victims, who were present at more than one event where a "poisoning" (using the word only as a placeholder now, until we could learn more) or accident had occurred was neatly laid out on a spreadsheet with the locations, dates and times of the events. Under each name was a summary of his or her statement about each occurrence, and their full statements were attached in an appendix.

Of the 47 incidents the police knew about, 19 involved victims connected in some way to the Gate City Playhouse, and five had taken place there. That was the concentration Blue talked about. The others were scattered among other people, events, and venues with no apparent patterns.

The obvious analytical theory was that if the perpetrator had to be present in order to trigger the poisoning or accident (although accidents could have been set up ahead of time like booby traps or triggered remotely somehow), then any witness who was present at all 47 events became a prime suspect. Of course, if there were two perps, most likely neither of them would be on the lists for all the events. However, one, and possibly both, would have to have attended more than half the events. Beyond that, there seemed to be no logical way to analyze the lists, especially since the two perps may have attended some of the events together.

If there were three perpetrators, the analysis would be a nightmare, a mathematical problem worthy of being included on a Mensa IQ test. But I didn't think there would be three. Two maybe, but not three or more. Why? I don't know. It just didn't seem likely there would be a whole team of people doing this.

In any case, Blue and I assumed no more than two at this point. In total, there were 674 witnesses. Blue had circled in red the names of five who had been at 50% or more of the events. No one had attended all the events, seeming to confirm that there were at least two perps. The most frequent flyer among the five had attended 29 events. He circled in blue seven others who had attended all of the 18 events not attended by the five. Crude, maybe, or maybe it was brilliant, but either way it was a reasonable place to start.

Three of the seven also attended some of the same events as the five, but that didn't seem important at this stage.

What kind of person attends 29 arts-connected events in a six-week period? That's almost five per week. Or even 18 events? Maybe somebody in a leadership or staff capacity at an arts venue? Somebody lonely and in need of frequent social contact of a particular kind? Or someone who wants to make trouble. Unfortunately, those categories were not mutually exclusive.

Blue and his team had checked the validity of each witness's identify—licenses, Green Cards, home addresses, emergency contacts who could vouch for them, etc.—trying to eliminate the possibility of the perp or perps wearing disguises and carrying fake IDs so as to pass as multiple different people. There were 34 whose identities could not be positively verified. Oddly, each of the 34 had been present at only one of the incidents. What did that mean, if anything?

None of the 34 was among the five or the seven. The police did not take photos or write descriptions of the witnesses, and only the Komedy Klub had video surveillance, so there was no way to have a look at those people.

Before taking a closer look at the five and the seven, I

spent some time reading the witness statements. Quickly, it became apparent they were remarkably similar, so instead of plowing through 674 of them in detail, I started scanning for anomalies. Such as, did anyone report seeing strange lights before or during the events? About 75 did. Brief flashes. Glints. Reflections. Colorless or white. Maybe reddish. Not bright. Sometimes as long as a minute or two before the event, sometimes immediately before it. Sometimes more than one flash, sometimes only one. Sources of the lights were indeterminate.

There were no other anomalies that jumped out. Brennan had attended four events, but they were not centered around the Playhouse. Monahan had attended none except the one at the Xomedy Xlub. Nevertheless, these two still bothered me.

Then I looked at the five and the seven. Sure enough, four of the five were employees or volunteers at the venues where the incidents had occurred. The same was true of five of the seven. Chances were they wouldn't jeopardize their jobs by causing mayhem at their places of employment unless they were disgruntled for some reason. So, while those nine weren't eliminated from suspicion, it did leave one of the five and two of the seven to focus on. The one, who turned out to be the 29-event veteran, was Charles Kelly, 42 years old and divorced, no children, who listed his job as an obituary writer for the *News and Record*. The two among seven were Lorna Gribble, 41, a single part time substitute elementary school teacher who lived with her mother and dabbled in watercolors, and Dr. Travis Humberto, 66, a retired ophthalmologist and widower who was writing a novel. Miss Gribble had attended 18 of the events, Dr. Humberto 15.

The doctor didn't strike me as a likely suspect. He seemed a "pillar of the community" type who wouldn't want his reputation sullied by involvement in any kind of mischief.

Miss Gribble, on the other hand, might be lonely and bored, maybe even angry over the hand life had dealt her, and therefore possibly vulnerable to a pitch from a persuasive representative of the dark side promising some excitement in her ostensibly drab existence, and also money.

Kelly could easily be a troublemaker too, if only as an escape from the morbid subject matter he encountered on the job every day. However, what got my attention about him was that he worked for the newspaper and had witnessed 29 attacks, and yet the paper had not done a story about it or even made inquiries to the police. Why would he keep it from the higher-ups, which he apparently was doing, maybe missing out on a career promotion opportunity, unless he was involved in the attacks himself? And he was Irish.

We'd need to keep an eye on Gribble and Kelly.

I did some more work with the numbers and the lists and then took the time to read carefully the statements of the nine employees/volunteers who had been present at so many of the incidents. They seemed quite pleasantly gruntled, thank you very much. No obvious motives for mayhem. We could ignore them for the moment.

The analysis had taken all morning and most of the afternoon, with a short break for lunch. I now had two persons of interest—Lenny Monahan and Michael Brennan—and two likely suspects— Lorna Gribble and Charles Kelly.

Another of my conclusions from all of it was a surprising one and was either Mensa-quality or simply wrong, so I needed to run it by Blue as soon as I could. But first I wanted to show Emily the Morrie Milburne video.

Congratulations! You have just waded through the most boring chapter in this book. That is, unless you are a numbers person. I am not. But it moved the story along, we made some progress on The Case, and I did warn you detective work is mostly tedious and boring. I promise things will pick up again after this. However, there will probably be no moments of sheer terror. No shots fired at me while I'm hiding in a dumpster. I hope you hope that's the truth, but you might be one of those people who likes hockey because of the fights and the prospect of blood on the ice or goes to a NASCAR race hoping for a spectacular crash. Of course, *I* already know what's going to happen later in the book. You'll find out soon enough.

Chapter Thirty-Two

"I don't want to sit through the whole thing," Emily said as I cued up the video on my PC.

"No, just Morrie Milburne's part, starting a couple of minutes before he comes on stage."

"Why a couple of minutes?"

"Just because of something I noticed in the witness statements. I don't want to prejudice you by telling you first."

She sat down and got comfortable in front of the screen. I started the video where Freddy the MC announces Milburne. There was Freddy bounding on to the stage and giving Morrie the energetic introduction, then the drum roll and cymbal crash as Morrie bounded out from backstage in his Groucho Marx glasses and took the microphone, bowing to the audience applause as Freddy bowed to Morrie and bounded off. Then the applause dying away, Morrie sticking the microphone in his mouth, throwing up, and falling down. I stopped the video.

"Anything?"

"What do you mean, 'Anything'?"

"I mean, did you see anything you thought was unusual?"

"I thought putting the microphone in his mouth, vomiting and falling down was unusual."

"Aside from that."

"Can I see it again?"

I played it again. I didn't have the ability to run it in slow motion. Blue could probably do that and send me a slowed-down version, but for now I was making do with what I had.

"Anything this time? I mean, anything else?"

"Give me a hint."

"Okay," I said with a sigh, "like a strange light or glint or a flash. Anything like that."

"Play it again."

I did.

"Can you pause it where I say to?"

"Yes."

"Play it again and wait for me to say 'pause.'"

I played it.

"Pause. Right there!"

I paused it.

"What?" I said.

"Look. There," she said again, pointing at the screen.

"What are you pointing at, exactly? Touch it."

She touched Morrie's glasses. Sure enough, there seemed to be a glint of something. A reflection of some sort of light. Not bright, but a light. Maybe that was what had been bothering me about the video all this time. An unexplained, out of place glint of light registering in my subconscious. My detective subconscious.

It was too small to make out what it was, and I don't have the equipment you see on TV where the tech lady blows up the image for the detectives and it's always perfectly clear when the script calls for it, or too grainy or pixelated to make out, depending on the story line. But there was one thing I could try.

I took a screenshot of the scene I had paused on. (Don't ask me how I did this. I can never remember how to do it, so when I need to I Google for the instructions, get the screenshot, and then promptly forget how I did it.) The screenshot was a digital picture file, so now I could make it bigger and zoom in, which I did.

There was the enlarged light reflection from Milburne's

Groucho glasses. I couldn't make out the light's exact source, but it looked like it was coming from the back of the Komedy Klub room. Near Lenny Monahan's T-shirt table.

Chapter Thirty-Three

The disguises had become a pain in the butt. How many now? Thirty-four and counting? Wigs, fake beards and mustaches, fake noses, tinted contact lenses, skin tints and makeup to let him appear black or Asian. Cotton wads in his mouth to puff out his cheeks. And the eyeglasses. Wire rims, plastic rims, no rims, even a monocle once. More eyeglasses than Elton John, or that idiot Morrie Milburne. He'd caught his act once at a nightclub in Toronto while on another job. Like Elton John only not as funny.

Hats, shoes, pants, shirts, jackets, ties, even scarves—34 complete changes of wardrobe, so far. His client would pay for them, of course, but buying and storing them, and then taking selfies to keep track of what he'd worn and looked like each time so he didn't repeat himself was tedious. It was easy enough to get fake North Carolina drivers licenses, but for each one he had to pose for the required photo, and each photo had to be different, so he'd had to put on each disguise once already just for that. He had started with a stack of 60 different licenses in his arsenal, and now he had 26 left. Once the 26 were used, he would tell his handler this job was done with; he wasn't about to get any more. Not only did he have to keep track of which fake ID went with which disguise, he had to record where each disguise and ID were used. It was an administrative nightmare. Norman Shartly was not administrative. It was killing him.

All that was not to mention sitting through endless boring

and ridiculous narcissistic poetry recitations by people who could use lessons in basic expressive reading. Apparently, it was the thing in poetry circles to read as slowly and somberly as possible.

Bush league play rehearsals. Dreary nightclub acts with gimmicks and lame jokes in place of real humor. He'd heard better stuff from some of his buddies in Special Forces, and especially whenever a USO troupe would come through. Although that guy Lenny Monahan hadn't been too bad. And Rwanda Forsythe was interesting. Innovative. But otherwise ...

Snoozing through alternately monotonous and cacophonous symphony performances that went on forever. At least the seats were comfortable. And the opera? People in ridiculous costumes screaming their heads off in foreign languages and dying, and then getting up and singing about it. Forget it!

Guided tours and open houses at art galleries were the worst. Paintings and drawings no better than his own doodling, truly weird sculptures where it seemed each sculptor's goal was simply to be weirder than the other sculptors, often featuring nudes with their body parts scattered in seemingly random fashion hither and yon. Hands where feet should be. Elbows bent the wrong way. Breasts replacing buttocks, and vice versa. That sort of thing. Pottery you might make for your mother's birthday if you were seven. Strange ugly faces on useless pieces—ugly mugs on ugly mugs. Clay pots too big or too small to be of any practical use, except maybe the big ones could be filled with water at a wedding and Jesus could turn it into wine. Not likely the sculptors' intent (although in one case it apparently was). No place to sit. Skimpy little *hors d'oeuvres* with soured wine and endless, and fundamentally nonsensical, prattling by the guide or the artists about What this Piece Means or What the Artist Was Trying to Say. Who cares?

Even worse, lately he'd been getting sloppy. A toupee coming loose. A mustache coming unglued. A tinted contact dropping into his drink. Tiresome, and potentially much more than embarrassing. Once he'd even swallowed a cotton wad. It did not digest completely.

And this absurd weapon they'd given him. Concealed in a Gate City Playhouse Rocks fountain pen that was hard to aim—worse even than a pistol. Squeeze the pen's "sweet spot," a clip which was supposed to work like a trigger, and seemingly nothing would happen, but if his aim was true his targets would do something crazy and fall down. Sometimes if they had a microphone they would stick it in their mouth and gag first. Sometimes they would put their hands over their ears and look around wildly before closing their eyes and swaying a little before collapsing.

It missed as often as not. He would aim for one person, squeeze, and nothing would happen. Or he would hit somebody else. He didn't keep a count, but he figured he'd hit his intended targets only a little more than half the time. He never made more than one hit per event, intended target or not. Then he would calmly wait for the police to take everybody's statements, including his, which he carefully tailored to fit his disguise *du jour*. Afterwards, he would drive his cement-colored but otherwise nondescript Toyota Corolla back to the cheap motel room he was renting in Kernersville, the next town west of Greensboro, removing his disguise as he drove so as to look "normal" and nondescript to anyone who might see him there more than once, like the desk clerks and the maids. (He couldn't believe there was actually a color called "Cement," but there it was on the used car lot, and it was perfect.) He paid for the room in cash. He kept his wardrobe, makeup supplies, fake IDs, firearms, and activity files locked in the Corolla's trunk.

Norman still didn't fully understand how the weapon worked. His handler had said it was "need to know" and highly classified. It was powered by one AAA battery (included) and had an effective range of about 150 feet. Was it a ray of some sort? Laser? Microwaves? He'd heard of such weapons while in the Army but assumed they had to be much larger and need a bigger power source.

He had several of the Playhouse pens and had been given six that contained the weapon. Even though the weaponized pens were noticeably heavier than the real ones, he was constantly mistaking them for each other. When he picked the wrong one, he'd squeeze and ink would flow out, staining his pants or a tablecloth or simply leaving a dark blue puddle on the floor that he would sidle away from so as not to be discovered and have to explain.

At least he got to pick his own targets, and nobody cared if he missed or hit somebody else, but God forbid he should accidently hold the thing backwards and shoot himself with it.

This was by far the worst engagement he'd ever had. Worse than the Middle East. The pay was good, true, but not enough to keep putting up with this crap much longer. And now, as if the disguises, the record-keeping and the stupid artsy stuff weren't already intolerable, to top it all off it looked like he wasn't the only one operating here. More than once, he'd observed someone becoming victim to an attack even before he'd gotten his Playhouse pen out of his pocket, made sure it was the right one, and got it oriented correctly. Most recently it was at the Komedy Klub. He'd picked out Morrie Milburne as his target, but somebody else got to Milburne first. Not that he was unhappy to see Milburne go down. That wasn't the point. Anyway, whenever somebody beat him to the punch like that, he would put his pen away and look around covertly to see if he could find the other assailant. So far, he hadn't spotted anyone. Who was it? Competition? An unspoken teammate his handler chose not to mention or maybe himself didn't know about? It was too much.

Yes, Norman thought, this whole job had become a raging pain in the butt.

He needed to kill somebody.

Chapter Thirty-Four

Thursday

"Three shooters?" said Lieutenant Blue. "Are you serious?"

"As a heart attack," I said. "I was as surprised as you are."

We had started calling them shooters for lack of a better term. Somebody, or somebodies, was/were doing something, and people were falling down like they'd been shot, only without the bullets and blood, so "shooters" seemed apt. "Perpetrators" or "perps" was still fine, but "shooters" seemed more in keeping with the times and was also more fun to say.

Eschewing McDonald's and Sharon's geriatric ministrations this time, we were breakfasting at the Panera Bread on Lawndale Drive. Now that I was beginning to circulate in the Greensboro arts community, I did have a concern about blowing my cover by being seen with Blue by anybody who might recognize me, but Blue pointed out that nobody was likely to recognize him. Greensboro Police detectives don't drive typical police-type cars like Ford Crown Victorias anymore, so there was nothing in the parking lot that would give him away. We settled into a relatively quiet booth.

It was Thursday morning and the art gallery event would be from 2:00 to 5:00, so I had plenty of time. Blue didn't and had arrived late, so we talked fast and were wolfing down our food. Actually, only Blue was wolfing. When I remembered I was not the one in a hurry I slowed down and chewed my

Bacon, Scrambled Egg, Vermont White Cheddar, Salt and Pepper on Artisan Ciabatta sandwich more contemplatively.

Blue's Egg Whites, Vermont White Cheddar, Avocado, Spinach, Vine-ripened Tomato, Salt and Pepper on a Sprouted Grain Bagel Flat, while healthy, was proving difficult to wolf. He kept washing it down with gulps of Light Roast Coffee (Soft and smooth with hints of citrus, roasted nut and chocolate. A blend of Central and South American beans. Light bodied with a bright sweetness. Freshly ground). I had chosen the Dark Roast (Rich and bold full body with dark chocolate notes and a nutty, sweet finish. Brewed from beans harvested from the volcanic soils of Costa Rica and Colombia. Freshly ground. [Not fuzzy]).

I saw antacid tablets in Blue's immediate future, but at least he wasn't publicly stuffing himself with donuts. We talked between bites and gulps.

"I agree there are at least two bad guys because of the way the numbers work," Blue said, "but why three?"

"It comes back to the 34 people with bogus identities, each of whom attended only one event. It doesn't make sense. Very few other witnesses attended only one event. Most attended at least a few. Those are people active in the arts community who participate regularly, as you would expect. Not these guys."

Wolfing, gulping and sipping. Thinking, but quickly.

"Maybe you mean, 'not *this guy*'?" offered Blue with what I took to be a slight twinkle in his eye.

"Exactly. I think it's the same person 34 times."

"Yeah, I can see that's possible, but think about it. So many disguises, so many different fake IDs. Maybe more to come. Gearing up for it and keeping track of it all would be, whatcha call it, an administrational nightmare."

"It also would take dedication. Commitment. I'm guessing the guy's a pro."

Wolf, gulp.

Sip. Contemplative chew.

"Could be," said Blue.

Belch.

"But maybe not a smart one," I said. "Look at the list of names and occupations he used."

I'd made a list of all 34 apparently fictitious names, ages and occupations. They were in chronological order of the dates of the events the suspect was at, not alphabetical. I handed Blue a copy and read a few aloud but then shut up while Blue looked through it.

Partial List of Unidentified Witness' Names

1   John Smith, 49, dentist.
2   Bill Smith, 48, truck driver
3   John Jones, 38, sous-chef
4   Norman Smith, 32, librarian
5   William Short, 42, pawn shop clerk
6   Fred Norman, 42, postal carrier
7   Ralph Shotky, 50, paralegal
8   Roman Billings, 45, martial arts instructor
9   Manfred Short, 37, optometrist
10 Walter Shores, 41, stockbroker
11 Forrest Normal, 45, bank teller
12 Sherwood North, 51, barber
13 Norman Frisbee, 39, insurance agent
14 Edward Namron, 45, insurance adjustor
15 Northwood Shirttail, 38, wild goose chaser
16 James Shortnick, 55, dentist
17 Manfred Tallman, 55, registered nurse
18 Hyman Shostak, 46, jeweler
19 Norwood Brown, 43, English teacher

20 Barry Norman, 39, physician's assistant
21 Shoney Mannor, 43, accountant
22 Shelby Ronnam, 46, bartender
23 Shandar Rodman, 36, hairdresser

"Okay," said Blue, setting the list down, "I can see where this might be just one guy, but why don't you tell me why you think it is."

"Is this what they call a 'teachable moment'?"

"Maybe."

"Look at the patterns," I said. "First of all, the ages are all within a 20-year range—early thirties to early fifties—making it easier for somebody who's actually in that age range to put on disguises that don't have to go to extremes."

"Okay."

"And the occupations—mostly lower- or mid-level jobs that could easily be held by people in that age range and ordinary enough not to raise eyebrows when showing ID and giving a witness statement. And all are the kind of people it would be easy to see having an interest in the arts on the side or as a hobby, like maybe as an artist, a writer, a musician, you name it."

"That ain't bad, but it could still be only random. What else?"

"The biggest clue is the names themselves. Look how he starts out using generic names—John Jones, Bill Smith. John Smith? C'mon, nobody's named John Smith anymore.[7] But then he transitions. See, he uses Norman a few times. Then variations or anagrams on Norman, like other names starting with 'nor' or ending in 'man.' One of them is Norman spelled backwards. One is Norman with the syllables reversed: Mannor. And several beginning with 'sh' or 'sho.' They're 'all of a piece,' as they say. Too strangely consistent to be a

---

[7] Of course, that's not true. Some of my best friends are named John Smith. But you know what I meant.

coincidence. And even though some of the names are unusual, they're mostly bland. No raised eyebrows. Except Northwood Shirttail. He must have had a laugh coming up with that one. But even there, he starts with 'nor' and 'sh.'"

"So, you have a theory?" Blue was persistent, but I appreciated it.

"I thought you were in a hurry."

"I was, but this just got interesting."

Sipping lukewarm coffee. Sliding empty plates and trash to the back edge of the table.

"I've read, or maybe heard on TV cop shows, I don't know, that criminals can be narcissistic. They often pick aliases that are variations of their real names. Maybe for some of them it also helps them remember the aliases, but mostly I think it's passive self-promotion, if that's a thing and if you can get past the idea that in the end it's pretty stupid. It's almost like a challenge: 'It's me! Here I am! Admire my cleverness! Come and find me if you can!'"

"Now I think you've read too many detective stories."

"And written one myself, if you'll recall."

"Yeah, well I don't know if that counts."

"Last week you said I hadn't read enough of them."

"Just testing you."

"Like now?"

"You betcha. So, what do you think?"

"I think his name is Norman something. I looked up Norman and it means 'northman,' and see, he uses North several times."

"Norman Something? I'll look him up in the phone book."

"Ha ha. But, yes, what about his last name? All the 'sh's and 'sho's might be a clue. And look, there's Short and Shortnick," I said.

"Okay."

"Tallman may be a clue too. Not sure why, but it stands out for some reason. And Hyman, which might be a play on 'high man.'"

"So maybe he's short, and he's trying to compensate?"

"Now you're into it," I said. "Wait a minute. Maybe his last name *is* Short."

"Could be."

"Or maybe, and this is a stretch, but since we're trying out ideas here, maybe it's a nickname, like Shorty, which he hates but is a play on his real name."

"Would make the Tallman thing make sense, I guess."

"But what could it be? Could just be Short, I guess. Or Shortly—is that a name? Shirtly? Shartly? Shurtly? Shertly? I'm out of vowels. Any of those could translate to Shorty as a nickname. Maybe 'ey' or 'ie' instead of 'y' on the end? Lots of variations."

"I've got a computer can help with that," said Blue.

"Well, please crank it up."

I felt we were on the right track with this, but what with the mayhem the attacks were causing and the unlikely names of some of the people I'd met, for all I knew the evil mastermind we were looking for was named Hap Hazzard.

"What else you got for me?" asked Blue.

I told him about narrowing down the lists of suspicious witnesses to two, Lorna Gribble and Charles Kelly, and why. My research on social media had turned up nothing for Kelly on LinkedIn or Facebook and Googling him had only turned up his address, an apartment on Yanceyville Street, not far from the Playhouse. Gribble was absent from LinkedIn as well but very present on Facebook. Her posts, except for family stuff, portrayed an unhappy woman with some talent as a watercolorist but who felt alternately mistreated or ignored by the world. Outside of some occasional small triumphs, she seemed to suffer a constant stream of disappointments by friends and other people she dealt with, but there seemed to be no particular target for her frustration. However, at least she had 179 Friends.

Blue listened patiently to my report about having taken the time to read some of Kelly's obituaries. They weren't bad. Just the right balance of fact and sentiment, I thought.

(Where does one go to learn how to write obituaries? What kind of person aspires to do so? I looked into it. According to Wikipedia, in 2018 there were 1,279 daily newspapers in the United States alone, plus a long list of weeklies and semi-weeklies, most of which presumably feature obituaries. So, the obituary writer community, while large, is widely dispersed. But no worries—they have an association called the Society of Professional Obituary Writers [SPOW]. The website is pun-filled fun ["Welcome to The Society of Professional Obituary Writers, an international organization created for folks who write about the dead for a living."], with videos ["Remembering the Passed"] and resources for the accomplished and the aspiring among them, plus an online Gift Shoppe and Bookstore. They hold an annual convention called ObitCon where they give out Grimmy's for the best writing. I am not making this up.

Are apprentice obituary writers encouraged to attend ObitCon? Are there critique groups for amateur obituary writers, like the Rhyme 'n' Time Again poetry group? Maybe I would speak to Betty Wright-Moore about that. They could call it, uh, never mind; I'm sure all the good obituary joke names have already been thought of. But I can't help thinking of the acronym as a cartoon sound effect: "SPOW! Take that, Mortal! SPOW! SPOW! Now you're Dead!"

I checked the SPOW Directory and Kelly's name did not appear.)

Blue reluctantly agreed we now had three promising suspects and promised to have a closer look at Gribble and Kelly and to mount an effort to identify Norman Something. Or maybe it should be Norman Shomething.

One other thing I noticed was that Gribble and Kelly had almost exclusively been found at events connected to the Gate City Playhouse while Norman's attendance was more generalized. Why would the two presumed amateurs concentrate on the Playhouse and Norman, the presumed pro, be less discriminating? That suggested they weren't all three working together. Or that Gribble and Kelly might be a team, but not working with Norman. What were the motives involved? Were the team, if that's what it was, and Norman operating on their own, or was somebody directing them? If so, who? And why?

Many questions, but still this was progress. Blue was happier now than when we'd entered Panera's. So was I. But the attacks were ongoing, and we had no way of predicting them.

"One other suggestion," I said. "I wish we had pictures of Norman in each of his disguises. From here on, can the police start taking pictures of the witnesses when they get their statements?"

"We might need their permission, but we can try. Anything else, Mr. Detective?"

I told Blue about the 75 witnesses who said they saw some sort of light before or during the incidents. Also, the reflection Emily and I saw on Morrie Milburne's eyeglasses in the ꓘomedy ꓘlub video, looking like they came from near Lenny Monahan's T-shirt table.

"What do you make of that?" he said.

"I'm pretty sure it's a clue."

"Aren't you the smartass."

"You and Bob Ausländer are on the same page there. Do you have anything for me before we go our separate ways?"

"Just a kinda funny story. You know how we went Canadian to disguise our radio calls about the attacks, right? Now some of the police scanner junkies are asking why we're putting 'eh' after some of the 10-codes. They think we're saying 'A,' and they want to know if we've got new codes."

"Makes sense."

"Funny part is, there are some Canadians here and they think we're making fun of them. They're offended."

"What are you going to do?"

"So far, we've been fainting ignorance about it."

Sip.

Sip.

"Coffee's gone cold."

"Mine too."

Chapter Thirty-Five

The tune sounded familiar but barely audible over the murmuring of the crowd. It was coming from an acoustic guitar, fiddle and bass trio tucked in the back corner of what apparently used to be the living room in the small, two-story building on State Street that had once been a private residence, maybe in the 1940s. The space was now the main showroom of The Framery, a well-known Greensboro art gallery that played frequent host to gatherings such as this one. The works of several artists were being celebrated, and the many rooms in the house were chock full of paintings in oil, acrylic, watercolor and mixed media. Most had little cards showing the name of the artist, the title of the work, the medium used, and a price. In another corner was a woman in a smock painting on an easel-mounted canvas. An artist, presumably.

Emily and I had visited this gallery a few times but never during an event. We'd never bought anything and certainly weren't in a position to buy anything today. Besides, I was On the Case. I signed a guest register in the foyer. There was a space for your email address if you wanted to receive information about upcoming events. I left it blank, but Emily grabbed a pen from a mug full of them and filled it in. Naturally, it was a Gate City Playhouse Rocks pen.

Guests stood shoulder to shoulder in some of the rooms, but everybody found ways to keep circulating. Veteran gallery-goers, no doubt, who had lots of practice maneuvering in tight quarters if there was art to see, people to see, people to be seen by, elbows to be rubbed, literally, and refreshments.

Speaking of which, Emily and I were partaking of mixed nuts, crackers, and cheese along with some slightly sour chardonnay (I had learned by then not to expect Monet, as that was more likely to appear in a frame than in a wine glass. My arts education was progressing.). Everybody was wearing paper stick-on "HELLO my name is" badges. I didn't see anyone I recognized, nor did anyone seem to recognize me. Maybe there wasn't much overlap between the fine arts community, the poets and writers community, and the standup comedy community. Emily thought she saw a woman from her church circle, but it turned out to be someone else.

"That tune sounds familiar," I said.

"Why don't you ask them what it is?" said Emily.

With me in the lead, we cautiously shouldered our way to the corner, holding our disposable plastic wine glasses ever so protectively. The guitar and fiddle players looked like they might be husband and wife, and the bass player had a gold wedding band but no wife in evidence. The men appeared to be in their late fifties. Both were clean-shaven and had salt & pepper hair tied back in ponytails, like Ryman Stanza without the goatee, while the woman had a short blond bob, making her look younger than she probably was. She noticed our approach and seemed to shrink back, almost getting behind her husband as we neared.

When the tune ended, I introduced Emily and myself using my GADC persona, here to promote the arts, and said we were enjoying their playing. The guitar man, who appeared to be the leader, smiled, and his wife seemed to relax a little. The bass man excused himself and headed for one of the refreshment stations. His gait suggested this wasn't the first time he had done so.

"Horace Vance," guitar man said, extending his hand. "And this is Cara."

Cara smiled demurely and nodded slightly.

"Cara's not normally shy, but she's a little wary today."

"Oh, I'm so sorry," said Emily. "May we ask why?"

"She got zapped at one of these gigs a couple weeks ago, so actually we're both a little on edge."

"Zapped?" said Emily.

"We're in the middle of a set, and she's playing her heart out, and all of a sudden she's sticking the fiddle bow down her throat, throwing up, and falling down. It was scary."

We nodded sympathetically. I vaguely remembered seeing the name Cara Vance in the lists of victims, but there were so many.

"Somebody called the cops, and the EMTs took her to the ER. She was okay enough to go home after a couple hours, but she was in bed with a headache until the next day. They couldn't find anything wrong with her, and nobody has any idea what happened, but we think somebody zapped her somehow. Don't know who or why. Happened to some other people we've heard about too, but nobody knows anything. I'm the worship leader at a small church, and Cara volunteers at the Food Bank, so we don't have insurance to cover most of the hospital bill."

"That's terrible!" said Emily.

"I'm only telling you all this," he said, looking at me, "because if you're promoting the arts community this kind of thing won't help."

"Obviously not. I've heard of a couple other cases like this too, and I'm looking into it. Can I ask you something? Or Cara?"

"Sure."

"The police probably already asked you, but did you

happen to notice anything unusual before or during your getting zapped?"

"They did ask," said Cara, "but I don't think there was anything."

"Nothing at all? Even if it was something really small and insignificant."

Cara knitted her brow and shook her head slowly.

"Maybe something like a light, or a glint, or a reflection—anything like that," I hinted.

"I don't think so. Is it important?"

"Eh, probably not," I said. "But thanks anyway."

The bass player was back, and Cara began to rosin her bow.

"Oh," I said, "the reason we came over here in the first place is I wondered what that tune was you were playing before."

"It was 'Hewlett' by Turlough O'Carolan," said Vance. "You know him?"

"Not personally, but I've heard the name, and that tune."

"It's from the show over at the Gate City Playhouse. I'm in the backstage band."

"That's where I heard it. Went to a rehearsal there the other day."

"Some people got zapped there too. Makes no sense."

"Well, you all sure sounded good. Thanks for being here."

"Glad you liked it," he said.

Emily and I circulated some more and then introduced ourselves to the hostess, a pleasant looking woman who was standing at the entrance to a tiny office area just off the foyer.

"Mr. and Mrs. Fairley," she said, glancing at our name badges. "Dylan Vivaldi told me about you when he dropped off some fountain pens the other day. I was hoping you might come!"

"That Dylan gets around, doesn't he?" I said.

"He's quite the character, but very supportive of what we're doing here. I'm Astrid Plonck."

Nice-to-meet-yous were exchanged as we shook hands all around. Her name badge was plastic, not paper, and gave her title as "Curator."

"What's a curator?" I asked.

She laughed. "Around here it means I clean up the mess these people leave so the real customers will think this is a nice place."

Emily and I chuckled politely.

"But really, I'm a co-owner of the gallery, with Amy Dellinger over there." She pointed to the artist at the easel. "'Curator' is just a fancy word for someone who's in charge of a gallery or museum and decides what pieces to show, that sort of thing. It's classier than saying 'owner' or 'boss'. And pretentious. Pretentious is important in the art world, as I'm sure you'll discover. I'm not the only black art gallery owner in town but probably the only one who's a Curator."

I liked Astrid. She proceeded to tell us a little about the history of the gallery and what they were trying to accomplish—basically trying to up the quality of fine art available in Greensboro, educate the public about it, and encourage talented emerging artists as well as beginners, while trying to make a living doing it. It seemed a daunting task to me, and I admired her for it.

"Have you had a chance to look around, talk to some of the artists yet?" she asked.

"Only a little, so far. We did speak to the musicians."

"Great. Circulate, enjoy yourselves, and come find me if you have any questions."

We shouldered our way back into the milling throng and tried our best to get unobstructed views of the paintings as we went. Since I'd encountered so many unlikely arts-people names by then, I fully expected to see a painting signed by Roy G. Biv. But I didn't.

On the whole, I thought the art was quite good. Several different styles were represented—impressionist, realistic, abstract, and so on. ("And so on" because I don't know all the styles and genres, so I'll admit my ignorance and get it over with. More than once, I resisted the urge to blurt "I don't know much about art, but I know what I like.") Some pieces were so good it was hard to believe they were done by human hands, some were mediocre (in my humble opinion) but perhaps encouraging to a budding artist who could say, "Hey, I bet I could do better than that," and some looked like the doodlings of a madman. It was a well-rounded show, expertly curated it seemed. Nothing jumped out at me.

We circulated some more, spoke to a few of the artists, and revisited a refreshment station. The wine had not improved, but since I was driving and didn't want much, it didn't matter to me. Emily was disappointed.

Suddenly, there was a piercing scream. "Amy!! Amy!!" It sounded like Astrid's voice. The crowd hushed for a moment and the music stopped, then shouts of alarm came from all over the house. A few people crouched down as if expecting gunshots, but there weren't any. Looking across the crouchers, I saw Amy Dellinger lying on the floor in front of her easel, apparently unconscious. Before I knew what I was doing, I waded into the crowd in her direction, shouting, "Call 911! Call 911! She'll be okay. It's all right. I've seen this before! She probably forgot to take her meds! Give her some space. She'll be okay!" Things like that.

Emily stood transfixed at the refreshment table, but Astrid was beside me in a flash with a wild look in her eye, a mixture of fear and rage.

"I've heard of this happening, but I never thought we'd see it here," she said through clenched teeth.

I said, "It looks bad, but she *will* be okay. Believe me. I've been through this before. Help is on the way." That seemed to calm her a little.

"Did you see what happened?" I asked the man standing closest to me.

He didn't respond immediately but finally shook his head as if waking from a bad dream. "Yeah, I guess so," he said. "We were watching her paint, asking her a few questions, you know, and then she stuck her brush in her mouth, gagged, and fell off her stool."

Looking closer, I did see what looked like pale yellow paint on Amy's lips and chin.

Evidently, someone had indeed called 911 because already I heard approaching sirens. The crowd was in a state of confusion, so I called out, "Everybody please stay where you are! The police will want everybody's statements." A mistake. As there was nobody to bar the door, several people scampered out and headed to the parking lot across the street. Lucky them. They'd be home enjoying dinner while the rest of us were still being questioned.

The sirens got closer and stopped, and to my surprise Detective Blue was the first to enter, making a beeline to me. He was good at beelines.

"Fancy you should be here," he said to me.

"Just doing my job," I whispered back so only Blue would hear me. "How did you get here so fast?"

"We knew about this event, so we were on alert, just in case. I've been sort of patrolling in the area. And here we are."

"Some witnesses got away."

"Doubt it. We've surrounded the parking lot. Our version of a dragnet. We'll get 'em all."

You can guess the rest. The EMTs hauled Amy away. Astrid went with her after Blue assured her the police would keep everything secure until she got back. All the witnesses were interviewed, and this time most had their pictures taken. It took a long time. We later learned Amy recovered and was back at work at The Framery on Saturday, finishing her painting, which, in its unfinished state, looked like it was going to be a self-portrait. "Portrait of the Artist as a Middle-aged Woman," would most likely be the title, I imagined. Oil on canvas. $650, framed. But who would want it except maybe her mother? Who probably already had one.

As Emily and I were leaving, Horace and Cara Vance came up to us, Cara trembling a little as she held Horace's hand. The bass man was packing up their instruments and equipment.

"This time we saw something," Horace said. "A light. Like you said. I happened to be looking at Amy when it happened. Just a faint glow on her forehead before she went down."

"Could you tell where it came from?"

"No."

"Okay, thanks. Did you tell the police?"

"Yes. Does that help? What does it mean?"

"Yes, it helps. And no, I don't know what it means. Yet."

Chapter Thirty-Six

"I've been here six weeks and went to 35 arts events, which, by the way, is an average of one every day of the week except Monday because I take Monday off. I've made 31 hits. I haven't been caught, no one suspects me, and in fact nobody has a clue what's going on. That's how good I am."

"You're good, you're good."

"Damn straight I am. In spite of the conditions I have to put up with, including this ridiculous weapon that's about as accurate as a rubber blunderbuss, plus now it looks like I've got competition. You know anything about that?"

"What's a blunderbuss?"

"Never mind that! I'm going nuts here, but I'm doing the job and doing it right, and now you tell me your client wants me to 'step up my game'? 'Step up *my* game'?! Who does he think he is? My life coach or something? What does he mean by that? Does he actually want me to kill somebody? I can do that. I'd like to do that. But not one every day. And it will cost a lot more. Help me out here, Eddie."

"No, he doesn't want you to kill anybody. He just wants you to do more than one hit at some of the events, that's all. You'll get paid extra, of course. I don't know anything about competition. What are you talking about?"

"Never mind that either. How am I supposed to do more than one hit at an event? I do one and all hell breaks loose and everybody's calling 911 and the cops come and then the EMTs, and everybody's looking at everybody else, and he wants me

214

to do it *again*? He's nuts, and you can tell him I said so! No, wait, I've got a better idea. I'll tell him myself."

The phone was silent for a moment.

"You can't do that, Norm."

"I can and I will. You tell me who he is, and I'll take care of it."

"I cannot do that, Norm. You know the drill. You agreed. It's like a contract. You know that."

"That was before I got here and saw what I had to put up with. I was misled. That makes the contract null and void."

"He won't like it."

"I don't expect him to like it. And don't worry, you'll still get your fee. I'll see to that. And one other thing. There's this new guy, Mike Farly or something. He's supposedly with the Greensboro Development Committee or something like that, and he's been sort of worming his way in among the artsy people. He doesn't fit. You know anything about that?"

"No, but I can look into it, see what I can turn up."

"You don't seem to know very much today, Eddie. But here's something you can know. I'm through putting up with this, and nobody tells Norman Shartly to 'up his game'! I talk to the client or I'm gone. Get it? You set it up. And stop calling me Norm!"

Chapter Thirty-Seven

"Well, that was a hoot and a half," said Emily as we drove to Chick-fil-A for some takeout on the way home from The Framery.

"I know. Too close for comfort."

She was upset and wanted to talk it out.

"What if it had been you?"

"But it wasn't."

"Or me."

"Not good," I said.

"No."

"They're not after me. I'm not artsy."

"You're getting artsy."

"Very slowly."

"But you are. And if 'your cover gets blown,' as the cloak and dagger types are so fond of putting it, you'll be their biggest target."

"I don't think it will. Plus, Blue has my back."

"Except at his best it still takes him at least two or three minutes to get to your back. And that's only *after* something happens."

"You're right. But even if something happens, I'll be okay in a day or so. No fun but nothing to worry about. And I'll ask for more money. Hazardous duty pay."

"Not funny. For somebody who calls himself a detective, you seem to thrive on missing the point."

"It's hard to miss the point when it's perched on top of the elephant in the room. I will be careful. I can't quit now. Probably nobody would hire me for anything ever again if they think I'm a quitter."

"What about that company in Charlotte?"

"Haven't heard from them. Didn't much like them either. So I'm not counting on anything there. Unfortunately."

Emily was quiet.

"Besides," I said, "we're finally making some progress."

"Like what?"

"We have three suspects and two what Blue calls persons of interest. Two of the suspects seem to be working together, and the other one seems to be working alone, but we can't rule out the possibility all three are working together somehow.

"We think there's some sort of weapon involved instead of poison—thank you again for questioning the poison theory—because some people report seeing glimpses of light before or during the attacks. You saw the reflection in Morrie Milburne's eyeglasses."

"Yes."

"I admit we still don't have a motive, why they are doing this. If they are not all working together, there may be more than one motive. We don't know if they're working for somebody or doing this on their own, although that doesn't seem likely. And we don't have a positive last name for one of the suspects."

"Oh, wonderful."

"But we're a lot further along than we were a week or so ago. Even Blue would admit that. And it's not a stretch to say he'd agree the police wouldn't have done it without my help."

"And mine," said Emily.

"And yours. You really do have a talent for this, you know."

The drive-thru line was short, so we got our sandwiches more quickly than usual. We'd supplement them with our own chips and drinks when we got home. Probably a beer for Emily this time instead of more wine. Maybe two beers for me.

Even though I would still go to the open mic on Saturday, and I did want to get back to the Playhouse and have a look around, it seemed less important now for me to meet more people in the arts community. It was time to focus on the suspects we'd identified, or thought we had, and figure out how they were pulling off these attacks, who was really behind them, and why. That meant starting with the suspects themselves. Which meant working more closely with Marshall Blue. I liked him, grumpy though he could be, and he seemed to be warming up to me because I had made some helpful contributions to The Case in my undercover role. So, I was looking forward to it even if Emily was skeptical.

Friday bright and early I called Blue and asked if he could meet me at the Playhouse.

Chapter Thirty-Eight

The morning United flight to Chicago from Greensboro's Piedmont Triad International Airport was uneventful except for the flight attendant singing the safety instructions instead of reading them. The crew's attempt to change things up a little, relieve the usual boredom of going through the procedures and also get the passengers to pay more attention than they normally would. Norman almost shot her with his clumsy little weapon but stopped himself at the last moment.

At Three First National Plaza, he checked the lobby directory for RayDact Corporation and boarded an escalator which took him to the elevator banks. He punched the 14th floor button and settled in for the ride up, suppressing a slight case of heartburn from the crappy airline coffee and muffin he'd had and the crappy cup of O'Hare coffee he'd consumed on top of that during the cab ride in. The collar of his Hugo Boss blue micro-stripe dress shirt was a little too tight, and his new Bally wingtips pinched a bit, but he looked good in his Regent Fit Plaid 1818 Brooks Brothers suit and red Brunello Cucinelli medallion wool-blend tie. His black Tumi Aviano Slim attaché case in ballistic fabric with leather accents and his Rolex Oyster Perpetual 41 watch completed the picture. With such a presentation, a man should need no introduction. Still …

"Namron Mannheim here to see Mr. Fostridge," he said to the receptionist. "He's expecting me."

"Namron?"

"Yes, ma'am."

"Mannheim."

"Yes, ma'am."

"Are you su–? Of course, you are. It's *your* name."

"Yes, ma'am."

"Oh, here it is. Sorry. They had it listed as Mannheim Namron."

"No problem."

"So, I was looking in the 'M's first. Not the 'N's."

"It's okay. It's fine. May I see Mr. Fostridge, please?"

"Of course. If you'll just clip on this Visitor badge and have a seat over there, I'll let his executive administrative assistant know you're here."

"Of course. Thank you."

"No problem."

He sat. There were no magazines to look at, so he looked around instead. He saw paintings on the walls. Every available space where there was no window and except for the wall with a three-dimensional RayDact logo behind the receptionist's desk was filled with framed paintings. Ghastly paintings. Even if he could ever settle for an office job, he could never work in a place like this, he thought. It would drive him nuts. These paintings were as bad as anything he'd seen in Greensboro, and to make it worse, they were bigger. His fingers tightened on the familiar and comforting shape of the Ruger SP101 .22 pistol in his pants pocket, one he'd retrieved from a locker at O'Hare by prearrangement with a sometime-associate in the Chicago area. It was outfitted with a silencer. He would return it before boarding his return flight. His Gate City Playhouse Rocks weapon pens got through Airport Security all right, but a real pistol would not.

There was no immediate target, so he relaxed his grip.

"Mr. Mannheim?"

"Yes." He stood.

"I'm Susan from Mr. Fostridge's office and I'll take you there if you'll just follow me."

"Thank you."

Fostridge had a super-large corner office with the expected luxurious furnishings and a sweeping view of nearby skyscrapers. And more hideous paintings.

"Would you like coffee, water?" said Susan.

"Um."

"Or hot chocolate? I think we may have some hot chocolate."

"Yes, hot chocolate would be fine," he said, thinking it might help with the heartburn.

"Would you like anything, Mr. F?"

"No thank you, Susan."

She left, closing the door behind her.

Jerome Fostridge offered his hand, which Norman shook, and gestured for Norman to sit in a chair opposite the ornate desk, which he did after handing Fostridge a business card announcing him as Sales & Service Vice President of Solar Plexis Industries at a bogus address in Norman, Oklahoma. Fostridge took it and sat behind the desk.

"How do you like the artwork?" Fostridge asked, gazing around the room.

"It's okay, I guess."

"It's part of a wonderful collection of pieces curated by the chairman of our parent corporation. You should see the ones on display up in their offices. Gorgeous stuff. I could get lost in it."

"Maybe you should."

"Excuse me?"

"I mean I'm sure you would enjoy it."

"I would," agreed Fostridge, picking up Norman's card. "Solar Plexis, eh? With an 'i'? Shouldn't it be with a 'u'?"

"It's just the way we spell it. We like it."

"Um, okay. Well, what can I do for you, Namron? Is it okay if I call you Namron?"

"It's fine."

"Eddie was quite adamant that I see you, but he was a little vague as to why. I understand Solar Plexis makes custom cases and containers for various kinds of weapons."

"Yes."

"We do most all of that sort of thing in-house."

"I imagine you do."

"I'm not sure I understand."

"You will."

Two soft knocks on the door and Susan entered carrying a mug of hot chocolate, a plastic stirrer, and a small paper napkin. She took a coaster from a stack on the credenza behind Fostridge, placed it on the edge of Fostridge's desk within easy reach of Norman and then set the mug on it, putting the stirrer and napkin to the side. "Are you sure you don't want anything, Mr. F?"

"Thank you, Susan. Not right now."

She left.

"What did you mean, 'You will'?"

Norman took a sip of the hot chocolate. Hot but not too hot. Just right. He stirred it a little.

"Is Eddie often adamant? Is he usually vague?" he said.

"Eddie provides me with many things. Customer leads, contacts with potential suppliers—like you—help with executive recruiting, Broadway show tickets, tips on where to vacation, that sort of thing. He's very well-rounded, but I wouldn't characterize him as either adamant or vague."

"But this time he was adamant. And vague."

"Yes."

"Let's talk more about the recruiting part."

Fostridge sat silently for a long moment. Norman took another sip. A bigger one this time because the liquid had cooled enough. Then he took another. He said nothing.

"You're *him*, aren't you?" said Fostridge.

"Him who?"

"You're the guy he sent to Greensboro for me."

"Bingo."

"But, but you're a hit man, right? An assassin."

"I haven't assassinated anybody for you."

"No, you're just supposed to stir things up down there. In the arts community. Make Greensboro a less desirable place to live."

"I don't see how it could be any less desirable than it is now."

"I agree with you there. It's like that old joke about Philadelphia: First prize is a week in Greensboro. Second prize is two weeks in Greensboro."

"I don't get it."

"But you don't like Greensboro."

"For one thing, the art stinks. It's the same as the stuff you've got here," said Norman, gesturing at the walls, "except smaller."

"You don't like this artwork?"

"No."

"Well, *à chacun son goût*, as they say."

"What?"

"It means there's no accounting for peoples' tastes," said Fostridge. "Anyway, you shouldn't be here. In my office. I can't be seen with you. I mean, uh, this just isn't done."

"Yet here I am."

"Why?"

"Because I am going to assassinate you, Jerome."

"Holy crap! But why?" Fostridge had gone white as a sheet. Or *blanc comme un drap de lit*, as they say.

"I don't like my job anymore."

"You could quit."

"I like the money."

"What is it; you want more? Why aren't you talking to Eddie about this?"

"Talked to Eddie. Told him I wanted to talk to you. He set it up. Apparently, he was adamant."

"And vague."

"Yes. Good for Eddie."

"I still don't see the problem."

Norman took a long swallow of the hot chocolate. "Problem is, you told Eddie I should, what did you call it, 'step up my game.' Nobody tells me that, Jerry. I'm offended."

"I admit, I may have said that. You're going to kill me over that?"

"Might. But that's not all. After everything I've done for you for the past six or seven weeks, and the conditions I've had to operate in, averaging one hit a day, six days a week, now Eddie says you want me to increase that. By maybe 50%. Can't do it. Won't do it."

"Why didn't you tell Eddie that?"

"Did. Eddie takes orders from you. I came to the source."

"You're not really going to kill me. Are you?"

Some of the color was returning to Fostridge's face.

"Depends."

Some of the color went away again.

"Look, you've gotta do this. Can I tell you why?"

"It doesn't matter to me why somebody hires me. But my plane's not leaving until this afternoon, so please, go ahead. Tell me why."

"Because I'll die if I have to go to Greensboro. If I'm gonna die anyway, I'd rather it be here than there. More convenient for my wife to make, you know, arrangements."

"Are you trying to be funny, Jerry? Ingratiate yourself with me?"

"Okay, it's not so funny. Here's the thing."

Fostridge explained his plight. He didn't want to move his company to Greensboro. The Chairman wanted him to. He'd made his pitch to the Chairman, hoping he would understand. The Chairman did not understand. The Chairman upped the pressure. Now Fostridge wanted to up the pressure for not going by upping the apparent cost of going by upping the chaos in the arts community, thereby ruining the chances for a good quality of life for RayDact and its employees, even though Fostridge himself didn't care one way or the other about that since nothing could make the quality of life in Greensboro good enough for him unless it magically turned into Chicago. Therefore, Norman had to up his level of activity.

"This is boring," said Norman, lifting his mug and draining the last of the hot chocolate. "And stupid."

Norman took the pistol out of his pocket, aimed it at Fostridge, and fired.

He missed.

"Are you crazy!!?" screamed Fostridge, diving under the desk.

"I missed, didn't I?"

"How could you miss from three feet away?"

"It was only a warning shot."

Fostridge's head appeared from behind the desk. Then, slowly, the rest of him.

"Look, maybe we can work something out," he said.

"Nothing to work out," said Norman. "I'll go on doing what I'm doing and you'll go on paying me, through Eddie of course, or I'll be back. With a bigger gun. See, I'm adamant. Like Eddie."

"But not vague."

"No."

"All right. I don't like it, but I guess I have no choice. Are we finished here?"

"One more thing." Norman put the pistol away and fished one of his special Gate City Playhouse Rocks pens from his jacket pocket. "Exactly what is this ridiculous 'weapon' you gave Eddie to give me?"

"It's top-secret technology," said Fostridge. "The irony is, if I tell you, then I'll have to kill you."

The pistol came out again.

"This time I probably won't miss."

"Okay, sorry. But jeeze, you put a hole in my credenza."

"I hear duct tape can fix anything. Now tell me about the weapon."

"Okay, well, it uses sort of a combination of laser and microwave energy. It was designed to be used in a larger platform to knock out enemy electronics without causing any apparent physical damage. Sort of like EMP, or electromagnetic pulse, only more portable and more precise. Surgical, sort of. Some of our guys were fooling around with it and somehow got it to work in something as small as that fountain pen."

"And of course, then you had to kill them."

"Now who's being funny," said Fostridge.

Norman shoved the pistol back in his pocket.

"I've never aimed at a radio, or my iPhone. From what I've seen, it just causes people to stick things in their mouths, upchuck and fall down."

"Yes, an interesting side benefit of the miniature model. Hallucinations. That's why I chose it for you. I got Eddie to send me a half dozen of those pens and had my guys refit them with the weapon. It only has an effective range of about 150 feet. You get about 50 shots before you have to change the battery. I sent all six back to Eddie, with extra batteries."

"Speaking of aiming, I told Eddie the thing handles like a rubber blunderbuss."

"What's a blunderbuss?"

"Never mind that. What can you do about it?"

"Nothing, I'm afraid. Not without mounting it in some kind of carrier with sights and a trigger or something, which would spoil the disguise. Besides, you're the hit man. Why don't you figure it out? Or do some target practice between hits."

"How would I know if I hit the target? How many radios and iPhones do I have to kill? It's not like laser tag or paintball or shooting at tin cans or targets with real bullets."

"We haven't developed a training course for it because it will probably never go into production, but here's a tip. It does emit a light. A dim one, and it's right at the upper edge of the visible light spectrum, or a human's ability to see it, but at close range you just might catch a glimpse of it on your target before you fire the thing. If you can hold the pen steady enough."

"Exactly."

Two soft knocks on the door and Susan stepped in.

"Can I get you gentlemen anything?"

Both men shook their heads.

"Did you enjoy the hot chocolate, Mr. Mannheim?"

"Yes, thank you. It was very good."

His heartburn had left, but there was a new worry causing it to return. Eddie had given him the half-dozen weaponized Playhouse pens all right, but after all these weeks he could no longer account for all six. Much worse than an unglued mustache, somehow three had gone missing. He would keep looking for them, of course. He wasn't about to tell Fostridge, or Eddie.

Chapter Thirty-Nine

Friday

"Thanks for meeting me on such short notice."

"No problem. It ain't like I had anything else to do today."

"What? No serving? No protecting?"

"Maybe tomorrow. Why are we here?"

When I called Vivaldi, Marcy Melnick said he would be out all morning but that it would be okay for Detective Blue and me to go wherever we needed to in the Gate City Playhouse as long as we were mindful of the *Christmas O'Carolan Songbook* rehearsals that were still underway. Cecil B.D. Miller, still favoring his right leg with a limp, wasn't pleased to see us but became cooperative when we told him we were looking into what might have distracted him enough to fall off the stage. Once we made it about him, he was happy.

"Miller talked about seeing a light from the back of the balcony before he fell," I said to Blue.

"Right."

"And the two musicians at the art gallery saw a light."

"Right."

"And you saw the glint on Milburne's glasses in the surveillance video."

"Right, after you told me about it. We blew up the image and tried to enhance it, but it didn't help. I sent my guys back to the Komedy Klub, but they didn't find anything. We didn't find anything suspicious at the art place, and they scoured the balcony here too and didn't find anything, like I told you."

"I know, but I want the two of us to get up in the balcony anyway and see what things look like from there. From the shooter's point of view, you might say. Assuming there even was a shooter."

"Suit yourself."

I did. We stood in the darkened balcony, in the walking space behind the last row of seats, so as to experience it the way a shooter would. As expected, we had a sweeping view of the stage and most of the auditorium except what was directly under us. The *O'Carolan* rehearsal was going full blast, and the balcony acoustics were good. I spotted Nigel Wilson, the young novelist and copywriter from Upshot Marketing. It looked like he'd gotten the part and was none the worse for wear from his experience as a victim.

After a few moments, I found a switch and flipped it, turning on the lights in the balcony. I hoped they wouldn't startle Miller enough to make him fall off the stage again.

"Oh, look," said Blue, bending down, "here's a couple of those pens."

"Stop!" I said.

Blue froze, then straightened up and glared at me. At least it looked like a glare, or maybe I was expecting a glare. Probably no one had ever spoken to him like that. "Gun!" or Duck!" maybe, if somebody was about to shoot at him, but not "Stop!"

"Sorry," I said. "Didn't mean to yell. It's just that maybe the pens are clues. Maybe evidence."

"I don't see how, since they weren't here when my guys checked the other day."

"Look how they're wedged behind the leg of that seat. And they're dark green—the same shade as the carpet. Your people could have missed them."

"Doubt it. How come we're finding them now?"

"I don't know. Serendipity maybe."

"Serendipity-do-da. Don't believe in it. For all we know they could have been here before Miller's accident."

Blue was right about that, I had to admit, but at least he was no longer defending his officers.

"But okay, let's say hypodermically they *have* been here only since then," he went on. "You think it means something?"

Was he testing me again?

"Maybe I'm not a real detective, but I'm allowed to have a hunch now and then."

"More like a hunchback, like that show about the screwed-up football player from Notre Dame."

Correcting him would be a losing proposition, so I plowed on.

"If somebody was up here, maybe they dropped the pens while making a hasty escape. Maybe they don't know they lost them. Maybe they haven't been back to get them because they didn't want to return to the scene of the crime."

"Maybe they don't care because you can get a handful of those pens anywhere around town, especially here at the Playhouse, and they're free," said Blue. "I agree the story about the flashing light and the door slam is suspicious, and I got excited about it at first, but if it was an attack, why didn't Miller stick something in his mouth, throw up and fall down like everybody else instead of stumbling off the stage?"

"Good question," I said.

"Thank you very much."

Blue used his iPhone to take a picture of the two pens *in situ*, then produced a handkerchief and used it to gingerly pick up the pens one by one and place them in separate clear plastic baggies marked "Evidence." He wrote the date and place on the baggies with his ball point. He was taking me seriously.

"That's strange," he said.

"What is?"

"One of these pens is heavier than the other one. See?"

I held both baggies and, sure enough, they didn't weigh the same. Taking a closer look at the heavier one, I noticed the clip on its cap was configured slightly differently from the lighter one. I took out my own Playhouse pen and compared it to the other two to see which one was different. Again, it was the heavier one. Its clip looked like it functioned more like those on some ball point pens where if you depress the clip the point retracts. Sort of like a trigger except it makes the point withdraw into the pen instead of ejecting it. I depressed the clip. Nothing happened. I handed the baggie with the normal pen back to Blue and held up the other one to get a better look.

It was difficult because the baggie was slippery, but I managed to unscrew the cap and place it over the barrel where it would normally be kept when the pen was in use. Blue and I both noticed immediately that there was no nib. I depressed the clip. A dim light shone out from where the nib should have been. Blue ducked even though nobody had yelled "Duck!"

"Don't point that thing at me!" he said.

He grabbed the baggie.

"I think this is a clue," I said.

Blue didn't laugh. We both knew what we had found.

Chapter Forty

Blue and I spent some time looking for more clues in the balcony but didn't find any. He was anxious to take the two pens to Police Headquarters to get them checked for fingerprints and then send the odd one to the State Crime Laboratory in Raleigh for DNA testing and to see if they could figure out what the heck it was, so he left while I went back down to explore the main floor and the backstage area. It didn't take long for Miller to spot me and ask if we'd found anything in the balcony. I dodged the question as best I could without making up an outright lie, and he seemed satisfied. I took a seat in the third row.

The unknown nature of the strangely configured pen nagged at me. Why would a flashing light from such a device be enough to cause victims to act the way they typically did? Why wouldn't you get the same results from a small penlight flashlight or a laser pointer or even one of those ubiquitous little LED flashlights you can put on your keychain that businesses use as promotional items? All were easily concealable. For all we knew that's all the strange pen was, a promotional gimmick. But if that were the case, why weren't they as numerous as the others Dylan Vivaldi had distributed all over town? No, it had to be something more than that.

Maybe a ray of some kind? I thought about RayDact, the defense contractor, and its cryptic website self-description. Unless "Ray" was the name of the company's founder, maybe it was indicative of at least part of the product line. Jerome

Fostridge was probably not the founder, and I didn't recall the website mentioning any other names in its brief gloss-over of the company history, so that line of thought was a dead end. But why would a company calling itself expert in "state of the art highly sophisticated countermeasures" waste its resources on a "vomit and fall down" ray? I suppose if you were looking for countermeasures against expressed creativity by an artist or performer, such a ray gun would be fine, but I couldn't see its use in national defense. Does America have any especially artsy enemies the general public isn't aware of? France? Italy? Jamaica has reggae music some people aren't crazy about, but it hardly seems like a threat to national security.

But if it were in fact exactly that, a vomit and fall down ray, why didn't it work on Miller? Was it a matter of effective range? All of the attacks I could recall had taken place in relatively small venues, except for the Playhouse and the Tanger Center. The shooters would have been within only a few dozen feet of the victims unless they were shooting through the windows from the parking lot, which was possible but didn't seem likely. Even at the Playhouse and the Tanger Center, shooters could get close to victims during performances and rehearsals or during breaks, use the easily concealable VAFD, and get away undetected. (Here I was, already calling it the VAFD, for "vomit and fall down" ray, unconsciously elevating it to the status of a bona fide government secret weapon merely by using an acronym.) But the back of the balcony was probably over 300 feet from the stage, so maybe the VAFD failed to have the desired effect at that range and merely caused Miller to be distracted by its light.

Still, why would RayDact make such a thing? And how did it get into a Playhouse pen? I couldn't believe Vivaldi would be involved, but who would be? And why? Which of

233

our three suspects and two persons of interest, if any, lurked in the darkened Playhouse balcony that day waiting for C.B.D. Miller to appear on the stage and fall victim to this strange weapon?

Suspects:
- Norman Shomething, probably 30-55 years old, the man who apparently attended 34 events where attacks occurred and used a different bogus ID each time. His presence was scattered seemingly at random among many venues in the city.
- Charles Kelly, the newspaper obituary writer who witnessed 29 attacks and still hadn't told his editor or a reporter about them. The attacks where his presence was recorded, while not exclusively so, were mostly at, or involved people connected with, the Gate City Playhouse.
- Lorna Gribble, the possibly frustrated and vulnerable substitute teacher who saw 18 attacks. The attacks where her presence was recorded, while not exclusively so, were also mostly at, or involved people connected with, the Playhouse.
- Persons of interest:
- Lenny Monahan, the overly Irish standup comedian with a chauvinistic chip on his shoulder
- Michael Brennan, the plagiarizing poet ostracized by Writer's Block

Except for Lenny Monahan's attendance at the Komedy Klub attack on Morrie Milburne, neither he nor Brennan appeared on the witness lists. So, either they weren't there or one of them was Norman Shomething in disguise. Or maybe one or both were the brains behind the operation and were pulling the puppet strings on the others. That didn't seem likely for Brennan. Monahan?

How would these people get hold of something as sophisticated as the VAFD ray gun? They don't come in Cracker Jack boxes. Not even Amazon carries them. No, somebody had to have supplied them to the shooters.

It was hard to think because of the noise from the *O'Carolan* rehearsal, so I went backstage where at least the sound was somewhat muffled. I found a folding chair and sat. I could see sandbags hanging in the rafters. I was not directly under any of them. Still not the best conditions for thinking through a knotty puzzle, but the surprising discovery in the balcony had catalyzed the process.

What would be a consequence of screwing up the arts community, besides the obvious, like night clubs closing, philanthropic supporters withdrawing their support, the public fearing to attend events, and artists themselves withholding their time and talent? Of course! The reason I'd been hired in the first place: RayDact would refuse to relocate its headquarters and manufacturing plant to Greensboro because "quality of life" would be unfavorable.

What would be a consequence of centering the trouble on the Playhouse? Dylan Vivaldi himself had stated it: The Playhouse production of *The Christmas O'Carolan Songbook, Volume 1*, would have to shut down.

Who would benefit from RayDact's refusal to relocate to Greensboro? There was no company remotely like RayDact already in town, so putting up a barrier to competition didn't seem the answer. Besides, competition doesn't depend much on physical location these days. I doubted any of the characters on our suspect and person of interest lists would benefit directly—unless they were taking orders from, and maybe being paid by, someone else: the someone who was supplying the weapons (I assumed there were more than one VAFD pen).

Who would benefit from shutting down the *O'Carolan* show? Somebody who didn't like Dylan Vivaldi? Or the Playhouse? Certainly, shutting down this show would be a blow, but Vivaldi would just put on another one. It wasn't a permanent solution to destroying him or the Playhouse. And besides, he had other businesses in town, and except for his two nightclubs there had been no attacks at any of those. No, it had to be someone who, for whatever reason, didn't want this particular show to go on. Maybe someone who failed to get the part they wanted? I'm told some artsy people have big egos and can be overly competitive, emotional, vindictive, and petty, but even so, the importance of losing a part didn't seem to rise to the level that would trigger the kind of sabotage we'd been seeing. There were probably exceptions, like Brennan the plagiarist, but the arts people I'd met so far were friendly, generous, encouraging, mutually supportive and seemingly willing to give their colleagues a hand up, not destroy them for competition's sake.

Was there something about the show itself?

I mentally reviewed what I remembered from the first act as I returned to my third-row seat and settled in to watch some more of that day's rehearsal. They were doing Scene Two again, which I'd skipped on my previous visit.

Chapter Forty-One

The Christmas O'Carolan Songbook, Volume 1

SCENE TWO

(Interior of O'Donald's Pub 20 years later. The only change is some different potato special signs and the slogan is now "Multitudes Served". Another sign reads, "We didn't invent the potato, only the potato sandwich." There are still potatoes scattered here and there. Characters from Scene One look 20 years older, in their 40s & 50s, as does CONOR, and a little more down-at-heel. CHRISTMAS is 20. It is early morning. Paddy is behind the bar drying tankards with a dingy towel. Christmas is seated alone at one of the tables, facing the audience, alternately playing a few notes on a blindharp and scribbling on foolscap with a quill. He is wearing oversize brogans. Music fades and there is a commotion offstage, then Mick, Sean, Jack and Conor enter, in good spirits.)

PADDY: Top o' the mornin', lads! I see you're still stoppin' at the IHOP first.

MICK: Conor here can't get enough of their bangers and mash.

CONOR: We've almost got enough Frequent Masher Miles for a trip to the Great Hall in Dublin.

PADDY: After 25 years I should hope so! And it's the only way you lads'll ever get there, that's for sure.

MICK: Such talk from the man who makes us entertain the evenin' crowd for nothin' more than a free pint now and then and the storin' of our instruments behind the bar.

CHRISTMAS: Paddy's no fool.

(They turn to look at Christmas.)

MICK: Ah, Christmas, me boy! Slavin' away at another song, are we? Tryin' to best your father, Turlough, still?

CHRISTMAS: Oh, I don't know about that. He's been at it a long time.

PADDY: Don't be so modest, young Christmas! I think you've got promise.

JACK: Still and all, it's a tall order.

MICK: You can do it, laddie! But what the dickens is that thing you're holdin'?

CHRISTMAS: (Indicating the blindharp) This?

MICK: Aye, that thing!

CHRISTMAS: This, Mick, is what's called a "blindharp."

(Christmas holds it up for inspection by the lads.)

JACK: Mother o' mercy, how did you come by that?

SEAN: And how does it work?

CHRISTMAS: You lads know how hard it is to make a living as a musician around here – unless of course you're my father – but I've tried. First, I had to pick an instrument. Noticing a surfeit of good fiddlers in County Meath …

(They look at him quizzically.)

PADDY: "An excessive amount of something, as in 'a surfeit of food and drink,'" or in this case, of good fiddlers.

CHRISTMAS: Thank you, Paddy. (Ahem) Noticing a surfeit of good fiddlers in County Meath, I resolved to learn a less popular instrument, but one that would produce both melody and harmony if played skillfully. That way, I'd face less competition. Although I must say it's harder to find students willing to pay me to teach them how to play it.

MICK: That would explain a harp, but what's this *blind*harp thing?

CHRISTMAS: See, it has slats instead of strings. You can vary the pitch of the slats with this little knob here, and you play it with these little mallets, like a xylophone.

(He demonstrates.)

CHRISTMAS: I looked high and low for one of these and finally found this one in the choir room of the church. Seems it was left behind by some travelling missionaries from Italy. From Venice, Father O'Malley says. He let me have it for a promise to come to Mass more often.

SEAN: So, then it's a "Venetian blindharp," I'd say.

(They pause contemplatively, as if letting the concept sink in.)

JACK: It does have a nice tone. There's a gentleness about it. Almost a sadness. Could we try a little number with it?

CHRISTMAS: Here's one I've been working on.

(Christmas hands Mick the foolscap sheet music, the instruments and music stand are produced from behind the bar, and they join in on "Christmas's Debut," an instrumental.)

JACK: It does sound nice, the blindharp, but it's a little cumbersome, isn't it? Are you sure there's a future in it for you?

CHRISTMAS: Ah, but don't you see? It's my father's instrument after all. If I master it, I can indeed follow in his footsteps and maybe succeed him someday.

PADDY: Uh, you don't see much of your father, do ye, lad?

CHRISTMAS: Well, what do you think? He travels so much. With Barry. It's been a long time.

PADDY: And this is your father's instrument, is it?

CHRISTMAS: Well, I don't suppose they call him Turlough O'Carolan, the Legendary Itinerant Blindharpist of Ireland for nothing now, do they?

JACK: (to the others) How do we tell him?

CHRISTMAS: Tell me what?

MICK: We just tell him. Christmas, me lad, sometimes I think you're the greenest leaf on the shamrock. I fear you've been deceived.

CHRISTMAS: What do you mean, deceived?

PADDY: Christmas, your daddy is blind. Since he was a boy. And he plays a regular Irish harp. He's blind, and he's a harpist, not a blindharpist.

JACK: Aye, Chris. We thought you knew.

CHRISTMAS: (stunned) No. I didn't. I guess that explains a few things. Oh my! I've played the fool here, in front of my friends. And what would my father say? This is quite sad, isn't it?

JACK: 'Tis the Irish state of bein', I'm afraid.

(They give Christmas some space for a moment.)

MICK: No need to stay sad forever! Look on the bright side, Chris! You're probably the only one in Ireland who plays a blindharp. As you said, no competition. Surely you can trade on that somehow. Look at the rest of us. Wastin' our days eatin' potatoes and playin' in pubs for a dram or a pint. At least *you've* got a future. Big shoes to fill. Speakin' of which, what are those things you're wearing?

CHRISTMAS: Never you mind my brogans, Mick. It's personal.

SEAN: Oh, it's personal, is it? Quite the introspective one, are we?

JACK: Ah, leave the lad alone. He's suffered a big enough blow already today.

SEAN: Well, if Chris won't cheer up, let's cheer ourselves up. Give me a big one, Paddy!

PADDY: (drawing Sean a pint) Do you want fries with that?

JACK: Give me an Old Harp, Paddy!

(Paddy picks up an Irish harp.)

JACK: No, Paddy, an Old Harp Ale!

(Paddy hands him a large mug of beer.)

MICK: Say, Jack, do you ever think about what you might do with the rest of your life?

JACK: Well, Mick, I sure don't see myself still comin' in here every night when I'm 64.

SEAN: You've been doin' it for over 20 years now already. What's another 20?

JACK: Nah, Sean, I think I'll settle down. Maybe find me a lass and take up farmin'.

MICK: You? But you don't have a farm! You don't have much of anything!

JACK: You're right. I don't. But I can dream. I'll save up and buy some farmin' tools. A man's got to start somewhere.

SEAN: That I'd like to see! And what would you do all day?

JACK: Well …

(They sing "The Potato Song" chorus. Christmas watches.)

Chorus
I'd plant me some potatoes
if only I'd a hoe.
I'd have a little garden
and plant them row by row.
I'd pray for rain and sunshine
and hope the buggers grow.
I'm Irish, yes, and I'd do me best,
if only I'd a hoe.

MICK: Sounds good, Jack! So, what kind of potatoes would they be?
And what would you do with them?

JACK: We all know the answer to that!

(They sing "The Potato Song" verses, to the tune of "The Irish
Washerwoman.")

Verse 1
Now there's Irish and Russets and Yellows and Fingerlings,
Pink Eyes and Pontiacs, tubers for everything.
Big Golden Wonders and Almonds and Chiloés,
Burbanks and Roosters and Désirées too!

And there's White ones and Blue ones and Murphys and Idahoes,
Jerseys, Atlantics, Clavelas and Congos and,
Royals and Kestrels, King Edwards and Fonteneys.
You find a new one, we'll name it for you!

Verse 2
Oh, we'll roast 'em and steam 'em and boil 'em in water, and
mash 'em with gravy or pour on the butter, or
bake 'em and stuff 'em with bacon and cheese, we'll
dice 'em or cube 'em and serve up a stew.

Oh, there's hash browns and French fries and chips for a dippin'
and
twice baked potatoes or scalloped au gratin. We'll
serve 'em in casseroles, just as you please.
I'll have potato cakes, latkes for you!

SEAN: Latkes!?

MICK: Latkes!!?

MICK, JACK, SEAN & CONOR: (in unison) Hey, hey, hey, hey!

(They break into "Hava Nagila" and dance around madly.)
(Hebrew lyrics omitted because everybody loves "Hava Nagila"
even if they don't understand the words.)

JACK: What the dickens was that all about?

SEAN: Didn't sound much like Gaelic to me!

MICK: So, what'll it be tonight, lads?

SEAN: How about bangers and mash again?

MICK: Let's vote on it. All for bangers and mash say, "Eye!"

("Eyes" enthusiastically all around)

MICK: The "Eyes" have it! Fill my cup and get out the spud peeler!

(They sing a reprise of "The Potato Song" chorus, toward the end of which MICK interjects:)

MICK: For the love of Mike, somebody get this man a hoe!

(The song ends.)

JACK: How are you feelin' about things now, Chris?

CHRISTMAS: I'll admit you've cheered me up a little. But when I think about how much time I've wasted … How will I ever catch up to my father, and with a stupid blindharp for Heaven's sake?

PADDY: Like the song says, you're Irish, you'll do your best. You'll find a way to turn your lemons into lemonade.

SEAN: Or in this case, your potatoes into gin!

CONOR: Paddy, when did you start serving lemonade?

PADDY: (ignoring Conor) I've got an idea! As sad as that blindharp sounds, but beautiful too, why not write a song and enter it into the annual All-Ireland Sad Song Competition? You'll be famous, and your future will be assured!

JACK: Aye, that's it! The All-Ireland Sad Song Competition!

CHRISTMAS: Oh, you know I could never win. My father walks away with a prize almost every year. How can I compete with that? I'll truly look like a fool, and not just in front of a few friends, but in front of the whole of Ireland.

PADDY: I can't think of anybody more likely to beat your father. There's much of Turlough in you, lad, and that gives you a head start. But you've got somethin' more, too, Chris, somethin' special. You're unique. There's nobody else like you.

JACK: And with that blindharp you're truly special.

CONOR: And extra sad.

MICK: So how about it? Will you do it? Will you at least try? For Paddy here, and the old O'Donald's gang?

CONOR: Maybe for the Gipper too?

CHRISTMAS: The who?

MICK: We're stuck away here in Ballyfoulmouth, the armpit of the world, where nobody's ever likely to hear of us. Here's your chance to do us all proud, and yourself in the bargain.

SEAN: Hey, we'll go with you! Be your backup band, The Travelling Spud Buddies. You'll sound great!

CHRISTMAS: I just can't. Not yet anyway. No.

(Lights go down as music comes up offstage: "Inisheer Waltz")

Chapter Forty-Two

Scene Two was clever, and again the music was good if a little rough in spots because it was still only a rehearsal. Miller worked the cast and crew hard, but he seemed well respected as a director if not as well liked as a person. I looked forward to the show's scheduled opening in a few weeks, assuming we had solved The Case before then. I tried to imagine what, if anything, might cause someone to want to sabotage the production. There was a vague feeling of unease about it right on the edge of my consciousness, but nothing was jumping out at me.

After seeing a blindharp on stage, it did occur to me that Dylan Vivaldi could have a bunch of miniatures made up to give away as promotional gimmicks for the play. I made a mental note to suggest it to him.

(I should mention here that I while I was Googling Monahan and the others and ignoring Facebook ads for ghost hunting gear, I also visited the *Christmas O'Carolan Songbook, Volume 1* website and found several more songs from the production. I've included them in an Appendix for your reading, and maybe playing, enjoyment.)

I stayed at the Playhouse through the morning's rehearsal and stuck around for a catered lunch of sandwiches, pizza and soft drinks, giving me a chance to say hello to Nigel Wilson and Horace Vance the guitar player, meet a few of the other cast members, and make small talk with Miller. He seemed pleasant enough once we got better acquainted, but he didn't

247

shed any more light on The Case than the one he had seen in the balcony on the day of his injury.

Friday afternoon turned out to be more exciting, although not for me. After I left, two sandbags plummeted from the rafters backstage, bursting and spewing sand in every direction, halting rehearsals for the rest of the day while the cast and crew cleaned it up. Nobody was hurt, but it was the third time this had happened at the Playhouse and frightening enough that two of the actors, one crew member and Horace Vance, quit on the spot. Miller was incensed because it would set the schedule back at least two weeks while they auditioned for replacements. He was on the verge of quitting himself, but in the end his "show must go on" philosophy prevailed.

Detective Blue heard about it from a distressed Vivaldi and sent a uniformed officer to inspect the ropes. Sure enough, they had been partially severed with a knife. That could have been done anywhere from hours to days before the sandbags dropped, which means the drops could have happened at any time, totally unpredictably, and someone could have been seriously hurt or killed. I thought it strange that both had dropped at about the same time, but I didn't read anything into it. The officer checked all the other load-bearing ropes, found them to be in good shape, collected brief, unrevealing statements from everybody, and left.

I learned about all this from Blue later in the afternoon when he called to let me know and to tell me that fingerprints found on the two pens from the balcony belonged to Charles Kelly and that he'd turned up some information on Norman Shomething.

He had checked on Kelly, Lorna Gribble and Michael Brennan but couldn't find much more on them than I had. None had ever been in trouble with the law except for a couple of old parking tickets Kelly had gotten downtown and a speeding ticket Brennan got on a stretch of Wendover Avenue where the speed limit is 45 but everybody routinely goes 60 anyway. I had mostly written off Brennan as a suspect by now, regarding him as a childish, lazy, frustrated wannabe, although why anybody would wannabe a poet without trying to write a poem was beyond me.

There was nothing new on Lenny Monahan either, besides what was on his website and the publicity material he'd given to Dylan Vivaldi before Vivaldi hired him, which Vivaldi had shared with me after he, Emily and I had met with him at Vivaldi's office. Monahan had a Nevada driver's license but no violations. Maybe that's because he flew almost everywhere he went, but boy were his arms tired.

Blue did have the home addresses for all four including Monahan's small rent-by-the-week apartment not far from the Komedy Klub.

"What about the mysterious Norman Shomething?" I asked Blue.

"Looks like we got lucky there," he said. "I ran all those aliases through the computer, and it spit up one name out of the database. Ninety-nine and forty-four percent sure the guy we're looking for is Norman Shartly."

"Shartly. How about that? Shartly is one we came up with when I was going through all the vowels. We were pretty close. So, who is Norman Shartly?"

"Former Army Special Forces officer with tours in the Middle East, honorably discharged about 10 years ago. Did some consulting work in the DC area for a couple years and then it's like he dropped off the map. Mom and Pop both deceased. No brothers and sisters. No address, no current credit cards, no driver's license, nothing on Facebook or Twitty or any of those."

"Like Jack Reacher."

"Who?"

"Nobody. What else do we know? What's he look like?"

"I've got pictures from when he was in the Army and school pictures from when he was in ROTC. He's what we call 'nondescript.' White, average height, average build, brown hair, brown eyes. No distinguishing marks like scars, moles, or tattoos. His Officer Evaluation Reports say he was good at his job but if you met this guy, you'd forget about him two seconds later."

"Not much help. Why would a guy like that need 34 disguises? Although I guess if you saw even a nondescript person 34 times, you might begin to recognize him."

"Beats me, but what do you wanna bet growing up the other kids called him Shorty?"

"You think maybe that led to his embracing a life of crime?"

"It happens. But here's the thing, poetry boy."

"What?"

"In the Army he was a sniper."

"What do you think that means?"

"It means, young Mr. Detective Mark, that we are probably dealing with a professional hit man."

"I bet nobody calls him Shorty anymore."

Underneath my flippancy, I felt a stab of fear. Maybe two stabs. One because it's scary to think about facing a professional killer. Two because I couldn't immediately think of a euphemistic way to tell Emily.

I said, "But he hasn't killed anybody here, at least not yet. Doesn't seem like he intends to."

"No, I agree with you there, but guys like that can be a little psycho, and I still don't have a report back on that weapon we found. You think him and Kelly are working together?"

"Looks like they're using the same kind of weapon, but I

250

doubt they're working together. The numbers don't support it."

"So what it boils around to is we got two separate cases here."

"That's the way I'm seeing it."

"Oh goodie. I'll ask for a raise," said Blue.

"Good luck."

I'd have to try that on Bob Ausländer, just to annoy him. But I wasn't ready to talk to Bob about any of this yet.

"In the meantime, what do you want to do about Charles Kelly?" I said.

"Finding his fingerprints only means he touched the weapon. Doesn't prove he used it. Could be he found it and then lost it, but I don't think so. I think he's guilty, and so is that Gribble woman, but somebody else is behind all this."

"What if you bring him in for questioning and then release him so he'll lead us to the big fish?"

"You mean like on TV?"

"Well, yeah, like that," I said.

"That's exactly what I'm gonna do. Sometimes on TV they get it right."

Chapter Forty-Three

"You tried to shoot Jerome Fostridge?!"

"I missed."

"You were sitting across the desk from him and you *missed*?"

"It was a warning shot."

"He says you ruined his credenza."

"Bullet had to go somewhere. I told him duct tape would fix it."

"You're a piece of work, Norman, you know that?"

"I am."

"Anyway, that's not the point. He didn't like it."

"Who would?"

"He's very angry."

"You told me he wouldn't like it. You were right. So what?"

"You've jeopardized the job."

"No, we came to an understanding. I keep working, but at my own pace, he keeps paying, you keep getting your fee, and he stays alive. Simple. You could have negotiated that yourself, Eddie. Maybe even without a gun. I do not want to do your job. Hard enough doing mine. Especially this one."

"In the end, he'll fire you and get somebody else."

"Let him try."

Chapter Forty-Four

Saturday

For the Saturday open mic at the Read-A-Spell bookstore, I didn't have to submit my haikus in advance. Since they were the same ones I'd brought to the critique group, all I had to do was print out a couple of copies, so Saturday was an easy day at the Fairley household. There were no voicemails from Bob Ausländer asking for updates and no voicemails or emails from the Charlotte company. Facebook was now showing me ads for vampire-hunting gear. There were 35 kits offered on Etsy alone, plus a half-dozen for finding zombies. I passed.

After lunch we called each of our three children. All were doing well in college as far as we knew. Colleges don't send grades to parents anymore even though we pay the bills. It's been declared an invasion of privacy. Knowing of our family's shaky financial position, all three had found part-time jobs near their campuses, and we were proud of them for that. Judy, the youngest, was a gofer at her university library, and William, the middle child, was unloading trucks at Home Depot, while Lisa, the eldest, was waiting tables at a restaurant the name of which she conveniently kept forgetting to tell us. Maybe it was a nightclub and she was practicing to become a standup comedienne, since Lenny Monahan says Lisa is a good name for one. We could only hope it wasn't a sports bar.

I confess I wasn't "up" for the evening's event since we had reached a turning point in The Cases (plural) with the identifying of suspects, the discovery of the VAFD weapon, some fledgling theories about motive, and a plan to rattle at least one suspect's cage. I didn't need to be spending a perfectly good Saturday evening at a bookstore. Nevertheless, I'd made the commitment, so I was going to show up. Who knows, I thought, maybe something else will jump out at me.

The Melnick brothers, Milton and Siegfried, own two independent bookstores, the Read-A-Spell on North Greene Street downtown and the Read-A-Spell-Too on Tate Street which runs along the edge of the University of North Carolina at Greensboro campus and is not to be confused with State Street, home of The Framery art gallery. At one time, the brothers owned three stores, including one in nearby Winston-Salem called Readers' Roost, but it burned down a few years ago and never reopened. Something about an alleged conspiracy involving the arson investigator and the insurance company, according to the Melnicks.

What was once a budding chain is now, as Lieutenant Blue might put it, just two broken links flying by the skin of their pants. The number of independent bookstores in the US has been growing for a decade, and sales per store have increased as well, except in Greensboro. That's because Greensburgers, as some of them like to call themselves, apparently do not buy many books. At least not from bookstores.

That is why, in order to attract customers inherently uninterested in buying books, Milton and Siegfried frequently host what are known in the trade as "events." In the case of the downtown store, overseen by Milton, the events are literary in nature. These might include open mic nights, poetry readings, author readings, book signings by authors of both local and national prominence, or wine and cheese lectures by professors of English or history from the many colleges and universities in the area. The idea is that the event-goers will somehow connect the literary goings-on with the fact that there are books, amazingly, right there among them, for sale. And then they might buy one or two.

At the Tate Street store, managed by the younger Siegfried, the events are musical. This is because the store is near the UNCG campus where the students and faculty are already so burdened with textbooks and assigned reading materials they are required to purchase at the university's own bookstore that they are not interested in, nor do they feel they have time for, any additional books. But they will find time to go listen to a local acoustic string band singing and playing folk and "coffee house" music while enjoying a glass of beer or wine, or several, or both, purveyed by the bookstore's on-premises licensed bar and café. In this case, the fact that it's a bookstore is almost irrelevant, although occasionally someone who has had one too many to drink will actually buy a book. All sales are final.

Neither store stocks my book, *The Accidental Spurrt*. I don't know why, and I've been meaning to speak to one or the other of the Melnick brothers about it.

Siegfried is a bachelor but has many friends in the coed community, while Milton is married to Marcy Melnick, Dylan Vivaldi's receptionist. Another of the many ways Vivaldi stays on top of things.

On the surface, Siegfried and Milton get along well as business partners, but, at least according to Dylan Vivaldi, Siegfried is jealous of Milton because Milton is operating "a real bookstore" while he, Siegfried, is stuck running a shabby college dive where his duties include cleaning up vomit in the alley behind the store after the customers have staggered out and gone home or back to their dorms. Added to that lately was the similar mess, made right in the store, when there were VAFD attacks during the musical performances.

My event was to start at 7:00 p.m. at the downtown store.

I arrived a few minutes early so I could look around, this being the scene of the first 911 VAFD call a few weeks before. I had visited the Read-A-Spell as a customer a few times long before The Cases arose, but like a true naturalized Greensburger, I had not bought anything. Maybe if I had been lulled into doing so while attending an event, I thought, but we'll never know. Unless I buy something this evening.

Nothing much had changed since my earlier visits. Beside the entrance were two large windows looking out on to the sidewalk, one filled with book displays to attract passersby and the other featuring a couple of small tables around which people were sitting and enjoying their choice of beverages and baked snacks from the small, tended bar right behind them. Across from the bar and near the entrance was the checkout counter, mid-chest high on an average adult and barely large enough to accommodate a cash register, a space to set down whatever you were buying, a few impulse-purchase items like fancy bookmarks, multicolored highlighters, gum, LifeSavers, or Tums, and a new item: a Read-A-Spell coffee mug full of complimentary dark green Gate City Playhouse Rocks fountain pens.

Books and magazines were stacked or displayed on every available surface and shelf. The aisles were narrow. It was an old building with uneven floors, so some of the bookshelves leaned slightly this way and that. As I passed them, I was afraid something might jump, or maybe drop, out at me, but nothing did.

Weaving my way through a veritable jungle of books in such categories as Literature & Fiction, Home & Garden, Religion, Self-Help, Children's, Gay and Lesbian, Biography, History, Local & North Carolina Authors, Arts & Music, Business, and Birdwatching, I suddenly reached the edge of a small clearing within which were three rows of folding chairs arranged in a semi-circle facing a lectern with a microphone. Almost everyone in the clearing was wearing a "HELLO my name is" badge. Those few who weren't were slowly clearing out. Several were holding or sipping from Read-A-Spell mugs or disposable clear plastic cups, presumably enjoying beverages purchased at the bar. Some were toying with Gate City Playhouse Rocks pens they probably picked up on their way in. More than one ink-stained index finger was in evidence. The clearing was dimly lit, but the atmosphere was convivial.

I grabbed a HELLO badge from a table displaying books by the "headliner" poets for the evening (Sadly, *The Accidental Spurrt* was not among them since I wasn't a headliner, only a lowly sign-up) and introduced myself to the woman womanning the table. It was Betty Wright-Moore, president of Writer's Block and the MC for the evening. She was a pleasant looking woman of about 55 with blonde hair and horn-rimmed glasses, librarian-like. We exchanged pleasantries.

"I can't wait to hear your haikus," she said. "Ryman Stanza says they were a big hit at the critique group."

"Hard to miss with haikus," I said modestly. "They're fun."

"Well, I'm sure the crowd here will love them. In the meantime, why don't you go ahead and mingle a little, meet some of the others. We're honored to have a representative from the GADC among us. I'll call everybody to their seats in a few minutes and we'll get started. I'm going to mix the sign-ups in with the headliners tonight, so you'll be, let's see, the fifth reader, if that's okay."

"Sounds good. Looking forward to it."

I had decided to make a point of looking at as many people's name badges as I could, even if I only had time to meet a few of them. After shaking hands and chatting briefly with two or three people with fairly ordinary names, I spotted what I was looking for. Sitting by himself in the chair nearest the store's rear emergency exit was a man whose name badge said "Norbert Shostakovich." It had to be Norman Shartly.

How do you strike up a conversation with somebody you think may be a trained professional hit man?

"Good evening. I understand you are a trained professional hitman."

"Why, yes, as a matter of fact, I am. How did you know?"

"Lucky guess. I did notice you were scratching your trigger finger."

"Itchy."

"Um, what's it like?"

"Being a hit man?"

"Yes."

"It's a living. You know. We all have to do something."

"Ha ha. I guess people are dying for your services."

"Oh, that's a good one. Never heard that one before."

"I bet nobody calls you Shorty anymore."

And so on. Until he kills you.

Of course, we didn't have that conversation. I said, "HI, I'm Mark Fairley," and held out my hand, which he shook, rising from his chair. He was of average height and build, gray-haired with rimless glasses, wearing jeans and a tan corduroy blazer with fake leather elbow patches, kind of like a stereotypical aging college professor.

"Norb Shostakovich," he said. "Nice to meet you."

"I'm sort of new at these things," I said. "Have you been to many?"

"Just a few."

"Well, they're letting me read some poems tonight, so I hope you won't be disappointed."

"I'm sure I won't be," he said, sitting back down just as Betty Wright-Moore stepped to the microphone and did the obligatory "One, two, three, testing, am I on?" speech to get everybody's attention.

At that moment, when his head was below me again, I noticed a wisp of brown hair peeking out from under what I then realized was a gray toupee. You might say it was a dead giveaway. Don't.

This was our man. I resolved to keep an eye on him the rest of the evening. Especially when I was behind the mic, although reading haikus while watching someone in the audience, let alone a professional killer who might VAFD me in mid-verse, could prove difficult. With that thought gnawing at me I didn't have the presence of mind to get out my phone and surreptitiously text Marshall Blue, "Come quick! He's here! He's here!"

There were about two dozen of us as we took our seats, mine five chairs to the right of and two rows behind my quarry.

"Good evening and welcome to our quarterly Writer's Block Open Mic Poetry Corner," said Betty. Then she lifted the microphone, stuck it in her mouth, vomited, and fell down.

I couldn't believe it. As usual, chaos ensued. An ear-piercing pulsating whistle sounded from the emergency exit. People stood up, aghast. Those in the front row scurried away from the vomit, knocking over chairs and crashing into the now standing people behind them, causing some of them to fall, leaving poor Betty alone on the floor. Plastic cups and coffee mugs flew, their contents splashing in all directions, and someone we later learned was Milton Melnick yelled, "Call 911!"

Recovering quickly, I looked around but saw no sign of our friend Norbert Shostakovich. He was gone. The whistle stopped.

"Greensboro Police!" someone else shouted. "Everybody stay calm; everything's under control! Please take your seats again. This is now a crime scene, and you are all witnesses, so I'm afraid we can't let anybody leave until we've talked to everybody and taken your pictures."

It was Marshall Blue!

Grudgingly, people started wiping wine, coffee and hot chocolate from their chairs with paper towels supplied by the bartender. Blue strode up to me.

"You again?" he said with a grin.

"Afraid so. How did you get here so fast?"

"Learned my lesson at that art gallery place. Took it one more step. Knew you were going to be here, so I came in dressed like a customer and waited to see what would happen."

Indeed, he was wearing jeans and a tan corduroy jacket with fake leather elbow patches but without a toupee. A coincidence? In this case, probably yes.

I heard sirens approaching. No doubt the EMTs to tend to Betty Wright-Moore.

"He was here!" I said. "I even spoke to him."

"I know," said Blue. "I spotted him too, while you were talking to him. Couldn't get to him before the hostess lady started the show, and then he ran out the back door. I've got two plainclothes guys at the front, but my man in the back wasn't in position yet. Went to the wrong building. Hard to tell which is which from the alley. Anyway, Shartly ripped his nametag off and dropped it back there and we picked it up. Must've been in a real panic to make a mistake like that."

"Can you get fingerprints off it?"

"We'll see, we'll see. But anyway, now we know for sure he's a player, we'll get him. We'll get him." Blue was excited.

I didn't see how we'd get him, since all the fingerprints could do was confirm he was Norman Shartly, not lead the police to him. The disguises had worked well for him, until now.

I said as much to Blue.

"You're right," he said. "So what would you do, Shylock?"

I thought a moment before blurting, "Well, his weakness is the narcissistic way he picks his aliases. Assuming this won't be his last attack, what if you take what you did tonight even further by stationing plainclothes officers at the next couple of events where he might likely show up? If the attendees have to register or wear nametags, have your people look for suspicious names like Norbert Shostakovich and disguises that look like disguises. Arrest him before he can do anything."

"Very good! You nailed it on the head that time. I guess I can dress my guys up so they look artsy."

"As long as they don't all wear the same thing, it shouldn't be too hard."

"Thanks for the tip."

"Shartly's toupee had come loose. Maybe he's getting sloppy."

I was happy Blue liked my idea. Or happy at least that my idea was the same as his, so I was thinking more and more like a real detective. But my warm fuzzies were short-lived.

"Okay, but there's something you should know," said Blue.

"Yes?"

"Speaking to him maybe wasn't such a great idea. He probably thinks he's been made. That's why he did his thing right up front this time and then beat it quick."

"If he thought that, why didn't he just sit this one out? Why take the risk?"

"Guys like him don't think like that. It's all about pride. And especially if he's getting paid by the hit. Or maybe he just don't like poetry. On the other hand, after this he may lay low for a while. But not for long, if I know my oatmeal. Then we'll be on him like honey on a bee."

"Can't wait," I said.

"But here's the thing I should mention. If he thinks you're the one who made him, you could be the next mic swallower."

I swallowed hard then, without a mic.

"But don't worry. We'll have your back."

"Right," I said. "What could go wrong?"

"Anything does, you can write a poem about it."

Chapter Forty-Five

"You're home early," said Emily, looking up from her magazine.

"I know. I saw your boyfriend running out the back door."

"Very funny." She rose and kissed me warmly. "What happened? Your poems were so bad they kicked you out?"

I thought about saying the poems had been "arresting," but you can only carry a pun so far. I told her what happened. She was not pleased, especially about Norman Shartly being a professional hit man.

"But on the bright side," I said, "Blue really did have my back this time, we've confirmed who one of the shooters is, and Blue has a plan to trap him at a future event where I don't have to be involved."

I didn't mention the part about Norman Shartly possibly trying to silence me if he thought I had recognized him because, on reflection, I wasn't too concerned. I figured Blue would have him locked up before he had time to come looking for me, so why worry Emily with it.

"What about the other two you think are still out there?"

"Lorna Gribble and Charles Kelly. I'm pretty sure they aren't professionals. We think they're probably working as a team but somebody else is giving them their orders. We don't know who. We don't think it's Shartly, and we still don't think they are working with him. That's why it's become two cases in one."

"A real bargain," Emily said with a note of sarcasm, "you should charge more."

"Yeah, and Blue said he should get a raise too, but he was kidding."

"You'd never get it out of Bob."

"That's for sure. Anyway, Blue is going to pick up Kelly for questioning and then release him. Follow him and see if he contacts anybody unusual."

"And you?"

"Not sure. I'm going to have a relaxing Sunday and not think about all this too much. Sometimes when I step away like that, things jump out at me."

"I hope nothing jumps out at you with that ray gun thing, or a real gun."

Sunday started out well enough. We went to church, stopped at IHOP for some pancakes after, and then went home. The sermon was about how God works in a mysterious way, His wonders to perform. Certainly true in my case since it's a mystery how I got into the detective business, and if it ends well it will be a wonder. Nevertheless, I was determined to relax, not think about The Cases.

But of course, that's all I could think about.

On the one hand, I no longer felt the need to interview the "Artsy 6" victims since we had three suspects and a weapon and now knew the source of the mysterious flashing lights. And the only other event I really had to attend was the Upshot Marketing Greensboro Arts Alive! kickoff fundraiser at the Greensboro Country Club coming up on Tuesday evening. On the other hand, we still didn't have any idea who was behind all this and what the motives were. Who would benefit if RayDact refused to relocate its headquarters and manufacturing plant to Greensboro? Who would benefit from shutting down the *O'Carolan* production at the Gate City Playhouse? Some ideas were forming, but there weren't quite enough dots to connect yet.

Maybe by Monday more dots would jump out at me.

Chapter Forty-Six

Monday indeed brought more dots, but not all of them were connectible.

The State Crime Lab report came back on the weapon Blue and I found in the Playhouse balcony. Blue had picked up Charles Kelly for questioning. The Charlotte company called, wanting to set up a second interview.

Blue and I met for lunch, this time at Stamey's Barbecue on Battleground Avenue. Stamey's is a Greensboro institution, a simple, bare bones kind of restaurant featuring Lexington-style pork barbecue with no attempt at atmosphere beyond the cheeriness of the blue-uniformed waitresses who call everybody "Honey." Their official motto is "93 Years and Still Smokin'." I love the place and Blue does too, so we at least have that in common. It's better, somehow, than both liking McDonald's and having that in common.

You might think it would be natural for a barbecue restaurant to take a promotional cue from Dylan Vivaldi and give away pens decorated with pictures of plump little pigs. But no, the folks at Stamey's are too smart for that. No point saturating the town with cheap writing instruments that would inevitably and immediately come to be known as Stamey's pig pens.

We arrived a little after 1:30 and the lunch crowd had thinned out, so we took a table in the middle of the room. Blue sat facing the door. I ordered the Regular Chopped Pork Barbecue Plate, and Blue had the Large Chopped, both "Traditionally served with Stamey's slaw and hushpuppies." Too-sweet Iced Tea for me and Diet Pepsi for Blue, topped off by both of us with Peach Cobbler n' Ice Cream, all but the drinks being "Stamey's Barbecue Signature Items." Stamey's may be the only barbecue restaurant in North Carolina that doesn't serve banana pudding. I don't know why. Obviously, it's some sort of esoteric tradition. They could add that to their motto: "93 Years and Still Smokin' and Without None o' That There Banana Puddin' With Them Soggy Vanilla Wafers In It."

"The Crime Lab traced the weapon back to that RayDact company," said Blue after we had got our food and commenced to eatin'. (Sorry, that's the last of the fake Southern dialect stuff, but I couldn't resist.)

"Are they sure?"

"It was hard, but they put their best forensic experts on it. Wearing sterilized form-fitting nitrile gloves, they carefully removed it from the pen casing with sterilized tweezers and using a state-of-the-art, highly polished magnifying glass they noticed the teensy-weentsy words 'RayDact Corporation Made in USA' etched on it."

I looked at him.

"You think I'm pulling my leg, don't you?"

"No, I definitely don't think that."

"It's some kind of ray gun all right. They tested it on some mice. The mice threw up and fell down."

"Did they give them tiny little microphones to swallow?"

"No."

"Okay, well what do they make of it? I mean how does it work and all that?"

"I've got the report right here and you can look at it, but they said it's sort of a combination microwave and laser thing.

Runs on a little battery. There was no patent number or anything, so they couldn't find it in any records or databases. That probably means it's hush-hush. If this is what Shartly and Kelly were using, we'll have to start with them or get somebody to pay a visit to RayDact. Time to find out if Vivaldi knows anything about it too. I know you don't think he's involved, but I've got to turn over every new leaf."

"Speaking of Kelly, how did that go?" I asked, shaking a few drops of Texas Pete hot sauce on to my barbecue.

Blue started to laugh.

"What?" I said.

"That was a joke, right?"

"What was?"

"The little microphones. For the mice."

"Yes," I said. "I was pulling my leg."

"Gotta admit, you got me with that one. Anyway, so I grabbed Kelly this morning outside his residence and took him to the station. Not under arrest or anything, just for questioning."

"How did he take it?"

"Wasn't too happy about it. Wanted to know if he needed a lawyer. 'Not if you ain't got nothing to hide,' I told him. He was surprised I had the two pens with his fingerprints all over them and said he wondered where they'd got to. He freely admitted being in the balcony but said he was just curious about the show they were putting on and didn't want to disturb anybody. I told him he was trespassing, and I confronted him with how many times he was a witness when somebody got attacked and how one of the pens was a weapon, and then I flat out accused him of being the shooter."

"Then what?"

Blue paused to drizzle some Texas Pete on his own barbecue and take a gulp of his Diet Pepsi.

"Said he hadn't noticed one of the pens was anything but a pen. 'They all look alike,' he said. 'They're all over town, and I could have picked it up anywhere. And so what if I like to go to a lot of arts events? Not my fault people are throwing up and falling down all over the place. In fact, some of us are taking bets whether it'll happen each time, you know? Besides, I work for the newspaper, so I like to keep up with current events.'"

"Cheeky."

"Yeah, it was like he was waving it in my face."

"He writes obituaries. I guess that's current events. Kind of."

"He's not careful, he'll be writing his own."

"That's a good one," I said.

"What is?"

"Nothing. Does he know Lorna Gribble?"

"Claims he's never heard of her, but I'm not buying it."

"So, what next?"

"We got no solid proof he's a shooter, so I let him go with a warning, which he pretty much laughed at, which I won't forget, and I've got a couple of my guys tailing him night and day, see where he goes. Sooner or later, he'll contact whoever's calling the shots."

("So to speak," I added silently.)

"You didn't happen to ask him if he knows Lenny Monahan, did you? I checked, and Kelly was one of the witnesses at the Komedy Klub incident when Morrie Milburne got VAFDed."

"VAFDed?"

"That's what I'm calling it. Vomit and Fall Down."

"That supposed to be funny?"

"No, just convenient. Sorry, I guess I hadn't mentioned it before."

"Well, I didn't ask him, but if he's connected my guys will find out pretty soon. Why the interest in whether he knows Monahan?"

"I don't know exactly. Like you, I'm trying to turn over new leaves, and stones. Looking for stuff to connect. Besides, they both have Irish names."

"So does almost everybody else involved in this thing, except you and me. They can't all be guilty."

"True, but I can't help thinking something is rotten in the state of the Greensboro Irish Community."

Chapter Forty-Seven

Tuesday

The first thing you notice about the Greensboro Country Club is that it is not out in the country. It is practically downtown, only 2½ miles north of City Hall. It is the central landmark on the high ground of a golf course surrounded by an upscale residential neighborhood laid out in 1909, a time when it was indeed out in the country.

The second is that people arrive early when there is a major event because otherwise there will be no place to park within a half mile of the clubhouse. I was right on time until I had driven around fruitlessly for about five minutes, finally finding a spot requiring me to parallel park, which I have never done since taking driver's ed when I was 15.

That reminded me of one of the questions on the driver's license exam. Like most of the others, it was multiple choice, and I am not making this up:

You are driving on a residential street, and there are children playing in the yards. What should you do?

A   Stop.

B   Slow down and proceed with extra caution.

C   Speed up so as to pass quickly.

I am pretty sure I got that one right by choosing B, but as would many a normal 15-year-old boy, I was sorely tempted to go with C just for the fun of it.

I walked the half mile to the clubhouse. That took about

10 minutes at a brisk pace in a light drizzle, holding my Glowery executive portfolio over my head because I had not brought an umbrella. I reached the shelter of the *porte-cochère* at 7:45 for the 7:30 event. Being fashionably late is not the thing in Greensboro high society, at least not for most.

It's a beautiful club, well-suited to hosting events such as this one. According to its website, "The Club facilities provide complimentary wireless internet, state of the art audio visual services as well as the finest in food and beverage offerings. The Club prides itself on flexible room setup to include classroom, conference style as well as an intimate executive boardroom setting." Since coming to Greensboro, Emily and I were torn about whether to apply for membership. On the one hand, I was curious about what it would be like to get intimate in the executive boardroom. On the other, I couldn't help remembering Groucho Marx's famous quote upon resigning from the Friars Club, "I don't want to belong to any club that would accept me as one of its members." Since we couldn't afford it anyway, especially now, it remained a moot question.

Tonight was the unveiling of the Upshot Marketing Grand Plan for promoting and raising support for revitalizing the arts in Greensboro. A major event. The movers and shakers and their spouses or significant others would be there. Yours truly was to be the featured figurehead. And I was late.

A smiling uniformed off-duty policeman held open one of the double doors for me as I hastened up the carpeted brick steps into the foyer and approached a second set of double doors. I was on my own with those but managed to negotiate them successfully, launching myself into a magnificent atrium lobby full of people who seemed to be milling about happily, drinks in hand, with no concern for what time it was.

I signed a register, quickly scanning the other names for

any likely Norman Shartly aliases but finding none. Then I made my way into the ballroom where the big event was to be held and beheld Frances Muldoon in the center holding a glass of red wine and talking with two men, one of whom I'd seen in a newspaper photo recently but whose name I couldn't recall and the other of whom was Bob Ausländer. She spotted me and beckoned. I approached with trepidation over my tardiness, but her smile suggested that as far as she knew I had arrived an hour early.

"Mark," she called, "I want you to meet Brian Gulliver, executive director of the Edmund and Chloe Fitzgerald Memorial Family Foundation. Brian, this is Mark Fairley, our liaison with the GADC."

Brian was a pleasant looking, slightly portly man in his seventies with balding gray hair and a bushy Rich Uncle Pennybags mustache, like from the Monopoly game, and the bow tie to go with it. Maybe that's why when Frances said, "the Edmund and Chloe Fitzgerald Memorial Family Foundation," I wanted to follow it with "and Storm Door Company,"[8] but I didn't. Gulliver and I shook hands and exchanged warm nice-to-meet-yous.

"And of course, you and Bob already know each other," she gushed.

"We do," said Bob.

"Yes, we do," I said.

"Well," said Gulliver, "Moira and I—that is my wife, over there by the *hors d'oeuvres*—are looking forward to hearing from Frances this evening. The arts are so important to the Fitzgeralds, you know."

---

[8] Apologies to Bob Newhart re his "The Grace L. Ferguson Airline (And Storm Door Co.)" bit. *Bob Newhart, The Button-Down Mind Strikes Back*, ℗1998, Warner Records Inc.

I didn't quite see how that could be, since as far as I knew Edmund and Chloe Fitzgerald had been dead for at least 20 years and never had any children, but I let it pass.

"I'm sure you'll be impressed by the presentation," I said.

"I must agree," said Dylan Vivaldi, joining the group. "And top o' the evening to you, Brian. Always good to see the Fitzgeralds represented."

"And I am happy to be doing it," said Gulliver. "By the way, how are the rehearsals for that *O'Carolan* show of yours going? I heard Mr. Miller took a bit of a spill. I hope he is recovering well."

"He is that," said Vivaldi. "I'm sure things will be back on track in no time at all."

"If you'll excuse us," Frances said, taking me gently by the elbow, "Mark and I have a few things left to check on before we begin."

She guided me toward a large projection screen placed where it could be seen from the rows of chairs set out for the audience, which I guessed probably numbered about 200 community leaders from a cross section of ethnicities, faiths and vocations, not counting the dozen or so uniformed bartenders and ushers and the servers gliding through the crowd with *canapé* trays. Almost all the guests were dressed at least to the eights and many to the nines. Brian Gulliver maybe a ten. I had on the ordinary suit I wear to weddings and funerals, not the fancy one I wore in Charlotte. So I gave myself a seven.

No one was wearing "HELLO my name is" badges. I saw several people I recognized other than Dylan, Bob, and Brian, including two Glowery VPs along with the Mayor, a couple of City Council members, other business people I knew from my years at Glowery, Betty Wright-Moore (looking a bit pale, but steady), my doctor, my dentist, my butcher, my baker, my candlestick maker, and some others. I spotted the estimable Frank Sheldon, Esq., my erstwhile attorney, and Don Bledsole, supreme commander of my Neighborhood Watch Committee. In addition to the doctors and lawyers, there was even a bona-fide Lumbee Indian chief. A star-studded evening.

Some of the people whose names I recognized had appeared on some of the witness lists, so they were definitely patrons of the arts in Greensboro.

There was a mug full of green Gate City Playhouse Rocks pens on the *hors d'oeuvre* table, and several people had them in their hands and were absent-mindedly toying with them or rubbing ink stains off their index fingers with handkerchiefs or cocktail napkins as they chatted. The presence of so many pens made me uncomfortable.

To one side of the screen where it wouldn't block anyone's view was a lectern and mic at which stood Donna Majors, the Project Director, gesturing to someone bending over a laptop balanced on a small table in an aisle about five rows back. It turned out to be Sarah, the "media and computer guru" in Donna's pod.

"Sorry I'm a little late," I said to Frances.

"Oh, were you? Well, no problem. These things never start on time. We give everybody a few minutes to mingle, socialize. You know, maybe have a drink or two and get relaxed before we reach into their wallets."

"Figuratively speaking, I presume."

"Of course! Anyway, the reason these people are here even this early is the chance to see and be seen. And also the parking problem."

"Are these people all members of the Greensboro Country Club?"

"A lot of them are, including Donna and me, but the rest are from all over. They'll use any excuse to come to the Club for a free event, even if it means having to make a pledge to whatever is the cause *du jour*, just to stay in the game."

It was a cynical way of looking at it, but there was probably a lot of truth in what she said.

"Hello, Donna," I said as we neared the lectern.

"Oh, hi, Mr. Farly!"

"It's Fairley, Donna," said Frances. "There was a little mix-up with the business cards."

"Oh. Right. I forgot."

"No problem," I said. "Anyway, again, call me Mark."

She nodded. If we were pod-mates, we should be on a first name basis.

"How are Brad and Nigel?" I asked.

"They're fine. Brad's probably at home, and I think Nigel is at an evening rehearsal at the Playhouse. They're trying to make up for lost time."

"I'm glad to hear he wasn't one of the actors who quit."

"We almost wish he was. It's almost like somebody's out to kill the show and doesn't care who gets killed along with it."

"Is everything ready?" Frances said to Donna.

"Yes, Ma'am."

"How do you want to handle this?" I asked Frances.

"I'll start it off," she said. "Then I'll introduce you and Donna and ask you to say a few words, and then if you will turn it over to Donna, she'll make the presentation. After that, I'll take a few questions, tell everybody how they can make their donations, and wrap things up."

The rest of the evening went as planned. Frances got the crowd comfortably seated, welcomed them, and thanked them for coming. She introduced Donna and me and turned the mic over to me. I told them how impressed I was with the publicity and fundraising campaign the Upshot Marketing people had put together and gave my words of official endorsement from the Greensboro Area Development Commission. Then I sat down as Donna took over.

Her presentation was fast-paced, entertaining, efficiently informative, and convincing, and she never lost the attention of the audience. Most of them were oblivious to the threat of anyone being VAFD-rayed, but it was all I could think of. In my mind, Lectern + Microphone = Danger.

Donna made the arts in Greensboro seem like a lot of fun, that it was fulfilling for the highly talented yet safe and welcoming for beginners, that it contributed greatly to the quality of life in Greensboro and that Greensboro Arts Alive!, the program they were being asked to support, would encourage more participation in it by both the artists and the public to the betterment of the overall community. She finished by deftly playing the *noblesse oblige* card to "garner more financial support by the more economically favored among us," just as she had put it the day I visited her pod.

Frances took over, conducted a brief Q & A, and told everyone how to give to GAA! Even I was tempted to make a pledge, though I am far outside the *noblesse* community.

In the end, I did so—a small donation, considering my economic circumstances. Mainly, I was playacting, holding up my pledge envelope for all to see as an example. "See, the GADC guy puts his money where his mouth is." I was rewarded with smiles from Frances, Donna, Sarah, Dylan Vivaldi, and even Bob Ausländer. Just doing my job. Should I put the donation in my expense report to Bob? Probably not.

It was a successful evening. The fundraising goal was exceeded. No one was VAFDed in the process. And Bob didn't rush over and demand a status report. He was too busy rubbing elbows and getting his rubbed in return.

As Frances and Donna mingled while Sarah packed up

their equipment, Dylan Vivaldi came over and thanked me for my small role in the festivities.

"You're welcome," I said. "Looks like you've gotten rid of a few more Playhouse pens tonight."

"Aye, everybody loves them."

"Just curious, but do you or someone on your staff inspect each of them before you put them out there?"

"Now why would we do that? They're just fountain pens. Why do you ask?"

"It's a half-baked theory I'm toying with. Blue and I are making progress, but there are still a lot of loose ends."

"You think the pens may have something to do with it?"

"Not sure yet, but if they do, you'll be the first to know."

"Now I'd better go home and have a Carolans Irish Cream before I go to bed or I won't sleep a wink. It's already bad enough thinking about what's happening to my *O'Carolan* show."

"I heard about that."

"One more incident will kill it, I'm afraid. Even Miller won't come back."

"All I can say is, again, we're making good progress, and maybe there will be a break soon."

"I bloody well hope so."

He didn't seem in a hurry to rush off, so I decided to ask him about something else that had been gnawing at me.

"Again, just curious, but how often has Lenny Monahan been to the Playhouse?"

"Now that you mention it, I don't think he's ever been there except when you and Emily came to meet with him after the trouble at the Komedy Klub. And then he didn't want to stick around to watch the rehearsals, which kind of surprised me. Him being so Irish and all and telling me he came to town mostly because of the *O'Carolan* show. Again, why do you ask?"

"Again, trying to connect some dots that may or may not be connectable."

At that point, one of the City Council members came up and, after giving me a nod of recognition, whisked Vivaldi away.

After hanging around to meet and greet a few more people for another half hour during which nobody offered me a job, I excused myself and began the half mile trek back to my car.

It had stopped drizzling, and the sky was clear. Once past the streetlights in the parking lot, it was dark. There was no moon and no clouds to reflect city lights from the nearby downtown. A couple of times I turned on my iPhone's flashlight feature to be sure of my footing. It is an old neighborhood. Over the years tree roots have grown under the sidewalks and heaved up the edges of some of the concrete slabs, creating opportunities to trip or lose my balance on the uneven surfaces. I stepped carefully.

It was also very quiet except for a strange sound I heard three times. A sort of "phut" followed a split second later by a soft "thunk" from a nearby tree, as if a woodpecker had taken one giant peck. Phut-thunk. Phut-thunk.

A fourth time, it was similar to a phut but, as I thought about it the next day, sounded more like somebody muttering a certain sibilant swearword. There was no thunk.

Chapter Forty-Eight

Wednesday

Although the Charlotte company had left a voicemail Monday afternoon, I didn't get around to calling them back until Wednesday morning. No excuse, really, except it clearly showed my interest was not high, even though I was indeed desperate for a real job with career potential. Never could I see myself paraphrasing Groucho Marx with "I don't want to work for any company that would accept me as one of its employees."

Emily, understandably, had higher interest and felt I should have returned the call sooner if only out of common courtesy. She was right, especially since it was GK3 himself who called and not some minion from HR. But did I want to make the 100-mile drive back down there and meet again with all the playacting Gatekeepers who never actually told me what position I was interviewing for? Maybe they would tell me this time. I would make it a condition of agreeing to go. I would also insist on meeting with someone more senior than GK3, even though he was a vice president. I wanted to meet the president. In addition, I wanted the option of rescheduling if rain was expected.

That being said, my detective Spidey sense was hinting that we might be on the verge of solving the VAFD pen mystery (I couldn't call it "the poison pen mystery" any longer.) and therefore I would be needing another source of income soon.

Of course, I could probably find a way to draw things out so I could stay on the GADC payroll a little longer—after all, we were given 60 days to clear things up—but I knew Lieutenant Blue would quickly figure out what I was up to, as would Bob Ausländer and even, eventually, Dylan Vivaldi. Dishonesty was not on the table. And I'm told Charlotte is a nice place to live if you can put up with the traffic.

I called GK3.

"Yes, we'd like to see you again," he said after we exchanged awkward pleasantries.

"So you think the first interview went well?" I asked.

"Well enough, I'd have to say, but there's been some back-and-forth discussion and that's why it's taken a little longer than usual to get back to you."

"I see."

"I must confess, I expressed some reservations about you, but my boss, our president, was impressed with your track record, and here we are."

"Spoken like a true gatekeeper."

"A what?"

"I mean, I understand. You just want what's best for the company."

"Don't we all? Also, your old boss, Mr. Ausländer gave you a good reference, and my boss liked that too."

That was a surprise. Emily would be even more surprised. I wasn't sure if I remembered listing Bob as a reference, but I suppose I must have. Hard not to.

"That's nice to hear."

"Yeah. Said you were kind of a, how did he put it, a wisenheimer? But you did good work."

"Well, I would like to come back, but I sort of need to know what to expect this time. You know, before I make the trip."

"Of course. We'll tell you exactly what position we have in mind, you'll spend some time with the president, and if it looks like rain you can reschedule at your discretion."

Either GK3 was a mind reader or he had driven I-85 in the rain a time or two himself.

"I've driven I-85 in the rain, and I know what it's like," he added.

"I appreciate that. You couldn't just tell me what the position is right now, could you?"

"It's … complicated. Better to wait 'til you get here."

I didn't like the sound of that, partly because it reminded me of Bob Ausländer's lack of candor when he asked me to meet him about the trouble in the arts community. Surely, they didn't want me to be an undercover detective in Charlotte. Surely.

There was only one way to find out. We set a date and time for two weeks away. Their president would be back from Cancún by then.

Chapter Forty-Nine

"You took a shot at Mark Fairley?!"

"Three shots, actually."

"With a real gun?!"

"Of course, with a real gun. My Glock G44 .22, with a suppressor."

"Norman, you *are* crazy! First Fostridge and now Fairley!"

"Relax. It's what I do."

"But you missed, right?"

"Yes. I do that too."

"Thank God!"

"Why? I think Fairley made me at the bookstore thing. I couldn't risk that."

"You *think* he made you?"

"The way he looked at me when he introduced himself. Like he *knew.*"

"How could he know? You're the master of disguises, Norman. Fairley doesn't know anything."

"I've been doing this a long time. I can tell when something's not right."

"Fostridge isn't going to like it. He already thinks you're becoming a liability."

"Fostridge isn't here."

"Do you realize what would have happened if you had actually shot him?"

"Yeah, my cover would be safe."

"No, your 'cover' would be a toilet seat. The cops would

be all over this. The newspapers and TV would get hold of it and make up whatever they wanted, and for all I know somebody would bring in the State cops, the FBI, the CIA and maybe the KGB!"

"It's not the KGB anymore. Now it's the FSB and the SVR."

"Whatever. The point is, disguise or not, you'd be rounded up with all the other witnesses and sweated until you had grill marks on your backside, and they *would* find you."

"Don't worry. I'm going to lay low for a while."

"Fostridge won't like that either."

"Fostridge can go jump in Lake Michigan."

Chapter Fifty

Ḣıscorıcaƚ Nocҽs

The Annuaƚ Aƚƚ–Ireƚand Sad Sonᵹ Compecıcıon

Each year from about 1650 until it petered out in the mid-19th Century, the annual All-Ireland Sad Song Competition was held to see who could write the saddest Irish songs. Anyone could enter as long as they were Irish and could prove it. Merely being sad was, in itself, not a qualifier.

Because the contest was not sponsored by the government, the organizers could not afford gold and silver for trophies. They could afford pewter, and the top prize was the Pewter Potato. It was awarded by a panel of six judges picked at random from among the townsfolk. They listened to songs performed by the composers (or stand-ins for those who could not sing or play an instrument or weren't sober enough to do so) in a local pub where drink flowed freely. This was to make it of no use for contestants to try to bribe the judges with alcohol.

Often a particular song would be heard more than once during the competition, which lasted about a week, either because the judges wanted to hear it again or because no one noticed that it had been performed already.

Points were given to songs based on sincerity, lyrics fitting or nearly fitting the meter of the music, intelligibility (does the song make any sense? – often a source of contention among the judges, especially near the end of the week), and sadness (does it bring a tear to the eye other than for poor musicianship or an over-dramatic presentation?).

Although it was the top prize, the Pewter Potato was actually for second place. The organizers felt a first-place prize should not be awarded because "No matter how sad the winner, we believe there is an even sadder song still out there somewhere that, sadly, has not yet been heard." Third place, fourth place and honorable mention were awarded the Pewter Barley Stalk, the Pewter Rye Stalk, and the Pewter Cow Pie, respectively. The song judged the least sad of all the entries was awarded the Pewter Turkey.

In 1736, Christmas O'Carolan (1693-1760) entered a song in the competition for the first time. Turlough O'Carolan (1670-1738), of course, had won more than once already with such songs as "Hewlett," "Luke Dillon," "Eleanor Plunkett," "Sí Bheag Sí Mhór," and "Ashokan Farewell" (later claimed by Jay Ungar). It is often said that in 1736 Turlough, in deference to his son who had never won anything in his life, entered a song that hardly anyone thought was very sad. Turlough denied that he purposely "threw" the competition and professed joy that his son's song, "Never Moor," went on to win that year. Turlough's entry has been lost, so we will never know which was truly the sadder.

In 1739, Christmas's song with a similar title, "Nevermore," won first prize in the newly established So Sad It Makes You Laugh category and was awarded the Pewter Funny Bone.

Irish Contribution to Music Theory

The Circle of Fifths

In music theory, the Circle of Fifths is a way of organizing the 12 chromatic pitches as a sequence of perfect fifths. If C is chosen as a starting point, the sequence is: C, G, D, A, E, B (=Cb), F# (=Gb), C# (=Db), Ab, Eb, Bb, F. Usually illustrated in the form of a circle, it is used for finding the key of a song, transposing songs to different keys, composing new songs and understanding key signatures, scales, and modes.

In the early Irish version of this, originating around the time of Christmas O'Carolan (1693-1760), musicians would get together in pubs and play for hours, standing each other to rounds of whiskey after each set, or, as the evening progressed, after each song. The empty whiskey bottles were placed in a circle in the center of the room, or as nearly in a circle as the musicians could manage, and this was called "the circle of fifths."

Chapter Fifty-One

"It took a while to find them, but we dug two 22-caliber slugs out of a couple of trees near where you parked," said Marshall Blue. "Never could find a third one."

"So I could be dead, is that what you're saying? The first to actually die because of all this?"

"Not saying anything. What I'm *thinking* is if he wanted you dead, you'd be dead."

"You think he was just trying to scare me? It worked!"

"I don't see how he could've missed at that range."

"Or maybe he's a bad shot."

"His military record says otherwise."

"If he was trying to scare me, why use a silencer? Why not just let the shots ring out, as they always say on the news? Boom! Boom! Or maybe Ding! Ding!"

Apparently, most journalists have only ever witnessed people shooting at bells.

"It was only a .22. Not very loud even without a suppressor. Plus, he probably didn't want to alarm the neighborhood. Plus, we know he's not too smart anyway. Plus, he probably figured you would know what 'phut-thunk, phut-thunk' meant."

"Well, I didn't until you told me."

"That's what I'm here for."

It was Wednesday afternoon, sunny, and Blue and I were leaning against his unmarked car parked under one of the huge oak trees that line Granville Road, half a mile from the Greensboro Country Club. That is, he was leaning, seemingly unconcerned; I was standing, concerned. No way was Emily going to hear anything about "phut-thunk" until she reads about it in this book. I had made that clear to Blue.

A mild breeze fluttered the American flags a few of the homes were flying and caused an audible rustling of the tree leaves.

At least two of these trees had taken bullets I feared were meant for me, so I guess in a sense I owed them. How do you repay an oak tree? A little fertilizer maybe? A judicious pruning now and then?

"No need to get hysterical," said Blue as if he was reading my thoughts.

I had called him that morning to let him know the GAA! event had gone well, and I happened to mention the odd noises I'd heard on the way back to my car. He told me what he thought they meant and quickly dispatched a crime scene unit to the area where I'd parked.

"Are you sure it's him? Not some nut job out to make a statement about people who belong to country clubs? Which I don't, by the way."

"Don't see how it could be anybody else. The slugs are pretty mangled, but we might get enough from ballistics to match them to his gun. If we can find him, and his gun."

"We've *got* to find him. Fast."

"Needle in a haystack. How do you suggest we do it besides waiting until he shows up at another event?"

"I have an idea," I said, barely noticing that Blue had actually spoken an idiom correctly. The idea was one I'd been thinking about for a few days.

"Let's hear it."

"We think he's using a pen weapon like the one Kelly had, right? The pen weapon connects him to RayDact, right?"

"Unless he bought it on the black market."

"No, somebody intentionally put that ray gun into a Gate City Playhouse pen. Apparently more than one. That's not a black-market kind of thing."

"Agreed."

"So, back to RayDact. Could somebody get hold of it without RayDact's knowledge? It's doubtful. I mean, it's top-secret technology. Somebody high up at RayDact has to know about this. It would take a team of people, inside, to deliberately engineer it so it would fit neatly into the pen. That's a conspiracy, and I doubt it could be pulled off in secret by a bunch of lower-level employees. And for what purpose? And why a Gate City Playhouse pen?"

"So you think it starts at the top." Blue stopped leaning and stood, now concerned.

"I think Norman Shartly may be working for Jerome Fostridge."

Blue thought about it.

"Could mean Kelly is working for him too," he said.

"No, I think there's something else going on with Kelly. Can't put my finger on it yet, but remember, we didn't think he and Shartly were working together. Doesn't mean they couldn't both be working for Fostridge, and, granted, I don't know how else he could have gotten his pen, but I still don't think he's connected to RayDact. Are you still watching him?"

"We're not monitoring his phone calls—waiting for a warrant for that—but the first thing he did after I released him was hightail it over to Lorna Gribble's place."

"So he was lying about not knowing her."

"We think they're itemized, if you know what I mean. Another thing I was going to tell you is there haven't been any incidents for the past few days. Well, except another sandbag fell at the Tanger Center, but that could have been set up weeks ago."

"They're all three lying low then. We've got them worried."

"That's a good thing," said Blue.

"Not if it means Shartly is going to use me for target practice again."

"Possible, but not likely. Anyway, there's one more piece of news."

"I'm all ears."

"Why do people say that? I've never understood it. Do you want to hear this or not?"

I nodded.

"A threatening note showed up at the Playhouse."

"Wow. Saying what?"

"Here, I'll show you." Blue took out his iPhone and showed me a picture of the note. It looked like a plain sheet of paper with individual letters cut from a magazine and glued on. The letters made up the words "Stop the show or else."

"Marcy Melnick found it at the back door this morning and Vivaldi called me, so I had it picked up and taken to headquarters, but I doubt we'll find any fingerprints."

"'Stop the show or else'? Looks like a 6th grader's idea of a threatening note. 'Or else' what?"

"Beats me. Maybe more attacks, or something worse. Vivaldi said this isn't the first note like this he's gotten. There were two more."

"You're kidding! And he didn't bother to mention them before now?"

"He said he didn't think anything of them. In his business, he says, you get all kinds of crackpot stuff. The first one came before the attacks started happening, so he didn't connect it to them until he got the second one. Besides, who's going to take seriously a note that just says, 'Stop the show or else'?"

"Is that what the other notes said? Do you have them?"

"He threw them out. But they all said the same thing. The

first one came in the mail. It was the original. The second one came in the mail too."

"What do you mean, 'the original'?"

"The original note, the first one, had the actual cut out letters pasted on it. The second one, and this latest one, were photocopies of the first one."

"So we have a lazy terrorist?"

"I doubt it. Maybe just an efficient one, sort of. And this one didn't come through the mail," Blue said, "so maybe there's some urgency to it."

"But at least it wasn't tossed through a window tied to a brick. Or a sandbag."

"It does confirm our theory that somebody wants to shut down the Playhouse."

"At least for the *Christmas O'Carolan* show. But we still don't know exactly who, or why."

Somehow, I knew it wasn't about the revenge of the busted ticket scalpers. I told Blue the rest of my idea. He liked it.

Chapter Fifty-Two

Friday

It took some doing, but Blue and I persuaded Bob Ausländer and Dylan Vivaldi to invite Jerome Fostridge down to Greensboro for a gala weekend of fun and entertainment. We finally convinced them with the same rationale we wanted them to use with Fostridge. After all, we told them to argue, this will be his new hometown, along with hundreds of his RayDact employees, and we want him to see the latest improvements in the downtown nightlife scene, new landscaping on the parkways, the opening of another new leg of the Interstate beltway around the city, and performances we believe can go on safely now because we've almost, but admittedly not quite completely, solved the business of the attacks on the arts community. In short, quality of life in Greensboro is well on the way to being great again.

"Why the urgency?" both Bob and Dylan wanted to know.

We didn't lie. We said, "You're just going to have to trust us on this."

We made no mention of Norman Shartly.

Of course, there were no changes to the nightlife, no new landscaping, no new Interstate leg, no new anything since Fostridge's previous visit a few months before, and we knew the attacks had probably only stopped temporarily. Nevertheless.

Fostridge had been hard to convince, but when Bob and

Dylan suggested they might also invite "Mr. Phillips," Fostridge's boss and Chairman of RayDact's so-far-unnamed parent company, to come along with him, he caved. He arrived by himself Friday evening in time for a cocktail party and dinner in his honor at the country club attended by about a dozen GADC dignitaries and their spouses who were hastily rounded up with a promise of free booze, free food, and an unexpected elbow-rubbing opportunity. Although not a dignitary, I put on my funeral suit and my own GADC hat and attended as well because I wanted to take the measure of Fostridge and because Blue wanted to hear my impressions of him.

A full slate of entertaining activities was organized for Saturday and Sunday before Fostridge was to return to Chicago early Monday morning. That would keep him occupied during the day, leaving him to be watched by us at night when theoretically he would be tired and let his guard down, if indeed he had his guard up in the first place. Other than to GADC members, Fostridge would be introduced as "a representative of an undisclosed big company that might be interested in moving to town." It was the same cover the GADC had used when Fostridge and his relocation team had visited on previous occasions. RayDact's secret identity would be protected.

After the dinner party, Vivaldi put Fostridge up in the "Impresario Suite" in the guesthouse next door to the Gate City Playhouse. That was Blue's idea ("make him feel extra important"), and we didn't tell Bob and Dylan the real reason, which was we could do a better job of keeping an eye on him there than if he were in a hotel. We figured if he and Norman Shartly were working together, they would likely make contact during the weekend. It would be Shartly coming to Fostridge rather than the other way around because Shartly wouldn't want Fostridge, or anyone, to know where he was staying. We wanted to be there for that meeting so Blue could nab Shartly and take Fostridge in for questioning as a Lucky Strike Extra.

That meant … a stakeout. And I meant to be in on it.

Which brought up the other issue we had pressured Bob Ausländer about. We wanted a Glowery truck for the stakeout.

"You're kidding, right?"

"No, I am not."

"You want to joyride around in one of my trucks?!"

"I promise you, no joyriding. Blue thinks he needs it, and again you just have to trust us that there's a good reason."

I couldn't tell Bob we were going to use it on a stakeout. A stakeout of Jerome Fostridge, Greensboro's high hope for a brighter economic future.

"I'm not sure our insurance would cover us if anything happened to a borrowed truck."

"Nothing will happen. Besides, you know Blue has the right to commandeer any vehicle for urgent police business, and that's what this is."

I wasn't entirely sure that was true, but it seemed to shift Bob's attitude.

"Can you even drive a truck?"

"Blue or one of his officers will drive it. I don't have a commercial license."

"All right," said Bob reluctantly, "I'll make a call and Blue can sign one out at the garage."

"You won't regret it."

"I'd darn well better not."

Chapter Fifty-Three

I was practically salivating at the prospect of going on a stakeout because I expected it to be like a "boys' night out" sort of thing, but Blue abused me of the notion quickly. The actual experience then finished the job of shattering my illusions.

I had pictured us, like on TV, partners with an unspoken mutual trust, as different from one another as night and day but like-minded and compatible, sharing quality time and bonding with sharp but good-natured ribbing over bitter coffee in paper cups and cheap but delicious burritos, or maybe donuts, wielding high-powered binoculars and a state-of-the-art digital camera with a telephoto lens while we awaited exciting action to take place right after the commercial break. The reality was that while Blue did have bitter coffee in a paper cup and a cheap, smelly but presumably delicious burrito, Emily had lovingly supplied me with a travel mug of lukewarm instant, not fuzzy, and three Nature Valley Chewy Peanut Butter and Dark Chocolate protein bars from Costco. No binoculars and no camera except on our iPhones. Although I trusted Blue, I doubted he trusted me. We weren't partners, and our like-mindedness extended only to solving The Cases, a fondness for Stamey's Barbecue, and a passionate disdain for stupid criminals. Plus, a shared inability to appreciate rap music, but that never came into play.

We were both awkward at making small talk, much less sharp but good-natured ribbing.

I had excused myself from dessert at the Fostridge dinner so I could get to the Glowery garage in time to join Blue when he signed out the service truck. This one was the *Titanic*. We had been sitting in the bright red and green truck with the smiling, larger-than-life caped G-Man on the sides since 8:30 p.m., having got into position in front of the guesthouse on Summit Avenue before Vivaldi brought Fostridge there after the dinner so as not to arouse Fostridge's suspicion by showing up after he arrived. Blue did a competent job of driving the unwieldy vehicle. It still handled like an elephant, but a sober one.

Vivaldi dropped Fostridge off at about 9:00 and neither man appeared to take notice of the truck.

It was now midnight. Three and a half hours of alternately sitting up or hunkering down in the uncomfortable front seats, wearing dark clothing and black ball caps with Atlanta Braves logos supplied by Blue, evidently a fan. My back was killing me. I wanted badly to fall asleep. Emily's coffee must have been decaf. Blue made it clear that if I needed to pee, I couldn't just waltz into the guesthouse and use the men's room in the foyer. There were two plastic bottles on the floorboards for that. One for him and one for me. His was still empty. Mine was already half full.

We weren't alone. Two uniformed police officers, Pirelli and Evers, occupied the cargo section, sitting on pails of industrial cleaner, dodging the hanging mops, brooms and other assorted disaster cleanup machines and tools and complaining of the smell. It hadn't occurred to me to ask the guys at the garage to empty the truck before we took it, although Blue told them to disable the interior lights, which they reluctantly did.

Each officer had an empty plastic bottle on the floor next to the remains of his own coffee and cheap but delicious burrito. I was glad Fostridge and Shartly were our quarry and not me because the two cops were in no mood to be trifled with.

Several cars had driven by, but none slowed and none looked suspicious. Our only excitement so far was when three teenage boys snuck up on the truck at about 11:00 and started letting air out of the tires. To say they were surprised to be confronted instantly by a couple of already disgruntled police officers with guns drawn would have been a gross understatement. They fled.

Other than that, it was boooring. I never want to do it again.

"Tell me again why we're in this truck instead of a nice comfortable car with plush, reclinable seats," I asked Blue at one point.

"I told you, Fostridge might be fooled, but a guy like Shartly would be able to spot an unmarked police car as quick as a regular one. On TV they always use a van made up to look like it belongs to the power company or something. Usually white, with bland markings. He'd be suspicious of that too."

"While something as outlandish as this wouldn't bother him?"

"You got it. And in Fostridge's case, even if he did ask about it, Vivaldi knows these are normally parked overnight all over town because they're like billboards for the company, and that's what he'd tell him."

We sat. And sat. I looked at my watch for the umpteenth time and saw 12:30 had come and gone. I yawned for the umpty-umpteenth time. The two cops in the back were snoring. My protein bars were gone, and I was hungry. Worst of all, there was no guarantee Shartly would show up.

"Speaking of Fostridge," said Blue, "what did you make of him?"

"Polite, well-versed in the social graces. Not cold, but not warm either. Almost but not quite aloof. I had the impression he didn't really want to be here but was just going through the motions as a courtesy to Bob Ausländer. Talked a lot about how much he likes Chicago, how things are done there, that sort of thing. Maybe a little disdainful of Greensboro."

"Did he ask about the troubles among the arts people?"

"No, and that was strange. Vivaldi brought it up a couple of times, but Fostridge didn't pursue it. You'd think it would be a top-of-mind issue for him."

"Fits your theory, don't it?"

"Yep."

"Get down. Something's happening," said Blue.

We hunkered. The cops in the back woke up. A small, gray car, lights out and almost invisible in the midnight darkness, drove by and slowed as it maneuvered around the *Titanic* and turned into the circular driveway of the guesthouse. It rolled up to the front door and stopped. The driver got out. A man of average height and weight, dressed in sneakers, jeans, and a dark sweatshirt but otherwise entirely nondescript except for a black ball cap with a Washington Nationals logo.

I thought I heard Blue say "Grrrr" when he saw the cap. Does anyone actually say "Grrrr"?

Cautioning me to stay put, Blue slowly got out of the truck. The two officers quietly exited from the rear, and all three took up strategic positions before the man noticed them.

"Norman Shartly?" said Blue sharply, his voice shattering the night stillness.

"No, I'm Namron Mannheim," the man said, startled.

"Yep, that makes you Norman Shartly all right."

"No, no, here, see? Take one of my cards."

"Hands where I can see them, sir. You're under arrest on one count of attempted murder and 34 counts of assault and battery. And that's just the stuff we know about. There will probably be more."

"I don't know what you're talking about."

"Of course you don't," said Blue. "Pirelli, cuff him, pat him down, read him his rights, and put him in the truck. Evers, run into the house there and ask Mr. Fostridge to come and join us. He's not under arrest, but make sure he's not carrying."

Pirelli and Evers did as they were told, and soon we had Shartly and Fostridge in the cargo section of the *Titanic* ready for a ride downtown. Both were already complaining about the smell, but Pirelli and Evers told them to shut up. Shartly was found to be carrying a Glock G44 .22 pistol without a concealed carry permit, so Blue added that charge to the 35 others.

At that hour, I would have expected to see Fostridge in pajamas, but he was fully dressed in the clothes he had worn to the dinner. It was clear he had been expecting his visitor.

Before we left, I excused myself and ducked inside the guesthouse to use the facilities. It took longer than normal, and Blue was tapping his fingers impatiently on the steering wheel when I returned, but he didn't say anything.

He started the truck and slowly pulled away from the curb. Very slowly. Too slowly. And stopped. And got out.

Three of the four tires were flat.

Chapter Fifty-Four

Saturday through Tuesday – Week 4 on The Case

It didn't take long for Officer Pirelli and Officer Evers to reinflate the tires using the electric pump we found in the back of the truck. That made me glad I had forgotten to ask the garage guys to take everything out.

Blue drove us to the police station where Shartly would be booked and Fostridge held for questioning. All the while, Shartly and Fostridge pretended they didn't know each other and had no idea what the fuss was about. Breaking my implied promise to Bob Ausländer, I drove the *Titanic* back to the Glowery garage where I would pick up my car and go home. The night shift garage guys were not happy about the coffee cups, burrito and protein bar wrappers, and other detritus they found and were especially offended by the three plastic bottles containing what might have passed for beer had it not been for the distinctive aroma.

"Stuff happens," I said, paraphrasing Bob's company strategy statement.

"Yeah, but not to us," they retorted.

I helped them clean things up.

A search of Norman Shartly's car and motel room turned up three of the weapon pens, over 300 rounds of .22 caliber ammunition, a suppressor for the Glock, several dozen fake business cards in various names including Namron Mannheim, 59 fake drivers licenses in as many different names, and enough paraphernalia to make a hundred disguises.

Ballistics testing confirmed it was his gun used in the phut-thunk attack on me. The names on the fake licenses matched those of the lone unidentified witnesses at each of the 34 relevant attack events.

Apparently realizing his goose was cooked, Shartly then claimed he had missed me on purpose so he would only scare me because I had identified him, that he had nothing against artsy people and no intention of actually harming anyone, and that the whole thing was Fostridge's idea. Lieutenant Blue at that point had no choice but to arrest Fostridge for conspiracy to commit all the crimes Shartly was charged with. Fostridge denied everything.

Shartly's traditional one phone call from the jail was to somebody he was overheard to call "Eddie." He pleaded with "Eddie." No Eddie ever showed up or tried to contact him.

At Shartly's arraignment on Monday morning, an attorney from the Public Defender's Office was appointed. The judge set bail at a million dollars, primarily because of the attempted murder charge and the flight risk and secondarily because messing around with the arts community offended the judge, whose wife is a leading patron of said arts. If memory serves, I had seen the couple at the GAA! Campaign kickoff at the country club.

From jail, Fostridge was overheard trying to phone his wife, but according to whoever answered in Chicago, she was apparently "out." Having failed in that attempt, he argued to the guards that he was entitled to a second, makeup, call. This was granted, and he was overheard calling someone named "Eddie." He pleaded with "Eddie." Neither Fostridge's wife nor anyone named Eddie ever showed up or tried to contact him. At his arraignment on Tuesday morning, a high-powered

Chicago lawyer appeared, but the same judge set bail at the same million dollars for the same reasons.

Needless to say, Fostridge's arrest caused no small commotion in the GADC and among those few other dignitaries who knew that Fostridge's RayDact Corporation was the big company from up north that was supposed to move to Greensboro. But no one else knew that. News reporters assigned to the courthouse knew only what had come out during the arraignments, which was limited to the charges against Fostridge and Shartly and included no revealing information about their victims or intended victims. The Police Public Information Office issued a brief statement acknowledging the charges and saying there would be no additional information released while the investigation was ongoing. Since this was no more than the media already knew, the reporters quickly became bored with the story and gave it only short and fleeting coverage. Fortunately for me, my name never made it into the news; so, again, Emily will not know I was the target of phut-thunk until she reads it here. Then she will probably shoot me herself.

Until Lieutenant Blue explained things to him in a conference room at Police Headquarters late Tuesday morning, Bob Ausländer wanted to blame me for destroying Greensboro's last best hope for economic development by fingering Fostridge for the attacks.

"Still," he said, now slightly mollified but ever the pragmatist, "three years of hard work and money down the drain. Plus, you made a mess of the *Titanic*."

"I did not. I helped clean it up."

"So you do admit it was a mess."

"Bob, you are conflating a current disappointing reversal of fortune which may still be salvageable with a maritime disaster that happened in 1912 and can't be."

"You're still a smartass, but I agree with the disaster part," he said.

Dylan Vivaldi was more forbearing and although he was still angry and frustrated by the unexpected turn of events, he wasn't jumping to conclusions.

"You're sure Shartly was working for Fostridge?" he asked.

"He claims he was, but Fostridge still denies even knowing him," I said.

"Let me hop in on that," said Blue. "Didn't have a chance to tell you before, Mr. Fairley, but I got the number from Mr. Ausländer and called Fostridge's office yesterday afternoon. Spoke to somebody named Susan and requested a list of Fostridge's visitors for the past month. It was a long list, but one name got my attention. It was Namron Mannheim."

"That's the same name Shartly tried to use the other night," I said.

"Bingo! They were working together all right. This Susan person also said when she went in Fostridge's office to remove an empty hot chocolate mug after Mannheim left, Fostridge was putting duct tape over something on his credenza. When he went to the men's room she snuck back in and lifted the tape. Said it looked to her like a bullet hole, but she hadn't heard any shots."

"You're kidding," I said. "Duct tape?"

Blue shrugged.

"So if the theory is that Fostridge hired Shartly to carry out these attacks and stage the accidents, my question is why," Vivaldi said.

"We don't know for sure yet whether he had anything to do with the accidents," I said, "but yours is still the right question."

"I hate to say it," said Ausländer, "but if the trouble in the arts community was the main reason RayDact was holding off on moving here, and the president of RayDact was behind the trouble, then it looks like he simply didn't want to move at all and was just stringing us along."

"Stringing somebody along, anyway," I said.

"But like I said, why?" said Vivaldi.

"Maybe he saw it as a comedown from Chicago," I ventured.

"No, I mean wouldn't he have realized sooner or later we would find a way to stop the trouble, and then what would he have for an excuse? Did he think he could keep it going forever?"

"Don't forget, he gave us 60 days to fix everything. So he had a failsafe deadline," said Ausländer.

"Oh, right. I did forget," said Vivaldi.

"You said something about this disaster being salvageable," said Bob, looking at me.

"Maybe I was just trying to find some encouraging words."

He scowled. I decided not to break into strains of "Home on the Range." I was discouraged about RayDact myself, but there was no need to wallow in it.

"But looking on the bright side," Vivaldi ventured, looking at both Blue and me, "it was good police work, and at least we can say the arts community is safe now that those two rapscallions have been put away, right laddies?"

"Um, well there is a little bit of a problem there," I said.

Bob continued to glare at me, and Dylan's face got as red as his beard. Blue jumped in quickly.

"It's like this, gentlemen. We have reason to believe Fostridge and Shartly weren't the only ones involved," he said.

"So now you're going to go on a fishing expedition so Fairley here can stretch out his time on the GADC payroll," said Bob.

"Hold on, Bobby," said Dylan. "Let's hear what the man has to say."

"Thank you," said Blue. "I know the fact we caught these two in only about three weeks since Mr. Fairley has been involved maybe makes it seem easy to you. And I know you want this to be over with. I do too because I like to solve crimes, and I'm getting a lot of heat from my boss, which means she and the chief have been getting it from the Mayor. So we're going to keep at it. But first I have to say, without Mr. Fairley it would have taken a lot longer, so you should be thanking him for the progress we've made so far."

"I'll thank him when we get some companies moving to Greensboro."

"That's our job, Bobby, not his," said Vivaldi.

"Why are you taking sides?"

"I'm not taking sides, boyo. I'm listening."

Without mentioning Charles Kelly or Lorna Gribble by name, Blue outlined our suspicions. He said we had two suspects but believed there was someone else in the shadows "pulling their strings like a ventriloquist." Bob and Dylan weren't happy, but there was nothing they could do about it except let us get on with our work.

"I hope you won't need to borrow another Glowery truck anytime soon," said Bob.

"I hope so too," I said.

"'Cause *Titanic* is my best truck. I use it to take my family camping at the lake. People see it and take off, so we have the lake to ourselves. They probably think the lake is polluted and we're there to clean it up, and I don't tell them any different. Next time, if there is a next time, I'll see you get *Chernobyl*. It's already a mess."

Chapter Fifty-Five

Vivaldi and Ausländer were two unhappy campers when they left at about noon. Bob went to deliver the bad news to the Mayor, which would mean still more heat on Blue. Dylan returned to a partially darkened Gate City Playhouse where C.B.D. Miller was gamely trying to keep the *Christmas O'Carolan Songbook* production alive by auditioning new actors and musicians to replace the ones who quit.

The warrant to monitor Lorna Gribble's and Charles Kelly's phone calls and get their records came through as Bob and Dylan were leaving, and Blue's tech team wasted no time getting over to the phone company. It would take them a while to go through the call records and set things up for monitoring, so Blue and I gobbled down vending machine sandwiches before walking to the Guilford County Detention Center where we had an appointment to interview Norman Shartly. There was no point interviewing Jerome Fostridge right away because he was still officially not talking.

We walked the two blocks from 100 Police Plaza at the corner of W. Market and S. Eugene Streets to the Detention Center on S. Edgeworth Street. It's a beautiful, relatively new five story building, and if it weren't for the police and Sherriff's cars parked out front and the weird-looking windows on each corner, you'd think you were approaching a hospital or a luxury hotel.

We entered and went through security where Blue turned over his service pistol and I surrendered the little red Swiss

Army knife I carry on my keychain (1½" steel blade, scissors, combination screwdriver and nail file, tweezers and plastic toothpick) and which, if I ever tried to hurt anybody with it, would likely cause more injury to me than to my victim. Thus safely disarmed, we were led to a bare, windowless room furnished with a steel table bolted to the floor and four steel chairs on two of which sat Norman Shartly in handcuffs and an orange jumpsuit and a pleasant looking young man in rumpled khakis and tan corduroy blazer with elbow patches with a scuffed briefcase who I presumed was Shartly's court-appointed lawyer. He stood, introduced himself as Derreck Respin, and handed us his Public Defender business cards before sitting back down next to his client. Blue and I sat across the table and took a long look at Shartly. It was the first time we'd seen him since the wee hours of Saturday morning. I wouldn't have recognized him; he was that nondescript. I wanted to say, "Are you sure you are Norman Shartly?" but I refrained. Blue wasn't so timid.

"You're sure you're Norman Shartly?" he said.

"I assure you, he is," said Respin.

"Hey, I'm right here," said Shartly, annoyed.

Lenny Monahan's standup jokes about detention centers popped into my head, making me wonder if Shartly had made any new friends in ours. Probably no making out though.

"Okay," said Blue, "well this ain't a formal interrogation or deposition. We just want to ask you a few questions to help us tie off a few loose ends." Blue took out a small notebook and a Gate City Playhouse Rocks pen.

"I'll be as cooperative as I can," said Shartly.

"My client will be as cooperative as he can," said Respin.

"I'm curious about why you're willing to be so cooperative," said Blue.

"You don't have to answer that," said Respin.

"It wasn't a question," said Blue. Although it was.

"Oh. Okay."

I had been wondering the same thing. My guess was Shartly figured he could make bail and then vanish again. In his line of work, I imagine he had a large nest egg built up. My question was why he hadn't bailed himself out already. Then I thought maybe it was because he'd had to come up with so many aliases he couldn't remember which ones he'd used to open his bank accounts and so couldn't readily access them. I decided not to bring that up just yet. Blue let it slide as well.

"Tell us about your relationship with Jerome Fostridge," said Blue.

"I advise you not to answer that," said Respin.

"It's a simple agent-client relationship. He needed a service performed; I performed it."

"Did he hire you directly, or was there a go-between?"

"I advise you not to answer that," said Respin.

"No go-between. My line of work, word gets around. Opportunities come my way."

"What about this 'Eddie' you called from the Detention Center?"

"I advise you not to answer that."

"Don't know any Eddie."

"What was this service you were providing?"

"I advise you not to answer that."

"Stir things up in the Greensboro arts community. Not kill anybody. Just make them sick, you know?"

"How?"

"I advise you not to answer that."

"Oh, shut up, Derreck! I know what I'm doing," said Shartly. "See, Fostridge gave me these fake pens that have some kind of ray gun inside. Just point it and press the trigger thingy and boom, the target goes down. Harder to aim than a rubber blunderbuss, but he didn't care so much about accuracy, only mayhem, which is what happened. It was fun for a while, but then it got boring."

"What's a blunderbuss?" said Blue.

"It's … never mind. Not important."

"I'll be the judge of that," said Blue. "How many pens did Fostridge give you?"

Respin started to speak, but Shartly held up a warning hand.

"Six."

"We only found three when we searched through your belongings."

"I lost three somewhere."

"You lost three?"

"Yep. No idea how. One day I had six and then all of a sudden I had three. But three was plenty. He gave me extra batteries too so it's not like I needed a big arsenal. Besides, I figured if somebody found the other three, they'd probably create more mayhem. In the Army we'd call that a force multiplier, so maybe losing them was a good thing. I think it was, in fact."

Blue made a note.

"Why did Fostridge want you to create mayhem?"

"His way of making it look like Greensboro was an unsafe place to move his company. So he wouldn't have to move. He hates Greensboro. And I can see why. Still, it's pretty stupid if you ask me. But, hey, I'm just the hired hand."

"You said it got boring after a while. Why?"

"You know, same thing over and over and over, day after day. All the disguises. The aliases. Hard to keep track. An endless stream of boring events with boring small talk, boring snacks, bad performers, bad art, bad everything. Boring. Tedious. Pain in the neck. Not my cup of tea. I'm all about one and done. One shot, that is. And then he wanted to increase the body count, so to speak. Wanted more for his money. I refused. We had a talk. Came to an understanding. I would continue, but no more moving the goalposts. All said and done, you know, your jail here is a welcome break from the crap I've been putting up with."

Blue offered me a turn at the questioning while he made some more notes.

"Did you really shoot Fostridge's credenza?" I asked.

"Bullet had to go somewhere."

"Were you trying to kill him?"

"Bite the hand that was feeding me?"

"Were you trying to kill me?"

"You'd be dead."

"Why come after me at all?"

"You made me. At the bookstore open mic thing. I couldn't have that. Needed to scare you away."

"How did you know who I was, that I was a threat?"

"That's a trade secret."

I suspected this Eddie person was involved somehow, but since Shartly was denying his existence I didn't think there was any point in pursuing that line of questioning just then.

"Mind if I ask you a question?" said Shartly. "How did you finally finger me?"

I looked at Blue. He nodded it was okay to answer.

"It took a while, but you made three mistakes that we know of. The police tracked 34 events and interviewed all the witnesses. At every event there was always one witness, and only one, whose identity turned out to be bogus. All the bogus witnesses had different names and different descriptions. That told us they were most likely all the same person, using aliases and disguises. It told us you existed, although we didn't know who you were yet. You should have used some of the same aliases and disguises more than once. We might never have noticed you."

Shartly was silent. I continued.

"Then we looked at the aliases you used. Almost all looked like they were probably some variation on your real name, or parts of it. Narcissistic, wouldn't you say?"

"But typical of a criminal," said Blue. "Talk about your 'criminal intelligence'!"

Shartly glared at him but said nothing.

I went on. "It didn't take long to narrow things down to a few names the computer could run through various databases until we came up with Norman Shartly. I must admit we did get a kick out of Northwood Shirttail."

Shartly snorted, glumly.

"Finally, that night at the open mic, not only did I find your name, Norbert Shostakovich, suspicious, I noticed your toupee was slipping."

"Yes, I admit I got sloppy. Too tired of the whole dumb routine, I guess."

"Let's circle behind to where you said it's good you lost the three pens," said Blue. "What did you mean by that?"

"I meant I think there's somebody else out there using those pens. I was working alone, or so Fostridge claimed, but more than once I'd get a bead on a target and before I could hit the trigger somebody in another part of the room would start gagging and fall over. It was eerie and I didn't like it, but it was helping Fostridge, so, okay. Too bad, gentlemen, but it looks like you still have some work to do."

"Why do you think this other person is doing that?"

"No clue, Mr. Blue, that's up to you. And, believe it or not, that's better than some of the so-called poetry I've been hearing around here."

"Thanks for the tipoff," said Blue. He wasn't about to tell

Shartly we already knew about the others. "One more question. Not to rub in it too much, but what do you think you'll do now that your hit man career is over? After you get out of prison, I mean."

"I advise you not to answer that," piped up Respin.

This time Shartly didn't.

Walking back to 100 Police Plaza, I asked Blue the same question.

"Nothing much else he knows how to do besides shoot people unless he learns another skill in prison. Like making license plates. Or becoming a lawyer. He's a one-horse pony."

Chapter Fifty-Six

Blue's two-person technical team were waiting for us in Blue's office. If you could call it an office. It was more like a closet in a row of several others like it built out from a windowless wall into a large open room full of desks and cubicles occupied by a dozen or more men and women, some in uniform and some in plain clothes, who were constantly coming and going, answering phones, hanging up phones, shouting to one another, ducking down so they couldn't be seen, popping back up, pounding on laptop computer keyboards, and drinking coffee. I didn't see any donuts, but it was afternoon so if there had been any they were long gone. Blue's office had a door with a large window so he could see what was going on in the big room and could be seen himself. Forget privacy.

There was a picture of the Governor on the back wall along with Blue's framed diplomas from UNC Greensboro and the Police Academy and a few photos of him with people who might have been his parents or his wife and children on what might have been a fishing trip. It was hard to tell. Another photo appeared to be Blue in uniform shaking hands with one of Greensboro's former mayors. There was a battered desk, an ancient wooden swivel chair, a desk lamp, a phone, a laptop, an empty coatrack, and two steel chairs like the ones at the Detention Center, all on a bare, painted concrete floor. It was light blue.

If there is a Lieutenant Green, does he have a green floor? Lieutenant Brown? What if your name isn't a color? Do you get to pick something meaningful, like red if you want to project a "don't mess with me; I'm dangerous" aura, or purple because you want to be thought of as royalty, or whatever is the predominant color in your family crest? But probably never yellow. Not in a police station. I'll never know, and I probably won't ask. However, I will say that no taxpayers' dollars were being wasted on luxury or frivolity here.

Blue grabbed another chair from an empty cubicle and carried it into his office. The four of us barely fit in the tiny space.

"What have you got?" said Blue.

"Not much," said the tech team leader, a thin, clean shaven young man whose name badge said Roger Wilkins. His assistant, a small pleasant looking woman named Madge Perkins who looked as if she'd graduated from high school only last week but probably had a master's degree from MIT, smiled and nodded in agreement.

"You can't have 'not much,'" said Blue.

"It's like this, Lieutenant. You think Kelly and Gribble are the ray gun shooters, but you don't know who they're taking orders from, right?"

"Right."

"Okay, well there are a lot of calls made by Kelly and Gribble to each other. So either they're an item or they're working together like you said, or both. Kelly calls his office a lot, and he gets other calls that look like they're from family members of people he's writing obituaries for. He made one call to his ex-wife. It was short. He calls his mother in Durham almost every day."

"A nice boy," said Blue. Madge nodded in agreement. Blue looked at her.

"Gribble gets calls from the school system," Wilkins continued, "probably about where to show up and teach when a regular teacher's out sick. She calls her mom occasionally too, usually late afternoon so maybe it's to tell her what time she'll be home. Both of them have the usual calls for doctor and hair appointments, pizza, and so forth. And that's it. Except for one thing."

"Except?"

"Except Kelly, and only Kelly, gets calls from burner phones."

"That's more than 'not much,' Roger," said Blue.

"Lots of robo-callers, telemarketers and scam artists are using burner phones these days, aren't they?" I interjected.

"Yes, sir, but so are more and more people with legitimate reasons. Say you want to use a dating service or sell or buy something on Craig's List but you want to be anonymous at first. A burner phone is good for that."

Madge nodded in agreement.

"I doubt Kelly is dating anybody but Gribble," said Blue, "although you never know. I doubt he's got anything to sell that he wants to keep secret unless it's the ray gun, and that don't seem likely. Everybody gets calls from telemarketers and bogus impersonators."

"But in Kelly's case it's lots of calls from the same three phones, sometimes multiple times a day. That's more persistent than most telemarketers, or scammers as the case may be. And he calls them back. Oh, and there was a lot of burner phone activity right after you brought Kelly in and then released him."

"You can trace the phones, can't you?"

"We can only tell you where they were purchased, but that's all."

"Well?"

"All three bought on the same day about two months ago from a Best Buy in Cincinnati."

"So maybe all bought by the same person?" I said.

"Be my guess," said Blue.

"And he's using all three because he thinks that will confuse us."

"Most likely."

"Are the phones still in Cincinnati?" I asked Wilkins.

"No, sir, they're here in Greensboro, but we can't give you a location except for which cell phone tower they usually ping off of. We could get closer if the phones were left on a lot, but they're always turned off unless they're in use."

Wilkins gave us the cell tower location. He said in an urban setting like Greensboro, the phones could be anywhere within about a two-mile radius of the tower. A lot of territory to cover. I didn't think we'd be going door to door. I said so. Madge nodded in agreement. Wilkins looked at her.

"Are you set up to monitor the calls from here on?" I asked.

"You bet. The equipment will record everything, including when the burner phones are in use. Madge or I will check on it every few hours, and the night shift team will do the same."

"Okay," said Blue. "Just let me know when there's traffic between Kelly and Gribble, or with the burners, or if anything new pops up."

"Roger that!" said Roger.

"Roger, did you just say 'roger'?" I said.

"A little tech humor, sir."

Madge … well, you know what Madge did.

Chapter Fifty-Seven

"In for a penny, in for a pound, if you'll excuse the English expression."

"Easy for you to say, Uncle. You're safely out of sight in your ivory tower, but I just got busted because they found my pen with my prints on it. Now, that Detective Blue is probably having me followed, and they're probably listening in on my calls."

"'Probably' being the operative word, lad, and I would agree, but you cannot be sure. And even if they have tapped your phone, mine are untraceable, so they will never know it is me you are talking to. Besides, they cannot prove a thing except you touched the pen, which you told them you did not know was a weapon and which, by the way, was rather dimwitted of you to lose."

"I didn't expect Miller to fall off the stage so dramatically. I didn't expect him to fall off at all, just throw up and fall down like all the others. But no. He's clutching his chest, moaning in agony, pointing and yelling about lights in the balcony. It startled me, and then I panicked and had to get away quick. My hands were sweaty, and the pens slipped out without my realizing it until I was in my car."

"Pens? Pens, plural?'

"Well, yeah, but the other one was an ordinary Playhouse pen, not the weapon."

"So now we are down to one weapon. I do not have another one to give you. You will have to share with Miss Gribble."

"Look, I don't want another pen, and I don't want to share with Lorna. I'm scared, and now she is too. We want out."

"You would abandon The Cause?"

"I love The Cause. You know I do. I just don't know if I'm ready to go to jail for it. And Lorna's basically just along for the ride. She's doing it for the excitement and because she likes me, but it's gotten too exciting even for her."

"Does she know about me?"

"No. She knows there's someone who gave us the pens, but she doesn't know it's you."

"Then get her pen back and let her go."

"Not that easy. She'll worry about me."

"Lie to her. Tell her you are getting out. Then keep up the good work."

"It's gotten too dangerous. Setting booby traps with sandbags, slashing tires, putting vegetable oil on staircases. It hasn't all been just 'point and shoot,' you know. Somebody could get hurt bad. Maybe killed."

"You write about death every day."

"Yeah, but I didn't cause any of it, and that's where this is headed."

"Now you are being as dramatic as you say Miller was."

"It was no fun cutting out letters from magazines and pasting them on that note either. And with gloves on. And then I had to shred the magazines, page by page, and put them in my neighbor's garbage can in the middle of the night. 'Stop the show or else'? C'mon, are we 6th graders? 'Or else' what?"

"Listen, my young lad. When you agreed to this, you were willing to face the consequences if it turned out badly. And may I remind you, consequences were much more dire for those involved in The Troubles. This is nothing compared to that."

"Maybe I'm not as Irish as I thought I was."

"You are Irish. You are my nephew. We are family. You cannot quit."

"Plus, it's getting too complicated. There's this guy, Mark Fairley. I think he's a ringer. Came out of nowhere and passes himself off as a GADC member trying to get to know the arts community so he can help promote it. The timing is too convenient. For all we know, he's a cop, and I think he knows too much."

"I agree. But you just let me worry about Mr. Fairley."

"What are you going to do, kill him?"

"You watch your tone with me, lad! I will have you know, finding those pens as I did was not mere serendipity. It was a sign from God. I had been searching for a means to reach our goal, and He provided."

"What do you mean, 'He provided'? You said you found those pens in the men's room at the Tanger Center."

"His ways are higher than our ways, Charles, and His thoughts higher than ours. He works in a mysterious way."

"I won't argue with that, Uncle. Not in your case anyway."

"There is no need for sarcasm. It doesn't become you. Besides, I risked my life discovering what the pens were."

"Oh, so God didn't tell you?"

"At first, I thought they were penlights, but they were too dim, so I replaced the batteries and tried them out again. Still dim, but I happened to point one of them at myself while testing it and suddenly I shoved the pen in my mouth, vomited and fell down. I had a headache for two days. I thought I would die. Was it the pen? I did not know. I pointed it at the stray cat who hangs around my back door, and it went crazy. Conniptions I think it is called. So you see, I have sacrificed as well. It has not been easy for me either, but I carry on. For Him, and for The Cause. As must you."

"I'm not sure how much you really need me and Lorna

anyway. Maybe you know, there is another shooter out there. More than once, I've aimed my pen at somebody but before I can shoot, somebody else collapses. Do you have another follower out there I don't know about?"

"Hmmm. Interesting. No, I did not know about that. I wonder if it is the person who lost the pens I found."

"Now that you mention it, it might be that guy who got arrested with his friend from Chicago. Weird name. Shortly, I think it was. Something like that. And Frostfridge. No, Fostridge."

"All the more need for you to continue your fine work, Nephew. If those two have been neutralized, then it is truly up to you, and you alone, to pick up the slack. For The Cause. For me. I am not as young as I used to be. I grow weary. It is up to you, the younger generation, to carry on. Steel yourself, lad! *Éirinn go Brách*, lad! *Éirinn go Brách*!"

"Let me think about it, Uncle. I promise I'll think about it."

"Aye, you do that, lad. You do that. Call me tomorrow."

"I will. Goodbye, Uncle."

"Until tomorrow."

"Nuts. *Éirinn go Break my Back* is more like it."

Chapter Fifty-Eight

Wednesday & Thursday

As expected, forensics turned up nothing on the "Stop the show or else" message. No fingerprints, no DNA, not even a watermark in the paper. The 17 letters were cut out of advertisements for well-known products and could have been from any of many popular magazines. By now, the sacrificial magazine or magazines had been recycled or were in the landfill, and no one was about to go looking for them. Still, we knew it had to be Charles Kelly or Lorna Gribble since Shartly and Fostridge were out of the way.

Because the burner phones were practically untraceable, we were getting nowhere with figuring out who was pulling Charles Kelly's strings. Lieutenant Blue didn't have the resources to put simultaneous 24-hour tails on Kelly, Gribble, and my favorite ringleader candidate, the self-proclaimed super-Irish Lenny Monahan. Though why Monahan would want to shut down the *Christmas O'Carolan Songbook* production was still a mystery.

How to flush out the kingpin, whoever it was, that was the question. We had no cause to question Monahan, and if he was the ringleader and we did question him about it, he would deny it and shut things down or keep lying low, and we'd get nowhere. Blue could bring Kelly back in and sweat him for a name, but, again, we had no good reason to do that and risk him lawyering up and claiming police harassment to the media.

I had an idea. It would still be police harassment, sort of, but it would be fun.

"Let's reply to Kelly's note," I said to Blue. We were breakfasting at the Panera on Lawndale again. We'd ordered and eaten without many words passing between us, and now we were at the finishing-up-with-lukewarm-coffee stage.

"You mean like write 'Return to sender' on it and leave it on some random doorstep and wait to see who picks it up?"

"Now you're joking," I said.

"Nah, I'm frustrated. Need to close this case once and for all."

"Copy that, as they say. As you say."

"I never say that. Anyway, what did you have in mind, Fairley?" At least he wasn't calling me Shylock or poetry boy anymore.

"Let's write a note of our own and leave it on Kelly's doorstep, then see what he does with it."

"Now *you're* joking, right? What, like 'Fess up, signed, The Police'? Oh, that'll work."

"No, I'd put a little more information in it—make him think we already know who his boss is and you'll go easier on him if he cooperates and gives him up."

"You gonna cut out the letters from a magazine?"

"Sure, why not?" I said.

"Waste of a good magazine."

"You really are in a mood this morning."

Blue stood up, stretched wearily, picked up our empty dishes and trash and took them to the dirty dish station by the exit. Returning, he shrugged as if to shed a burden from his shoulders and sat back down.

"Okay, I'll bite it," he said. "What's this note gonna say?"

Very early Thursday morning, Blue and I sat parked in his

personal car at a fire hydrant across from the door to Charles Kelly's Yanceyville Street apartment. It was another boring stakeout, but this one promised to be relatively short and without the drama involved in borrowing a Glowery truck. I had no interest in experiencing whatever delights *Chernobyl* had to offer anyway. Blue had what looked like a peanut butter and jelly sandwich on white and a large "bubba-size" travel mug, presumably full of coffee. Emily had fixed me her version of an Egg McMuffin, which was excellent, and supplied me with a normal-size travel mug of coffee. I made sure it was hi-test this time, not decaf.

I hadn't had to pee yet, but I did have a bottle. Blue didn't. I wondered briefly if his bubba mug might be capable of double duty but quickly dismissed the idea.

Not bothering with cut-out letters, I had handwritten a note for Kelly on a blank sheet from the legal pad in my Glowery executive leather portfolio and given it to Blue before we left Panera's. I used a Gate City Playhouse fountain pen, of course, not that Kelly would even notice, or care. Blue asked one of the uniformed patrol officers on the night shift to place it on Kelly's doorstep by 5:00 a.m. weighted down with a stone, and it looked like she had done so.

The note said, "Tell us who your boss is or else! Hey, hey!" and included Blue's cell phone number.

Blue thought it was stupid and didn't understand the "Hey, hey!" part until I explained it. He still thought it was stupid, but he went along. Time would tell, and what did we have to lose?

We hunkered down every time a car went by. Fortunately, there wasn't much traffic at that early hour even on Yanceyville Street, by day a busy thoroughfare, so the hunkering was short and not too frequent. Still, if you're not used to it ...

At exactly 7:46, Kelly appeared in the doorway. We

hunkered down again. He was tall and thin. Because of his occupation, you might expect me to say he was cadaverous, but he wasn't. He wore business casual—khaki slacks, sport coat, blue dress shirt, no tie, and black wingtips. Appropriate for dealing with the bereaved beneficiaries of his obituaries, apparently. He carried a briefcase in one hand, and with the other he held a cell phone to his right ear.

As he stepped on to the small front porch, Kelly tripped on the stone holding the note. He went down face first and hard, briefcase flying one way, cellphone another. (SPOW! Take that, Charles Kelly!) He didn't get up right away.

"Clumsy," said Blue.

"I think he hurt himself," I said.

"At least he didn't puke."

After another moment, Kelly sat up. He looked around as if to make sure no neighbors had witnessed his embarrassment, and then he slowly stood. He looked back at the porch, obviously in search of the offending impediment, and spotted the rock. It was, we had to admit, a big rock. Not what you'd call a boulder, but big. Much bigger than required for a simple paperweight. Maybe the zealous patrol officer figured Kelly might not see a smaller stone and would step right over it. She couldn't risk that. Dereliction of duty.

Limping slightly, Kelly retrieved the briefcase and phone and checked his clothing for rips and grass stains, tidying up the scene so everything would look normal. (I'm okay. Everything's fine. I fall down like this every morning. Nothing to see here.) Only then did he bend over and remove the note from under the rock. He read it. He looked around again as if to see if whoever left it was still in the area. He read the note again. We remained hunkered.

He pressed some buttons on his phone and held it to his ear, presumably completing the conversation that was interrupted by his stumble. That done, he pressed some more buttons and held the phone to his ear once more.

Blue's phone rang. He answered it.

"Lieutenant Marshall Blue, serving and protecting. How can I help you?"

"Okay, let's talk," said Kelly.

We unhunkered (dishunkered?) and got out of the car. Kelly didn't seem surprised to see us.

Chapter Fifty-Nine

"You want to go in your apartment, or would you rather sit in my back seat?" Blue asked after we had introduced ourselves, Blue as a police detective and me as a Concerned Citizen. Kelly seemed to know who I was already. "It's either that or we go downtown. Your choice."

"I knew it would come to this," said Kelly. "I guess I always knew it. Let's go inside, away from prying eyes."

I was a little stiff from all the hunkering, as was Blue, and Kelly was still limping a little, but we all managed to get inside the apartment without tripping on the rock.

"I'll call the office, tell them I'll be late," said Kelly.

"You do that," said Blue.

It was a tiny apartment with a living/dining room combination and a see-into kitchen on the first floor and stairs leading to the second floor where presumably a bedroom and bath resided. It was sparsely furnished and not at all like you'd imagine a man cave to be. (I had no expectations about what a bachelor obituary writer's apartment would look like.) A large flat-screen TV dominated one wall, directly opposite a leather reclining chair which looked slippery to me, so I wasn't about to sit in it.

In one corner was a stack of old copies of the *News and Record*, maybe the beginnings of a collection of Kelly's best obituaries that he would one day publish in a book, making him rich and famous (and not the first to do so—see the SPOW website). He could title it *Whistling Past the Cemetery:*

An Outsider's Hilarious but Compassionate Journey into the Shrouded World of Obituaries (Because All the Real Insiders are Dead). There are already two or three books titled *Whistling Past the Graveyard* on Amazon.com but *Whistling Past the Cemetery* is available. The cover might show tombstones with some of the most common obituary clichés engraved on them in a Gothic Font. Such as DIED DOING WHAT HE LOVED, HER SMILE LIT UP THE ROOM, LIVED LIFE TO THE FULLEST, CHOSE HIS OWN PATH, SORELY MISSED, AN INSPIRATION TO US ALL, or HAD A ZEST FOR LIFE.

Or if he wanted to include fake obituaries he made up for the book, the tombstone could say "Here, lies". If he is worried about alienating future *News & Record* obituary clients, he could publish under a pseudonym like Stoney Chiselle, Dearly Depardieu, Luv Dwan, or Lou O'Flowers. Of course, then he'd have to write a fake bio for the cover, but that would be fun too. Alas, I digress.

Framed still life prints on the walls and a decorative vase of starting-to-wilt flowers on the coffee table suggested a woman's touch, probably Lorna Gribble's.

Kelly sat in the recliner but did not recline, and I took the sofa, which wasn't leather and looked safe enough. Blue stood.

"Well, this is awkward," Kelly said to Blue when he had finished his call.

"For you maybe. Not for me. I'm a happy man. You read the note?"

"I read it. As a writer, I appreciated the irony, although I didn't quite get the 'Hey, hey!' reference. Were you mocking me?"

"Well, we're not sure anymore," I said, "but it looks like we're beyond that now."

"Right. You gentlemen want anything? Water, coffee?"

"No, I'm good," said Blue.

"Me too," I said. "Is your bathroom upstairs?"

"Yeah, feel free."

"Thanks, I'll wait a while." I didn't want to miss anything.

"You want to know who my boss is."

"We do," said Blue.

"What do I get in return?"

"A crystal-clear conscience is what."

"No, I mean is there a deal we can work out here?"

"Here's the deal," said Blue. "One, two, three, you tell us who your boss is, I pick him up, and you both go to jail. How do you like that? Oh, and you can give us Miss Gribble too."

"I want immunity."

"You want immunity, get a flu shot."

"Look, this is really hard. Isn't there anything you can do?"

"Mr. Kelly, it's not my call. You cooperate and this goes down the way I hope it will, I'll put in a good word for you with the DA, but that's the best I can do. Okay? Now spill."

"It's my uncle. He's the one you want."

"What's his name?"

"See, that's just it. It's family. I can't be the one to give him up. I'd be the black sheep forever. He has to do it himself."

"He wants to give himself up? Turn himself in?"

"All I know is I can't, I won't, tell you who he is. Even if you throw out some names just to see if I'll react, I won't. Even if you take me to jail. Anyway, he's technically not really my uncle, just a very close friend of the family, and I've called him Uncle all my life. But I think he might be ready to meet with you. With you both, actually."

Blue and I looked at each other incredulously. I shrugged as if to say, "Don't look at me; I'm just the Concerned Citizen here."

"I'm supposed to believe that?" said Blue.

"Honestly, I think he's tired. I worry about him. He thinks

God told him to do all this. I know God works in mysterious ways, but this doesn't seem right. I told him I want out."

"You would set this meeting up?"

"Of course."

"Okay, I'll give it a shot in the arm. Meanwhile, we're still going downtown. And I'll send somebody to pick up Miss Gribble."

"No, please, leave her out of this."

"She's just as guilty as you are. Multiple counts of assault with a potentially deadly weapon. Premeditated. Maybe sabotage. She's going down."

"No, no. Look, here's her pen."

Kelly opened a small drawer in the coffee table. Blue assumed a ready-for-anything-he-might-pull-a-gun stance, but Kelly merely rummaged through an assortment of Gate City Playhouse pens until he found the one he was looking for and handed it butt first to Blue. Blue produced an evidence bag, placed the pen in it, and zipped it closed. Then he wrote something on it with a Sharpie.

"You already got mine. That one is hers, but I've wiped her prints and handled it myself, and I'll testify it's mine too. Now she's in the clear. All you've got on her is hearsay or circumstantial."

"We'll see about that. Time to go. Turn around please."

Blue handcuffed Kelly and read him his rights, and we headed out to the car, locking the apartment behind us and once again avoiding the rock on the porch.

There was a ticket on the windshield. Parking by a fire hydrant. Blue looked disgustedly to see which officer's signature was on it. The overzealous Officer Big Rock had struck again.

Chapter Sixty

Friday

You know how in every scary movie or TV crime show whenever there is a closeup of a character it means he or she is about to be (a) hit over the head, (b) grabbed from behind and dragged away, (c) strangled, or (d) given a good noogie. Well, maybe not so much option d. But this is a book. There are no closeups. So I will describe to you yet another tried and true cinematic device, but one that doesn't require a closeup. This is the one where the character gets into his or her car. Through the windshield we see the character's face as he or she goes to start the engine, and we know for certain that (a) the car will explode, (b) the villain will suddenly pop up in the back seat with a gun and a menacing remark, or (c) the character's cell phone will go off and it will be his or her mother asking some inane question at a most inopportune time. Let us consider option b for a moment. Because that is what happened to me on Friday morning.

After accompanying Blue and Kelly to Police Headquarters and waiting as Kelly made a call to his mystery "uncle" to set up a meeting with us, I had gone home for a restful rest of Thursday and some well-deserved, I thought, domestic tranquility. Roger Wilkins from Blue's tech team had dutifully reported that Kelly's call had gone to one of the burner phones, but they still couldn't trace it beyond the nearest cell tower. Madge had dutifully nodded in agreement.

Nevertheless, The Cases were well on their way to being solved. In fact, one of them had already been, and seemingly only one more step remained in solving the other one now that we had Kelly's cooperation. So I took a break.

Emily and I had leftover spaghetti for lunch. I skimmed the newspaper, skipping the obituaries, and leafed through a couple of magazines, *National Geographic* and *Smithsonian*, both of whose subscriptions would expire soon and would not be renewed unless I found a job. I read them scissorsless and with no intention of cutting out any letters. I updated my expense report and painfully paid a few bills. I sent out no new résumés, and I gave scant thought to my upcoming second appearance in Charlotte. That evening we dined at Lucky 32 ("Earnest Food and Hospitality in an Upscale Joint") using one of the $10-off coupons they mail out every month or so.

And so it was that after a good night's sleep and a light breakfast of orange juice and yogurt with Grape Nuts, topped off with a mug of hot fuzzy coffee and a warm kiss from Emily, the last thing I expected as I prepared to back out of my garage to head off to the pre-arranged rendezvous with Marshall Blue and the mystery uncle was someone in a ski mask suddenly popping up in my back seat with a gun and a menacing remark. The menacing remark was, "I have a gun. Be quiet and do not turn around."

I don't know what would go through your mind if this happened to you, but I can tell you what went through mine. A million thoughts, in rapid succession and not in alphabetical order: What the …?!! I'm going to die! I'm too young to die. I'll be late for my meeting. Who is this person? What will I tell Emily? At least I won't have to do my taxes this year. Death and taxes. Hmm, I'm getting low on gas. Where is Blue when I need him? I'm going to die! I'm too young to die. Will it hurt? Is that a spider on the windshield? Emily will have to do our taxes. She's going to kill me. No, this guy is going to kill me. Somebody's going to kill me. Why isn't my whole life flashing before my eyes? Oh, wait. It is. Gee, I don't remember *that*. I wish I'd gone to church more. I hope this isn't another of God's mysterious ways. What do I do now? What if I mash the accelerator and crash us into the back of the garage? No, that's stupid. What if I back out real fast and when he's thrown to the front I grab the gun and turn it on him? No, that's stupid. I'm going to die! I'm too young. I may need to change my underwear. What will Emily say?

I'll never know why I did it, but I blurted, "How do I know you have a gun?"

Backseat Man reached forward and displayed a revolver. It looked real, although it had a lot of filigree on the barrel and the handle grips look plastic and discolored, as if with age.

"It shoots too. Want to hear it?"

"No, thanks."

"Then shut up, slowly back out of the garage, and when you get to the street turn right and keep driving. Do not speed or do anything to attract attention."

"Whatever you say."

I drove.

"Left on Constitution, left on Bessemer, and right on Summit. Got that?"

Something about that voice. I'd heard it before.

"Hey, hey, how do I know that's a real gun?" I ventured.

No response. Cagey.

"It's not a real gun, is it?"

"Listen, it's old and I haven't used it in a long time, and I am nervous, as you can probably understand, so anything could happen. Do not push me. Keep driving."

I still couldn't place the voice.

"I'm supposed to be meeting someone, maybe you in fact,

now that I think about it, behind the library on Benjamin Boulevard. We are not headed toward the library."

"Change of plan."

"My arms are getting tired," I said.

Silence. But I figured at least he wouldn't shoot me while I was driving. I was banking on him being rational and not completely deranged.

I turned left on Bessemer, then right on Summit. It appeared we were headed for the Gate City Playhouse. Sure enough, as we passed the guesthouse and approached the Playhouse parking lot, Backseat Man said, "Turn in here." I did.

"Park by the back door. Get out of the car slowly and walk inside. I will be right behind you. With my gun."

We entered the Playhouse, walked around to the lobby, and took the elevator up to the reception area where Backseat Man, who I'll now start calling Ski Mask because he was no longer in my back seat, pointed the gun at Marcy Melnick and invited her to join us as we went back down in the elevator and made our way backstage. It was early and Marcy was apparently the only one in the building.

"Where's Vivaldi?" demanded Ski Mask.

"I d-don't know," said Marcy. "Maybe at the Komedy Klub. He had a m-meeting scheduled."

"Call him. Get him here, quickly."

"I left my phone upstairs."

"Use his," Ski Mask said, pointing the gun at me.

She did.

"Now you," Ski Mask said to me, "call that detective and tell him the meeting is here and he had better come now or else. And no weapons!"

I did.

"Now, both of you, get some of those folding chairs and

arrange them in a semi-circle, facing me. We are going to have a little show."

We arranged the chairs. I should have used the occasion as an opportunity to observe Ski Mask's clothing and mannerisms in an effort to identify him, but, frankly, all I could focus on was the mask. And the gun.

Then we waited, seated, while Ski Mask paced, at one point putting the gun in his pocket, which made Marcy and me feel relieved, but then he thought better of it and took it out again. At least he wasn't pointing it at us now. Eventually— it could have been five minutes or an hour, I don't know—Blue arrived. He had Charles Kelly with him and a uniformed police officer to guard him. It was Officer Pirelli. Not Officer Big Rock. Pirelli's holster was empty, and I didn't see the telltale bulge in his jacket where I knew Blue usually carried his service pistol. At a gesture from Ski Mask, they all sat.

"Hello, Charles," said Ski Mask.

"Hello, Uncle," said Kelly, still not giving him away.

Vivaldi walked in about a minute later. He saw Ski Mask's gun and stopped.

"Are you okay, Marcy?"

"Y-yes, sir."

Just then Cecil B. D. Miller appeared with his safari jacket, red scarf and riding boots and a "What's going on in my theater?" expression, still favoring the right leg. I suspected he was using the limp for dramatic effect at this point. Ski Mask motioned for him and Vivaldi to sit with the rest of us. They did.

All we needed now was Bob Ausländer. No, actually, I thought, he would only try to take charge, and we would probably all die. Taking charge was Blue's job, and I was sure he was thinking about it even though he was without his gun. Cops always carry backup guns, don't they? I hoped Blue did. And maybe Pirelli too. I hoped Ski Mask didn't know that.

"Police always carry backup guns, do they not?" said Ski Mask. "Let me see them, now, or the lady will be our first casualty of the day."

Blue and Pirelli complied, each laying a small pistol on the floor and kicking it toward Ski Mask. Blue's face was a mask itself, betraying no emotion. No smile, no frown, no sign of anger or concern. Maybe the best poker face I'd ever seen. Pirelli was clearly angry, as was Miller. Vivaldi looked confused but composed. Marcy had shrunk to approximately two-thirds her normal size.

"Thank you," said Ski Mask.

Ski Mask picked up the two pistols, looked at each, and pocketed the smaller of the two along with his own revolver. That told me his own gun was in fact most likely a fake, a toy. If only I had known. Of course, it also meant he now held a real gun on us, Blue's I think, and was probably even more nervous about it.

Even though he apparently no longer had a weapon, Blue's presence must have helped restore my confidence a little.

I said, "Is this the part where you say, 'I suppose you're all wondering why I called this meeting'?"

"I have told you to shut up," he said. "Now do so!"

"Or else?"

Marcy looked daggers at me, horrified. Blue smiled. Ski Mask raised Blue's gun in frustration and waved it around, and I thought he was at least going to fire a warning shot, which no doubt would have enraged Miller to the point of some sort of inappropriate violent reaction. Or the bullet would sever a rope and a sandbag would come down, which would startle Ski Mask into firing wildly at random. Or both. But he calmed himself and continued, lowering the gun.

"All right. Let us all stay calm. This will not take long, and no one will get hurt, unless Mr. Fairley persists in his impudence."

I hadn't been called impudent since I was 12. It brought back memories.

"Let me start by saying this meeting is long overdue," said Ski Mask.

"Is that why it was originally supposed to be at the library?" I said.

Blue snickered. Marcy shrank some more. This time, Ski Mask seemingly ignored the remark.

"My message is simple: This travesty of a musical comedy production, this most foul *Christmas O'Carolan Songbook, Volume 1*, must shut down immediately!"

Of course, Blue and I had figured out that was the motive for the mayhem of the past several weeks, but the question was still, Why?

"'Why?' you might ask. 'Why?' I will tell you why. I represent a proud people. A people with a rich cultural heritage that has in turn enriched the world with music, literature, theater, exquisite cuisine, and, yes, fine Irish whiskey, to name only a few blessings. Did you know, Henry Ford was the son of an Irish immigrant? Harry Ferguson from Northern Ireland invented the modern tractor. So also did Irishmen invent color photography, the nickel/zinc battery, the tank, the monorail, and milk chocolate. And yes, even the modern submarine, at the request of Winston Churchill during World War I. Ernest Thomas Sinton Walton, a physicist from Dungarvan, County Waterford, won a Nobel Prize and became the first person to artificially split the atom. You did not know that, did you now?"

"Boring," I said, although it was actually interesting. He ignored me again, but I could tell it took some effort.

"No, I doubt you knew. You people think of the Irish only in terms of shamrocks and leprechauns and potatoes and whiskey and drunken carousing day in and day out by a bunch of ne'er-do-wells with peculiar accents who are sad all the time, never happy unless they are inebriated. You make fun of the tragic history of her people, her heroic survival of the Potato Famine, her bloody sacrifices to drive the English oppressors from the land, her plight during The Troubles.

"And that brings me to The Gate City Playhouse, an institution that once was, and can be again, a proud bastion of the arts in Greensboro. But today it is the belly of the beast itself. We Irish revere Turlough O'Carolan, the legendary blind harpist of Ireland, but here you have cast him as an adulterous buffoon and endowed him with a fictional illegitimate son whom you have cast as a fool, a clown.

"Dylan Vivaldi, you should be ashamed of yourself! I have warned you three times, and now, unfortunately, it has come to this."

I said, "Who is going to take seriously a note that says, 'Stop the show or else'? Are we in the 6th grade?"

Out of the corner of my eye, I noticed Blue carefully easing his hand into his jacket. Slowly, very slowly, he withdrew his hand and in it was a Gate City Playhouse Rocks pen.

"The notes were not meant for you, Mr. Fairley," said Ski Mask. "Dylan understood them, I'm sure. But no, 'The show must go on!' Isn't that right, Dylan? Isn't that right, Mr. Cecil B. D. Miller? No matter how insulting, how disrespectful to the Irish and our fine heritage and all we stand for even today."

What was Blue waiting for? Shoot! Shoot!

"But it got rave reviews in Roanoke and Cincinnati," piped up Vivaldi.

"In Roanoke and Cincinnati, they are cretins. I was in Cincinnati and saw the show, hoping for an uplifting evening. I was disappointed to say the least."

"But we think it's brilliant. We chose it to honor the Irish, not to disparage them. And after all, I'm half Irish myself."

"Yes, but half Italian, Dylan, and that is only the beginning of the hypocrisy."

"What hypocrisy?" Vivaldi sputtered.

Now I wanted Blue to hold off a little longer so we could hear the answer. I also wondered why nobody had come into the Playhouse yet and stumbled upon our little tableau. Where were the actors and musicians for the day's rehearsal that must surely have been scheduled to start by now?

"What hypocrisy indeed!" bellowed Ski Mask. "I'll tell you what hypocrisy. First, this play, supposedly about the Irish, was written by Foster Wood, an Englishman. What an insult. And that is only the beginning. The director, your Mr. Miller here, is English."

"I am not!" cried Miller, rising and stamping his riding booted right foot repeatedly. (I was right about the limp.)

"Take it easy, Cecil," said Vivaldi. "Let him finish."

"Thank you, Dylan. According to my nephew Charles, you have cast one Nigel Williams, indisputably an Englishman, in a key role impersonating an Irish character. And he is not the only non-Irish person in the cast.

"The central comedic device, the so-called blindharp, is Italian.

"The very name of *Christmas* O'Carolan desecrates a sacred event. It is sacrilegious, not funny. The premise is absurd. The music is amateurish and not representative of the quality of original O'Carolan works. The lyrics are silly and disrespectful. You have cast any shred of authenticity to the four winds. It is a shameless parody, an abomination both to the Irish and to God Himself!"

"I grant you it is parody," said Vivaldi, "and meant to be funny. But also to honor its subject. If we Irish, or even half Irish, or any other national or ethnic group, cannot make fun of ourselves, what's to become of us all?"

"Yes," said Miller, "lighten up, sir. Lighten up."

Kelly sat with his face buried in his hands and appeared to be sobbing.

Now I was again eager for Blue to strike. Ski Mask continued his rant.

"And maybe worst of all, worst of all, there is a black man in the band. There were no black people in Ireland until late in the 18th Century."

"Who are you?" asked Vivaldi. "What do you want from us? You can't keep us here forever."

"I have no such intention. And I confess I have grown weary of the struggle. All I want, Dylan, is your simple promise as a gentleman to close down this insulting farce. Once you have stopped the rehearsals and announced that the show will not open, I will reveal my identity and turn myself in. I am …"

Blue finally aimed the Playhouse pen and pressed the clip. Ski Mask stopped in mid-sentence, a look of astonishment on his face. Then he stuck his gun in his mouth. Was it part of the typical vomit-and-fall-down sequence or he was going to shoot himself? Blue rushed forward, followed closely by Officer Pirelli. Before they could get to him and just as he was beginning the vomiting part, apparently not intending to shoot himself after all, a sandbag dropped from the rafters and slammed him to the floor, unconscious, the pistol and his breakfast flying.

Marcy screamed.

Kelly yelled, "Uncle!"

Blue yanked off the ski mask and stepped back.

There before us was Brian Gulliver, esteemed executive director of the Edmund and Chloe Fitzgerald Memorial Family Foundation.[9]

---

[9] (And Storm Door Co.)

Chapter Sixty-One

"Obviously nutty as a fruit, that's all I can say," said Detective Blue.

The EMTs had taken Gulliver to the hospital after Officer Pirelli relieved him of Blue's and Pirelli's pistols, his own vintage nickel-plated Gene Autry .44 cap gun, and a burner phone and after he woke up long enough to say, "This is not over," before collapsing again. Pirelli had taken Charles Kelly back to jail. The Playhouse backstage crew had arrived and were cleaning up the mess under Cecil B. D. Miller's close supervision. Marcy Melnick had run to the ladies' restroom to "fix her mascara" and was presumably back at her desk upstairs. I had checked myself carefully and found I didn't need the men's room just yet. Blue, the only-half-Irish Dylan Vivaldi, and I were doing sort of a post-game wrap-up, being careful not to stand under any sandbags.

"I don't get it," said Vivaldi. "He must have cracked, all right, but how much pressure could there be in a job managing millions of dollars in the name of a long-dead family, with nobody looking over your shoulder, spreading joy with every grant or donation?"

"I've seen it before," said Blue. "Most likely, his whole identity was wrapped up in the job. It gave him status in the community. He probably had nothing else but that and his Irishness. But he'd built himself a house of cards without a deck."

"Maybe you're right," said Vivaldi, ignoring the off-center

metaphor. I actually thought it was a good one, for Blue, and shrugged off the need to add "So to speak."

"He and Moira have no children," Vivaldi went on, "and it's well-known their marriage is shaky. I guess he'd built up the importance of defending Irish authenticity for the dead Fitzgeralds to the point where anything challenging it was a personal threat, and *The Christmas O'Carolan Songbook* pushed him over the edge. Too bad he couldn't see how respectful we're trying to be, even while poking fun."

"I have to admit, all along I thought it was Lenny Monahan," I said. "All that talk about being super-Irish."

"Aye, old Lenny was a big talker and all, but that's all it ever was. Big talk, little action. Anyway, he wrapped up his contract at the Komedy Klub last night, and today he's flying off to Pittsburgh."

"I hope his arms don't get too tired," I said.

Blue looked at me. Vivaldi laughed.

"Well, anyway, looks like you saved the day, Lieutenant Blue," I said, bowing toward him in mock obeisance. "Good thing you remembered to bring one of those pens."

"I just figured if anything went wrong I'd need a backup for my backup. Had to get this one out of the Evidence Locker. It's the one we found in the balcony."

"Obviously, you knew something was wrong when I called to change the meeting place."

"Didn't surprise me. I had some of my people lined up, just in case, and by the time Miller walked in, I had the place surrounded. Gulliver wouldn't have made it out the door."

"So that's why the actors and crew never showed up to interrupt the meeting."

"They were cooling their shoes in the parking lot. Not too happy about it either."

"The sandbag was a surprise."

"Yeah, somebody must have come back and rigged it after my guy inspected the ropes the last time."

"One thing still bothers me, lads," said Vivaldi. "Gulliver's last words were, 'This isn't over.' What do you suppose that means?"

"Probably an empty threat," said Blue, "but we'll do a thorough bomb and booby trap search this afternoon."

"Well, I want to thank both of you," Vivaldi said. "I confess I didn't have much faith in the idea of putting an outsider like Mark here on the case, but it's worked out well for sure. I guess we have you to thank for that, Lieutenant."

"Just doing my job," said Blue. "Sure beats collaring ticket scalpers."

"Bobby Ausländer will be pleased. I'll call him when we're done here."

"The chief and the Mayor will be off my back, too," said Blue.

"Aye, and it'll be grand to see things getting back to normal," added Vivaldi.

Chapter Sixty-Two

It is taking a while to get completely back to normal, but still it was a mostly happy ending for all, except for Norman Shartly, Jerome Fostridge, Brian Gulliver, Charles Kelly and Lorna Gribble. Gribble was brought in for questioning but due to a lack of evidence was never charged, so I guess that's semi-happy. Even so, she lost her boyfriend, at least temporarily, and her substitute teacher job. Now she volunteers at the downtown Green Hill Art Center coaching children in watercolors, and her mother has had to go back to work to support both of them. She's a weapons instructor at a local firing range. Go figure.

The others have joined the convicted felons community, serving sentences of various lengths depending on their crimes, Shartly the longest (apparently having been unable to access his nest egg so he could make bail and disappear), followed closely by Fostridge but in a federal facility, and Kelly the shortest.

In Kelly's absence, I understand the unwritten obituaries are piling up at the *News & Record*. Apparently, they don't have a succession plan in that department. At first, they assigned it to an intern who was oblivious to the nuances of the art ("Blanche Fraser, 92, died, but she was old anyway. Her husband, Ralph, and their two children, Amelia Draper and Geraldine Smith, along with six grandchildren and eight great grandchildren, were very sorry to hear it. She was cremated."). Then they gave a couple of their sports writers temporary double duty ("After a good run around the bases of life, Ronald Johnson, 74, slid home peacefully yesterday. He was cremated." "It was fourth down and 20 for Jeffrey Owens last week in his longtime fight with a pancreatic hernia, but a last-minute Hail Mary medical field goal by his spirited healthcare team scored him an extra three days, throwing his game into an overtime which lasted until Thursday. He outlived his twin brother Samuel by two years, making it Jeffrey 67, Samuel 65. He was cremated."). So far, they haven't pressed their humor columnist into service ("Gladys Wentworth, 55, died of a failed Heimlich Maneuver on Saturday. She was well liked by everyone except those who knew her. She was cremated.").

I'm sure they'll figure something out soon.

Brian Gulliver was deemed competent to stand trial, but he is serving his sentence in a residential mental facility. His wife, Moira, is the *de facto* executive director of the Fitzgerald Foundation and is in the process of dissolving it.

Magnanimously, she is using some of the money to set up a fund for reparations to VAFD victims who choose not to sue anyone. And the lawsuits are flying like bats from a cave at dusk. Or as Marshall Blue might say, like moths to a sweater. They are wasting their time and their legal fees. No one will ever find Shartly's money. Apparently, he can't even find it himself. Fostridge long ago put all his assets in his wife's name, and she is divorcing him. Kelly is poor as a church mouse. Gulliver's personal assets are bullet proof because of his mental state. Moira's reparations fund is their best bet. Maybe Kelly will benefit as Gulliver's pseudo-nephew and possible heir.

As soon as it was all over, Bob Ausländer formally terminated my temporary employment with GADC. He did it late on a Friday afternoon, in an email.

For a while, I was still undeservedly in the doghouse with Bob because of the loss of RayDact. There would be no bonus check. Then, to the unspeakable delight of Bob, Dylan Vivaldi, the Mayor, the City Council, the Greensboro Area Development Commission, and the Governor, "Mr. Phillips" came to town and announced that RayDact Corporation and its new president, a woman named Edith Dremel, would indeed be relocating to Greensboro after all. (I haven't met Ms. Dremel yet, but when I do I will ask her if she needs a strategic planning person.) After that, Bob did grudgingly give me a nice bonus, much to my and Emily's delight. I hope it is enough to lessen her ire when she reads this book and discovers the full extent of the perils I faced, though never on purpose.

The police have yet to identify "Eddie" or determine his exact relationship to Shartly and Fostridge. I have my suspicions and have related them to Marshall Blue, but he says I have been reading too many detective novels. He says that a lot. I don't think he means it. He also claims he knows what a blunderbuss is but just asked the question because he wanted to keep Shartly off balance. I believe him.

Blue said he might buy a copy of my book, *The Accidental Spurrt*. Maybe he was hinting I should give him a copy. I think I will. I double checked and confirmed I did spell his name right.

A full schedule of arts events has resumed in Greensboro. It's a happy community, if still just as fragmented, or amorphous, as before. The GAA! Campaign was a success. Frances Muldoon and everyone in Donna Majors' pod at Upshot Marketing are happy as … as, uh, clams, I guess, although those aren't found in pods. A bed of clams? That's the correct name, but I doubt they're going to change the name of their work area to Donna Majors' Bed.

A *shellf* of clams?

Betty Wright-Moore, fully recovered from her VAFD

ordeal, is still firmly holding the reins at Writer's Block and is back to, you know, writing more.

The Framery reopened with an exhibit called "Swallows," featuring local artists' interpretations of the VAFD events, rendered in a variety of mediums. Emily likes the impressionistic watercolor of a mustachioed man in a suit and bow tie pointing a long, green, nib-less fountain pen at a young girl who sticks a flower into the barrel. My favorite is a large canvas depicting countless bloated green pens coming from a point of indeterminate origin as from an aerial fountain and descending on different parts of the city like missiles, starting fires wherever they impact.

A fountain of pens? Why not? If we can have group names for animals, why not for inanimate objects? A sharpening of pencils. A luxury of sedans. A raging of debates. A ringing out of shots. A garbage of dumpsters. A dumpster of garbages. A plethora of haikus. A confusion of communities. A mixture of metaphors. And of course, although normally they are not inanimate objects, a sleuth of detectives.

But I digress.

Other venues are buzzing with activity too, including open mics, various writing critique groups, book signings, concerts both indoors and out, dance recitals, craft festivals, and pottery demonstrations, just to name a few, and of course, birdwatching.

I returned once to the Rhyme 'n' Time Again poetry critique group at the library, and Ryman Stanza and the others welcomed me warmly, Betty Wright-Moore having told them of my role in the crime-solving process. They forgave me for being an imposter, which I gathered is not quite so serious as being a plagiarist. It was like a class reunion of sorts. I shared my backup set of haikus, which they said were "unique." That's good enough for me.

The Xomedy Xlub brought The Spectacular Morrie Milburne back for an encore performance week. Lenny Monahan was also invited, but he declined, pleading health reasons. Maybe he sold out of T-shirts. Or maybe his arms were too tired to make the trip. I still don't fully trust him.

The Christmas O'Carolan Songbook, Volume 1, opened at the Gate City Playhouse three weeks after Brian Gulliver's arrest and got great reviews. Emily and I were treated to complimentary front row seats on opening night plus free wine for her and Guinness for me during the intermission, courtesy of Dylan Vivaldi. No one was VAFDed, and no sandbags fell. The first 100 ticket holders were given small Pewter Potatoes to commemorate the event. Ours are displayed on our mantel.

I never got around to suggesting to Vivaldi that he sell actual genuine Gate City Playhouse rocks in the lobby. Probably just as well. On the other hand, at my urging he did have a bunch of souvenir miniature blindharps made up for sale as potato slicers. I didn't get a cut, so to speak.

The news media did finally get hold of the story. Every fact they reported was wrong.

Sheriff Belton called from Spurrville to congratulate me, as did Fanny Spurr herself and Detective Jake Keil from Raleigh. "I read about it in the papers," Keil said. "At first, I didn't know who Markell Farley was, but I finally figured it out."

The Spurr Nutritionals initial public offering has been delayed, so my stock is still worth practically nothing. Nevertheless, I splurged and got another haircut.

I have yet to hear from the estimable Frank Sheldon, Esq., my erstwhile attorney, but I expect he will call any day now.

One weekday at lunchtime, Emily and I went back to the McDonald's at Westridge and Battleground to see how

Sharon/Evelyn/Eileen/Maw-maw was doing. That day her name was Frederica, and she was happy to see us. As soon as we sat down with our food she launched into a new (to us anyway) story about her exploits in the French Resistance during WWII and a kiss she received from Winston Churchill on Paris Liberation Day. I think she should try standup comedy. Or in her case, sit-on-a-stool comedy if that would be more comfortable. Maybe her great grandson, Lester, could at least sign her up for an open mic at the Read-A-Spell before her wonderful imaginary historical insights are lost forever.

I did travel to Charlotte for my second interview. I did meet with the president. They did tell me what position they were interviewing me for, and, surprisingly, they offered me a job. As grand and exciting as it may sound to some, I could not see myself as a public relations manager, so I turned them down. Emily is not happy about that, but I know something better will come along. I am revising my résumé again.

There remains at least one loose end I can think of regarding The Cases. Lieutenant Blue hasn't said anything, but I'm sure he's aware of it because he doesn't miss much. I was adding up the pen weapons. We got three from Norman Shartly, Blue found one in the Playhouse balcony belonging to Charles Kelly, and there is the one that Kelly took back from Lorna Gribble and gave to Blue. That makes five. Shartly said he started with six that Fostridge gave him and misplaced three, two of which are no doubt the ones Brian Gulliver found and gave to Kelly and Gribble. So there is one still unaccounted for.

Unless it's been destroyed somehow, somebody is in for a surprise.

Epilogue

The town is crawling with cheap Gate City Playhouse Rocks fountain pens. They're everywhere, and ordinarily he wouldn't bother adding another one to his collection, but this one needs rescuing. He spots it while late-night cruising through the now-empty parking lot at the Tanger Center, a handy shortcut from N. Elm to N. Greene if you want to avoid the stoplight on W. Friendly. It is an unusual place for such a find, which makes it interesting, and although it looks like it has been here for a while, it has not yet been run over and flattened. He doesn't want that to happen, so he stops and picks it up.

Wait a minute. This pen is different from the others. A little heavier. He unscrews the cap. No nib. Apparently, it is a penlight, but why so dim? Maybe it is his tinted goggles with the yellow-smoke lenses. He takes them off and has another look. Still dim, but this time when he clicks the little clip on the barrel he is hit with a strange feeling. Not like the one he is already enjoying from the weed he smoked only a few minutes before setting out for the evening, and definitely less pleasant. He feels an urge to swallow the goggles. He resists. He feels vaguely nauseous, but he resists. His legs begin to feel rubbery, but his stable position prevents him from falling.

He wonders, "Hmmm, what if I point this at someone who is not wearing tinted goggles?"

There is only one way to find out.

Before the night is over, the mysterious masked, black-clad, helmeted motorcycle mugger will strike again.

The End
(except for the Appendix)

Appendix

Additional Songs from *The Christmas O'Carolan Songbook, Volume 1*

Christmas's Debut (Instrumental)

While this may not be the first song Christmas O'Carolan (1693-1760) composed, it is an early one and was personally given this title by him. It has a fanfare-like feel to it, as if Christmas were indeed announcing himself to the world. Nevertheless, for this early stage in his development it is still rather pedestrian and not yet reflective of his later musical style. For example, he wrote it in 4/4 time instead of 3/4 or 6/8, the officially sanctioned sad music time signatures of Ireland. A rookie mistake. One can almost hear him straining to make it sound like a waltz or a jig, first by using a syncopated beat and then, seeing how that fails by itself, adding many eighth- and sixteenth-note flourishes. Still, it is an interesting piece and one that does have historical significance. The lyrics, if there were any, have not survived.

Two Left Feet

Christmas O'Carolan (1693-1760) was in fact born with two left feet. This gave him a tendency to walk in clockwise circles, especially if he hadn't had enough sleep after performing in pubs of an evening. Because most social dances of the day had the motion going counter-clockwise, Christmas often found himself literally out of step, which was a handicap when courting and the main reason he didn't marry until his late

351

40's. He tired of wearing oversized regular left and right brogans to mask his condition, and this song was his attempt to "come out of the closet" and at the same time begin to promote the affliction as an acceptable alternative lifestyle.

Part 1a
Ah, fancy that we should meet, for
I've a secret to tell, my sweet.
Needs you know, perhaps,
Something I've been keeping under wraps.

Part 1b
Now dance with me to the beat, for
'Tis good that we had this chat.
I've got two left feet,
Not that there's anything wrong with that.

Part 2
Left, left, left, left, left, left, left, left.
And I'll dance circles around
Any right-lefted man in town!

The Bellyful Whale

Christmas O'Carolan (1693-1760) originally wrote this drinking song as a children's story, or so he claimed. It started with nonsensical rhymes that popped into his head and that he used as placeholders for the lyrics he would later write to fit the melody. However, in the end he liked them, and they were never replaced. Some have tried to ascribe a more adult meaning to the song (not unlike "Puff, the Magic Dragon" by Peter Yarrow), but Christmas always denied that that was his intention, allowing only that "bellyful" *might* be a wordplay on Ballyfoulmouth, his hometown.

Verse 1
Come close and I'll tell you a tale
Of a man and a maid and a bellyful whale
And how they danced to a fiddler one night
'Til the whale ate the maid 'though she put up a fight.

Chorus
The fiddler he ran, and that left the man
Who tickled the tail 'til the whale made it right.
The maid he spit out from his big waterspout;
Then the fiddler poured ale, and they drank until light.

Verse 2
"Pray, tell me now what did you see
In that bellyful whale of an evening with me?"
"'Twas dark and lonely as ever I've been,
And I never saw Jonah, if that's what you mean."

(repeat Chorus)

The Bishop's Britches (Instrumental)

There was and still is a strong element of impudence employed in the naming of Irish songs. "Whiskey before Breakfast," "Britches Full of Stitches," "A Fig for a Kiss," "Catch Her in the Rye," "Kiss My Blarney Fife," and almost anything beginning with "Planxty" are good examples. It is a pity there was never an All-Ireland Impudent Song Title Competition.

Christmas O'Carolan (1693-1760) was fond of satire and wrote this song to call attention to Catholic Ireland's struggle to resist domination by Protestant England. One presumes the britches in question belonged to an English prelate, not an Irish one, but there are no surviving lyrics to confirm this or to shed light on what might have made the britches interesting to Christmas and his listeners, assuming any such reason were required. This is one of only a few songs of Christmas O'Carolan (1693-1760) that were politically motivated. "Parliament Stinks" is another, but it, too, has been lost.

Whiskey before Breakfast (or The Musicians' Lament)
Clearly a drinking song, this favorite tune of fiddlers and listeners alike is officially designated as a "traditional" Irish reel, but a case can be made that it was a Christmas O'Carolan (1693-1760) composition originally attributed to his fictitious alter ego, Blind MeLon O'LeMon. The lyrics are definitely Christmas's, however. They express the simultaneous joy of making excellent music and the frustration of being poorly rewarded for it in material terms, a typically Irish condition.

Verse 1
Life is hard when there's nothing to do.
When the days are long and the jobs are few.
Play the fiddle and the flute when there's time to kill,
'Cause musicians don't have any marketable skills.

Verse 2
Playin' all night, drinkin' all day,
Lord, I wish there was another way.
Stokin' up your body with beer and gin.
Then you get up early, start it all again.

Verse 3
Nobody's happy in the old farmyard.
The weather's crappy and the ground is hard.
Play for a pint, play for a 'tater;
Everybody plays somethin' sooner or later.

Verse 4
Midnight comes and we're havin' good fun.
At the all night pub? Aye, that's the one!
While you're still sleepin' like a log,
We're up lookin' around for some hair o' the dog.

Chorus
Well, it wears me out like a marathon contest.
Up all night and we never get no rest.
Need to start the day with something that's high test.
That's why it's whiskey before breakfast.

Christmas's Debut

(R2)

Christmas O'Carolan
(1693-1760)

Fallen and Can't Get Up

Christmas O'Carolan
(1693-1760)

The Robbers of Nobber

Two Left Feet

Never Moor

Christmas O'Carolan
(1693-1760)

Look how the wind sweeps a - cross to the sea, as it
Gone and no rea - son, no re - course to save, off to

beats you for - ev - er e're far - ther from me. Grass turn - ing am - ber like
find you a new world, a new road to pave. No more the com - fort we

old sheaves of grain; aye, the moor mocks me gent - ly to add to my pain. For I
shared as of old, now my hope's ren - dered brit - tle; it shat - ters with cold As the

know in my heart nev - er more will there be aught but bit - ter - sweet
Sun dim - ly sets be - hind clouds dark with rain, fad - ing dreams are the

sor - row you've set your - self free
last place I'll see you a - gain

The Bellyful Whale

Christmas O'Carolan
(1693-1760)

The Bishop's Britches

Christmas O'Carolan
(1693-1760)

Play Part A twice, then Part B once with 1st ending; then Part A once and Part B once with 2d ending.
Then repeat the sequence.

Nevermore

Christmas O'Carolan
(1693-1760)

Whiskey before Breakfast

Or The Musicians' Lament
(to the tune of Whiskey before Breakfast)

Traditional Irish Reel
(Or Blind MeLon O'LeMon?)
Lyrics (above) by Christmas O'Carolan (1693-1760)

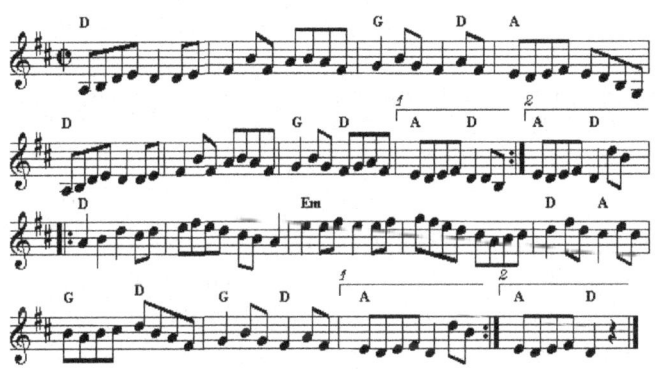

Potato Song Chorus

Christmas O'Carolan
(1693-1760)

plant me some po-ta-toes if on-ly I'd a hoe. I'd have a lit-tle gar-den and plant them row by row. I'd pray for rain and sun-shine and hope the bug-gers grow. I'm I-rish, yes, and I'd do me best if on-ly I'd a hoe! (Well I'm) I-rish, yes, and I'd do me best_____ If on-ly I'd a hoe!

WALT PILCHER

Verses Lyrics by Christmas O'Carolan (1693-1760)
Tune of The Irish Washerwoman
("Traditional" Irish jig but possibly by Blind MeLon O'LeMon)

Verse 1 (tune of The Irish Washerwoman, Part A)
Now there's Irish and Russets and Yellows and Fingerlings,
Pink Eyes and Pontiacs, tubers for everything.
Big Golden Wonders and Almonds and *Chiloés*,
Burbanks and Roosters and Désirées too!

And there's White ones and Blue ones and Murphys and
Idahoes,
Jerseys, Atlantics, Clavelas and Congos and,
Royals and Kestrels, King Edwards and Fonteneys.
You find a new one, we'll name it for you!

Verse 2 (tune of The Irish Washerwoman, Part B)
Oh we'll roast 'em and steam 'em and boil 'em in water, and
Mash 'em with gravy or pour on the butter, or
Bake 'em and stuff 'em with bacon and cheese, we'll
Dice 'em or cube 'em and serve up a stew.

Oh there's hash browns and French fries and chips for a
dippin' and
Twice baked potatoes or scalloped au gratin, we'll
Serve 'em in casseroles, just as you please.
I'll have potato cakes, latkes for you!

(Repeat Chorus & out)

About the Author

Walt Pilcher is a former CEO of Leggs®, the pantyhose in the plastic eggs. His comedy writing and his business writing were often indistinguishable. He was twice "downsized" long before it was cool. Walt is the author of *On Shallowed Ground, including Dr. Barker's Scientific Metamorphical Prostate Health Formula® and other Stories, Poems, Comedy and Dark Matter from the Center of the Universe* and the comedy novels *Everybody Shrugged* and *The Accidental Spurrt®*, all from Fantastic Books Publishing. His non-fiction book, *The Five-fold Effect: Unlocking Power Leadership for Amazing Results in Your Organization* (WestBow Press), was a First Horizon Award finalist in the 2015 Eric Hoffer Book Award competition.

Walt holds a BA from Wesleyan University and an MBA from Stanford University. In his spare time, he ghostwrites book cover blurbs from his home in High Point, North Carolina (USA), where he lives with his wife, Carol, an artist.

LinkedIn: www.linkedin.com/in/waltpilcher
Facebook: www.facebook.com/walt.pilcher

Listen to the Music

By now, you may have discovered that there is no website for *The Christmas O'Carolan Songbook, Volume 1.* Not to fret. Recordings of most of the songs in this book, and a few others, can be found on Soundclick.com at

www.soundclick.com/artist/default.cfm?band
ID=946465&content=songs

These are not professional quality productions, but you may enjoy them anyhow.

Post a Review! Browse the Fantastic Books Bookstore!

If you have enjoyed this book, please consider posting a review on Amazon or at the Fantastic Books Bookstore (www.FantasticBooksStore.com) to let the world know what you thought of Walt's work. While you're there, why not browse his other books and the rest of the entertaining offerings from Fantastic Books Publishing?

Books by Walt Pilcher

*The Fivefold Effect: Unlocking Power Leadership
for Amazing Results in Your Organization*
(WestBow Press)

*On Shallowed Ground, including Dr. Barker's Scientific
Metamorphical Prostate Health Formula® and other Stories,
Poems, Comedy and Dark Matter from the
Center of the Universe*
(Fantastic Books)

Everybody Shrugged
(Fantastic Books)

The Accidental Spurrt, a Mark Fairley Mystery*
(Fantastic Books)